Quatrain

by John Medler

Publisher: Rocket Books, LLC 2010

ISBN 978-0-6159-7964-9

"Although, my son, I have used the word 'prophet,'
I would not attribute to myself such a title...."

—Nostradamus, in a Letter to his son César,
in the Preface to *Les Propheties.*

PROLOGUE. BLOODLINE.

April 1429. Vaucouleurs, France.

Cate was afraid. This was her first birth, and her mother Isabelle was gone. The pain in her swollen stomach was like a blacksmith's molten poker. Her fever had not broken in the last two days. The midwife had told her that this kind of pain was normal, but she didn't think so. She knew that girls her age often died in childbirth, but she wasn't worried about herself. Her Savior would take care of her if anything happened. Cate was worried about the baby. If the baby should die before being baptized.... No, she could not think of such things. She stretched out on the small wooden cot, trying to get comfortable. Each position was worse than the last. Her white cotton robe was saturated. The midwife tried to calm her by rubbing her wrinkled hands on her neck and pressing wet strips of cloth onto her forehead. Cate wished that her sister....

Her thought was interrupted by an agonizing convulsion of pain. Her scream caused villagers in the fields to turn their heads. Blood started pouring out between her legs. She grabbed the midwife's blue shirt in desperation. "If it is a boy, I want his name to be Jacquemin, after my brother...." Cate didn't get time to express her name preference if the child was a girl. Before she blacked out, all Cate could see was the grimaced look of concern on the face of the midwife.

Ann, the midwife, had seen cases like this before. The placenta had ripped from its moorings. She acted quickly, using a metal tool to pry the infant's head through the birth canal. Seconds counted. She expertly removed the umbilical cord from around the child's neck and the mucous from the child's mouth. The infant looked a little blue, but within a few seconds, the infant gasped and began wailing. Success. The infant was a girl! She had beautiful red hair, like Cate's sister. She placed the child and the umbilical cord in a pre-arranged bassinette. Her assistant Marie attended to the child while Ann attempted to save the mother, but there was not much she could do. Cate had lost a lot of blood. She kept placing water on the girl's face, but after a few minutes, she realized Cate was lost. Her soul was now with Jesus Christ. She sent for the local priest.

Jean Colin, Cate's new husband, was a young tax collector for the duchy of Bar. He was the son of the Mayor of the nearby town of Greux. He was not a horrible man, and he had his tender moments, but for the most part, he was someone who thought of himself first and everyone else last. He had not even wanted children, seeing them as a nuisance and an expense, but his beautiful wife Cate had insisted that God's plan was for them to have children. Colin had fallen for her as soon as he had seen her pale cheek, her long blonde tresses, and her beautiful blue eyes. Cate's father was a tax collector like him, and her dowry had been sufficient. She was by far the fairest young girl in Domremy. His hope was to move to Chinon or even Paris someday, where he might move up the ranks and improve his position.

Ann left the birthing room and went out to see Colin, who was nervously waiting in the hall.

"I am terribly sorry, Monsieur Colin, but your wife has passed."

"What?" demanded Colin. "What do you mean she has passed?"

"Sir, the Lord has taken her. There was nothing we could do. She had lost so much blood."

"No!" Colin pushed passed the hefty midwife, and rushed into the birthing chamber, where his wife lay on the cot, in a clump of sweaty and bloody sheets.

"No!" Colin lifted up his wife's head, and looked for any signs of life. He could see she was gone. He didn't cry. He was just numb. "My God! Cate, I love you so! Do not leave me!"

Ann watched from the hallway as Jean Colin cradled his wife's body, willing her to return to him. Ann brought over his baby daughter in a blanket, hoping that the sight of the newborn would comfort him.

"Monsieur, you have a baby girl. She is just as beautiful as her mother."

Colin took the infant in his arms gingerly, worried he would break the small thing. She was so tiny. Colin was happy to see his new child, but the loss of his wife was devastating. And he had to admit he was disappointed that the child was not a boy. All of his plans were dashed. He looked down at his daughter. A baby girl— what could he do with a baby girl? He was certainly not going to raise a baby girl by himself. That was for sure. He resigned himself to thinking it might all work itself out somehow.

For the next several months, as was the custom, the child was raised and breastfed by the midwife. Colin went about his tax collecting business for the most part, and visited his daughter once or twice a week. He seemed to take some comfort in the fact that the child had her mother's beautiful blue eyes and his sister-in-law's red hair. He loved his daughter, but he realized that he would soon either have to re-marry or do something with the child. By early July, Colin had heard news of the battles at Fort St. Loup, Fort St. Jean le Blanc, and Les Tourelles. Fearing that the English might kill him or his child if they learned that his sister-in-law had a surviving heir, Colin arranged for a traveling group of Visitation nuns to secret the child to Bordeaux in the south of France. Before he surrendered his daughter, Colin gazed at the wicker basket and gave his daughter one last tender look. She should have something to remember him by. That was only proper. He took out a small cloth. On it was stitched the Colin family crest—a shield of blue stripes, a knight's helmet, and swirls of blue and silver. He tucked the cloth around the child like a blanket and kissed her goodbye. The nuns, believing they were doing God's work, agreed to the mission, and by October 1429, young Jeanette Colin, niece of Joan of Arc, was safe in the convent in Bordeaux.

CHAPTER 1. VISION.

March 1538. Agen, France.

God had given her a glorious day. After a long, bitter French winter, spring was finally here. The light breezes of Gascony carried the sweet scents of almonds and honeysuckle. Children watched their wooden toy boats bobbing on the River Garonne. The peacock-blue sky and towers of cumulus clouds beckoned anyone who was still indoors to come outdoors and breathe the fresh air. Young Henriette loved days like this. On these days, her father would relax in quiet meditation on the green banks of the Garonne, smoking his pipe, eating cheese, and reading stories written in Latin. But the twelve year-old French girl would rather be in the fields. Just a mile or two out of town, hillsides filled with cheery sunflowers danced next to vineyards brimming with purple grapes. Agen was, after all, only a short distance from the world- renowned vineyards of Bordeaux, the bosom of French wine making. Henriette loved to pick flowers and twist them into pretty arrangements for her mother, Andiette. Henriette took in a deep breath of spring air, smiled, and hurried down the dirt path with her little terrier Pierre. Today Henriette would visit the almond trees, sprouting their white and pink blossoms, swaying in the wind, blowing buds around her like a springtime shower of pink and white confetti. Henriette planned to lay down with Pierre in the grass between the trees, letting the blossoms fall on her face, smelling the almonds, and eating slices of her mother's nut bread. And if she got around to it, she might write a story. Henriette had an active imagination and cherished making up stories about far away lands and princesses and castles and stories of love. Her father had given her a white feather and bottle of India ink for her birthday. Papa was like that. He was always so considerate. She had borrowed some pieces of vellum from her father's study to start her next story. She had also brought her Bible. The Lord's Word was not only important for feeding the soul, but also a great source of inspiration when she got writer's block.

Henriette scaled a small hill, pushing her way through thigh-high grass. When she reached the top of the hill, she saw the rows of almond trees ahead and her heart leaped. Surely no one could deny the Savior after seeing such beautiful wonders! "Come on, Pierre!" she beckoned to the brown and gray pup. She carried a small basket which contained some of her mother's nut bread. She was trying to learn to cook these days but she had so much to learn. Mother had taught her last week how to make rabbit stew. How Michel had liked that! She thought of how savory the broth was when her Mother made it. She took in another breath of almond air as she skipped to a small clearing between the rows of trees. Henriette took the small blanket out of her basket and laid it on the ground, making sure there was no mud here which would ruin it. The grass here, though, was not wet and the spot was suitable. She pulled up her white cotton dress near the fringe and lay down on her back, staring up at God's beautiful sky. What a day!

She thought of her mother and father and how much she loved them. She thought of her husband Michel. He seemed like a kind man so far, and he seemed so dedicated to his medical patients. Papa had assured her that Michel was not only a man of means but also a man of wit, and Papa never said that about anyone. Her father had become such close friends with Michel. The two talked often for hours, discussing the need for a book on grammar or the best cure for a plant rash. They had become inseparable. She did not mind being married to Michel. He seemed very smart, and marrying Michel made Papa happy. She just didn't like the "consummation." She had only had her first blood come out six months ago, and she was just not that interested in having a naked man on top of her. She did not understand why people were supposed to enjoy intercourse at all. It hurt and Michel's underarms smelled and his beard was scratchy and it was just… well, not enjoyable. But Mother said girls must marry when they are twelve and can bear children, and sex was the only way to have children, so that was that. Henriette did look forward to having her own child, however. "How wonderful it will be to carry a child inside me," she thought, "And then to have a tiny face smiling back at me, just like one of Jesus' angels? What joy!" Her mother had told her that when God put a child inside her, the bleeding between her legs would stop. She wondered about that, because her blood had not come two weeks ago. Could she be pregnant?

She put such thoughts out of her mind and stared with wonder at the billowing clouds. She mentally drew a line between several of the clouds, picturing herself constructing a giant house of cotton fluff, where she would entertain pretty lady giants over for tea and make nice comments about the weather down below and serve almond cakes. She closed her eyes and faded off, almost asleep….

The vision fiercely gripped her, making her eyes pop out in fear. Even though her eyes remained open, it was as if she was asleep. If this was a dream, it was the most realistic dream she had ever experienced. She seemed to be seeing into another time—when, she did not know. There were two figures in the room. One paced back and forth on the floor, clearly agitated. The room was round, and the walls were cream-colored, with grand drapes the color of mustard. The floor was a deep blue color. In the middle of the floor was a crest of an eagle. The eagle was carrying a leaf in one claw and arrows in the other. Around the eagle were letters in a language which was not French, and which Henriette did not understand. As the scene unfolded over the next several hours, Henriette saw many things, very horrible things, and shook until her body turned cold.

When she woke up, she looked around her and noticed that it was night! How long had she been dreaming? The cool breeze felt good, because she was covered in sweat. Her arms and legs and face felt badly sunburned. She was exhausted. She felt like staying here under the stars and resting until morning, but she knew her mother, Papa and Michel would be worried about her. Henriette sat up and picked up her basket, but as she did so, she noticed her Bible was missing. She looked over to the blanket and saw her Bible was on the ground in the grass, opened. Next to the Bible in the grass was her white feather, blackened at the bottom, and an empty bottle of India ink. She looked at her hands and they were covered in ink, as was much of her white dress! That would be difficult to get out! Henriette looked at her Bible. There was handwriting-her handwriting!—all over many of the Bible's pages. The Bible appeared to contain verses of some kind of poetry. For the life of her, she could not remember writing any of this. Henriette looked around her, wondering for a moment if someone was playing a trick on her and writing the verses in her hand to trick her. However, that was plainly not the case. No one knew she was even here, and there was not a soul around anywhere. She read the verses, and they appeared in some places to reference what she had just dreamed. But how could she have written all this and have no memory of it at all? The young girl worried she might be going crazy. She remembered hearing stories her Mother told her about Joan of Arc, and how she at first believed she was crazy when she heard the Lord speaking to her. Like Joan, if the Lord wanted her to write this vision down in her Bible, then she would do God's will. It was not for her to question God.

Was some handwriting in a Bible more fantastic than speaking through a burning bush or parting an entire sea? No, of course not. Henriette vowed to ask her father and her husband what this all meant.

Henriette found herself momentarily distracted by her hunger and devoured a piece of nutbread. Her hunger satiated, she packed up her things. Badly shaken and confused, the young French girl set off with her dog for the trail that would take her back to the village of Agen to her husband Michel de Nostradame, the man the world would later know as Nostradamus.

January 15, 2013. Salon-de-Provence, France.

The burly workman hired by Father du Bois aimed his sledge hammer at the stone wall in the basement of l'Eglise de St. Michel. After his last swing, the last remnants of the stone wall came down. Father du Bois aimed his flashlight in the murky black space beyond the wall. There was something back there, all right. The priest entered the room behind the wall and shined his light around. There was a staircase, leading downward to an old wine cellar. Huge, centuries-old, wooden wine casks ran along the wall. The groundwater leaking into the basement of the church was coming from a hole somewhere up in the rafters of this wine cellar. The next call was to the plumber, who would need to caulk the hole where the water was entering.

The workman asked the priest in French if he needed any more help. No, the priest said, the workman could go. Father du Bois looked through the labyrinth of cobwebs running across the room. With a broom, he whisked the webs away and went down the stairs. When he got to the bottom of the steps, he inspected the wine casks. Behind each cask was a small, wooden fleur-de-lis nailed to the wall, which bore the name of the wine which had once rested within the cask. Father du Bois shined his light on the labels over each cask. That was strange. One of them looked different from the others. Father du Bois went back through the hole in the wall to get a ladder. What he would later discover would change the course of history.

CHAPTER 2. MASSACRE

September 28, 2012. Cincinnati, Ohio

They called him Mash'al, or "The Torch." He was an Islamic extremist and a paranoid schizophrenic, a dangerous cocktail. Since the time he was a teenager, Mash'al began finding his own personal secret messages from Mohammed in the Qur'an. When he was young, the Prophet only needed him to do minor tasks, like removing all the brown bottles from the local convenience store or catching mice and putting them in a duct-taped Slurpee cup. But that was small potatoes. The Prophet was calling him to do something important, that was sure. Mash'al's parents in Iran had given up on him long ago. The father had a fairly respectable job working for a petroleum company. His mother did a good job raising Mash'al and his three brothers. But Mash'al was too much for them to handle. One day, his father would find Mash'al high on opium lying around the house. The next day he would learn that his son had vandalized a fruit stand, throwing the fruit all over the bazaar, claiming that the Prophet was calling him to cast out all the evil fruit pits. Left to his own devices, he was easily recruited by Al Qaeda. This next mission for Islam was something only a certifiable lunatic would do.

The Planner had mailed the anti-psychotic medications to his small apartment in Cincinnati. The Planner insisted that Mash'al take the medicine. If he did not, he would not become a true Abisali, a Warrior of the Faith. Mash'al did not want to take the pills, but he knew if he did not, he would let down the Master. Incredibly, the pills gave him a focus he had never experienced. The inner voices, constantly screaming at him that he was not worthy, that he was a mangy wolf, that he had too much hair.... they had all died down. The silence from the voices was most welcome and allowed him to focus. The only downside was the drugs made him a little lethargic, but Mash'al was in good shape. He would be fine.

Today was the day Mash'al would fulfill his destiny as the spear point of jihad. He could not wait. Mash'al opened the door to the lobby of his downtown Cincinnati apartment building and met the UPS man. He was terribly excited to receive the brown package. He bounded up the steps two at a time until he reached 2J, then opened his door with the key and dashed to the kitchen table. He ripped off the paper covering with a knife, and opened the cardboard package. Inside, wrapped in cellophane was a set of gray janitor's overalls, with a red and white emblem on the shoulder which read "Mills Janitorial". There was also a red baseball cap with the same emblem. Also included in the package were a black .45 Beretta and silencer, and an orange key to a storage locker.

Mash'al could barely breathe, he was so excited. This was really happening. The Prophet was practically demanding that he complete his tasks today. He quickly donned the baseball cap and put the overalls over his clothing, zipping himself up in front. The overalls were the correct size. He grabbed his keys and, checking the hallway to make sure no one saw him, ran down the stairs and out the door to the parking lot.

In a half hour, he had arrived at the Store-A-Lot storage facility in downtown Cincinnati. He parked his beat-up Mazda in front of locker 73. Taking out the orange key, Mash'al unlocked the powder blue door, and then, from the inside, swung up the corrugated metal garage door. There was only one thing in the locker, a white plastic trash barrel with the words "Mills Janitorial" stenciled on the side. Mash'al lifted off the lid and peaked inside. Seeing what he expected, he quickly shut the lid, looked around and smiled. The barrel was heavy, but he managed to drag it over and roll it sideways into his hatchback. Today, the Prophet would be proud.

September 28, 2012. Kirkwood Elementary School, Cincinnati, Ohio

Eleven year-old Justin Idris was excited about his Science Fair Project. His project was about bees. He had stayed up until midnight with his mom the night before making the hive out of paper maché. It looked so real! The pieces of honeycomb were expertly glued to the side. All the parts of the bee—head, thorax, and abdomen—were labeled. His notes of his interview with the beekeeper were pasted into his yellow and black Project Notebook. And, in colored yellow and black marker, he had drawn on the side of the project boards numerous "Fun Bee Facts", including:

—the average colony has 45,000 to 70,000 bees

—90% of the food consumed by humans depends on the pollination of honeybees

—the honeybee eats seven pounds of honey to produce 1 pound of wax

—the flight speed of a honeybee is 9 miles per hour

—the bee makes as many as 24 trips a day when collecting nectar from flowers
—50% to 80% of flying bees are collecting nectar.

Amy Idris, Justin's mother, was a single mom and a police officer for the Cincinnati Police Department. As usual, she was running late. She checked her makeup in the rearview mirror, and, as she did so, looked at her small son in the back seat. He had black glasses much too big for his head. She had pleaded with him to get less conspicuous eyewear, but Justin really liked the black glasses. He said the glasses made him feel smart. The Science Fair project was lying on the passenger seat of their tan Chevy minivan. She could see that Justin was looking at the seat in front of him nervously, obviously concerned that the bee project would suffer some mishap on the way to school.

"Don't worry about your project, sweetie. I am taking good care of it up here."

Kirkwood Elementary had two separate entrances. The first entrance was used by parents dropping off children in the morning. The second entrance was used by the bus drivers. Occasionally, parents racing to get to work on time would cheat and go in the bus driveway so as to avoid the traffic in the other lane. Today, the line in the first driveway was packed with minivans and SUVs, so Amy passed it and cheated her van into the bus driveway.

"Mom, you're not supposed to go that way," complained Justin.

"I know, but if we wait behind all those cars, we are not going to get your bee project in by the deadline. They said it has to be in the gym by 8 o'clock."

Justin's mother glided the minivan around one bus and in front of the other, and then put on her flashers.

"OK, quick, sweetie. Jump out and get your project. I am holding up traffic."

Justin quickly unbuckled, opened the sliding side door, and from the outside, opened the passenger door in front. He gingerly extricated the tall science fair project and closed the door with his foot.

"Bye, honey! I know your project will do great!"

"Thanks, Mom! Love you!"

Justin hurried through the front door of the school. Justin was a little guy, so the big three-paneled cardboard science fair project was a huge thing for him to carry. He was sweating a little bit, and his glasses slid down the bridge of his nose. He pushed back his glasses and forged on. He knew he had to get the project into the gym by 8 a.m. or it wouldn't be counted in the competition. It was five minutes to eight. He had better hurry. As he hustled down the hall to the gymnasium at Kirkwood Elementary School, he couldn't see where he was going because the boards of the science fair project were blocking his view. Running blindly, he plowed right into a plastic trash barrel placed against the white cinderblock wall of the hallway. His science fair project went flying and fell in a heap. The hive became disconnected from the branch and fell off. Some of the chicken wire and honeybee models he had glued to the board also fell off. "No!" pleaded Justin, visibly upset that his project was damaged. He started crying and whimpering, trying to re-attach the broken bee paraphernalia.

One of the science teachers, Mrs Willoby, was at the end of the hall and saw Justin collide with the trash barrel. Justin was so cute, in his green plaid shirt and those goofy black glasses. She would help him fix his project.

"Don't be upset, Justin, I will help you."

"But it won't be in the gym by 8 a.m.!"

"Don't worry, Justin. I will tell Mr. Yost what happened and he will let you bring it in a little late. I have a glue gun back in my office. We can get that hive put back together in no time." She brushed her hand on Justin's messy brown hair, and felt good that she had cheered him up. As she bent to look at the broken science fair project, she glanced over at the trash barrel. The lid of the barrel had fallen off and the barrel lay on its side in the hallway. Something was blinking red in there. A toy maybe? She walked over to the barrel, righted it back up, and peeked inside. She saw a flashing red light, a series of wires, and beneath that bricks of some kind of gray clay. She was, after all, a science teacher. It took her brain three seconds to make the mental synapse.

"OH MY GOD! IT'S A BOMB!"

Justin looked at her in panic. Her first thought was that she should evacuate all the children. No, that would take up too much time. How much time was left? She gently lifted up the housing with the red light and peered underneath. A red digital timer underneath the housing read TWELVE SECONDS!!!! ELEVEN, TEN.... "Oh God, Oh God, Oh God...." She grabbed the edge of the trashcan and yanked it as hard as she could, dashing down the long hallway. NINE, EIGHT, SEVEN, SIX.... The trash barrel was heavy, and she was not that strong. My God! All these children!

She could see the doorway at the end of the hallway. Oh, God, she was going to die today! What about her husband? Her children? She did not want to die!

FIVE, FOUR...

Only thirty feet left. She hauled the trashcan as fast as she could. She was ten feet from the exit.

THREE, TWO, ONE..... She threw the barrel towards the exit and then tried vainly to leap in the opposite direction.

The explosion which followed leveled half of the red-bricked school instantly. A huge ball of black smoke hurdled to the sky, as bricks went flying in all directions. Raging walls of fire consumed much of what was left of the school. The eighty or so students and teachers who were at the far western end of the building when the blast went off were the only ones not killed in the initial blast. The teachers and students, deafened by the sound and impact of the explosion, tried desperately to orient themselves in the darkness, as their ears began ringing and everything went deathly silent. The few teachers who could make sense of what had happened tried to find children in the flame, smoke and rubble and carry them to windows or stairwells. Many of them collapsed from smoke inhalation or falling debris with children in their arms. Miss Kiki Johnson's math class was trapped underneath piles of stone and brick, their classroom door walled shut by falling debris. Within minutes, the class of helpless crying children suffocated in the smoke. A resourceful gym teacher named Joe Wallace, a big six-foot 275-pound former high school football lineman, managed to carry, pull and lead about thirty children to a western art room on the second floor. He pulled a child's black North Face jacket from a hook and placed it underneath the door to prevent smoke from coming in the classroom. Then, in the dark, he ushered all of the children to the windows. He opened one of the windows and heard a lot of screaming below. He waved down one of the bus drivers in the school's front driveway, who came beneath the second-story window to try and help.

"Stay there. I have thirty kids up here! I am going to try and pass them down to you one at a time." Gus, the bus driver, looked around at what was left of Kirkwood Elementary. There was fire everywhere. The teacher had better hurry.

Most of the kids were crying, their faces blackened by the soot and smoke. Some had significant lacerations.

"I can't jump that far! I am too scared!" said one.

"It will hurt when I fall!"

Joe Wallace thought for a moment. He looked out the window at Gus. It was too high up. They would get hurt pretty bad if he threw them out the window.

"The coats!" he said. "OK, kids, this is important, I want all of you to stay next to the windows and try and breathe the air from the windows. Do not go anywhere but the windows or I won't be able to find you in the darkness. OK?"

The children nodded and crowded to the windows. Wallace crawled in the dark over to the far wall where the children had all hung up their coats. He grabbed fifteen coats. Then he returned to the children by the windows.

"Shoelaces! I need everyone wearing tennis shoes with shoelaces to take out their shoelaces and hand them to me." The children obeyed.

"I don't have shoelaces. I have Croc's," said a young girl.

"That's OK. I just need you to give me your shoelaces if your shoes have shoelaces." Just then another explosion rocked the school from the far side of the building. The children all screamed and huddled to Coach Wallace, petrified with fear. "Come on guys! Focus! Give me your shoelaces!"

Coach Wallace used the shoelaces to tie the arms of the light fall jackets together, in a daisy chain, making a long rope. When he had about ten coats tied together, he started to throw one end out the window. Wallace got the entire rope out the window.

"OK, now this is just like gym class. Remember when we all climbed the rope in gym class. This is no different. I want you to climb down the rope and when you get near the bottom, jump off. Jimmy Seigel, you go first." The Coach picked the strongest and most athletic of the children, hoping he could easily scale the coats to the bottom and give the others confidence that they, too, could do it. Jimmy took the rope of coats and climbed out the window. He was down the rope in no time and jumped into the arms of the bus driver, who showed him where to run to get away from the building. One by one the children went down the rope. The smoke was starting to pour in through the bottom of the door.

"Come on guys, we have to hurry," said Wallace. Just then, the glass on the classroom door shattered and smoke poured into the room. The children screamed again."Hurry, hurry, hurry!" he yelled. Wallace ripped off his own shirt, and used it as a bandana over his nose and mouth. The children began scampering down the rope as fast as they could. The last two children, a boy and a girl, had passed out from the smoke. Fire poured into the classroom and engulfed the far wall. There were only seconds left. Wallace picked up both children over his right shoulder, and tried to muscle down the rope with his left hand. He got about five feet down when one of the arms of the coats ripped free, sending Coach Wallace falling to the grass with both children. He fell so that his back was on the grass and the children were cushioned from the fall by his massive frame.

Gus Gentry, the bus driver, immediately picked up the two fallen children, each by the scruff of their collars and dragged them across the grass fifty feet away from the building. He laid them down on the ground and performed CPR on each. Both of the children coughed within a minute or two. They were out of the woods. He ran back for Coach Wallace, who seemed stunned and unable to move from the fall. With the help of a second bus driver, he frantically tried to pull Wallace out of the way. Just as they got him to the driveway where the buses were parked, the entire rest of the school building exploded and collapsed in a cloud of brown and black smoke. Fire engines, with sirens wailing, were pulling in next to the buses.

Priscilla Wills was on the switchboard at the Cincinnati Channel 19 Fox News Desk when the call came in from her brother Dan.

"Priscilla, have you heard about the Kirkwood Elementary School Bombing?"

"What bombing? What are you talking about?"

"A guy at my work said that his kid goes to Kirkwood Elementary School, and ten minutes ago, the entire school blew up in a bomb. It might be a terrorist thing! I checked with the La Grange Fire Department, and they are confirming that their fire trucks are responding to an incident at the school. That's what they called it, 'an incident'."

"Jesus!" said Priscilla. "A school! Now they're attacking schools!" She thanked her brother and hung up. Priscilla stood in the middle of the news room and yelled as loud as she could. "EVERYONE! I NEED YOUR UNDIVIDED ATTENTION. THERE HAS BEEN A BOMBING AT KIRKWOOD ELEMENTARY SCHOOL! WE NEED A CRISIS TEAM ASSEMBLED NOW! WE NEED TO GET THIS BEFORE ANYBODY ELSE GETS IT! THIS IS NOT A DRILL, PEOPLE! THIS IS BIGGER THAN 9-11! GET MOVING!"

The news room office was in sudden pandemonium. Everyone dropped what they were doing and reporters and cameramen went scrambling for the door. Priscilla could not believe it. A terrorist attack in her own city, in a swing state, in the final month of a neck-and-neck Presidential race. Their ratings were going to rock!

Anna Scall, the Governor of South Carolina, was the Republican candidate for Vice President and the running mate of Tim Woodson, the Republican Governor of Nevada. Their campaign against Barack Obama and Joe Biden had gone well so far, but they were still behind by three points in most polls. They only had one month to close the gap, and some of their funding was drying up. Scall was a strikingly beautiful woman. She was 5' 6" with long, wavy brown hair and a long, graceful neck. She wore skinny light-framed eyeglasses, the kind that made one look either smart or German. She had long legs and flat abs that most women would kill for. She was a workout freak, and spent two hours every day exercising and lifting weights. When she talked, all of South Carolina came out, and her hometown charm won most people over. In addition to being a former Miss South Carolina, she was also a great pie maker, and each year was the hands-down winner at the Lexington County Fair. Her favorite pie was the blackberry cobbler, a recipe given to her from her mother. She wasn't keen on all the details of national politics, like the name of the leader of the Congo or the meaning of a health care cooperative, but she was excellent at hammering home talking points. If someone gave her a script, she could hit it out of the park every time. And she studied a lot when Woodson gave her the nod as VP. She was not about to let Katie

Couric make her look stupid. Her interviews with the major news outlets, including The Today Show with Matt Lauer, went very well. Audiences loved her.

Her three girls were nine, ten, and thirteen. Her husband, a dentist in Charleston, South Carolina, was a little strange. He was seven foot two inches tall, with somewhat freakish blonde hair which stood on end, and looked like a cross between Ichabod Crane and Albert Einstein. All Tim Scall liked to do in the world was ride bikes. When they met, Anna had enjoyed bike-riding with him, but her interest in riding bikes had faded long ago, so they did not have much in common left. He hated politics. He did not mind the occasional family photo, and he was proud of his wife, but he much preferred riding bikes with his girls and helping them with their homework. He and his wife had stopped having sex long ago.

Today her campaign manager, Matt Suba, had scheduled Scall for a rally near Findlay Market, Cincinnati's 160 year-old produce market. Suba had picked the site due to the diverse racial and ethnic crowds known to frequent the market. If some blacks, Latinos or Asians showed up in the crowd at the rally, he would have cameramen ready to take their pictures. Ohio was going to be a critical swing state this year, and the campaign needed every vote it could.

Scall, Suba, and the campaign staff had set up temporary quarters before the rally in a downtown Cincinnati Hyatt hotel suite. As they were going over last-minute details for the rally, Suba got a phone call from his friend Priscilla Wills from Channel 19.

"Matt, has Governor Scall heard the news about Kirkwood Elementary?"

"No, what news?"

"There was a bombing—maybe a terrorist bombing—at Kirkwood Elementary School in suburban Cincinnati. Hundreds of little kids are dead."

"Prissy, is this a joke? Because if it is, I am really busy right now."

"Matt, it is no joke. The entire school blew up. Our news van just arrived on the scene. Turn on your television."

"Where is Kirkwood Elementary?"

"It is located at 2419 Manchester Road. You are about fifteen minutes away by car!"

"Thanks for the tip, Prissy, I owe you big. I'll call you back."

Suba ran for the TV. He turned on Fox Channel 19 and saw a picture of a burning building, with fire trucks spraying water. The byline at the bottom read: "BOMBING AT KIRKWOOD ELEMENTARY. HUNDREDS OF CHILDREN PRESUMED DEAD."

Suba ran to the adjoining room and banged on the bathroom door.

"Anna, get out here now! There's been a bombing at a school! Hundreds of kids are dead, and we are FIFTEEN MINUTES away!"

Suba ran back to the center of the room.

"Sheila, I need Anna's tightest jeans, and a Cincinnati Reds sweatshirt with a hood. We need her hair changed to a ponytail. Make her look like a suburban mom. Cut down on the makeup but give her just enough to look good.

"Jimmy, cancel the rally today. Send out a press release stating that due to today's tragic bombing Governor Scall will be canceling the rally and putting all her efforts into helping the victims of this tragedy.

"Danny, get working on a statement for Anna— terrible thing, possibly terrorists at work, dark day for the parents of these small children, our campaign will do everything in its power to bring these madmen to justice, blah blah blah, get on it.

"D.J., juice up the Suburbans and have them ready in three minutes. The address is 2419 Manchester Road. We are going to Kirkwood Elementary immediately. Also call Secret Service. We are going to need an escort through the police and fire blockades.

"Manny, I need as many first aid kits as you can lay your hands on, bottled water, disinfectant, Neosporin, blankets—red ones, cots—we need lots of cots. Contact the closest big hospital to the school with a burn center, maybe Mercy Hospital, I don't know. Hell, call all of the hospitals within a fifteen mile radius of the school. You tell them that Governor Scall will pay from her own personal resources the medical bills of any child whose parent does not have insurance. Then go down to Toys R Us, and start buying every stuffed animal they've got. I need Gameboys, Barbies, whatever you would play if you were a kid between kindergarten and fifth grade, however old that is. We need them ready to be taken to the hospital. Find the best Cincinnati pizza place, and start buying pizzas, take them to the hospital and to the school for the families, courtesy of the campaign. I need photographers at the hospital, because Anna will go there later today. Have them take video and stills of the pizzas, the toys, stuffed animals coming into the hospital. Got it?

"Jim, call the LaGrange Fire Chief and the Chief of Police. I want round-the-clock updates of the details of this bombing. How many kids are dead? How many are injured? Where was the bomb located? Who is a suspect? How did the bomb get in the school? What was the mechanism of the bomb—plastic, fertilizer, what? You got it? Get me everything. Ditto for the FBI and Homeland Security. Find out who is running the case on the Fed side."

Anna Scall dashed out of the bathroom in a towel. Her aide Sheila handed Scall her skinny jeans and a Cincinnati Reds sweatshirt. "Here, put these on," she said. "Matt says your hair needs to be in a ponytail, halfway on the makeup."

"Got it," said Scall, grabbing a ponytail holder from the dresser and running back to the bathroom.

Suba was still barking orders. "Poll guys. Come here." Two thin men in t-shirts and jeans, one with horn-rimmed glasses, ran over with their Sony VAIO laptops. "I need polls on how this bombing affects the opinions of voters on which candidate to choose. Does this give us a bump or not? Does this help Obama or us? What if we attack Obama as being soft on terrorism? Does that help us or hurt us or should we take the high road and let Hannity and Beck blast him? What themes will bump us up? Go, go, go, I need this yesterday!"

Ten miles away, a sleepy-eyed college freshman at the University of Cincinnati working part-time at Adriatico's Pizza hung up the phone. "Hey, Donny! We just got an order from the Woodson Presidential Campaign for a hundred cheese pizzas!"

Donny was dumbfounded. "A hundred?"

"Yep. They said they would be here in thirty minutes to pick them up!"

"Holy shit!" He turned to the assistant manager. "Mary, call every part-time guy we can find and get them in here now. We've got some pizzas to make!"

When President Obama heard the news about the Cincinnati Massacre, he was numb. Hundreds of children dead, on his watch. Those poor families. It sure sounded like a terrorist attack. He wondered whether the bomber was home-grown or foreign. Whoever he was, he would make sure this guy was caught.

Obama looked at the television and watched the injured children being carried out from the school. He was in Santa Fe, New Mexico today because New Mexico was going to be a critical swing state in the election. He was about as far away from Cincinnati as he could possibly be. And Scall was in Cincinnati today. She was going to have a field day with this. He called his entire staff in to work out an action plan. Obama considered his present location. It would take at least twenty minutes to get to Air Force One and probably four or five hours at least to get to Cincinnati. Who did he have on the ground in Cincinnati?

"I am sorry, sir," said the LaGrange Police officer at the yellow horse barricade. "The fire chief says no one gets in."

Suba, a Howie Long lookalike with a huge muscled chest, buzz cut, and wire-rimmed glasses, tried to size up the officer. Suba had forced his way through the frantic crowd of shoving parents, each of whom was screaming that it was their child in there and to please let them in.

"Officer, I have Governor Scall in the suburban behind me here. She is very interested in the welfare of these children. She is also still a registered nurse, and she has extensive experience in helping trauma victims. She is not trying to make speeches, Officer. She's just trying to help."

"I'm sorry, sir," said the lanky officer, "I have my orders. The paramedics are already in there taking care of the wounded. I just cannot let anyone else in."

He could see he was going to get nowhere with this squirrel. "Could I speak to your supervisor, Officer?"

The young policeman considered the request, and then spoke into the black radio on his shoulder.

A few minutes later, the police captain approached the barricade.

Suba showed the man his credentials. "Captain, I appreciate your consideration. Governor Scall is here and she just wants to lend a hand."

The Captain said, "Where is she?"

Suba escorted the Captain through the angry crowd of parents and over to a double-parked black Suburban. Governor Scall quickly jumped out of the back seat, looking like a perky soccer mom.

"Isn't this a tragedy?" she said to the Captain, in her thickest Southern drawl, and gently picking up the Captain's right hand. "Captain, if you could just grant me access to those poor souls in there, so I can lend a helping hand, I can assure you our campaign will arrange for a charitable donation to your department. Maybe you could use some more police cars or increased pay for your officers for all the fine work they do?"

The Captain leaned over so that only Scall and Suba could hear him, and spoke in a hushed tone.

"Governor, you're the only one in this campaign that seems to get that we have a war going on against these Muslim bastards. Look at this today! All those little kids killed because the Democrats want to read these bastards their Miranda rights! Come with me, I will get you where you need to be."

The Captain ushered Scall, Suba, and one camera-man passed the yellow barricade. As they did so, the parents became furious that someone else besides them was getting access to the school. Anna Scall turned back and walked over to the anguished parents. "Captain, can we let just three of these parents through? I will make sure they stay out of the area of the fire. And then we can use them to go report back to the other parents?"

The Captain did not like the idea. The crowd was anxious, awaiting the Captain's response.

"Captain, what would you do if you were one of these kind souls here, and it was your child in there?"

"Well, I guess it's OK," he said.

Scall quickly picked the closest two mothers and one father and grabbed them past the barricade. As she walked toward the school, she turned to the parents and said, "I promise I will be back with an update on your babies."

She quickly ran with the Captain, Suba, the camera-man, and the three parents to the closest fire engine. Fire-men were running everywhere in the black smoke with hoses and ladders. Scall quickly dashed past the first fire engine and onto the lawn in front of the school. Temporary cots had been set up on the lawn, some with body bags and some with injured children or teachers, awaiting transport in an ambulance. She quickly made her way through the crowd, trying to comfort everyone she saw. Suba, meanwhile, was getting an update on what law enforcement knew from the Assistant Fire Chief, the Chief of Police, the FBI, and Homeland Security.

Amy Idris, mother of the little boy with the science fair project, was a police officer, so she had no trouble getting through the police barricades. She dashed over to the front lawn of the school. The fire-men were taking the injured children in ambulances. The bodies of the children and teachers who didn't make it were lined up in body bags in three rows on the front lawn of the school. Idris started crying, repeating, "Oh, my God! Oh, my God! Justin, where are you?" She looked in each of the bags but did not find her son among the bodies. Initially, this gave her optimism. Many days later, she would learn from an FBI Forensics team that Justin's small remains had been identified through dental records. He did not make it.

Governor Anna Scall scanned the place where the red-brick school had once stood. It was a crumbled pile of bricks, mortar, and debris. She decided to jog around behind the school to see if anyone else was there. What was left of the jungle gym and playground was in the back. She started to walk around some of the rubble, seeing if there were any survivors. She soon came upon a gray Little Tikes plastic molded castle, the kind little toddlers use as a fort. The castle had a secret hidden brown door in the back, so that someone inside the castle could sneak out. It was dark, but sticking out from the little door was a foot and a tennis shoe of a child. Scall quickly peered over the top of the castle, and curled in a ball inside the castle, underneath a dozen bricks and stones, was a little boy, blackened with soot. Anna Scall's heart leapt for the boy. Could she save him in time? She reached over the top of the castle, and, with her waist on the top of the castle wall, reached under the boy's shoulders and yanked up with all of her might. It took a few tries, because he was wedged, but on the third try she grabbed him and pulled him over the wall. She held the boy in her arms and ran into the side yard of the school where she could find a patch of grass to lay the boy down.

"ABC, ABC," she told herself. "A" was Airway. She tilted the boy's forehead back and put her cheek over his mouth. She could not feel any breath and his chest was not rising. "B" was breathing. She bent down and gave the child two rescue breaths. "C" was circulation. She checked his pulse. She could not feel anything through his blue Kirkwood Elementary shirt. She put her palms out and began giving the boy chest compressions. 1, 2, 3, 4, 5. Then two breaths. 1, 2, 3, 4, 5. Two breaths. 1, 2, 3, 4, 5. She was not giving up. She had done about ten rounds when paramedics rushed over with electric paddles. They shuffled Anna out of the way, juiced up the battery, yelled "Clear!" and shocked the boy's chest. The boy began immediately coughing and sputtering. One of the paramedics placed an oxygen mask over his mouth, and, winking to Governor Anna Scall, carried the boy off on a stretcher over the yard to the school's driveway. Governor Anna Scall sat back on the grass, exhausted. When she got her wits, she realized that she just saved the boy's life. Her cameraman, Ramon, was standing next to her, grinning from ear to ear.

"What is it?" she asked, confused.

"I got the whole thing, boss! You are going prime time!"

The headline of the *Cincinnati Enquirer* the next morning said it all:

CINCINNATI MASSACRE

HUNDREDS OF CHILDREN DEAD IN KIRKWOOD ELEMENTARY BOMBING

HERO GOVERNOR SCALL GIVES CPR TO BOY, SAVING HIS LIFE

When the dust settled, it was clear that 240 of the school's 300 children, and nearly all of the teachers, had been killed. No one had claimed responsibility for the bombing.

During the next month, the video of Governor Anna Scall rescuing the young soot-covered twelve year-old boy from the castle, giving him CPR, and modestly accepting the weeping thanks of the boy's parents, was played hundreds of thousands of times on television news channels and the Internet. The poll numbers started to turn, and the Woodson campaign was out in front.

Barack Obama had reassuring words for the country and harsh words for the bombers. He vowed to find them wherever they were and obtain justice. But so far, the FBI and Homeland Security had turned up nothing. There were no cameras at the school. No parent or bus driver remembered seeing anything suspicious. And the physical evidence was buried under a mountain of rubble. The FBI would find what they needed eventually, but it would take time, and in the homestretch of a Presidential election, that was a luxury the President could not afford. Hannity, Beck, O'Reilly and the rest of the Fox News gang were merciless in accusing the President of incompetence and demanding to know the identity of the terrorists. Dick Cheney returned to the "Talking Head" circuit, quacking to anyone who would listen that he had told them so, and that if the country had not gone soft on water-boarding terrorists, we would not be in this position. But more importantly, all across America, mothers became very, very worried. An attack on a government building or a skyscraper was one thing. This was an attack on suburbia, on an elementary school! If the terrorists could strike in Cincinnati, they could strike anywhere. A wave of panic set in, and Tim Woodson stepped into the fray of paranoia nicely, assuring voters that he was in a better position than the President to protect America. By Halloween, Woodson and his running mate, heroic South Carolina Governor Anna Scall, were ahead by three points in most polls.

On Halloween, the lead investigator in the bombings, FBI Chief Detective Rudyard "Ruddy" Montana announced a lead. A hiker had found a Mills Janitorial Company white plastic trash barrel under a small bridge in a creek bed a few miles from Kirkwood Elementary. The barrel contained a number of discarded pieces of paper that clearly came from Kirkwood Elementary. The FBI concluded that the bomber must have posed as a janitorial worker, taken one of school's trash barrels and put it on his truck, and then replaced it with an identical plastic barrel full of explosives. Later, driving down the road away from the school, he must have stashed the barrel of trash from the school under the bridge. The FBI searched for fingerprints on the barrel and began combing through the records of Mills Janitorial.

However, while the discovery bumped the President's approval ratings back a point or two by Election Day, it was simply too little, too late. Voters turned out in droves to elect the candidate best equipped to battle terrorism. On Election night, the State of Ohio put Tim Woodson over the 270 electoral vote threshold needed to win the Presidential Election.

January 16, 2013. 2 a.m. Washington, D.C.

Two months after the election, the one called "Mudabbir," or the Planner, sat up in his bed at 2 a.m. He was frantic. He had seen something important in his dreams. The Ancient Prophecy had never been extinguished. Now, the prophecy was out in the open. This could ruin everything. He quickly picked up his cell phone and started making international calls.

CHAPTER 3. DEBATE.

January 17, 2013. Los Angeles, California.

"Nostradamus was most certainly not a prophet," intoned UCLA History and Anthropology Professor John Morse, scolding his debate opponent across the stage. "The best that can be said about him is that he accidentally cured some very sick people during his lifetime. The worst that can be said about him is that he was a charlatan, snake oil salesman, and a liar, and the great weight of the historical evidence points toward viewing him in an extremely negative light. But whatever he was, he was not, as you say, 'the greatest seer whoever lived,' and I challenge you to come up with any facts—as opposed to after-the-fact rationalizations—to prove it."

John Morse was quite at ease in front of the lectern, and, in his own mind anyway, was badly beating Los Angeles best-selling author Erika G. Flynn in their debate entitled "Nostradamus: Prophet or Quack?" which was televised over Time Warner's local interest television channel in Los Angeles. It was astounding to Morse that this woman's books on Nostradamus garnered fifty times the sales of his own books on the subject. She simply had no compelling facts to support any of her wild assertions, yet the audience seemed to hang on her every word. Listening to her tell it, Nostradamus predicted the French Revolution, Hitler's atrocities, Saddam Hussein, 9-11, Osama Bin Laden, the election of Barack Obama, global warming, and the death of Michael Jackson. Yet ask her to predict any specific future global event based upon the sixteenth century figure's *Les Propheties*, and Flynn suddenly became very short on details.

Morse knew his stuff. He had read over two dozen scholarly books on Nostradamus (many of them in their original French), and had visited Nostradamus' birthplace in St. Remy-de-Provence, his home in Agen where he met his first wife, and his home in Salon-de-Provence where he had gone on to write his famous "quatrains," or four-line verses. Nostradamus organized his prophetic quatrains into ten groups, or "centuries." Each "century" had 100 quatrains. However, the seventh Century only had 42 quatrains. The missing 58 quatrains from Century VII were either never written or were lost by the publisher. Morse had poured over handwritten manuscripts attributed to the seer, as well as letters written by Nostradamus' son César. And he had been called upon from time to time to authenticate centuries-old French artifacts believed to have been once possessed by the psychic. Morse was fairly well-versed in astrology and was familiar with the ancient astrological texts which had been used by Nostradamus in the sixteenth century. But after over a decade of research, Morse became quite convinced that there simply was nothing of substance to Nostradamus, and that the seer had managed to somehow hoodwink centuries of followers concerning his so-called psychic gifts. To Morse, Nostradamus was a fraud.

Morse had become interested in Nostradamus and other psychics about eleven years ago, just after his wife Lola died. Now there was a person who should be remembered through the ages. Lola was like a perfect day—when the sky is blue and the breeze is cool and every traffic light turns green and an unexpected check arrives in the mail. When he woke up next to Lola each day, Morse felt flabbergasted at his luck. She was incredibly beautiful, way above him in the looks department. He had met her on a trip to Peru. He had planned to visit Machu Picchu with a group of other professors and some graduate students. But after he walked into the cantina and saw her 1,000-watt smile, her beautiful thick dark hair and cocoa skin, he couldn't remember why he had even come to South America. She was thin in the waist, big in the bust, and had a rear end that looked fantastic in her tight blue cotton dress. She liked to dance and flirt and dazzle everyone around her. She could speak English fairly well, although she regularly used a "b" instead of a "v"—"you are berry interesting." She often mixed up present tense and past tense and could not seem to get the distinction between "much" and "many." But when she rolled her "R's," Morse was delighted. And the best part of Lola Carrera was that she was crazy about John Morse, a boring, overweight, white-haired History and Anthropology Professor, with nose hair and ear hair, and bushy pepper eyelashes and a bad sense of fashion. The two shared several rounds of pico sours, and Morse never looked back. After several months of letter-writing, Lola had managed a visa to Los Angeles to visit him. They had married at the Venetian Resort and Casino in Las Vegas two weeks later. John and Lola Morse had gone on to have two children, Zach and Zoey. And John Morse had been very happy.

Lola had been much more religious than Morse. Morse tended to believe in things which were supported by evidence, facts, or at least a good hypothesis. He did not believe in all-powerful bearded beings living in clouds, winged angels with harps, talking serpents, or virgins giving birth. Lola had taken the kids to Catholic mass every week. That was probably good, Morse thought, in that it gave the children some structure and peace of mind. Morse would be there to help Zach and Zoey when they could reason for themselves, and help them understand the Big Bang Theory, evolution and DNA. Morse never understood how his wife could believe in all the Catholic teachings but at the same time chart horoscopes, read Tarot cards, and bet the same six numbers every week on the California Lotto drawing. The Catholic thing and the mystical thing seemed inconsistent to Morse, but he wasn't one to quibble. He had a happy life and did not want to rock the boat. When Zoey was just a baby, Lola had begun reading books on prophets like Nostradamus, Jeanne Dixon and Edward Cayce, and she had become convinced that certain people could sense future events. Lola had told him once that she believed she herself had the gift of foresight. Morse burst out laughing. That was one of their few bad fights. He had tried to reason with her, but she had felt truly insulted.

He did have to admit that she was skilled at reading people upon meeting them the first time. She could usually divine whether a woman she met at the grocery store or the gym was having problems with her husband, was interested in another man, or had money problems. Morse chalked those up, however, to a keen observation of people's facial expressions and body language, not psychic powers. If a woman came into the gym with her eyes red and a sad look on her face, chances are she was sad about something. It did not take Nostradamus to figure that out.

In August 2001, Lola had learned that her brother James was coming to the United States for a visit. James had followed much the same path as his sister. He had wavy, dark hair and beautiful features, and he had met his lover on a vacation to Peru. James' boyfriend Greg was an advertising executive for a large bank in Boston, and the two had arranged for a trip to Provincetown on the Cape that weekend. Provincetown was a small beach town on the tip of Cape Cod, Massachusetts. In the last few decades, the small town had become a gay and lesbian Mecca. Lola begged John Morse to go, but he refused. At first, he did not understand why he had refused, but later, when he honestly analyzed the facts, he concluded that he had refused to go because he did not want to spend all weekend with gay men going to drag comedy shows and gay bars. He was a Californian, and a fierce Democrat, and he thought gay people should be able to marry and have equal rights, but he just did not like going to the shows and elbowing well-built men in the A-Bar. Call it his last vestige of homophobia. It was a stupid concern, he later realized, and he should have gone, but he didn't.

His wife had gone to Provincetown by herself and had enjoyed a great time with her brother and his new boyfriend. They had gone fishing on a small island off Provincetown, and had eaten clam chowder and lobster. Greg turned out to be a sweet person, and Lola had been very pleased at her brother's happiness. On the morning of her return trip home from Boston, as the stewardess closed the door of the plane, Lola Morse had experienced a momentary panic attack. She had a feeling of dread, something she could not put her finger on but was sure was real. She had learned always to trust her instincts— that is what her mother in Peru had told her. She had called her husband John on the cell phone.

"John, I have a very bad feeling about this flight. I am worried there is something wrong with the plane."

"Nonsense," John had said, brushing her off. "Do you see any fire on the engine? Do you hear any sounds indicating the plane is malfunctioning?"

"No."

"All right, then, you have no evidence at all that anything is wrong. Everything will be fine."

"OK, it is probably my active imagination. John, I love you. Will you kiss the kids for me? I cannot wait to see you tonight."

"Will do."

American Airlines Flight 11 left Boston on a clear day on September 11, 2001. At 8:42 a.m., the airplane crashed into the north tower of the World Trade Center, ruining John Morse's life forever.

For the last eleven years, John Morse had been raising his two children alone, and trying to get past the pain and grief of losing his wife. He never even considered marrying again. She was too perfect. Any other woman would have been an anti-climactic disappointment, like losing the Mona Lisa and getting the Dogs Playing Poker in return. He had been haunted by his wife's last premonition, and had questioned himself every day about why he had not told her to get off the plane. Morse's psychiatrist, a fellow professor at U.C.L.A., had assured Morse over the years that the death was not his fault; that even if he had told her to get off the plane, the doors had already shut and the airline would never have let her get off.

Her intuition, he had been assured, was just a coincidence, and not any reason to torture himself with guilt. Morse had an affinity, of course, for logical arguments, and his friend's advice made sense, but he still could not let the matter go. He could not understand how he could be given a woman so perfect, and have a life so happy, and have it all taken away in an instant by a group of madmen.

Even though he did not believe in heaven before, in the weeks following his wife's death, he flirted with a belief in the afterlife, probably because the belief gave him comfort at the possibility that somewhere after death he could be reunited with Lola. He went to Catholic mass for a while, and for the first year, it had given him some relief. But in the end, he was a man of science, a man of logic, and the meaningless prayers and Friday meat-eating bans had caused him to lose interest. He returned to a life of academics, but this time with a slightly more cynical, angry eye and jaundiced view of the world. He now viewed the world as one random, often harsh, series of unrelated events, with no purpose or meaning. The only things left which gave him any real joy were his children and his work debunking the mystical world.

He started writing books on Nostradamus and other psychics, attempting to shine the light of logic on fantastic claims of mysticism and prophecy. His first book on Nostradamus, called "*The Man Who Saw Nothing At All*," was popular in the Los Angeles area, and enjoyed by his many students, but he could not seem to crack the Best Seller List like this nutty woman he was debating.

Erika Flynn tightened her jaw as she listened to the UCLA Professor. She was short, and had an odd, blonde bowl-cut which made her look a little bit like a cross between Carol Channing and skater Dorothy Hamel. It was hot under these bright lights in her red turtleneck sweater, but she tried to remain as calm as she could. She was not going to be criticized by this nobody professor who hadn't even sold 10,000 books. Her books, "*The Man Who Saw Through Time*" and "*Nostradamus' Prophecies*" had sold millions of copies and had each reached the New York Times Best Seller List. One of her earlier books on Nostradamus had been made into a movie which was frequently aired on the History Channel. She was a Somebody. She regularly appeared on Fox News as a commentator when public events made people scared of terrorism, Y2K, global warming, or some other crisis. Flynn felt that the evidence of the accuracy of

Nostradamus' prophecies was quite convincing.

"Professor Morse, as someone who has read all the prophecies of Nostradamus, you must be aware that Nostradamus foretold numerous famous events in history hundreds of years before they occurred. The prediction of the death of Henri II in a jousting tournament is the most obvious one. In Century I, Quatrain 35, Nostradamus writes:

The younger lion shall surmount the old,
'Midst martial battlefield in a single duel.
His eyes he'll put out in a cage of gold—
Two wounds joined—then a death most cruel.

As we know, in June 1559, King Henri II, as part of a royal wedding festival, participated in a joust with the Captain of the Scottish Guard, Gabriel de Lorge, the Count of Montgomery, who was younger than Henri. During the third encounter, the Count's lance splintered and entered the king's eye, piercing his brain. He died in agony ten days later. The king's helmet, it is said, was made of gold. Both men wore shields embossed with lions. And the two wounds are the wound to the king and the wound to France. In Century III, Quatrain 55 of the Propheties, Nostradamus himself predicted '*By the grain of Blois his bosom-friend is slain, the kingdom placed in doubt and trouble double.*' The word '*l'orge*' in French means 'barley,' which is a type of grain. Nostradamus, then is essentially using the specific name of the Count—Lorge. And it is beyond dispute that Lorge and the king were friends. Surely even you cannot contest the accuracy of that prediction."

"I most certainly can contest it," countered Morse. "First, we should note that this quatrain is the one that is most quoted by Nostradamus' enthusiasts. It is the 'best case,' if you will. So if this is the best evidence there is for Nostradamus' psychic gifts, this prophecy should be a really good one. Alas, it is not. Let's address this business about the shields having lions on them. The French never used lions in their crest. There is not one bit of factual evidence supporting the claim that their shields had lions on them. Henri at the time was only 41, hardly what anyone would describe as 'old.' There is also no evidence that the king's helmet was made of gold. It would be unlikely to have been made of gold, as gold is a metal which is too soft to provide any protection. And your translation about 'two wounds joined' is incorrect. The French word '*classe*' means a fleet or force. You are using the Greek word '*klasis*,' which means a fracture or wound. You cannot just jump to Greek when it suits your purpose. The last line refers to two fleets of ships, which obviously fits nothing with regard to this event. Your reference to '*Lorge of Blois*' is also incorrect. The verse as originally printed was 'Le grand de Bloys" NOT 'Le grain de Bloys.' '*Le grand*' in French meant 'lord.' And let's keep in mind that before Nostradamus ever started printing his quatrains in the Propheties, he printed up a yearly Almanac which would list the important events for the year ahead. His Almanac for the Year 1559 mentioned absolutely nothing about Henri II dying. In fact, he referred to Henri in the Almanac as 'Henri the Most Invincible' and said that '*France shall greatly grow, triumph, be magnified, and much more so its Monarch*.' If Nostradamus was so gifted that he could see centuries into the future, one would think he could have at least gotten the next year right."

Flynn was not the least bit ruffled, but decided to make a different point. "Professor Morse, Nostradamus quite successfully predicted the events of 9/11, in one quatrain referring to the 'hollow mountains,' which is surely a reference to the twin towers. In another, Century VI, Quatrain 97, Nostradamus writes:

Latitude forty-five, the sky shall burn:
To the great "New City" shall the fire draw nigh.
With vehemence the flames shall spread and churn
When with the Normans they conclusions try.

Obviously, New York City is the New City. The fire from the sky is an obvious reference to the airplanes hitting the Twin Towers and causing fire and smoke in the buildings and throughout the Manhattan skyline. How can you say Nostradamus is a quack when predictions like these are so accurate?"

Morse grimaced somewhat at the reference to 9/11. This woman obviously did not know how his wife died. He could not imagine anyone would be that insensitive to pick the 9/11 example. He composed himself, and then responded, "First of all, Ms. Flynn, I think you suffer from a profound lack of knowledge as to basic geography." Morse held up a map of the United States with latitude lines. "As you can see, Latitude 45 degrees is in Maine, some 300 miles north of New York City. So if this is supposed to reference New York City, Nostradamus needs a lesson in geography."

The small crowd chuckled. Flynn quickly retorted, "Professor Morse, I am quite familiar with the latitude lines, and I think what you are missing is that Nostradamus was obviously referring here to 40.5 degrees, not 45 degrees, latitude, which, if you know your geography, happens to be the exact latitude of Central Park in New York City."

"The actual French phrase used by Nostradamus, Ms. Flynn, was '*cinq et quarante degres*' or 'five and forty degrees,' which is a strange way to say 40.5 degrees. Putting aside the fact that the decimal system had not even been adopted in Europe in Nostradamus' day, the French have never expressed decimal places using this type of language. But even if we were to assume that '*cinq et quarante degres*' means 40.5 degrees, this quatrain could just as easily refer to the eleventh-century Norman invasion of Naples (from the Greek word '*neapolis*' or 'new city'), which also lies at 40.5 degrees latitude, in Southern Italy. And next to Naples, of course, is Mount Vesuvius, which had lava flows several times in the eleventh century, and could be what Nostradamus referred to as the '*fire in the sky*.' And that interpretation would certainly account for the reference to 'Normans.' But if we were to assume, as you claim, that Nostradamus did mean the 9/11 tragedy, why didn't Nostradamus tell us about a five-sided building being attacked? I would imagine if Nostradamus could really see into the future, a five-sided building shaped like a pentagon would look rather odd, and would be an important detail to include, wouldn't you agree? Why didn't we hear about metal birds going into a building? Surely, Nostradamus must have thought the jetliners looked rather strange and would have attempted to describe them in some way? Why don't we have a date? And what, Ms. Flynn, on earth, does the reference to 'the Normans' mean—because, as far as I know, no Normans were involved in the 9/11 attacks on New York City."

The crowd laughed again, which infuriated Flynn even more.

"A prophet, Professor, often cannot see all events as clearly as one might see a motion picture. The prophet may only get bits and pieces of the future, which may be difficult for the prophet to understand, especially because the world changes significantly over time. One cannot expect Nostradamus to get every detail correct. But surely you must admit that

Nostradamus has mentioned by name Generalissimo Francisco Franco in Century IX, Quatrain 16, Louis Pasteur in Century I, Quatrain 25, and Adolf Hitler in multiple quatrains."

"I will not admit that," said Morse. "Regarding Franco, the reference in the quatrain is to '*castel Franco*,' so the word Franco could refer to a place just as easily as a person, and the remaining part of the verse is so vague it could mean almost anything. Regarding Pasteur, the word 'pasteur' is not capitalized. 'Pasteur' is the French word for 'pastor' or 'clergyman.' There is nothing in the quatrain referencing the scientist's first name 'Louis' or anything having to do with science or germs. It states in the quatrain that the pastor shall be 'treated as a demigod.' Say what you want about the contributions of Louis Pasteur, I think it is an overstatement to say that he has been treated as a demigod. In Century VI, Quatrain 28, there is a reference to '*le grand pasteur*' or 'the great pastor,' which is quite likely a reference to a pope, and not to Louis Pasteur. And you are incorrect when you say that Hitler was mentioned by name in Les Propheties. What Nostradamus did mention was *Hister*, with an "S," which is the Latin word for the Danube River. And it is quite clear Nostradamus is referring to the river, not the man. In Century I, Quatrain 68, Nostradamus refers to Turkish and North African armies meeting those '*from the Rhine and Hister*.' That obviously means a river. In Century II, Quatrain 24, Nostradamus refers to the great battle '*encontre Hister sera*,' which clearly means 'along the banks of the Hister River.' In one of Nostradamus' Almanacs, he states, '*A very learned man in his last quarter, while walking along the river Hister, also called Danube, the ground subsiding, in the said river shall be lost.*' In fact, a councilor of Vienna named Gaspar Ursinus Vellius had actually fallen into the River Hister and died when the ground gave in. Nostradamus wrote about the drowning incident in his *Traité des fardemens* in 1552. So no, Nostradamus was not referring to Franco, or Pasteur or even Hitler by name. And if he was referring to Hitler as 'Hister,' then, in addition to being quite poor in geography, he was also a very bad speller!"

Flynn was getting quite annoyed. This debate was not going the way she had planned. "Professor, as I am sure you know, Hitler's youth was spent in the city of Linz in Austria, which sits along the River Danube. So by referring to the River Hister, Nostradamus was obviously using the Latin version of the name of the river as a word play on the name Hitler.

Nostradamus was very fond of word plays, so this is not unusual. For example, in Century VIII, Quatrain 1 Nostradamus writes that '*Paul, Nay, Loron will be more of fire than of blood.*' The letters of 'Paul, Nay, Loron' rearranged becomes 'Napoleon Roy,' or 'Napoleon the King,' who was certainly a man of war rather than royal lineage. The next two lines refer to the imprisoning of the 'Piuses,' which is a clear reference to Napoleon's imprisonment of Popes Pius VI and VII."

"The problem with word plays, Ms. Flynn," said Morse, "is that it leads inevitably to Humpty Dumpty's quote in Lewis Carroll's *Through the Looking Glass* 'When I use a word, it means just what I choose it to mean.' You appear to be taking the letters in the names 'Paul, Nay and Loron' and changing them around to mean Napoleon Roy. If you take the word 'dog' and change the letters to read 'god,' then of course, it means something entirely different, as I will most certainly not pray in church to my dog or buy a pooper-scooper for my God. But if we are free to take all the letters of the words used by Nostradamus and switch them around however we like, then we can say the quatrain means whatever we want it to mean. For instance, in your books, you claim that Nostradamus identified three Antichrists in his prophecies. The first was Napoleon, the second was Hitler, and the third was supposedly someone from the Middle East named 'MABUS.' I have heard some authors claim that if you take the name 'G. W. BUSH' and invert the 'g' and the 'w' you get 'AMBUSH.' Then, if you knock off the 'H' and mix up the letters, George W. Bush becomes the third Antichrist. Now if you are a Republican, never fear, because you can take the name 'OBAMA,' knock off the first and last letters, add "U.S." for the United States, and switch the letters, and now Barack Obama is the Third Antichrist. So this kind of word play where we knock off and add letters and mix them around is really silly and pointless."

"Professor Morse," chided Flynn over her reading glasses, "The names 'Nay' and 'Loron' are not exactly names like 'Bob' or 'Bill.' It is obvious he put those names together as an anagram for Napoleon. The mention of imprisoning Piuses in the very next line confirms that by the context. Nearly every scholar but you agrees on this point."

"Really?" snapped Morse. "Let's play the same word game you just played with Napoleon's name." Morse took out a sketch pad and a black magic marker and wrote "ERIKA G. FLYNN" in bold, block letters. If we cross out one of the "N's," and then rearrange the letters of your name 'Erika G. Flynn', we get: 'LYING FAKER.' Perhaps when your parents named you, they were trying to deliver a cryptic message to the world about your future theories."

Flynn was furious. "Well, I thought we could have a civil discourse about an important historical topic, but I can see you are only interested in hurling *ad hominem* attacks and making sophomoric jokes. This debate is over." Flynn stormed off the stage, leaving the producer scrambling to figure out how to fill the last five minutes of the show. The M.C. started talking about how good debates often stir people's emotions, especially when the topic is so vital to our everyday lives, and other filler material until the producer was able to cut to commercial. John Morse shrugged his shoulders, packed up his sketch pad and briefcase and walked off the set to talk to the producer.

"Hey, Professor, good stuff, but next time, can you tone it down on calling people liars and fakers? Now I have to find five minutes of Nostradamus filler for the end of the show. And next time, press your jacket, it looks a little rumpled."

Morse felt bad about the last crack about Flynn's name, but the ignorance of some people really irritated him sometimes. It was nearly 10 p.m. Satisfied with his performance, he left the building and headed for the parking lot. He looked at his Seiko wristwatch. He had just enough time to get home and kiss the kids good night.

As he crossed the parking lot, his cell phone rang.

"Hello?"

"Monsieur Morse?"

"Yes."

"I am calling from France. It is urgent that I speak with you."

Morse put his phone on his ear, beeped the lock open on his Audi, and hopped in the front seat.

"Who is this and how did you get my number?"

"*Pardonnez-mois, monsieur*. My name is Father Jacques Du Bois, Pastor of L'Eglise-St. Michel. I called your house tonight and your daughter Zoey was kind enough to give me your cell phone. We have made a most unusual discovery in Salon."

"Salon-de-Provence? Where Nostradamus lived?"

"*Oui,* Professor Morse. Earlier this week, an underground vault was discovered beneath the Eglise-St. Michel. We believe the vault may have long lost artifacts from Nostradamus himself."

"Is this a practical joke? Are you serious?"

"I assure you I am most serious, Professor. We have not attempted to gain access to the vault until we called you. I can send you my credentials by e-mail to your computer, so that you can verify I am who I say I am."

"Really? Interesting. A lost vault? Why summon me?"

"It is not I who has summoned you, Monsieur Morse. It is Nostradamus himself."

CHAPTER 4. SNIPER.

January 18, 2013. Abandoned soccer field. Williamsburg, Virginia.

His code name was "Haytham," the "Young Hawk," named for his sharp eyesight. Fifty-one year-old assassin Mohammed el Faya lay down on his stomach, looking through the scope of his long-range sniper rifle. He calmly breathed in and breathed out, lining up the site. Six hundred yards away was a large toy monster truck. Attached with duct tape to the side monster truck was a six-foot tall plastic red rod. At the top of the rod was a red and white target. El Faya pressed a button on a remote control, and the monster truck began moving from one side of the soccer field to the other, with the target bobbing up and down on the swinging red stick. When the truck moved to a point near the goalie box, el Faya calmly pressed the trigger in rapid succession. The red and white plastic target was annihilated. But even more impressive, every bullet also hit the white goal post behind the truck. El Faya was ready. He rested on his back, and pulled out a Marlboro, contemplating what lay ahead of him in two days. He was happy The Planner had not given him the Kirkwood school assignment. He thought the killing of children was wrong under any circumstances, and thought for a moment about his small brother, killed at the hand of Saddam Hussein. No, he was glad that another Abisali had been chosen for that assignment. He could not kill a child. He only had to kill one person, an unworthy and bad person, a defiler of the faith. He would not lose any sleep. His untraceable phone buzzed, indicating a text message. It was from The Planner. "Phase Two Ready. See attachment for planned route." He opened the attachment, and viewed the map where his target would be traveling in two days. He thought for a moment about vantage points. He would have to case the area, but he believed this was doable. He sent a text message, "Confirmed." He put his phone away and took out a cloth, and cleaned his gun. His aim would be true this time. This time....

July 8, 1982. Dujail, Iraq (50 miles north of Baghdad).

Eighteen young, angry militants from the Iraqi Shiite Dawa Party gathered in the small stone house which they had converted into a temporary headquarters. Every man in the room hated Saddam Hussein. Every man in the room had a relative who had been imprisoned, tortured or killed by Saddam. Mohammed el Faya, a tall, lanky brown-bearded 20 year-old with piercing brown eyes and a sharp nose, was especially interested in the mission. Two years earlier, Mohammed's brother Salmon, who was then eight years old, had been playing football on a small dirt street in Dujail when he had experienced the inhumanity of Saddam Hussein's Revolutionary Guard. Salmon el Faya had been given the soccer ball from a traveling Red Cross worker, and it was his pride and joy. He carried it everywhere. He had mastered the flip throw-in and even the scissors kick. He was far better at football than any of the older boys, and he hoped one day to play on the Iraqi National Team. On that afternoon two years ago, he had been practicing flipping the ball over his head and onto his shoulders, where he attempted to cradle the ball between the top of his shoulder blades and the back of his neck. It was a tough move, but Salmon felt he could master it. No one had known then that President Hussein would be coming through town that afternoon with his motorcade. Had his family known, Salmon most certainly would not have been playing in the street. Oblivious to the oncoming Mercedes Benzes, Salmon flipped the ball from his foot to his thigh, then back to his foot, then over his shoulder, where he kicked it with the outside edge of his foot, attempting to pop the ball over his shoulders for the neck-shoulder-blade move. He lost control of the ball and it went down the dirt street and under the lead car of the motorcade. Salmon had not wanted to lose the ball, so he ran toward the front car. The car honked loudly at him and a man stuck his head out the window telling Salmon to move. Salmon tried to explain to the man that his ball was under the car. It was at this time that Mohammed el Faya heard the news about the motorcade and ran from his house out onto the street to find his brother. The crowd was thick and was being corralled to the side of the street by Saddam's armed guards. Mohammed tried to yell at his brother, but the crowd made too much noise for Salmon to hear.

The next moment was like a slow-motion dream that he had seen a hundred times in his sleep since then. A burly guard exited the car, armed with an AK-47. Without the slightest hesitation, the guard sprayed a volley of automatic fire into Salmon's head, chest, and legs, killing him instantly. The lead car of the motorcade then drove over the boy's lifeless body, which thumped loudly under the wheels of the Mercedes. The crowd was outraged, but the guard wasn't hearing any complaints. He sprayed another set of rounds in the air as a warning, threatening anyone who dared to challenge him or Saddam's authority. Before Saddam left the town, he stopped his car and walked to the edge of the street, where he plucked a small child from the hands of its mother like a friendly politician. Saddam paused, smiling, holding the child up. Another guard took out a Polaroid Instamatic and took a picture of Saddam with the child. Saddam turned to the frightened mother and, returning her child to her, said, "It is so nice to see the children of Dujail." Saddam patted the child on the head and drove off in his car.

Mohammed ran into the street wailing in anger and grief, holding his dead little brother, his small white cotton shirt drenched in red blood. At that moment, holding his brother, he vowed to get vengeance on Saddam Hussein. He promised that he, Mohammed el Faya, would put the bullet through Saddam's brain.

For the next two years, he trained extensively with firearms. He learned to use American weapons, Russian weapons, and cruder models. However, he was most interested in sniper rifles. He had been a very good shot as a child. His father had let Mohammed and Salmon guard the family's small flock of sheep from coyotes and other predators. Mohammed had incredible vision, the kind that comes once in a generation. He was determined to be skilled at the most sophisticated long-range sniper weapons. His father had given him his Accuracy International sniper rifle, and Mohammed soon became expert in shooting it.

Four months ago, some of the young men in town who had similar grudges against Saddam decided to form a team to stage an assassination. They recruited an older Shiite military fighter from the town called Sabat to plan the mission. Sabat's son had been taken to one of Saddam's prisons five years ago and had never returned. He had a salt and pepper beard, and, even though he was grossly overweight, he had the full respect of all the young men. The first part of Sabat's plan was to plant spies in as many places in Baghdad as they could. The sole mission of the spies was to learn when Saddam would be coming again to Dujail. Sure enough, last week, a Dujaili spy working at a restaurant in Baghdad had overheard two generals in the Republican Guard talking about Saddam's plan to travel to Dujail today. Saddam was planning to give a speech thanking local conscripts in Dujail for fighting against Iran in the Iraq-Iran War. Sabat quickly organized the men to finalize plans for the assassination attempt. There was a place in the town very near the place where Salmon had been gunned down where the main road ran through a very narrow stretch between several houses. The plan was to wait until the convoy reached the chokepoint between the houses, and then one of the men would drive a large truck out of an alley at high speed and smash the lead car. A second man would then drive a petroleum truck behind the back car of the convoy. Then Saddam would have nowhere to go. Rocket launchers would then be used from the roofs of the houses on the remaining cars. There was a metal water tower just on the edge of the town. The militants built a small perch on the tower for the marksman, Mohammed. He would take out Saddam if they tried to clear him from the cars. The remaining men would rush in from the date orchards on the side of town and shoot anything that moved coming out of the cars.

Many in the town of 75,000 knew of the plan, but everyone was sworn to secrecy. Sabat rallied the eighteen men at the planning meeting.

"I want each of you to look at that dirty, flattened soccer ball nailed to the wall." started Sabat. Sabat put his hand on Mohammed's shoulder. "All of you remember little Salmon el Faya, Mohammed's brother. He was one of the finest football players this country has ever seen. I have no doubt he would have made the National Team. And he was everything young Mohammed had in the world. And we all remember the day two years ago when Saddam's men mercilessly gunned him down in the street for NOTHING! Nothing at all!" The crowd of men became agitated and started nodding. "He was eight! And each of you has a similar story. Malik, Saddam took your father and grinded him to a pulp in a wood chipping machine! He, too had done nothing at all! This man Saddam Hussein is a monster, the most evil man on earth! And I am sure you all know the story of my son, who was taken from me in the night, with no charges, no trial, and no word. And every night, I worry that he is being tortured by Saddam in some dark prison somewhere. Our country is paralyzed in fear by this man. No one will take action because everyone is afraid. That is why the ones who must kill Saddam are those who have nothing left to live for and nothing left to fear—the ones Saddam has rendered walking ghosts. We are those men. Saddam will be killed this day, I swear to you. And when we have killed him, and have spit on his grave, we shall dance and rejoice, and then, and only then, will we inflate this dirty little soccer ball and have a grand game in little Salmon's memory!"

The men erupted in cheers, waving their guns in the air.

"To your stations! And may Allah guide your sights so that your aim is true!" The crowd of eighteen men filtered out of the house, determined to carry out their mission and rid the world of Saddam Hussein.

With his sniper rifle bag slung over his shoulder and his magazine of cartridges in a canvas pouch tied on a string around his neck, Mohammed began the long climb to the top of the water tower. The tower was over four football fields away from the place where Saddam would be passing, but that was well within the 870-yard range of his Accuracy International Arctic Warfare bolt action sniper rifle. Mohammed was a skilled climber, having practiced climbing on the rugged hills near his home in Dujail. This tower had large bolts at regular intervals, which served as excellent handholds. Normally, climbing the tower would pose no problem.

Unfortunately, however, this morning, Mohammed had woken up with an incredible pain on the left flank of his lower back. For the last two weeks, he had an incredible amount of difficulty urinating. This morning, however, was worse than anything he had ever experienced. What Mohammed did not know was that he had a kidney stone, a rather large one, and it was blocking the opening from his ureter to his bladder. Kidney stones often were caused by a lack of water, and that certainly was the case here in this town with frequent temperatures over 110 degrees. As he grabbed on to one of the metal struts during his climb, the pain stabbed at him. He began sweating and was feverish, but he was steadfast in his determination to kill Saddam, so he forced himself through the pain until he had scaled to the top of the tower.

At the top of the tower, there was a small flat metal perch, which had been broadened earlier in the week by some of the men in the town with pieces of plywood and 2 by 4s. Mohammed unrolled a two-foot square, black, rubber mat near the edge of the perch. This was to stop the gun from sliding on the plywood. Mohammed took the rifle out of the black canvas bag and set the bag behind him near his feet. He unfolded the integrated bipod of the slender weapon and set it down on the mat. The Arctic Warfare sniper rifle was built in 1988 by a British company as an upgrade to the Precision Marksman rifle specifically for use by the Swedish Army. Because the Swedes often needed to work in cold environments, the specially designed rifle featured special de-icing features allowing it to be used at -40 degrees Farenheit. The stockhole, bolt, magazine release and trigger guard on the rifle were made bigger so that they could be used with heavy winter mittens. Even though the rifle was originally intended for cold climates, however, it became a popular sniper rifle even in warmer climates, and was used in conflicts around the world. Many such rifles had been used in the Afghanistan War and the Iraq War. Mohammed's father had smuggled the gun out during his service in Saddam's army before he had to retire for disability reasons.

Mohammed removed from his pouch the ten-round detachable box magazine filled with .338 Lapua Magnums and connected it to the chassis of the rifle. He hoped he only needed a few shots. He laid down on his stomach and peered through the German-made Schmidt & Bender PMII telescopic sight. He focused the sight and was quickly able to see the critical section of road through the intersecting black lines in the scope. If Saddam got out of the car, his job should not be too difficult. Now all he had to do was wait.

As he lay down on his stomach, his midsection was entirely uncomfortable. His pain in his back was getting worse. "Why do I have to get sick today?" he thought. "The one day when I am needed most." It was unclear when Saddam's convoy would be coming. All they knew was that it was sometime in the morning. Mohammed's thoughts began to turn to Salmon. They had been so happy together. He remembered happy times around the family dinner table, eating his mother's lentil stew, Salmon telling jokes and his mother laughing. There was the time Salmon had been stung by a bee, but was convinced it was a scorpion. And there were times spent in the hills, just he and his brother, talking and wondering what their futures might bring. Anger swelled within him again as he remembered the soccer ball incident with Saddam Hussein. He tried his breathing exercises, slowly breathing in and out to obtain the focus and clarity needed for the shot. He would only get one or two shots at most, and they better be good.

He waited for about an hour and a half, and now he was getting concerned. The pain in his back was incredible, but that is not what bothered him. He could withstand pain for his brother. It was the constant urge to urinate. He was tapping his foot back and forth and trying to think of math problems or anything else he could think of to get his mind off the problem. He could not leave his post now. Saddam could be here any minute. He thought of a story his mother had once told him about three goats, a wise man called Azaram, and a pot filled with never-ending food. He liked that story. He started thinking of the story to keep his mind off his physical problems. Soon, however, he could hold it no more. He moved the gun back and forth to survey the surrounding countryside with his rifle scope. As far as he could see, Saddam's convoy was nowhere in sight. If he just left for a minute, he could surely make it in time.

Mohammed El Faya stood up and walked to the back of the platform. Mohammed pulled down his brown trousers and began to relieve himself off the back of the platform. Just then, he heard a commotion in the town below. He turned his head to look over his shoulder and saw the dust cloud of the motorcade coming down the road to Dujail. "Of all the luck!" he thought. He finished his business and then quickly spun around to get back into position. As he did so, he caught his foot on the strap of the rifle bag and he tripped. When his weight came crashing down on the board, the plywood tilted upward, knocking the gun on its side, and sending it sliding down the plywood where it began to veer towards the edge of the board.

Meanwhile, Saddam's line of white Mercedes Benzes was getting close to position. The huge gray dump truck driven by his friend J'aana screamed down the alley at high speed and smashed the lead Benz into the wall of one of the houses. The men inside tried to lower their windows to shoot but the windows were jammed against the side of the truck.

Mohammed slid quickly across the platform and dove for the gun. He managed to catch it by one of the legs of the bipod just before it fell off the tower. However, this left Mohammed half on the plywood, and half off, with one leg dangling. He threw the gun up on the platform first and then hoisted himself up.

The silver petrol truck pulled from an alley five streets away and blocked the exit of the caravan of white cars. Inside Saddam's vehicle, which was in the middle, his Chief of Security, a dark, tanned, burly man with a mustache much like Saddam's, quickly surveyed the scene and could see they were in an ambush. If the petrol truck exploded, they could all be incinerated. The only safe course was to get President Hussein out of the vehicle. He would have to shield him with his body, in case there were snipers on the roofs. With grim determination, he reached for the door handle.

Mohammed quickly re-set the gun on the mat. The two trucks were in position. Damn it! He lay down on his stomach, but he was still sighting the scope when Saddam's Chief of Security dashed him from the car. Mohammed fired quickly, much more quickly than he would normally take to aim, and his first two shots hit the bullet-proof glass of the open door, forming spider web cracks, but not shattering the glass. As the Chief cleared the door with Saddam, he was within Mohammed's sights. Mohammed fired again, this time cleanly hitting the Chief of Security in the head. There he was, Saddam! Out in the open, he was ducking and heading for the door of a house! Just then, Saddam's guards started filling the streets, shooting at anything that moved with automatic weapons. He had a millisecond to aim and put Saddam down. Saddam yanked open the wooden door of the house and Mohammed shot three bullets in rapid fire succession through the door frame which splintered the wood, destroying half the door. Each of the three bullets missed Saddam's head by an inch. But he was too late. Saddam was safely inside the house. Mohammed cursed himself and then turned towards Saddam's guards. He took four more shots and managed to take down one more guard but then his magazine was out of bullets. He reached over to put in the next magazine and then realized with horror that the other three magazines had slid off the tower during his fall. He had no ammunition left. He would be a sitting duck up here. He still had some time before the guards got to the tower, as they were busy fending off gunfire from his other comrades who were coming in from the orchards. Mohammed packed up his weapon in the canvas bag, and began to scale down the tower.

The gunfire between the Republican Guard and the Dawa militants continued for about fifteen minutes. It was hard for Mohammed to tell who was winning. Mohammed was about half way down the tower when he heard the chopper blades. Saddam was sending in reinforcements. He looked towards the horizon and saw clouds of dust near the road. He shimmied down the rest of the tower as fast as he could.

Five minutes later, Saddam's reinforcements arrived. Dozens of troops fanned out in the streets, shooting at everyone, even women. When they reached the petrol truck, they fanned out through the houses, looking for the President. They found him in an upstairs bedroom, hiding in a closet. They formed a phalanx of soldiers around him, taking him up to the roof of the small house, where they set up a perimeter. Their first concern was snipers. In about one half hour they had shot and killed everyone in the vicinity who was on the rooftops. The only other high vantage point was the water tower outside town, but when they looked through their binoculars, they could see no one at the top of the tower. They took Saddam across several rooftops, jumping from building to building. After jumping over about five houses, they led Saddam down a series of stairs to the ground floor. A military Humvee sped right in front of the door. The soldiers put down ground cover and then hustled Saddam into the Humvee. Safe inside, Saddam cursed in anger at the Dujaili people. The Humvee went through the backstreets, and was able to get back to the main highway. Saddam's soldiers killed the remaining militants in the firefight, which lasted another three hours. The assassination attempt had failed.

Three days later, Saddam returned to Dujail, this time with dozens of armored vehicles. Saddam ordered large transport vehicles into the main part of town. Hundreds of soldiers went from door to door, rounding up townspeople. Soldiers grabbed young boys out of the arms of their mothers, who were screaming and clawing at the soldiers to stop. Over 393 men and 394 women and children were placed in the transports and imprisoned at Abu Ghraib. Most of the men, and some of the women, were mercilessly tortured. Forty men died during interrogation. Over the next few months, 148 of the captured men confessed to having some part in the attempted assassination attempt. On July 23, 1984, Saddam Hussein signed the death sentences for 96 of the 148 men. He also ordered that their homes, buildings, date palms, and fruit orchards be razed to the ground. In 1989, on orders of Shu'bat al-Mukhabarat al 'Askariyya, Saddam Hussein's Directory of the Department of Military Intelligence, ten children from Dujail were executed.

Mohammed el Faya, however, was not among those captured, tortured, or executed. He had fled the town in guilt after the failed assassination attempt. He vowed that day that he would find some way to murder Saddam Hussein for his crimes. But that would have to wait for another day.

What Mohammed could not imagine that day was that sometime in the future, he would hate someone even more than Saddam Hussein.

CHAPTER 5. CODICIL.

June 19, 1566. Salon-de-Provence, France.

Nostradamus only had twelve more days to live. The gout was taking him. The gut pain had gotten worse and worse every day. He had vomited blood in an iron bucket this morning. Nostradamus grabbed for a shirt, but the crippling arthritis in his hands hurt when he tried to fasten the clasps together. His doctors were all waiting for him in the next room. He could have asked them for help, but he did not. He was a proud man and hated to be in this pitiful state. If only his body were as fit as his mind, he thought. This morning felt worse than before.

Nostradamus rolled out of the bed and struggled to dress himself, pulling his long, black robe over his crisp white collar, and ran his hand through his long, sweaty gray beard. He looked at himself quickly in the glass. What a mess. The disease had really taken its toll. His eyes were bloodshot and the deep creases under his eyes showed the weeks of sleep deprivation.

Nostradamus broke away from his reflection in the mirror. He had to get dressed. He thought of just going into the study in his bed clothes, but then decided against it. He had to get up to meet with the lawyer, who was coming this morning. It wouldn't do to meet a lawyer in one's bedclothes. Nostradamus pulled his velvet cap off the wooden peg near the nightstand and placed it on his head. God, he was hot in here. How hot was it in this house? It felt like a furnace. He slid into his buckled brown shoes and stumbled down the hall, grimacing at the stomach pain. Where was that idiot Chavigny?

"Chavigny! Where are you? Come here, you dunce! Have you summoned Joseph? Where is he? Time is most pressing!"

Jean-Aime de Chavigny, a lawyer and former magistrate in Burgundy, had been Nostradamus' secretary and personal apprentice these last twelve years. Chavigny certainly had a fine career ahead of him without the help of Nostradamus. He had schooled with the great Greek scholar Jean Dorat at the Principal of the College de Coqueret in Paris, and had earned his own reputation as a theologian and thinker. He had also dabbled in the magical arts. However, as he had explained to his wife many times, his career would have to wait. Clerking with Monsieur Nostradamus was simply too great an opportunity to pass up. He was willing to withstand the petty slights and menial work for the opportunity to work aside a real genius. He, Chavigny, had actually gotten to assist the Master with *Les Propheties*! This morning, Chavigny had been asked to summon Joseph Roche, the wills and trusts lawyer. It seemed that Nostradamus had gotten into his mind to prepare a last-minute codicil to his will. Chavigny wondered if there might be something of value for him in the new will. After all, Nostradamus had amassed quite a fortune here in Salon after his successful canal project. And Nostradamus' second wife, the old battle-axe, had come from money as well. Chavigny had once seen a balance sheet lying on the Master's desk. He had well over 3,400 crowns! Even if Nostradamus left most of the fortune to his three boys and three girls, surely there was something left over for loyal Chavigny for his dedicated decade of service to Master Nostradamus? Well, he would know soon enough, judging from the bucket of blood he cleaned up this morning.

"I see Monsieur Roche and the witnesses coming down the street now, Master. I shall bring him into the study momentarily."

Nostradamus had written 942 prophecies of future events. All that was missing were the final 58 verses, which would be his crowning achievement. Unfortunately, the 58 verses were still back in Agen, the town in Southern France where he had married his first wife. Nostradamus' new publisher was waiting on the final 58. Nostradamus hated publishers. Du Rosne, his first publisher in Lyon, had published the first few centuries. Du Rosne's version had so many typesetting errors one could hardly read it. His second publisher, Benoist Regaud of Lyon, was lazy. Even though he had been given several hundred of the quatrains five years ago, Nostradamus had not seen a single edition printed. At this rate, Nostradamus would die before he saw his entire masterpiece printed. By switching to a third publisher, he hoped to get the entire 1,000 in print.

Nostradamus looked at the letter lying on the night stand beside his desk and thought of its implications. The letter, delivered by a small eleven year-old boy yesterday, was written by Joseph Justus Scaliger, the son of Nostradamus' late mentor and former friend, Julius Caesar Scaliger. The letter was dated May 1, 1566, and read:

Dear Monsieur Nostradamus:

I have reviewed your most recent correspondence from last fall. As I have told you several times before, I do not have your poetry. I have no idea what these "58 verses" are to which you constantly refer. I personally collected my father's effects for the estate when he died, and I can assure you that I did not see any of your poetry. I wish I could help you, Michel, but alas, I cannot. Perhaps you can create some new verses? I have heard you have been a most prolific writer in recent years.

I know that you and my father were once the closest of friends. It is a shame that you had a falling out. On his death bed eight years ago, he was still filled with vitriol for you, Michel. I do not know what your offense was, as the whole matter occurred when I was just an infant. Whatever it was, however, my father never forgave you, even in his last breath. Just before he died, he wrote you a letter. I have not sent it before now because it is filled with anger, and, as a gentleman, I did not want to cause you further insult. However, in your most recent correspondence, you beseeched me to please give you anything of any description which my father may have left you. So, with some reluctance, I attach my father's last letter to you, written some eight years ago. I cannot imagine what comfort it would give you, but I send it anyway because of the urgency of your request.

The lad who brought me your last letter from April 5 of this year stated that you are in ill health. I am sorry about your condition, and I wish you a healthy recovery.

Michel, you must understand that as a man of science and letters myself, my business is most pressing, and I will not have another opportunity to write you again regarding your poetry. I trust that you may now be in peace. May God be with you.

Truly,
Joseph Justus Scaliger
May 1, 1566

Separating the letters of the father and his son was a piece of brown wrapping paper, which Nostradamus discarded to the side of the desk. Nostradamus then pulled out the attached letter with enthusiasm. Julius Caesar Scaliger's last letter to Nostradamus read as follows:

Dear Michel:

As I look out my window, I long for another spring, when the white almond flowers dance through the blue skies of Agen and the smell of honeysuckle fills the air. However, I fear I have seen my last spring on this earth. I am not in good health, Michel. I fear the morgue awaits me. By the time you read this, I probably will be in the ground, my bodily organs the daily feast of earthworms.

You, on the other hand, will be hawking another edition of your prophetic drivel. Many of your verses, Michel, are simply plagiarized from prophets of earlier ages. The remainder of your verses are drafted in such vague and indecipherable terms that they may mean almost anything to anyone. It astounds me that masters of the written word like Vergil are attacked by critics on a daily basis, while you make riches off verses so poorly written and so poorly constructed that one would think that the literary critics would be armed with pitchforks at your gate. Yet, for some reason, they have prepared the fatted calf for you. And while true prophets are ignored, you shamelessly convince the world that you can predict future events by looking at the stars. You know, Michel, that I see through you. I know for a fact that the great "predictor of pigs" cannot predict future events. If you could, your wife and children would be alive today. And I plan to reveal to your centuries of followers what a charlatan and liar you really are. You may think this is a big game, but when I get finished with you, you will regret your abandonment, fraud, and plagiarism.

Michel, the wind of change is upon us. The world and the Catholic Church face true evil ahead, and I must stop it. My task is difficult. To hold in one's hands the future of mankind is an awesome responsibility. However, despite the danger to myself and my family, I must press forward, like two oxen pulling a plow through a rough field. Through the divine Word of God, the world will be warned and humanity will be saved from destruction. And even though I am only one frail human voice in the cacophony of misdirection and mendacity, I will be here through the ages to make sure that the words of the true prophets, and not the false ones, are heeded.

If you are the clever man I hope you to be, Michel, then you, too, may be an instrument of change. If you repent and show the world who you truly are on the inside, future generations may avoid the evil that awaits them.

Truly,
Julius Caesar Scaliger
October 14, 1558
Agen, France

Yesterday, Nostradamus had scowled at first when he had read the letter. He truly respected Julius Caesar Scaliger, and it pained him to hear his angry words. It appeared the man was never going to forgive him. He read the letter over and over again, hoping to find some hidden meaning, but he could find none. He picked up the brown wrapping paper, preparing to discard it into the trash basket. However, as he did so, he noticed some small cut marks or perforations on the paper. He brought out his magnifying glass, and studied the brown paper. Sure enough, there were little brown indentations in the shape of ovals at various places on the brown paper.

"Aha!" he thought. He quickly pulled out a small knife from a drawer and began cutting along the perforations, creating numerous oval holes in the paper. When he was finished, he laid the brown paper with the holes over the letter from Julius Caesar Scaliger. Only a dozen or so words peeked out through the holes. Nostradamus thought for a minute and then realized the meaning behind the remaining words.

"Ah!" he exclaimed. And then another thought dawned on Nostradamus, and a hearty smile crept across his face. "The old man had a soft spot for me after all!" he thought. Could he get back to Agen in time? Surely not, in his health. If that blasted Joseph Scaliger had only sent him the letter sooner! However, there might be another way.... Then his legacy would be secured after all!

Nostradamus then wrote long letters to his oldest daughter Madeleine and his oldest son César, giving them detailed instructions on what to do after his death. He gave these letters to Chavigny, instructing him to give the letters to Father De Neve of the Chapel of our Lady of the White Penitents of Salon as soon as possible. Father De Neve would be instructed by Chavigny to safeguard the letters and give them to the children upon Nostradamus' death. He had written a separate letter to Father De Neve.

As Nostradamus struggled to finish dressing himself this morning, Chavigny welcomed Monsieur Roche and his briefcase of scrolls and quills through the front door. Along with Monsieur Roche came Jehan Allegret and Jehan Giraud de Besson, two locals who would act as witnesses to the codicil.

"Good morning, Monsieur Roche," welcomed Chavigny. "The Master and his doctors are waiting for you in his study. Let me show you in."

Roche had been somewhat perturbed at his summoning this morning. Roche had an office full of clients waiting for him at the other end of town. He had just spent an entire day with Nostradamus just three days ago preparing his will. As was his custom, Roche had been most thorough, conducting a complete inventory of all assets and covering Monsieur Nostradamus' wishes as to distribution with respect to each item. There was obviously the house in Salon, as well as some decent furniture, various astrological tools and devices, and a whole library of books. His treasure trove of currency—crowns, rose nobles, simple ducats, German florins, imperials, marionettes, crown-pistollets, Louis XII crowns, golden lions, and other coins were all kept in three large coffers in the house. Three different men in the town were entrusted with the keys to the coffers. As Roche had transcribed into the original will written on the 17th, most of Nostradamus' fortune would go to his wife Anne Ponsarde. His son César would receive the house, his gilded silver cup, and his wooden and iron chairs. Madeleine, the eldest, would receive 600 golden crowns. Anne and Diane, then eight and five years old respectively, would receive 500 crowns upon their marriages. Charles and Andre, his youngest sons, would receive 100 gold crowns each on their twenty-fifth birthday. There had also been individual bequeaths to the Chapel of our Lady of the White Penitents of Salon, the Brothers of St. Pierre-des-Canons, and the Minor Brothers of the Convent of St. Francis.

He had been so detailed in the preparation of the will, Roche thought. Had he done something wrong in the drafting? He hoped Master

Nostradamus was not upset with him. What could have changed in three days? Had Nostradamus had a falling out with the wife? If Monsieur Nostradamus was not paying Roche an obscene fee, he would not have made this speedy house call this morning and ignored his other clients. But one must go after the money if one is to succeed, after all. At least that is what is father had taught him.

Roche entered Nostradamus' study, which was a scattered garbage heap of parchment, scrolls, astrolabes, maps, astrological tools, candles, and, most of all, books. Books stood in huge stacks on the desk, in the bookshelves, and all over the floor. There was Virgil's *Eclogues*, Pliny the Elder's histories, Livy's *History of Rome*, and Abraham Ibn Ezra's *Livre du Monde et des Conjunctions*. There were books on the conquests of Caesar, a chronicle on Constantinople, and a history of cataclysms. There were books regarding the interpretation of omens and the alignment of planets. There were books on mythological monsters, meteors and magic talismans. Dozens of texts, some open, some not, many annotated and tabbed and scribbled on, were scattered all over the room. Roche saw Nostradamus hunched over a work bench, in obvious pain. Tending to him were Antoine Paris, doctor of medicine, Guillem Eyraud, apothecary, and Gervais Berard, a surgeon from Salon. These doctors had been unsuccessfully attempting to cure Nostradamus over the last several weeks but they, too, could see the writing on the wall.

"Monsieur Nostradamus, I have brought the will which you executed three days ago. Is there some problem with its execution?"

"No, Joseph, nothing like that. I just remembered that I have a few special items which are particularly important to my eldest children. So I wish a codicil be prepared to dictate the specific bequeaths of those items."

"Certainly, Monsieur," said Roche. Roche laid out a scroll on the table. He plunked down a copy of Stadius' *Ephemerides* on one end of the scroll so that it would not curl back. Roche wrote out the legal jargon necessary for the establishment of a codicil and then asked the seer about the personal items.

Nostradamus responded, "To my eldest son César, I wish to give my great gold ring, inset with the stone of cornelian, as well as my astrolabe, which I treasure dearly. I have also written this epistle to César, which I wish to be given to him upon my death. In addition, I wish to bequeath the contents these two walnut chests to my daughter Madeleine absolutely and immediately." Nostradamus pointed to the chests lying under a pile of books in the corner of the study.

"I entrust the keys to the chests to sire Martin Manson, Consul, who shall deliver them to my daughter Madeleine immediately upon my death."

Roche nodded his head and wrote in the appropriate language in a very sloppy French cursive. Nostradamus signed at the bottom, grimacing at the arthritic pain as he grabbed the quill. When he was finished, everyone but Jehan de Giraud signed at the bottom as witnesses. Roche took custody of the keys to the chest and the newly executed codicil.

"Very well, Monsieur Nostradamus," said Roche, preparing to leave, "Everything is in order. You can trust me that this matter will be promptly handled."

Nostradamus thanked the man and handed him a handful of French crowns.

Eleven days later, on the evening of July 1, 1566, Nostradamus gave one more fond look to his study, and pulled out the Ephemerides book from the desk where Roche had left it and wrote on it "Hic prope mors es," which, in Latin, means "Death is close at hand." He then got into his nightclothes and summoned Chavigny to his bedside. Chavigny quickly came to his master's side.

"Chavigny, you have been a dear friend and a good student. I am sorry if I have ever mistreated you. Make sure you carry on my work because I will not live long."

"Do not say that, Master Nostradamus," said Chavigny. "Surely with the surgery you can recover."

"No, son," said Nostradamus, "You will not see me alive at sunrise. Summon the pastor for Last Rites."

Chavigny quickly left to summon the local priest. As Nostradamus lay in agony awaiting the local priest, the door to his bedroom silently opened. A dark shadow appeared in the doorway. In the dim light, Nostradamus could barely make out the figure of a tall, broad-shouldered man wearing a hooded monk's garb. His hard, chiseled face, narrow eyes, and silent snarl told Nostradamus that this was not the parish priest.

The man whispered. "Where is the prophecy?"

Nostradamus replied, "If you mean *Les Propheties,* they are with my publisher."

The monk was agitated. "Not that drivel, you idiot. The real prophecy. The one written in Agen."

Nostradamus looked terrified, "I don't know what you are talking about."

The man sat on the edge of Nostradamus' bed and put his face an inch above Nostradamus' mouth.

"Old man, you can either tell me where the prophecy is now, or I will kill every member of your family."

Nostradamus again protested that he did not know anything. The monk then took his two giant muscular hands and began strangling Nostradamus. Nostradamus stiffened, his eyes bulging out, gasping to breathe. After thirty seconds, Nostradamus stopped fighting and his body slumped. Just then, the monk heard a commotion at the front door. It was the local priest and Chavigny. Several moments later, Chavigny and the parish priest entered the bed chamber. Chavigny thought it was odd that his master's bedroom window was ajar. That draft would not be good for his master's condition. Chavigny closed the window and looked fondly down at the seer. The priest bent over the bed, making incantations and blessing Nostradamus with holy water. After the Last Rites were administered, the parish priest left and Chavigny retired to bed. True to Nostradamus' prediction, when Chavigny visited his master the next morning, he was dead.

CHAPTER 6. TRANSITION

January 18, 2013. The Wynn Resort and Casino. Las Vegas, Nevada. Headquarters for the Transition Office of President-Elect Tim Woodson.

Tim Woodson, the Republican Governor from Nevada, had done the unthinkable—he had beaten Barack Obama in the race for President. And to think that in July, Obama had a 12-point lead.

It was now shortly before Inauguration Day. Woodson was meeting with his advisors to continue his meetings to pick the next Cabinet. Attending the meeting was Woodson's new Chief of Staff Chance Bixby, a short, slight man with a big smile, thinning brown hair combed in a preppy cut, who wore an expensive blue Polo suit, red and blue striped tie, and shiny brown loafers. His campaign manager, Bobbie MacDougall, was here, but was not planning on adding much. Her job here was largely done, and she was spending most of her days here in Las Vegas fielding calls from lobbying firms across the country. After her big win with Woodson, she had her pick of the litter and could not wait to start making serious money.

Due to the terrorist attack in September, Woodson felt that responding to that threat was going to be Number One on his agenda, so appointing the Director of Homeland Security, the Director of the FBI, the National Security Advisor, and the Director of the CIA were going to be his first picks as the new President. Bobbie would handle press inquiries for now until the President-Elect had decided on a Press Secretary. Also present were some of the top lieutenants from the campaign, including Bill Dominic, who handled foreign affairs questions, T.J. Donovan, who handled domestic and economic issues, and Roger Tippins, Woodson's attorney, who handled legal issues. Also present were the Vice President-Elect, her Chief of Staff Matt Suba, and one of their advisors, Tommy Mitchell.

They were staying at the lush Wynn Resort and Casino in Las Vegas, the only hotel in the world to receive the Mobil Five Star Rating, the AAA Five Diamond Award, and the Michelin Five Red Pavilion Award. The huge suite in the Tower Suites had tangerine walls, cream sofas and chairs, over a dozen flat screen TVs, shiny marble floors, several cream-colored Jacuzzis, gigantic glass-walled showers, and dozens of vases of fresh flowers. The suite looked out onto Wynn's breathtaking and manicured golf courses, complete with waterfalls, pine trees, and stone-rimmed lakes. Three dozen villas bordered the golf course, each with its own outdoor pool and massage tables. Well wishers and patrons seeking favor had flooded the President-Elect's suite room with gift baskets of caviar and brie, fresh mangos, and bottles of expensive wine. Woodson had his own Secret Service security detail now, and over a dozen agents covered the inside and outside of the suite to make sure no one else crashed the party.

One of the expansive suites had a large granite conference table, and the interested parties had gathered with their briefing books and notes to discuss the selection of the next Administration. Woodson folded his tan arms onto the table, and addressed the team.

"We have already selected the DHS, the NSA, and the head of the CIA. Now we need to pick the Director of the FBI. Frankly, anybody we pick will be better than the clown we have in there now. You have my three possibilities, but I want to know if you guys have come up with anybody better."

"Mr. President -Elect... Wow, it feels really great to say that," Bixby cooed.

"It feels great for me too," joked Woodson, as the yes-men in the room all giggled.

"Of course, all three of your selections are excellent, Mr. President-Elect. The only other one we came up with was Tony Delano from Missouri. As you recall, he narrowly lost his Senate run against Claire McCaskill, so he needs something to do. He is an up-and-comer in the Party, very smart, some say he is a real egghead. He is a former Missouri Highway Patrol Officer and he served as a JAG in the Gulf, so he has law enforcement experience. He is a total straight arrow, goes to Catholic Church every week with his doting, ugly Italian wife and a couple brainy kids. He has no skeletons. All in all, I think he would be a safe pick. Here's his photo." Bixby slid the 8×10 over the table to the President-Elect. "Other than Delano, we have your three picks, Mr. President-Elect. That's all I have."

None of the other members of the group had any other suggestions. Then Anna Scall's Chief of Staff, Matt Suba, spoke up. Suba had been golfing earlier in the day, and so was wearing a yellow short-sleeved golf shirt. His biceps were bulging from the sides of the shirt. He always tried to wear tight short-sleeved shirts whenever he could. He had a brown buzz-cut, tight abs and one of those chiseled faces that women loved. He obviously was not afraid to speak out, even across the table from the

President-Elect of the United States.

"Mr. President-Elect, there is one other gentleman we might consider for Director," said Suba. "His name is Rick Thomas. He is currently the Sheriff of McCormick County, South Carolina. Now I know what you are going to say, too small town. But this is the officer who cracked the case of that young lady who killed her whole family with rat poison. I know Rick very well, and he is a straight law-and-order guy. He also has no skeletons. I cannot think of anyone better to be the Director of the FBI."

T.J. Donovan, one of the young, slick-haired, East Coast political science junkies who was on Woodson's staff, almost laughed at the suggestion.

"Look, Matt, no offense, we love South Carolina and everything, but this is the most important post in perhaps the entire country. This is the guy who is going to find the terrorists from Cincinnati. We just had perhaps the worst terrorist attack on our nation. And you want to entrust the nation's safety to some hillbilly sheriff from the backwoods? That's crazy. Once they see his beer gut and hear his twang, he will get eaten alive on MSNBC. We will never get him through."

"Well, T.J...." Suba spit the word "T.J." with as much contempt as he could muster. "I know you don't like Southern accents, but America seemed to have no problem electing a South Carolina beauty queen with a Southern accent as their next Vice President. And while you were making a fool of yourself on Hardball with Chris Matthews, our Governor from the South was administering CPR and saving a little boy's life. And contrary to what you may have learned in your vast three years of experience in Washington, T.J., not all of us in the South look like Boss Hog, drink moonshine from a jug, and sport beer guts. So why not open your mind and at least give the guy a chance?"

"Look," said Donovan, clearly miffed at the experience comment, "I have been around Washington D.C. a lot longer..."

"Gentleman, gentleman," Bixby smiled patronizingly. "This is getting us nowhere. Look, whoever gets this appointment needs to be a sure thing, someone no one will argue about. If we cannot even get agreement around our own table on a candidate, he is obviously not the one for us. We already have four great candidates, so let's just stick with those four for now, but Matt, we appreciate your input and keep the ideas coming. OK, let's go pro's and con's for each one of these guys. Roger, what are your thoughts?"

Suba smiled and said nothing, but inside he was thinking about the best way to smash Donovan's face in. Suba took out his cell phone and text messaged Anna Scall next to him.

"If you become President someday, and I smash that little punk's face in, will you give me a pardon?"

The Cabinet Selection meeting went on for another two hours. When it was finished, Anna Scall went back to her hotel room and took a shower. The soaps and shampoos at this hotel were amazing. They all smelled like fresh fruit. After she got out of the shower, she popped a bottle of Dom Perignon champagne (another expense for the Transition Committee) and drank down a few glasses of the golden liquid. That felt good. She went over to the luxurious marble bathroom, and bent over to one side, drying her long brown hair with the dryer. She stood up straight and teased her hair with a brush so that it was big and full, and then applied her false eyelashes. She applied a full coating of deep black mascara and coral lipstick to her full lips. She looked at herself front ways and sideways in the mirror. She still had it. Her abs looked awesome. She turned her fist out and backwards, so that she could see her tricep in the mirror. God, she looked good. She went to the drawers of her bedroom and pulled out a yellow, French brassiere and matching lace thong. She put on her four inch black heels and pranced around the room for a minute or two, drinking another glass of the Champagne. She went to her closet and pulled out a rather drab chocolate brown dress. She wished she could wear some sexier dresses, but the voters would never approve of a Governor of South Carolina (or a Vice President! She still could not believe how far she had come!) who was too overtly sexual. There would be another late meeting tonight, but she had a few hours to kill.

Just then, there was a knock on her door. She walked from the bedroom into the living room of the suite, across the orange and cream carpet and onto the cream marble floor near the door to the suite. She asked who it was. It was Matt, her Chief of Staff. He was still in the golf shirt from this afternoon. He must not have changed after the meeting. He was carrying a large gray briefing book.

"Madame Vice President-Elect," he said, crossing the room and putting the briefing book down on the glass table in the living room. "I have some things here to go over before the meeting tonight." Anna Scall crossed over into the living room.

"And take off that ridiculous dress!"

Anna Scall complied, taking off her dress and sauntering over to Matt Suba. He admired her yellow undergarments and said, "That's better." He kissed her deeply for a minute and then with his strong hands, spun her around so she was facing away from him, and forcefully pushed her back down so she was bent over the end table. Looking into the huge suite wall mirror, he took off his pants and shirt and entered her from behind. She looked back at him in the mirror, lusting over his huge chest and standing ready to obey any command which he had to give.

CHAPTER 7. BUILDER.

January 19, 2013. Midnight. Georgetown. Washington, D.C.

Hector Santiago worked silently at his large work bench. Earlier this week, he had prepared his own homemade batch of C4 plastic explosives. He had avoided the C4 produced by most commercial manufacturers because explosives manufacturers frequently added chemical markers, such as "DMDNB," which could be easily picked up by the Secret Service in a security sweep. He needed to be absolutely sure that this C4 went undetected. Next to his work bench were several barrels of RDX in powder form, which had been smuggled out of an Alexandria, Virginia chemical plant. RDX, or "royal demolition explosive," was the active explosive material in C4.

Last week, in a makeshift chemical lab in his dingy two-bedroom Georgetown apartment, Santiago prepared the C4. In a large basin, he added water to the powder RDX to form a white slurry. Then, in a separate bowl, he dissolved the polyisobutylene binder into a solvent. The binder made the explosive material much more resistant to force and heat, rendering the C4 more stable. By adding the binder, the C4 could handle rough treatment without exploding. Santiago knew that even a rifle shot at the clay material would not cause it to explode. Only a detonator or blasting cap could do the trick. Santiago combined the binder and RDX and whipped the mixture with an industrial sized cake mixer. Then he added the sebacate "plasticizer," which gave the material its malleability and the texture of modeling clay. As Santaiago had learned in the camps in Afghanistan, the recipe was 91 parts RDX, 5.3 parts di(2-ethylhexyl) sebacate, 2.1 parts polyisobutylene, and 1.6 percent motor oil. Once the parts were mixed together adequately, the solvent and water had to be removed. Through a series of handmade mesh and cheesecloth filters, Santiago strained out the solvent. Finally, the material was left out to dry under heat lamps, which removed most of the water. Santiago collected the material on large aluminum sheets, and then cut the final product into a series of white clay moldable bricks.

In his training, Santiago learned that C4 had become the weapon of choice for terrorists. Due to its stability, it could be carried relatively easy. Its soft composition made it easier to smuggle through lax security posts. And its malleability allowed it to be transported in any number of shapes.

For example, C4 could be molded to appear like plastic black wheels on a suitcase. In October 2000, terrorists used C4 to attack the U.S.S. Cole, killing 17 Navy personnel. In 1996, terrorists used C4 to blow up the military barracks in Saudi Arabia. A terrorist had even attempted to smuggle C4 on a commercial airliner in his shoe.

Laying on its side, in the middle of Santiago's artist's work bench, was a nine foot-tall plaster statue of St. Anthony of Padua. He was pictured in a plain brown hooded monk's robe, with a rope around the waist. St. Anthony was holding a small haloed child in one hand and a copper-colored Bible in the other. Earlier this afternoon, Santiago had taken the bricks of homemade C4 and meticulously applied a layer of C4 explosives around the entire statue like a mud mask. With his fingers, he gently molded the material into the grooves and indentations on the statue. After the coating was complete, Santiago then placed another layer of plaster over the C4 layer, gently painting the white mix over every inch of the statue. Without the DMDNB chemical marker, it was extremely unlikely that the Secret Service would ever notice the C4 layer. That was the easy part. The difficult part was hiding the wire and the detonator. Because those items were very dense, they would get picked up in any X-Ray scan.

But Santiago had thought of that. He was The Builder, after all. The wire and detonator would go in the Bible. With a small rotating saw, he gently cut the Bible away from the statue. In its place he put a rectangular wooden box with a copper skin. Along the length of the Bible's spine, Santiago placed a slender blasting cap about the size of a harmonica. He had specially carved the metal housing of the blasting cap so that it blended in perfectly with the Bible's spine. To anyone waving a security wand over Bible, it would look merely like an ornate metal spine. The wire ran from the detonator through a small hole at the top of the Bible, into the Saint's arm, and finally into the layer of C4. When he was finished, he took out a portable X-ray machine that he had stolen last year when he had worked at a local hospital as an X-ray technician. He passed the portable scanner over the Bible.

In his training several years ago as an X-ray technician, Santiago had learned all about X-ray machines and how to avoid detection. X-ray machines were made to detect the density of objects. Some objects have low atomic density, called "low Z." Other objects had high atomic density or "high Z." X-rays worked by passing photons through an object. If the object being scanned had high Z, the photons would be absorbed. Otherwise, the photons would be scattered. Through special software, the X-ray machine could recreate a black and white picture of what was within an object based upon its density. An object with a recognized shape, like a gun, could be readily identified. However, individuals attempting to trick security personnel succeeded when they made dangerous objects appear to be everyday, non-lethal objects with similar density. That was Santiago's plan here. By disguising the detonator as parts of the Bible's spine, he hoped to avoid detection. As he ran the portable scanner over the Bible, he looked at the picture on the screen. He was convinced that the blasting cap would go undetected.

He placed the new explosive copper Bible against the Saint's hand and arm and secured them temporarily with small pieces of clay and plaster. Then he applied Crazy Glue, securing the Bible in place permanently. After the final layer of plaster was added, the statue was left to dry alongside the Builder's other masterpieces: Jesus Christ and Joseph of Arimathea. The detonator on Jesus was hidden within a metal crown of thorns, which Santiago thought was most appropriate, given the amount of suffering he and the others planned to unleash on the arrogant infidels.

It was now midnight and St. Anthony was ready for painting. Santiago also loved the irony in hiding the C4 and detonator within St. Anthony of Padua, who the Catholics believed to be the patron saint of lost items. If you lost your keys or your wallet, this was the saint to whom you were supposed to pray. And now the saint could not even find a load of explosives buried inside his own body! These Americans with their ridiculous beliefs. Who would waste Allah's time with prayers to find car keys? Santiago removed a color glossy 8×10 picture of the original statue which he had taken this morning. Out of a nearby desk, he took out an artist's palette and squeezed out a dozen globs of different colored paint. He used a brush and mixed some of the paints together to obtain more realistic hues. Then, copying the colors in the photograph, he began to repaint the statue of St. Anthony of Padua so that it resembled the original. He had to work quickly to get the statue back in the Church by 5 a.m.

As he painted, Hector Santiago reflected on his long journey to this point. His real name was not Hector Santiago, of course. That was just the name given to him on his fake ID. A lifetime ago, he had been known as Shabaz Ma'ak Lom. His name "Shabaz" meant "hawk," a name his father decided upon after first seeing his infant's hazel eyes. He had two brothers, Suhaim ("arrow") and Saif al Din ("sword of faith"). He lived in the Shaab residential district in northern Baghdad and his father sold produce in the local outdoor bazaar. His father kept his head down and stayed out of politics. The father told all of his children to do the same. If you were asked, you did not know anything, you did not see anything, you did not hear anything. By taking this approach, the family had largely avoided the crazy edicts of Saddam Hussein. They had a simple life and a happy life. Shabaz went to school in northern Baghdad and learned Arabic, math, and astrology. The family loved to eat their father's fruit, and many a family meal was spent telling stories and devouring ripe melons and delicious figs.

When the President of the United States announced that he would be invading Iraq in March 2003, Shabaz's family couldn't believe it. They had seen saber-rattling before, and they assumed that if the United States attacked, they would be going into downtown Bagdhad, where Saddam was, not here in the Shaab district. So for Shabaz and his family, life went on.

On March 26, 2003, a few weeks after the invasion began, Shabaz's entire family was working with their father at the produce stand. Shabaz had been sent on an errand by his father to pay another merchant for a delivery of grapes. He was about a half mile away from the fruit stand on his bicycle when he saw the two silver American warplanes with the red, white, and blue stars fly over his head at an altitude which was extremely low. "What are they doing?" He wondered to himself. "There are no Republican Guard troops here. This is a shopping area filled with women and children." And then he saw the big cylindrical objects fall out of the bomb bay doors of the aircraft. In a moment of dread and disbelief, he looked towards the area where his family's fruit stand was, and there was a gigantic explosion of orange flame, followed by a tumultuous cloud of pitch black smoke and soot. "No!" he shouted, dropping the bags of grapes and pedaling as fast as he could back to the bazaar. He could not get more than a few hundred feet before he was knocked off the bike by a panicked and hysterical mob. People were running everywhere in the smoke, screaming. When Shabaz finally fought through the crowd, there was a crater as big as a football field where the bazaar used to be. That was the last day he saw his father, mother, and two brothers. The subsequent news reports confirmed it: fourteen civilians dead and thirty wounded. There was not one military target here. And yet the Americans did not seem the slightest bit apologetic. Their Secretary of Defense brushed off the reports, calling it necessary "collateral damage." These people were monsters and needed to be stopped. That was the day Shabaz answered the call for jihad.

Over the next five years, Shabaz trained in camps in Afghanistan. The leaders there were most impressed with his ability to build things, so he was immediately trained in the art of demolition and explosives. One day, he was informed by his spiritual leader that Osama Bin Laden, an engineer himself, was impressed with his work and had ordained a special task for him to complete. He was given the ceremonial name "Ammar" ("the Builder"). He was told that he was one of a handful of chosen ones, called the "Abisali," or "Warriors of the Faith," who would be given the honor of going to America and striking at the heart of the enemy. All would be explained once he arrived in America. There was a convert in America, he was told—someone very high in the government who believed in jihad and would provide instructions. This last Abisali would be the leader of the group and would act as the planner. He was appropriately named "Mudabbir" ("the Planner"). In 2009, the group of foreign-born Abisali—one from Iran, three from Pakistan, and two from Iraq—traveled on a freighter across the Atlantic Ocean to Mexico, where, with fake passports and identification cards, they posed as Mexicans. This was when Hector Santiago was created. They worked in Mexico for about a year, and then, in late 2010, hooked up with a gentleman who specialized in obtaining student visas. The Abisali entered the United States on student visas, but never showed up one day on campus. The men eventually assimilated themselves into the fabric of America, blending in and taking odd jobs in restaurants, hotels, and landscaping companies. Later, one of the Abisali would take aviation training and would get a job as a private pilot. Two other Abisali would get jobs as over-the-road truck drivers. Another found a job as an X-ray technician, and later as a maintenance man. It would not be until July 2012 when the Abisali would be summoned by Mudabbir to meet and prepare for the destruction of America.

The meeting had taken place in a Red Roof Inn in St. Louis. Each had received a hotel key, a letter with the typed word "Abisali," and the address of the hotel. When they arrived at the small hotel, Mudabbir was nowhere to be found. About a half hour after the last member arrived, however, there was a phone call to the room, stating that room service had arrived. The bewildered men opened the door to their room and saw a room service tray with a gray dome used to keep food warm. Under the dome was a DVD. The men quickly took the room service tray in the room and watched the DVD on the DVD player.

The last Abisali never showed his face and had used typed words on the screen to narrate the plan. The DVD set forth the nature of the targets, the responsibilities for each man, the method of accomplishing each task, the materials needed, and the timeline. The date of the attack was set. At the conclusion of the DVD, the men were given instructions to crush the DVD into dust with a mallet and dump the pieces of refuse in the hotel dumpster.

The wheels were set in motion. Step 1, the Massacre in Cincinnati, was already completed successfully by the first of their group. Step 2 would be the Assassination on Inauguration Day by Haytham. Then it would be Ammar's turn.

Mudabbir had given Ammar instructions to become a parishioner of St. Anthony of Padua last year. Ammar then snuck into the church at night and dirtied up the place, so that the existing maintenance man was fired. He quickly volunteered to act as the parish's maintenance man for a salary so low that the priest could not afford to turn him down. His new job gave him keys to the Church at night and full run of the place. Ammar had not been told by Mudabbir why this particular church was so important, but all of the Abisali were told by the spiritual leader that it was not up to them to question the plan of Mudabbir. So each night, like a dutiful parishioner, Ammar, pretending to be Catholic, had cleaned the Church. But tonight was the night he would switch the three statues. He was sure none of the parishioners would notice the switch. Unlike the followers of Islam, these Americans would spend half their time asleep during the prayer services and the rest of their time checking Blackberrys or watches, wondering when mass would be over so they could go to the Redskins game. Ammar did not feel bad. These Americans were all the same. They were no different than George Bush. "They all deserve to die," he thought, as he painted the last bit of yellow acrylic paint on the child's halo.

The paint had to dry, so he turned on his heat lamps to low, and went to bed, setting his alarm for 4 a.m., when the paint would be dry.

Father Timothy Rourke was the pastor of St. Anthony of Padua in Georgetown. Father Timothy was a good man, and did a fairly decent job preaching on Sundays. This particular parish had a lot of rich Washington politicians, lawyers and lobbyists, so parish fund raising was not too difficult. Two Senators, the Secretary of the Treasury, a few members of the Secret Service, and even a Supreme Court Justice were all parishioners. Father Timothy also liked the energy and optimism of the young people. Situated on Prospect Street, the church was just down the road from Georgetown University. His one vice was the bottle. He ordered all the wine for the weekly Church ceremonies and picked the orders up personally from Dick's Liquor. He always made sure to throw an extra bottle or two of Scotch in with the parish order, and no one had ever been the wiser.

This past month, Father Timothy had been hitting the sauce pretty hard. Christmas always did that to him. For most people, the Christmas season warmed the heart, but for Father Timothy, he mostly felt the pain of loneliness. His sister had passed last year, and none of the parishioners had invited him over for dinner. In the old days, he would get invited over all the time, but recently, everyone seemed so busy that they kind of forgot about the friendly parish priest. He had prayed to Jesus, of course, for strength, but in the end, he was a man and sinned like anyone else. During the past week, he had drained the three bottles of Scotch that were supposed to last him for another two weeks.

At 3 a.m., he woke up with night sweats. He had to have a drink. He went down into the rectory kitchen, where the wine for mass was kept. He found a bottle of cheap red jug wine and sat down at the small kitchen table. He took the wine over to the small family room and turned on the cable. There was nothing on except old re-runs of Seinfeld. That would have to do. He unscrewed the lid and poured the liquid down his throat. The wine was very poor quality and much too sweet, but it was good enough. After thirty minutes, he had completely drained the entire jug of wine, and he was smashed. He decided to go for a walk to clear his head. He took his ring of keys, put on his navy blue parka, ski gloves, and blue winter cap, and walked from the rectory across the parking lot.

There was a basketball hoop which was missing its net on the parking lot. He searched the grass near the edge of the lot to see if there was a basketball but he could find none. Oh well. He staggered a bit, tipping into a chain link fence by the edge of the lot, and looked up at the stars. He felt bad about the drinking and decided to go to the Church and ask God for forgiveness again. Father Timothy opened the Church with his ring of keys, turned on the lights, and walked down the aisle between the pews. It was so beautiful in the Church when no one was here. There were no sounds, and one could focus on silent prayer. As he made his way to the front of the Church, he thought that something looked odd. What was it? Then he saw it. St. Anthony's statue was missing! Had someone stolen it? As he looked around the Church, he noticed that the statue of Jesus and Joseph of Arimithea were also missing. Who would steal a statue? He decided he needed to report this to the police, but surely not now, at 4 a.m. in the morning. How would he explain his intoxication? He prayed for about ten minutes in silence, but then he found himself nodding off to sleep. He did not want any parishioner to find him passed out in the Church, so he decided to stagger his way back to the rectory. As he wandered back across the Church parking lot, he decided to say a prayer to St. Anthony of Padua to help him find the missing statues. After all, Father Anthony was the patron saint of lost items. Then he started giggling, thinking how ridiculous it was to pray to a saint to find himself!

He made it all the way back to the rectory, where he set his alarm and passed out on the couch. In his stupor, he never saw the gray van which pulled onto the parking lot with its lights off about forty-five minutes later.

Ammar pulled the van as close as he could to the side doors of the Church. With his janitor's keys, he opened the side door and propped it open with a wooden wedge. Then, under cover of darkness, he took the large, newly painted statue of St. Anthony coated with C4 and carried it into the Church, where he set it back on its stand. He walked back the van, and took out Jesus. On the third trip, he took out St. Joseph of Arimathea. When all three statues were in place, he inspected each one closely. He could not see any trace of the detonators or wires. There was no extra paint anywhere. He went back to a point in the middle of the pews, and stared from different vantage points at the statues. He was confident that they looked exactly like the originals and that no one would notice. Ammar quickly went back out the side door, locking it as he left. Then he drove his van back to Georgetown. He spent the rest of the morning until his prayer time disposing of all the materials in his makeshift laboratory. After all of the refuse was deposited in a local dry cleaner's dumpster, he washed down his entire apartment with bleach. He vacuumed the carpet and then removed the bag from the vacuum cleaner, placing it in the trash barrel outside his neighbor's apartment. Then he took a hot shower, washing off the last remnants of plaster and acrylic paint. The Builder's job was complete.

Father Timothy Rourke woke at 6 a.m. to prepare himself for 7 a.m. mass. His head was splitting. He took some Motrin with a glass of water from the rectory kitchen sink. He showered and donned his black trousers, shirt, and collar, glanced at his sermon notes, and trotted off across the parking lot. When he entered the Church, he was dumbfounded. The statues were there right where they had always been! He knew he was really drunk, but he had never hallucinated that badly before. Father Timothy crossed himself, and said a quick Hail Mary. He was certain that God was giving him a warning, and he vowed to stop drinking again.

CHAPTER 8. VAULT

January 20, 2013. Salon-de-Provence, France. 7 a.m. Paris time

"*Est-ce que vous faites du tourisme*?" <Are you sight-seeing?> asked the cab driver on the ride from the hotel to Salon-de-Provence.

"*Oui*," said Morse. His two children, Zach and Zoey, did not speak French and looked at him quizzically.

"*Qu'est-ce que vous allez voir*?" <What are you going to see?>

"Nous espérons voir la maison de Nostradamus." <We hope to see the home of Nostradamus>

"*Ah, le Grand Prophète. J'espère que vous vous amuserez, mais il n'y a pas beaucoup à voir. Vous pourriez peut-être emmener les petits à Euro Disney faire les montagnes russes."* <I hope you have fun but there is not much to see. Perhaps you could take the little ones to EuroDisney and ride the roller coaster.>

Zoey's ears picked up. "Did he say EuroDisney?" Zoey grabbed her father's arm in the backseat. "I think he said EuroDisney. Are we going to EuroDisney?"

"He says we should go to EuroDisney and ride the roller coaster."

"Can we? Can we, Dad? That would be so much more fun than looking at a dumb old French house."

"I told you, Zoey," said Morse. "We are here on business. I am only taking you two along because I have no place else to put you while I am gone. I am not making any promises on roller coasters. That is not why we're here."

Zoey pushed her father's arm away in a huff, swinging her long brown hair towards her brother. "Uuuuuuuh! You're mean. I am so bored!" Zoey had brought along her acoustic guitar, which was in her lap. She brought her acoustic guitar everywhere. She was just learning to play and was not by any means an expert yet, but she hoped one day to be in a rock band. She had an electric guitar back at her house, and a huge 60-watt amp that would shake the chandeliers when she played.

Her brother Zach, age 15, looked out the window, taking in the bright green hills of the French countryside, his eyes barely able to peak out through his blonde-streaked, Zac-Efron-like hair which he always wore halfway across his face. He wore a dark blue American Eagle hoodie and a skater cap on sideways, and was clutching his "long-board" (an extra-long wooden skateboard with lime green wheels) to his chest. Between the long-board, the guitar, and the three passengers, the back of this French taxi was very crowded.

"Z, chillax. Don't be buggin' on Pops."

Zach spoke some form of strange hip-hop-rap-speak which his father did not understand. The taxi rambled on through the town of Salon-de-Provence. As the taxi rolled over the cobblestones, Zach began loudly beat-boxing and singing a Jay-Z rap song. Morse could make out something about bee stings and shoestrings, but the rest sounded like gibberish.

"Stop doing that!" chided Morse. "Not only does the song make no sense, if you sing it, people will take you for an imbecile. Is that what you want?" Zach was annoyed.

"Right, Dad," he said sarcastically. "I am a real imbecile. I have straight A's, you know, unlike dimwit here, who be bo-janglin' like 24-7." Zach elbowed his sister.

"Shut up, Zach! You're a jerk!" Zach paused for about three seconds, and then started mumbling the same rap song again quietly toward the glass of the window.

Salon-de-Provence sits on a large rock plain called the Crau, between the confluence of the Rhone and Durance Rivers. In the center of the town is the Château de l'Empéri, a 9th century cream-colored castle, with two large towers, one wide and one narrow, with medieval battlements. Morse pointed out the window of the taxi to the castle.

"Look at that, guys," said Morse. "That's the Château de l'Empéri. At one time, that was the home of the Archbishops for the Holy Roman Emperors. That's where it gets its name from. In 1660, this is where Nostradamus would have come to meet Catherine de' Medici, who was the Queen Consort of Henri II of France. If you want later, we can take a look at the castle. It might be fun."

"Thrilling," said Zoey sarcastically, rolling her eyes and resting her head against her guitar, wishing she were anywhere else but here.

"Pops, why is that castle so freakin' high?" asked Zach.

"The castle is perched on top of a great rock called the Rock of Puech."

"The Rock of Puke!" exclaimed Zoey, laughing. "That's hilarious. Do you puke if you go on it?"

"No," said Zach, "Unless you look at your face! Hoooooooo! You is busted, shorty!"

"Funny," said Zoey, punching her brother.

"Not 'puke,' 'Puech'," said Morse. "However, if you go to the top of the tower in the castle and look down, you might get queasy. And what does 'busted' mean?"

"It means she's ugly," said Zach, grinning at his sister.

"Zach, don't call your sister names. And stop using such horrendous grammar. I know you know how to speak correctly. Why do you insist on pretending that you have a second grade education?"

Zach began improvising his own rap lyrics, which he often liked to do. He beat-boxed a rhythm: "Umm, sucka, umm, sucka, umm." Then:

I am the man and my sista is a loo-zuh.
If I had the choice, I would never want to choose huh.
I am so fly, and we trippin' by this castle,
But my sista with her git-ar is just givin' me a hassle.

Pops, he's a stressin' and he's poppin' out a vein.
He wishes that his kiddies were real smart and not a pain.
He holds out his hands and he gently tries to calm us,
But Zach's in the Hizzle, with his Homeboy Nostradamus!

Umm, sucka, umm, suckaa, ummm....

Morse laughed. "That was actually not half bad." This talent of spontaneous rhyming has to be worth something in later life, he thought.

The taxi went down the Boulevard Jean-Jaurès, turned right on the Cours Carnot, and followed the line of what once was the northern wall of the city, to the Place Crousillat. Morse pointed out to the children La Fontaine Moussue, an exquisite moss-covered fountain that looked more like a tree than a fountain. The taxi then let them out on the Porte de l'Horloge, the French word 'horloge' meaning "clock", so named because of the magnificent seventeenth century clock tower which crowned the former northern gate of the city.

Morse thanked the driver, paid the fare, and took his duffel bag of equipment out of the back of the cab. They then walked down the narrow street passing toward and under the Porte de l'Horloge. The old buildings lining the narrow street were refurbished with bright yellow, tan and mustard-colored paint, with pale green and dark green shutters on the top and small shops on the bottom. The Porte de l'Horloge looked like a cream-colored, boxy triple-layer cake, topped with a metal cage and crucifix and a large ornate clock face just below it.

A man on a motorbike zipped by them as they walked along the stone street, past a hat shop and a camera shop. Zach took out his long-board and jumped on. He skateboarded on the flat sidewalk ahead of his father and sister and rolled through the archway at the base of the tower. Morse yelled after his son to be careful on the rough street. Once through the archway, the group made a turn at the town's former fish-market and proceeded down "La Rue Nostradamus," or Nostradamus Street. The small non-descript tan-stoned building which was the former home of the most famous prophet in the world was on the right. It had been rebuilt by the City of Salon and looked hardly anything as it did in Nostradamus' day. A large rectangular doorway greeted them, with three arched windows above it. Waiting outside the doorway was a solidly built, tall Catholic priest, with brown hair, large sideburns, bad teeth, and a tanned, friendly face. He was wearing a gray winter coat and scarf over his black priest shirt, collar and trousers.

"Welcome, Monsieur Morse," said the priest, extending his hand. "I recognize you from your picture."

"My picture?" asked Morse.

"Yes, on the back of your books. I assure you that your books on Nostradamus are most popular here. Although it is a shame that you do not have faith in the predictions of our city's most famous prophet," he said, smiling.

"Are you Father Jacques du Bois?"

"Yes. It is nice to meet you."

The priest eyed the two youngsters standing next to Morse. "This is somewhat delicate, Monsieur Morse. You have little ones here. May I speak to you privately for a moment?" Morse moved over to the side to speak privately with the priest.

"I did not know you were bringing little ones. We will be going into a dark underground room. I just want to make sure they will not be too scared."

"Oh, don't worry about them," said Morse. "They will be fine."

The priest eyed the children with concern. "Very well, then. Shall we proceed?"

"By all means," said Morse, following the priest. The group walked a few hundred yards down Rue de Nostradamus to the ancient thirteenth-century Église de St-Michel, a tan and cream stone edifice with a three-story pointed belfry and thick walnut doors. Father Jacques led Morse and his two children through the ornate, arched entrance inside the church. The walls contained arches of white granite, sloping from each wall and meeting in the middle in a criss-cross pattern. On the ceiling, hanging from red velvet cords, were glass chandeliers. Behind the altar was a giant wall of gold with two gold pillars on each side, framing a picture of Jesus and several angels. Father du Bois took them in front of the altar and around it, then through the sacristy, and finally to a rickety wooden stairwell which led into the basement of the church.

The basement was a rectangular, musty room with stone walls and a stone floor. On the northern wall was a large red tapestry. At the foot of the tapestry on the floor were two piles of stone bricks, one on the left corner and one on the right corner.

"This room was an old basement beneath the church. In the Vernègues earthquake of 1909, much of the room collapsed. At the time, the Church did not have the money to repair the basement, so the pastor at that time just boarded up the door and walled over it. However, the priests responsible for St-Michel remembered that the room existed. December 14, 2003 was the 500th anniversary of Nostradamus' birth, so, as part of the bicentennial celebration, the City of Salon raised funds to restore certain historic sights in Salon. One of these sites was St-Michel. The funds were finally released for the restoration of St-Michel in 2004, and after several delays in obtaining bids from contractors, the restoration work began in earnest in 2005. The restoration of the exterior of the church and the worship areas of the church were obviously the most important projects, and so those were completed first. Finally, however, the city hired a contractor to restore the basement. By the end of 2006, the debris was cleared and the basement was capable of being used for storage. We put a rug down here and used the room mainly for storage.

"However, this month, when I came down here, I noticed a mold smell. I walked on the rug, and noticed that it was wet. I traced the water to this northern wall, and I saw that water was coming out of the bottom of the wall pretty steadily. I thought we had a water pipe leak behind the wall possibly, so I hired a local contractor to break through the stone wall to see if we could find the leak. This is what we discovered." Father du Bois lifted back the tapestry on the wall, and there was a smashed-out hole in the wall big enough for a person to walk through. Father du Bois gave Morse and the children flashlights.

"This way. Be careful with the children. It is very dark down here."

The priest ushered Morse and his children through the hole in the wall. When the foursome walked through the wall, they were at the top of another wooden staircase. The priest led them downward again, and Morse could see there was a large room down here with a tall, vaulted ceiling. It looked like an old wine cellar. There were over a dozen huge oak wine casks along the wall.

The priest pointed his flashlight to the ceiling. "You can see we have a small crack up near the roof of this room, and I believe water from the outside of the church during rains was entering the small crack and pouring down the wall toward the wall we just went through. Mystery solved."

Father du Bois walked in front of the oak casks, and led the group to the cask which was third from the end.

"Priests have long enjoyed their wine, especially priests in the south of France. It would not have been unusual at all for the priests of this Church in centuries gone by to run a vineyard in Salon and keep the wine stored here in this wine cellar. Of course, when I checked the casks, there was no wine left, but I believe there must have been wine in these casks at one time. You should know, Professor Morse, that the only ones who know about this underground room are the contractor, you and your children, and me. I thought it better to let you investigate first before calling in any authorities, who will only delay us with construction permits and regulations. Whatever Nostradamus wanted to tell the world, I think it is important that we know immediately. Do you agree?"

Morse nodded. Father du Bois moved to the end of the row of casks.

"Do you recognize anything strange about this particular cask?" asked Father du Bois. Morse and his children studied the cask. Nothing looked particularly strange about it. Upon a second glance, however, Morse noticed that the fleur-de-lis affixed on the wall behind the cask seemed to shine a little more than the others.

"The fleur-de-lis on the wall looks a little different."

"Ahh, very good Professor Morse, and so it does. I thought it looked strange, too. So, I got a ladder and went up for myself to investigate."

Father du Bois pulled over an eight-foot green aluminum ladder, which had been resting against one of the casks. "Shall we?"

"Dad, can I go up there?" asked Zach. "That looks tight."

"No. You stay here with your sister and shine the light, and don't go anywhere. It is really dark down here and I do not want to lose you."

Zach went back to beat-boxing.

For climbin' up on ladders, the Zachster is so tight,
But Pops is a scaredy, and says, 'Zach, hold the light.'
Pops is a downer and he's takin' all the fun,
But maybe he will let me climb the ladder when he's done.

Ummm, sucka, umm, sucka, umm.

Morse looked down at Zach witheringly from the fourth step of the ladder. "Please, Zach, not now, okay? You will get your turn."

While the priest held the aluminum ladder, Morse climbed up on top of the cask and, sitting on his knees on the roof of the cask, examined the fleur-de-lis. It was clear there had been dust on it which had been disturbed, as if someone had recently touched it. This fleur-de-lis looked slightly golden in color, unlike the drab wooden fleur-de-lis markers behind the other casks. Morse shone his flashlight on it, using his hand to clear away the remaining dust. "Merlot" was inscribed on it. Nothing strange there. Morse felt the edges of the fleur-de-lis with his hand. As he applied a little force to it, it appeared to slide and move slightly. He applied more force and the fleur-de-lis turned in a clockwise direction, clicking into place. In a second, a hinged wooden trapdoor in the top of the cask opened, and Morse crashed downward into the belly of the cask. Startled, with his back a little bruised, Morse found himself in total darkness inside the old wine cask. He shined his flashlight around it. To his astonishment, the wooden back of the cask was missing, and beyond appeared to be some kind of stone passageway. Morse felt his pulse quicken. Just then, the trap door in the roof of the cask opened, and a light shined downward towards him.

"Isn't it incredible?" asked Father du Bois, grinning above him. "I am sorry I did not warn you, but I thought you would be more excited if you found the passageway the same way I did. Did you get hurt in the fall?"

"No, I'm fine," said Morse sheepishly. "I just wasn't expecting that!"

The priest turned toward the two children staring in excitement near the bottom of the ladder. "Come on, kids, climb up the ladder. It is safe."

Zach left his long-board on the ground and scampered up the ladder, but Zoey refused to part with her guitar. The priest tried to convince her to leave it below, but Zoey insisted. She was not leaving her guitar anywhere. Father du Bois helped Zach and Zoey up to the top of the cask, and then lowered them down to their father. Then, the priest jumped with surprising athleticism to the bottom of the cask.

"It is like Indiana Jones, yes?" asked the priest excitedly.

Zach was impressed. "Pops, this is sick! We are kickin' it down here."

Zoey was scared. She vice-gripped her father's arm. "Are there rats down here? This is like really scary. I want to get out of here."

"If there are any rats, I will save you," Morse assured his daughter.

"Z, stop bein' a punk. This is so fly down here. Ooonce, oonce, oonce," said Zach, making an indecipherable beat-boxing sound. As he shined his flashlight around, he invented another rap:

We're through a secret door, like a bunch of Hardy Boyz.
Pops is really clumsy and he fell and made some noise.
But Zachster has the answer to this riddle in the bones.
For Zach's off the hook just like Indiana Jones.
Ooonce, momma, oonce, momma, oonce....

The priest turned to Morse, grinning. "Does he always do that?"

"Yes," said Morse. "All day long."

The priest and his three guests walked down a cold damp stony corridor about twenty feet to a door which appeared to be wedged into the stone walls of the corridor. In front of the door was a large stone, cemented into the floor, which contained an inscription in Latin:

"*Hic iacet bona Nostradami, vatis docti, servata a pueris, Madeleina Césareque, in memoria patris. Haec cella aperietur triginta diebus post diem Magnae Transitus Magni Dubitantis, I.M.*"

Morse studied the inscription, running his hands over the letters "I.M." Zach looked at the strange words.

"Pops, what does it say?" asked Zach.

Morse replied, "It is Latin. It says:

Here lie the personal effects of Nostradamus, learned prophet, preserved by his children Madeleine and César in their father's memory. This vault shall be opened thirty days after the date of Great Transition by the Great Doubter, I.M.'"

Zach looked at his father. "What is 'the date of great transition'?"

Morse looked at his son, clearly troubled. "The date of 'great transition' was an important date in the Mayan Indian calendar. Its Long Count calendar began in 3,114 B.C., marking time in 394-year periods called Baktuns. Thirteen was a sacred number for the Mayans, and the 13th Baktun ended on Dec. 21, 2012. In addition, the Mayans knew that once every 25,800 years, the Earth's axis wobbles slightly. That anniversary occurred on December 21, 2012, the date when the sun lined up with the center of the Milky Way. Some crazy people on the Internet claimed this was the Mayan equivalent of Armageddon—the end of the World."

"Oh yeah," said Zoey, "I saw that movie with John Cusack called 2012, when like the whole world blew up."

"Right. Same thing. Obviously, though, it was not the end of the world because we are still all here. For the Mayans, though, December 21, 2012 was not doomsday. What it really meant was that the great cycle of life is restarting, as if we are starting over into a new age. In addition, according to Mayan scholars, the New Age is supposed begin at the very moment of the winter solstice, which is precisely 11:11 a.m. Universal Time, or, 12:11 p.m. Paris time. So, if I had to guess, I would suggest that the best interpretation of 'The Date of Great Transition,' is December 21, 2012."

Zach pulled out his iPhone and looked at the date. "Dad, it says this vault is going to be opened up thirty days after the date of the Great Transition. Thirty days from December 21, 2012 is January 20, 2013."

"So?" said Zoey, obviously not understanding the significance.

"So? January 20, 2013 is today!"

Morse looked at his son somberly and then looked at the priest. "I know."

"And I.M., the Great Doubter," said Father du Bois, "can only mean one person, Professor—you."

"Father du Bois, my Dad's name begins with 'J,' not 'I,'" said Zach.

The priest looked at Zach. "In Latin, Zach, the letter J is spelled with an 'I.' The Great Doubter 'I.M.' can only mean 'Iohannus Morse.'"

January 20, 2013. 6:11 a.m. Washington, D.C.

According to the United States Constitution, the Electoral College meets to elect the President of the Untied States on the Monday after the second Wednesday in December. In 2012, that date was Monday, December 17, 2012. According to tradition, after the ballots are completed, the signed Certificates of Vote are sent certified mail to the then-sitting Vice President of the United States—in this case, Joseph Biden. A staff member from the Vice President's office then places the Certificates of Vote in two special mahogany boxes. The votes from Alabama to Missouri, plus Washington, D.C., are contained in one box, and the votes from Montana to Wyoming in the other box. On Wednesday, December 19, 2012, Vice President Joseph Biden received the Certificates of Vote for the 2012 Presidential Election by certified mail. On Friday, December 21, 2012, Skip Thompson, a senior member on Joe Biden's staff, organized the Certificates of Vote and, at 6:11 a.m., placed them in the mahogany boxes.

Thirty days later, at 6:11 a.m. Eastern Standard Time, President-Elect Tim Woodson straightened his tie in the mirror, running over in his head what he would say during his Inauguration Speech. He could not wait to be President.

CHAPTER 9. FLIGHT

April 2, 1520. Bordeaux, France.

Andiette de Bisson was eight years old. She was the last female heir of the Colin family line. Andiette lived with her parents and brother Henri in a small cottage in the outskirts of Bordeaux. They were quite poor. Their ramshackle stone house was freezing in the winter and stifling in the summer, but Andiette was not one to complain. She loved her hard-working father and mother, and relished time with her mother performing household chores. Her parents were very simple people, and very devout Catholics. The family spent much of their time when they were not working praying in the town chapel. The plague, which Andiette's family attributed to the Devil, had taken many in the village. Andiette's family felt that the best way to ward off the Devil was to pray.

Andiette loved the chapel. She loved how the soft wooden pews smelled after they had been cleaned. She loved the beauty of the candles, strung on metal chains above the pews. She loved the solace and peace with God that she felt when she was in the chapel alone. She felt that the church was the one place she could go and feel totally safe. Some Sundays, after the mass, Andiette would stay behind in the chapel and ask the pastor if she could do anything to help. Today was one of those days. She knelt before the statue of Mary and put some flowers at the Virgin's feet. She began praying to Mary, asking Her for help, asking that She divinely inspire her to do good works. She prayed for a good hour, and the longer she prayed, the more intense the experience became. She began to feel very close to the Virgin Mother, as if she could speak to Her.

Just then, she gasped and couldn't breathe. It was as if someone had cut off all oxygen to her throat. No one was in the chapel, so she could not ask anyone for help. She looked around wildly, holding her hands to her throat and trying to breathe. She had a floating sensation, and then fell onto the floor between the pews. She saw the boy's face under the water. He was about ten years old, close to her age. His head was thrashing back and forth under the water, his eyes bug-eyed and desperate. His hair floated silently like a ghost in the water. It was Petit Paul.

Suddenly, she woke up and could breathe again. She dashed out of the chapel as fast as she could back to her house, where she saw her father Charles de Bisson relaxing in front of the fire.

"Papa! You must come quick! Little Paulie is drowning! His own father is killing him! You must come quick!"

"Little Paulie? What are you talking about? I just saw him this morning in church."

"Papa, I am telling you! I saw it! Paulie will be killed today if we do not help! You must help me!"

Andiette's mother frowned. "Now, Andiette, shame on you. You stop saying things like that. That's the Devil talking. Why, Paulie's father Anton is a Christian. I saw him in church today. How dare you make up such things! Now go back to the chapel and pray for God's forgiveness."

"I am telling you, Mama! I know I am right! The Virgin gave me a vision this morning. If my vision came from the Virgin, how can it be the Devil's work? It must be right!"

Her mother rebuked her. "Now I am not going to hear another word of this! You get yourself to church right this instant!"

Andiette was frustrated but left the cottage. She started to go back to the chapel, but then stopped. No, she was sure she was right. There was no time. She went out into the shed behind her house and stole her father's hunting knife and ran into the woods.

The villagers called him "Petit Paul." Paulie was short for his age, but was a nice boy, although incredibly shy and quiet. He did not play very much with the other children, as he spent most of his time working for his father in their field. Paul liked to build things out of metal. He hoped to be a blacksmith someday and spent much of his free time watching the local blacksmith hone his craft. This afternoon, it had thunderstormed much of the day, so there was no plowing work to be done. Paul went out behind the cottage, underneath a piece of wood that he had strung up on a post to give himself shelter, and, took out the crude metal plow that his father used for the fields. His father's plow composed of three parts; the long metal piece which attached to the yoke for the horses, the chassis of the plow, which slid along the ground, and the sharp metal blade which cut the earth. Paul had gotten the idea to attach large metal wheels to the plow. It should not be too difficult to weld on the axle and then attach the wheels. If he could successfully add wheels, he figured he could reduce his time in the fields substantially and make his father happy.

Paul's father, Anton, was never happy. He was an insecure man who took out his feelings of low self-esteem on his son, frequently beating him mercilessly. Anton was not a very good farmer, and when he finally got out of bed to plow the fields, he usually quit after a short time and went into town to drink. Paul lived in constant fear, but he hoped that with one of his inventions, he could someday win over his father's love and respect.

He took out a long metal pipe which he planned to use for the axle. He slid the center of a wooden wheel down the length of the metal axle and fastened it in place with a metal washer, which he welded onto the axle with a hot poker that he had taken from the fire. Then he took the cutting tool and punched holes in the metal chassis of the plow. Unfortunately, however, when he punched the second hole, his hand, slick from the rain, slipped and he sliced the open palm of his hand with the cutting tool. The pain was pretty bad. He ran inside the cottage to ask his mother for something to cover the wound. He was binding his wound with his mother when his father came through the door. He clearly had been drinking wine all day with some of the other men in town. He was drenched with rain and smelled badly.

"This cursed rain! It's been raining for five days now. How can we plow the fields with all this rain?" He looked over to his wife and his young son, who was now looking up with a frightened look on his face. The father gave a suspicious look, clearly sensing that something bad had happened.

"What is this?" he demanded, pointing to his son's hand. "How did this happen?"

"I was fixing your plow," Petit Paul stammered, "And I cut myself."

"My plow? What was wrong with it? It was working last week."

"I was trying to improve it," said Paul.

"You what?!" yelled his father. He grabbed his son angrily by the back of the neck, forcing him outside the cottage into the rain. "Where is it?!"

"It is behind the house. But you have to understand, I have not gotten it fixed yet. Once I do, your plowing is going to take half as long."

The angry father dragged his son out behind the house, and looked at the plow under the lean-to. He saw the two holes in the plow's body and exploded.

"You destroyed my plow! That is the one thing I need to put food on our table and you intentionally destroyed it! You filthy piece of garbage!" The father smashed the head of his son with his fist until he fell into the mud. But his anger was not quenched.

"You think you can destroy me, you little worm! You are the one who is going to be destroyed!" He picked his son up by the collar and dragged him, crying and protesting, down the hill from their house to the Bonnes Creek. "Father, I am sorry, but I promise I can fix it!" Paul pleaded. But his father was not hearing any of it.

He took him down to the creek, intent on teaching him a lesson he would never forget. When he reached the water's edge, he pushed aside a leafy branch, grabbed his muddy son by the shirt color and thrust his head under the icy water. After submerging him for about ten seconds, he pulled his head out of the water. Petit Paul gasped for air, spitting out water from his lungs, pleading with his father to stop.

"I'm sorry! I'm sorry! Please stop!"

He dunked him again, this time for fifteen seconds.

When Paul came up the second time, he was frantic, and became convinced his father was trying to kill him. In a vain effort to free himself, he lunged out at his father with his right hand, scratching his face with his fingernails. It was a very weak blow, and hardly hurt at all, but Paul's father became enraged that his own son would try to strike him.

"You want to hit me, you little worm! I will kill you!"

With that, the father dunked his boy under the cold water a third time. As he forced his son's head under the water, the father heard a rustling behind him. He wheeled around, just in time to see a hunting knife impale him in the eye. The father fell back in agony, blood spurting from his eye socket, and fell into the creek. Andiette quickly pulled Paulie's head out of the water and threw him back on the bank. Anton grabbed his eye as the current swirled around him, pulling him down the creek. Blinded, Anton was oblivious to the large log sticking across the creek. His head hit the log in the water and his head went under. As his legs passed, his belt got caught on the log, and he stayed there, in the middle of the rush of water, his bloody head pinned under the water. It did not take long for him to drown.

Andiette and Paulie watched the scene in horror. Neither moved. Paul was drenched and shivering. Andiette was stunned.

"Is he dead?" asked Paulie.

"I think so," said Andiette, horrified. "Mon Dieu, what have I done?" she asked.

"You had to do it," said Paulie. "You saved my life. If you had not come along, he would have killed me."

"I think I am going to be sick. I have killed a person. My God, that is a mortal sin. My soul is lost! What will I do?" Andiette began rocking back and forth, crying, and shaking her head in disbelief at what she had done. "My Mother was right! The Devil has made me kill! *Oh Mon Dieu*!"

Petit Paul suddenly seemed to be less afraid now that he knew his father was finally gone. He knew he should feel bad that his father had died, but for some reason, he felt nothing. In fact, he almost felt happy. He felt courage coming back to him for the first time he could remember. He must take care of this girl who had saved his life.

"We won't tell anybody what happened. I'll just tell people he fell into the creek, cut himself on the log, hit his head and went under. There was nothing I could do. No one will even know you were here. Come on."

He picked up Andiette and walked her back to the village. When Andiette got back to her house, she was shaking. She walked quickly past her mother into the back of the cottage where she slept. Her mother could see that something was wrong.

"Andiette, what has happened to you? And what is all this blood all over your dress?"

Andiette could not lie to her mother. It was not in her nature. She told her the whole story, and her mother became very worried. She was worried her daughter might get accused of murder. She was worried the people in the town would exile them. But mostly she was worried about how her daughter knew in advance that Paulie's father would try to kill him in the creek. She must surely be possessed. If that were true, then the Devil Himself was in her own house!

"Andiette, tell me again how you knew Paulie would be drowned in the creek?"

"The Virgin told me."

"The Virgin Mary?"

"Yes!"

Andiette stroked her daughter's wet hair.

"Andiette, what have you done to welcome the Beast into your soul?" she asked gently.

"I don't know! I was praying to the Virgin, and I saw a vision of Little Paulie being drowned by his father in the creek, and all I could think about was saving him."

"But why did you have a knife?"

"He is a big man. I am just a girl. How would I stop him?"

"But don't you see, Andiette? You had a vision, then you grabbed a knife, and you committed murder! Surely it was the Devil who possessed you to do this! You have never hurt a person in your entire life, and now you are cutting up strangers with knives! You are possessed, child! Don't you see you are a danger to our entire family now? I cannot have the Devil Himself living under my own roof! I must send you away!"

Andiette began sobbing, begging her mother not to send her away.

"Please, Mama! Don't send me away! I promise I will be good. I will pray every day. I know the Virgin will forgive my sins if I pray hard enough!"

"I am sorry, child. This is for your own good. If you stay here, our neighbors may conspire against you and you will be hanged for sure. I know a friend who works for the Archbishop of Agen. Agen is not that far away, only several days journey. I will send you to the Agen Cathedral, and the Archbishop will give you sanctuary. In a few years, you can find a nice husband in Agen and settle down and raise a family, and no one here will know where you went."

"Shall I go alone… by myself into the wilderness… with no one to protect me from bandits and thieves?" Andiette whimpered, wiping her nose and eyes. .

"We shall send Henri with you. He is fifteen. He is strong and a good rider. He will protect you."

"Mama, please do not send me! I am afraid!"

"Enough! It is decided."

Henri was told that evening. He was obviously upset. His whole life was about to change, but he loved his sister dearly, and knew she was not equipped to ride the countryside on horseback all by herself. He would ride with her to the Agen Cathedral tonight, and then ride onward to Nice to make his fortune.

Three days later, Henri and Andiette arrived in Agen. The Archbishop took the girl into the Church and gave her temporary quarters, while Henri continued onward to Nice. The next week, the Archbishop requested a wealthy Agen merchant, Pascal de Roques Lobejac, and his wife Marie d'Encausse de Rocques Lobejac, to adopt the young girl. They had no children of their own and were happy to take the child in. Andiette lived with her adopted family for the next five years. Andiette tried to put the incident with Petit Paul and the man she killed behind her forever. However, she secretly never forgave her mother for abandoning her and forcing her to leave her family and everything in the world she loved. If she ever had children, she would never treat them that way.

What she did not know was that shortly after she left her village near Bordeaux, a High Inquisitor from the Grand Inquisition named Pere Guillame de Jobert had heard the rumors of a girl who had visions from God. The Inquisitor priest visited the town of Bordeaux and questioned Andiette's parents about her visions. Andiette's parents refused to answer. The Inquisitor responded by taking red hot branding irons from the fireplace and burning them into the parents' flesh.

"Talk!" he screamed. "Where is the witch?"

When the parents refused to yield, they were accused of supporting witchcraft and hanged in the public square. Their house was burned and all their possessions seized by the Church. As Petit Paul stood in his doorway, watching the black smoke rise into the night sky from Andiette's former house down the street, he felt a sudden pang of guilt, and hoped his friend Andiette had made it to safety.

CHAPTER 10. CONSTELLATIONS

January 20, 2013. Salon-de-Provence, France.

Just behind the floor inscription, the stony passage went back another twenty feet. There was a glow of light near the end of the passage. As they got closer, Morse could see that someone had brought down a battery-powered flood light, which was resting on yellow legs. Just past the floodlight, the passage opened somewhat and was taller. In the middle of the passage was a high, narrow table similar to a podium, but with a flat top. On the table was an astrological instrument of some kind and a man's gold ring. Ten feet behind the podium was a huge floor-to-ceiling oak vault door. The edges of the vault were embedded in the stone walls of the underground chamber. On the right was a large copper vault handle. Across the top of the door was an inscription in French:

SEULS PEUVENT ENTRER CEUX QUI ONT
LE COEUR PLEIN D'AMOUR

"What does the thing on the top say, Pops?" asked Zach.

"It says '*Only those with love in their hearts may enter*,'" his father said. As Morse studied the door, it looked clear to him that it was going to take a lot more than love to figure out how to open the door.

Beneath the inscription on the top was a series of ten top-to-bottom brass dials, like an ancient version of a slot machine. The door dials spelled out "BMRDAAATMD." Beneath the ten dials there was writing carved into the stone. The door looked like this:

Professor John Morse picked up the astrolabe on the table and studied it in wonder. He turned to the priest.

"I realize you must have brought the light down here."

"Of course."

"But other than that, is this exactly how you found this vault a few days ago?"

"Yes, Professor Morse. Absolutely. I mean, I tried to open the door, of course, with no luck."

"Other than that, nothing has been moved from how you found it?"

"No, it has not."

Morse shined his flashlight in the corners of the stone passage.

"Father, I don't know what kind of game you are playing here, but you are not telling me the truth."

"I don't know what you mean."

"This podium is tall and narrow. This astrolabe and ring are sitting on top of the podium. If, as you say, there was an earthquake in 1909 violent enough to damage the room where we were earlier standing, this podium would have most certainly tipped over, and the astrolabe and ring would have fallen to the floor. So if this podium and other articles were not planted by someone, then they most certainly would have been found on the floor, not up here nice and neat where they stand today. And I notice that the wood on the podium near the top is slightly damaged on the left side, which would probably have occurred if it had fallen."

"Ahh, Professor, you are quite the detective. Of course, when I came in, they were on the floor, as you correctly note. And I found the astrolabe and the ring over there in the corner on the floor by the bottom of the door. They got a little wet and I wiped off the water with my robe. But when you asked if I had changed anything, I thought you meant had I altered the writing on the door or altered the astrolabe or something like that. I merely picked the podium up and placed the items back on it where we assumed they had previously rested."

"Father du Bois, your explanation, of course, makes sense, but you must know that I am a man of science, and not of faith. I have only met you ten minutes ago. I have no idea if this stone which says the vault will be opened by 'I.M.' was planted here a month ago by someone attempting to play some kind of practical joke on me. I am not prone to accept on faith that a man over 500 years ago was able to predict who would open this vault and when. Frankly, to tell you the truth, it seems very far-fetched to me. But like any scientist, I will keep an open mind."

"I assure you, Professor," said the priest. "This is no joke. When I read the inscription I thought there could only be one man who was a famous doubter of Nostradamus whose initials—at least in Latin— were 'I.M.' So I contacted you immediately. But as a scientist, Professor, answer me this. Does it seem unusual to you that someone would call a person half way around the globe, whom he has never met, just to play a joke on him? What would our religious order gain by, as you say, 'being the wolf in the sheep's wool?' And I suppose there is a way to carbon date the stone monument or the door or the astrolabe, correct? That way we could determine scientifically how old it is."

"Yes, we have ways in which to verify these things. But it will take some time and additional equipment which I do not have with me here."

"Well, Professor, you have examined ancient artifacts before. Is there anything about what you have seen here which tells you this was fabricated in some way?"

"No," admitted the Professor, looking around and studying the astrolabe further. "This is most certainly a medieval astrolabe. Whether it is César's astrolabe I cannot say at this point."

"Julius Caesar?" asked Zach.

"No, César de Nostradame, Nostradamus' son. César was named after Nostradamus' long time friend and mentor, Julius Caesar Scalinger, a scholar and doctor who lived in the town of Agen in southern France. About a week before Nostradamus died, he prepared a codicil to his will, which we still have today, which made rather sudden bequests to his eldest daughter Madeleine and his son César. Madeleine received two walnut chests and César received his father's astrolabe and a special ring."

"What's an Astrolabe?" asked Zoey, giggling. "It sounds like a Space Dog, like Buzz Lightyear's dog or something."

"No, it is not a space dog, Zoey, but you are correct that it has to do with outer space. An astrolabe is an old fashioned instrument used by astrologers to measure and observe the stars. It has been used by people for hundreds and maybe thousands of years. In fact, some say that the three wise men—Balthazar, Gaspar and Abednego—used an astrolabe to find the Star of Bethlehem and Jesus' birthplace."

"Ah, yes," said Father du Bois. "We just celebrated the Epiphany two weeks ago. I had not heard about the astrolabe."

"In any event," continued Morse, "Nostradamus was very interested in astrology. His astrolabe was one of his prized possessions." Morse looked at the engravings on the side of the astrolabe. "I would have to study this further to see if this came from the seventeenth century, when Nostradamus lived, but it certainly looks that old." Morse turned to Father du Bois and they examined the artifact together.

Zach went over to the oak vault door. He tried with all his might to open the door. When it did not budge, he tried kicking it.

"Zach, stop that!" warned Morse.

"Pops, this is an Epic Fail. That door is not opening. Maybe we should get dynamite or something."

Morse had no idea what an "epic fail" was. "No, we cannot use dynamite, because we could damage forever whatever lies on the other side of that door. And, Zach, do me a favor, don't touch the ancient artifacts, OK? You don't want to break something. We have to be very delicate with everything here."

Morse went over to the door and gently placed his hand over the inscriptions. Which were carved into the stone. He placed his hand on the first metal dial and it turned in his hand like a wheel. As he did so, the letters began to read "BCD" then "CDE" then "DEF." He gradually turned the wheel and saw that it contained all the letters of the alphabet. After the letter "Z," there was a cross symbol, and then the letter A again. He and Father du Bois checked all the other dials, and they were the same.

Father du Bois spoke. "It appears clear that in order to access the vault, we need to spell some kind of word with the dials. And these verses below give us the clues to the word."

"Yes, I believe you are correct," said Morse, studying the inscriptions. Morse took out a field notebook, and began sketching the door. He took out a tape measure, and took measurements of the door, the inscriptions, the vault handle, and the verses etched into the stone. After he completed the sketch, he wrote out the verses in French, and then in English. The English translation of the verses in Morse's notebook read:

She regrets her foolish boasts, and almost loses her daughter.
Once a terror of the sea, now only a statue.
He tries to kill his mother, then tries to save her.
Hatched from eggs, guardians of sailors.

He was sent by Mother Earth to save the wild beasts.
Tricked by the king and punished by the queen.
His father appears as a shower of gold.
A pitiful distraction, it harbors bees.

He weeps a river for his foolish friend.
He hunts the greatest game and is slain by the least.

Four slayers, four slain.
Two mothers, two monsters.
The father of the gods
And four of his sons.

"Some of this I think I understand," said Father du Bois. "The father of the gods—since god is plural—must mean Zeus, the Greek father of the gods. But frankly, most of the other verses sound like gibberish to me."

"I think I have a good idea on the answer for many of these," said Morse, putting his hands again gently over the script.

"The first one that hit me was the father appearing as a 'shower of gold.' That can only mean Zeus. In Greek mythology, Zeus seduced Danae by appearing to her as a shimmering shower of gold, and the result was a son named Perseus. So I think we have nailed down one of the four sons."

Zach was now finding the puzzle interesting. Zoey, on the other hand, was bored to death and was sitting cross-legged in a corner, rolling her eyes, strumming her acoustic guitar, and waiting for this ordeal to be over. She softly sung a Demi Lavado song.

"So you're saying this Zeus guy is hitting on a woman by dressin' up like a gold shower? That is whack. Why would a girl want to do it with a shower? That don't make no sense."

Morse stood there in puzzlement, more in awe that this was his offspring than that a seer from 500 years ago was giving him riddles to solve.

"Zach, if you would read a book every once in a while, you might learn that this Zeus was quite the ladies' man. In fact, he cheated on his wife Hera dozens of times. He had dozens of illegitimate children. And he frequently liked to dress up as other things to fool the young maidens he was about to seduce. One time, he dressed up as a white bull and hid among the cattle. The woman he was attempting to seduce thought a white bull was rather odd and quite beautiful, so she put a garland of flowers around the bull and rode on his back down to the sea, where Zeus, dressed as the bull, promptly kidnapped her across the ocean to Crete, where he turned back into a man and raped her. As a result, the townspeople of Crete began to worship the bull, and the bull became sacred on the island. In fact, they liked bulls so much that the king's wife actually mated with a bull."

Zoey stopped playing her guitar. "Oooooh! Dad, you are so gross! Talk about something else!"

Zach started laughing. "Wait, wait, wait, wait. A lady and a bull?

That's hilarious! I have never heard that in school before."

"Sure you have," said Morse. "Their offspring was called the Minotaur, half-man and half-bull, who was kept in a maze until Theseus killed it. And if you look out into the night sky you can still see Zeus dressed up as the white bull. That's the constellation Taurus, one of the twelve zodiac signs."

"OK," said the priest. "So we have nailed down that the father of the gods is Zeus, and this gold shower is Zeus. Could the word be Zeus or the Roman name for Zeus—Jupiter?" The priest counted out the letters in Jupiter. Seven letters, too short.

Morse was not listening to Father du Bois. When he mentioned Taurus, he began scratching his head, realizing something.

"Of course," he said. "Perseus is a constellation. These clues have something to do with the constellations. That is why the astrolabe is here. We are obviously supposed to use the clues to find constellations, and then use the astrolabe somehow to get our word." He began studying the script again, sure he was right.

He put his hand on the first line of script. "This first line, I think that must be Cassiopeia. *She regrets her foolish boasts, and almost loses her daughter.* Cassiopeia was a queen of Ethiopia who boasted that her daughter Andromeda was more beautiful than the Nereids, the beautiful sea nymphs who were daughters of the sea god Nereus, who was often seen accompanying Poseidon. This angered Poseidon and as punishment, Poseidon sent a great sea monster called Cetus, whose name means whale, to destroy the town. The King, Cepheus, consulted the Oracle of Zeus, who said that the only way for the kingdom to avoid disaster was to sacrifice the life of their daughter Andromeda. Forced with losing his kingdom or his daughter, the king chose to sacrifice his daughter. He chained her to a rock for the sea monster to eat her."

Zoey looked up from the corner where she was sitting, and came over and grabbed her dad's arm, looking at him fondly. "What a jerk! Daddy, would you ever chain me to a rock and let a monster eat me?"

"Of course not," said Morse. "I would not let you get eaten by a sea monster."

"So did the sea monster eat her?" asked Zach.

"No, luckily for the king and queen, our hero Perseus was on his way back from chopping off the head of the gorgon Medusa. Medusa had a head of snakes and the sight of her could turn anything into stone. Flying on his winged horse Pegasus, Perseus flew up to the monster, unveiled Medusa's severed head, and the monster turned to stone. In their gratitude, the king and queen allowed Perseus to marry their daughter Andromeda, who was saved. So the person making the foolish boasts who almost lost her daughter must be Cassiopeia, which is also a constellation."

Father du Bois quickly read the next line. "Professor, you have also solved the next line. *Once a terror of the sea, and now only a statue.* That can only mean the sea monster Cetus! Is Cetus a constellation as well?"

"Yes it is," said Morse, now having a lot of fun. "It looks like a giant whale."

"*'He tries to kill his mother, then tries to save her.'* What does that mean?" asked the priest."Hmm," said Morse. "I cannot think of anyone offhand who tried to murder their mother. Let's go on to the next one.

Father du Bois read the text aloud. "*Hatched from eggs, guardians of sailors.*"

Morse looked at the text. "Hmmm. I can think of a woman who was hatched from an egg."

"Like Horton Hatches an Egg?" giggled Zoey.

"Yes, sort of. Helen of Troy, the most beautiful woman in all of Greece, the woman who 'launched a thousand ships' and was responsible for the famous Trojan War, was said to have hatched from an egg."

"I had never heard that," confessed Father du Bois. "Why did she hatch from an egg?"

"Well, this is another wonderful tale of Zeus' infidelity and bestiality. Zeus decided that he wanted to sleep with a woman. I cannot remember her name, I think it was Lena or Lydia or something. Anyway, he disguised himself as a swan, and when she went to embrace the swan, he mated with her."

"Ooooh! Yuck! Stop talking about this! It is gross!" said Zoey. "These Greek guys are all perverts."

"Woa. Woa. Woa. Pops, you're saying this same guy who was doin' ho's in a gold shower and raping women dressed as a bull is now getting' together with a lady dressed as a duck? Why would any woman want to be with a duck?"

"It was a swan, and yes, I have no idea why a woman would want to have sex with a swan, but she did, and as a result, her daughter hatched out of an egg." Zach thought of his next rap.

Zeus, on the loose, he can't keep it in his pants.
He likes to dress up and put shorties in a trance.
First, he's disguised as a shiny, golden shower.
Just like George Clooney, getting' ladies every hour.

His wife gets mad and Zeus she's water-boardin'
So he changes to a bull, and I don't mean Michael Jordan.
Then he hooks up with ladies while he's dressed like a swan.
This Zeus is a perv and he likes to get it on.

Oonce, baby, oonce, baby, oonce.

" ZACH!" yelled his father. "Stop it! Right now! No more rap songs until we are back at the hotel, understand?"

The priest patted Morse on the back. "These young kids today, they are a handful, *non*?"

"Yes, I agree. They are quite a handful."

"Is their mother here to help you?" the priest asked.

"No, my wife died about eleven years ago, Father. She was one of the victims of 9-11." Zach and Zoey suddenly got very quiet and serious.

"Oh, *pardonnez-mois*, Professor. That is quite tragic. These terrorists, they are truly evil people. I did not mean to upset you. Perhaps we should return to our puzzle. You were speaking about Helen of Troy, who hatched from an egg."

"I have a Helen in my class. Did Helen have like feathers or anything?" asked Zoey.

"No, Zoey, she was quite beautiful. In fact, she was so beautiful that two countries went to war over her. Each country had a leader who wanted to marry her. That was the famous Trojan War."

"Like the one with the Trojan Horse?" asked Zach.

"One and the same."

"So is there a constellation for Helen of Troy?" asked Father du Bois.

"No, but there is one for the swan. It is called Cygnus, and it looks like a cross in the night sky."

Father du Bois seemed skeptical. "But that doesn't fit, Professor Morse. As far as I know, Zeus was not the guardian of sailors. That was his brother Poseidon, god of the oceans. I do not think anyone would call Zeus a guardian of sailors."

"Hmm," thought Morse. "You are correct. That does not seem to fit. But I know Helen came from an egg, so that seems right. I don't know." Morse turned to Zach. "Zach, can you get a signal on that iPhone of yours?"

Zach flicked on the phone. "No bars down here. Must be all this rock."

"Zach, can you try and go back into the wine cellar where we just were and see if you can reach the Internet from your iPhone. Try putting in 'hatched egg Greek mythology constellation' into Google and see what you get. Then come back here and let us know if you find anything." Morse then went over to Zach and huddled with him for a moment, whispering in his ear.

"OK, sure."

"Can I go with Zachster?" asked Zoey.

"Sure," said Morse. "Zach, watch your sister."

Morse studied the door once more. "Also, put in 'Orion constellation Greek mythology' into Google and see if you can figure out how the great hunter Orion died. I have a feeling Orion might be the hunter referenced in the last line."

Morse looked at the last line. He did not know who was sent by Mother Earth to save the wild beasts. The next line was also drawing a blank. "*Tricked by the king and punished by the queen*" could mean a lot of people. That was obviously a reference to Zeus, who was always tricking women into sleeping with him, and the queen of the gods, Hera, who wrought her vengeance any time she learned of Zeus' infidelity.

"*A pitiful distraction, it harbors bees.*" Morse did not know of any bees constellation. "*He weeps a river for his foolish friend.*" That was not ringing a bell, either.

Morse looked at the last four lines. *Four slayers and four slain.* The four slayers they had so far were Perseus (who slew Cetus), whoever the hunter was in the last line...the identity of the other two he could not fathom. The four slain included Cetus (slain by Perseus). He did not know who the other three were.

The next line talked about two mothers. Cassiopeia, mother of Andromeda, was one. Who was the other one?

The priest pointed toward the wall. "It says here there are two monsters. One of the monsters was Cetus, the sea monster. Are there any other monsters which are constellations?"

"Yes," said Morse. "There is Draco, the dragon, who guarded the golden apples in the garden of Hesperides, which were given to Hera as a wedding gift. One of Heracles' twelve labors was to steal the apples. He asked Atlas to help him fetch the apples. Atlas said he would help, but he was busy holding up the whole earth, and plus there was the matter of the dragon. Heracles killed the dragon, temporarily relieved Atlas by holding up the earth, and then when Atlas had found the apples, Heracles gave the earth back to Atlas to hold. Draco is at the very top of the northern sky."

"Are there any others?"

"Leo was a big lion but I do not think that would qualify as a monster. Hydra is the longest and biggest constellation. That was a multi-headed beast fought by Heracles, who finally killed it by burning the stumps of the severed heads with a torch. Ummm, let me think. The only other one I can think of is Cancer, the giant crab, who was sent by the gods to hassle Heracles when he was fighting the Hydra. Heracles killed the crab pretty easily, too."

"He killed it easily, heh?" asked Father du Bois. "So then you would say it was almost a 'pitiful distraction?'" "Yes, that fits," admitted Morse. "But what about the part about harboring bees?"

"The only story I am aware of about a monster harboring bees is Samson, who killed the lion with his bare hands and then the honeybees built a hive in the lion's body. Do you think that could be it?"

"Possibly," said Morse. "But most of our other hits have been Greek myths. It would seem weird to suddenly jump out and look at a Bible story. Also, I would not describe a lion as a pitiful distraction."

Just then, Zach and Zoey came running back down the tunnel, with Zach holding his iPhone up in triumph.

"Dad, we've got it! I put in the search you told me, and it came back with that story about Zeus being a swan."

"Yes, we know that already," said Morse.

"But then it said that after the lady fooled around with the swan, she had three kids, not just Helen. Her other two kids were Castor and Pollux, who also hatched from eggs. Castor and Pollux are known as The Twins. Dad, the clue means Gemini!"

"Ahh, of course. And by any chance did it say that they are guardians of sailors?"

"Yep. In fact, it said that when you use the phrase, 'By jiminy,' whatever that is, you are repeating an old sailor's prayer to the Gemini."

"Let me see that, if you don't mind," said the professor, viewing the iPhone screen. He paged down on the webpage with his finger, until he found something else interesting. "It says here that Castor and Pollux later got into a dispute with their cousins over who were the rightful owners of certain cattle. One of the cousins, Idas, hurled a spear at Castor, killing him. Pollux later was so upset that he asked to be killed so he did not have to be without his brother. So Castor and Pollux were both sons of Zeus and one of them was slain. Looking at our count on the bottom of the door, the four sons of Zeus are Perseus, Castor, Pollux, and we need one more. The four slain are Cetus, Castor, and we need two more."

"What did your iPhone say about Orion?" asked Father du Bois.

"It said that Orion was a great hunter, and that he wanted to hook up with these seven hot sisters. He started bragging that he was going to bust a cap in all the animals on earth, and then Mother Earth came along and sent a scorpion to kill him. It said because the two were such enemies, Scorpio and Orion could never be seen in the sky at the same time."

"What does 'bust a cap' mean?" asked Father du Bois.

"It means kill," said Zach.

"Of course," said Father du Bois. "Zach, you have solved another one.

He was sent by Mother Earth to save the wild beasts. That has to be Scorpio. Because Mother Earth sent the scorpion, all the wild beasts of Earth were protected."

"He has solved two of them," said Morse. "*He hunts the greatest game and is slain by the least.* The least game is the scorpion. That has to refer to the constellation Orion. That brings our count of the slain to Cetus, Castor, and Orion. We only need one more. And Orion, as a hunter, is also a slayer. Since Scorpio killed Orion, that makes it a slayer. So that means our four slayers are Perseus, Scorpio, Orion, and we only need one more."

"Hey Pops," said Zach. "One other thing. I put in 'swan' and 'Greek mythology' 'cause I wanted to read more about that dude who hooked up with the duck, and there was this other story about this guy Phaethon. Apparently, the other kids in school were hatin' on him that he really wasn't the son of Apollo, the sun god, so he took his dad's ride out for a spin. His dad had this like Sun chariot or somethin', and Phaethon ended up crashing the car and burning up deserts and leaving polar icecaps everywhere and stuff. And Zeus was annoyed and hit him with a thunderbolt and killed him."

"That's all very interesting," said Morse, not following how the story was relevant. "What does that have to do with this?"

"Well, it turns out that Phaethon had this crybaby friend of his who was so bummed that his friend died that he starts crying into this river and he dives into the river flailing around for his buddy, and he looked like this swan flappin' around. So the gods took pity on the loser and put him in the sky as a constellation. His name was Cycnus. The name of the constellation was Cygnus, the swan."

"Of course! You've got it, Zach. Good work. *He weeps a river for his foolish friend.* That is Cygnus. Some of these constellations have more than one story associated with them. So here, Nostradamus was referring to Cygnus both with the story of the seduction of Leda—Leda, that was her name!—and the story of weeping Cygnus. Fantastic!"

"So what other constellations are there?" asked Father du Bois. "What are we forgetting?"

"Let's see, there's Aquarius, the water bearer. Capricorn, the goat. Centaurus, the centaur. There is Canus Minor and Canus Major, the two hunting dogs. There's Cepheus, the father of Andromeda. What else….."

"The only stars I know of are the Big Dipper," said Zach.

Morse thought for a moment. The Big Dipper. Of course, that was it. The other mother….Morse excitedly re-read the text on the door again.

"I've got another one! You've nailed it again, Zach. The Big Dipper is called that because it looks like a giant ladle. And then there is the Little Dipper, which looks the same, and at the end of its handle has the star Polaris, the North Star. But those constellations are known by a different name, Ursa Major and Ursa Minor, the Big Bear and the Little Bear. According to Greek mythology, Zeus was interested in sleeping with a woman named Callisto, who was very beautiful. Callisto was a follower of the goddess Artemis. So Zeus dressed up as the goddess Artemis herself…."

"Woa! He is a cross-dresser, too! This guy is like King of the Pervs," said Zach.

"Anyway," continued Morse, "He dressed up as Artemis, and Callisto....uh, as you would say 'hooked up' with him."

"Dad, stop talking about gross stuff!" screamed Zoey, throwing her hands up.

"After they finished..." Morse continued, but hesitated, as he saw his daughter glaring at him, "Anyway, then Callisto had a son named Arcas, who became head of the Arcadians. Zeus' wife Hera was so mad at Zeus that she turned Callisto into a bear. Now, it turned out that Arcas was a herdsman and a hunter himself—hey, there's our fourth slayer!—and as he walked through the woods, he came upon his mother as the bear. The mother was overjoyed to see him so she stood up on all four legs. Arcas thought his mother was an attacking bear, so he prepared to kill her. At the last second, Zeus saved the day, turned Arcas into a little bear, grabbed him by the tail as hard as he could, stretching it out. Zeus yanked Callisto up as well, throwing both mother and son into the night sky. However, Hera was still mad, so she made it so that the constellations were so high in the sky that they could never have rest or peace. And that's why the Big Bear and the Little Bear can be seen in the northern sky all year round.

He tries to kill his mother, then tries to save her. That has to be Arcas, the Little Bear.

Tricked by the king and punished by the queen. That has to be Callisto, the Big Bear."

"And Arcas," said the priest, "Must be the fourth son of Zeus!"

"All we need to know is what harbors bees," said Morse. "The pitiful distraction sure sounds like cancer to me. Zach, go back into the wine cellar room and when you get a signal, plug in 'Cancer constellation bees.' And see what you get."

A few moments later, Zach came back, triumphant again. "Whazzzup! Zach's in the Hizzle! Guess what I found?"

"Spit it out," said Zoey.

"Right in the middle of the constellation Cancer is a cluster of stars that look like a bunch of bees buzzing around a hive. It is called the Beehive Cluster."

"That's it!" exclaimed Morse. He scratched out some notes on his notebook. Here is what they had:

She regrets her foolish boasts, and almost loses her daughter. CASSIOPEIA
Once a terror of the sea, now only a statue. CETUS
He tries to kill his mother, then tries to save her. URSA MINOR
Hatched from eggs, guardians of sailors. GEMINI
He was sent by Mother Earth to save the wild beasts. SCORPIO
Tricked by the king and punished by the queen. URSA MAJOR
His father appears as a shower of gold. PERSEUS
A pitiful distraction, it harbors bees. CANCER
He weeps a river for his foolish friend. CYGNUS
He hunts the greatest game and is slain by the least. ORION

Four slayers (SCORPIO, URSA MINOR, PERSEUS, ORION)
Four slain (CETUS, ONE OF GEMINI, CANCER, ORION)
Two mothers (CASSIOPEIA, URSA MAJOR)
Two monsters (CETUS, CANCER)
The father of the gods (ZEUS, AS CYGNUS, THE SWAN)
And four of his sons. (URSA MINOR, GEMINI (2), PERSEUS)

The list was complete!

All four in the cave silently stared at each other. What were they supposed to do now? How did this give them the word to open the vault? Morse stared at the names of the constellations, looking for a pattern. He did not have a clue where to begin.

January 20, 2013. Miami, Florida.

Amy Idris had not been able to get over the loss of her son Justin in the Cincinnati Massacre. She had gone to grief counselors, a psychiatrist, and even to her fellow ministers at her church. She had been ordained herself three years ago, but her calling gave her no strength in the wake of this tragedy. She was filled with an equal amount of rage and despair. After a few weeks, the only remnants of her son's body the FBI provided to her for burial were some of his bigger bones and a skull. Fire investigators told her that her son had been very near the blast when it went off. She kept thinking that if she had only been a half hour later to school that morning, Justin would be alive today. She was always late. Why couldn't she have been later that day? She blamed herself and went through dozens of scenarios a day, thinking how things could have been different. Justin was her whole life. Amy's parents were worried about her. She was drifting into a deep depression.

The only thing that kept her sane was her maddening desire to avenge her child. She couldn't do that as a police officer. Her therapist recommended that she get a job as a Federal Air Marshal. That way, she could be on the front lines in the War on Terror. She thought it was a great idea. Her training classes in Miami lasted five weeks. After the classes, she decided she liked the weather so much she would remain living in Miami. Three weeks ago, she started taking flights, armed with a Beretta revolver. She was ever vigilant on her routes, desperate to find some way to stop future terrorist attacks. Today was a flight to Cincinnati. She switched routes with another Air Marshal. She could not bear to go back to Ohio yet. The pain was too raw. She packed her bags and rolled her suitcase down the ramp for the flight today to Phoenix. She would have six hours to think about her beautiful lost son.

CHAPTER 11. ASSASSINATION.

January 20, 2012. Washington, D.C. 6 a.m. EST.

President-Elect Tim Woodson was super-charged with energy, even though he had not slept at all last night. The last time he remembered when he could not get to sleep due to excitement was when he was six years old on Christmas Eve. It felt like that. He could not wait to take the reins of the nation, to be the most powerful man in the world. He looked at himself in the mirror of the bathroom at the Watergate Penthouse Suite. Damn, he looked good. Freshly tanned from the Las Vegas tan spa at the Palms Hotel, Woodson combed back his slicked salt-and-pepper hair. He was wearing his lucky red tie, with the little blue dots. This was the same tie he wore on Super Tuesday, when he decimated Rick Perry and Rick Santorum and all the other Republicans. This was the same tie he wore on the day of the Cincinnati Massacre, when Anna Scall was giving CPR to the boy in Cincinnati. What luck that she had been campaigning in Cincinnati that day. When he rolled up his sleeves and started comforting parents at the hospital in Cincinnati later that night, he looked like the kind, father figure every woman wanted. His team was able to arrive on the scene as the heroes, angrily denouncing the terrorists, before Obama even knew what was going on. His subsequent campaign ads attacking the Obama administration's efforts to curb terrorism were brutal. Ahhh, Ohio. He loved Ohio.

He had to admit that he could not wait for all the suck-ups and starlets to start genuflecting when he walked by, to get tickets to any concert or football game or boxing match he wanted, to travel the globe with a parade of staff members picking lint off his jacket and hanging on his every word. Even the food was going to be good. He heard that you could order whatever food you wanted any time you wanted, and the five-star chefs in the White House Kitchen would have it ready in a heartbeat.

However, above all else, he was excited to be President to bring about policy change and return the country to where it was before Obama and the lefties drove the country off the tracks. Fortunately, with the Republicans hammering the Democrats just before Election Day on the terrorism issue, they had picked up seven seats in the Senate and dozens of seats in the House. With the right amount of concessions, he could woo a few Blue Dogs over to his side and get some good legislation passed.

Obama's so-called "anti-torture" order would be the first thing to go. How could the Democrats possibly think we can stop terrorists if we have to give root beer and Nintendo to these animals trying to kill us? No, Cheney was right. Severe interrogation techniques had to be in the arsenal for the worst terrorism suspects. Then he was going to try and water down the 2010 Health Care Act before it officially kicked in. Insurance companies had poured money into his election war chest and they deserved some consideration. His friends in the insurance industry had told him that this health care thing was going to kill them. Why should 85% of the country who have worked so hard to get jobs with health care have to sacrifice everything and pay higher premiums so that a tiny few who did not obtain health care could get it for free? It made no sense to him. And he planned on showing the other world leaders that America was not going to cower with France at the United Nations. America was going to be strong again, and he planned on taking the country there.

His wife Gloria was finished dressing and stood behind her husband in the mirror. "You look so Presidential. I am so proud of you.""Thanks, honey," said Woodson. "And I know America is going to love its next First Lady."

"Aww." She adjusted her husband's tie in the mirror. "You are going to forget about me the first time you get back to the Oval Office."

"Not true."

"All I ask is that you remember our wedding anniversary. If you forget that, even the Secret Service is not going to be able to protect you."

Woodson laughed, and walked over to the coffee table, picking up the sheets of paper containing his inauguration speech. He looked it over again.

"This is going to be an inauguration to remember," said his wife, smiling. "Just don't let that little Southern bitch steal the spotlight from you. This is your day."

Mohammed el Faya opened the door to the small business office at 6 a.m. He had to set up his sniper perch. The twelve-story building was owned by Channel 7, a local D.C. news channel. The small 1,200 square foot office at the end of the hall on the top floor was completely gutted, with a plywood floor and wires hanging from the ceiling. The building owner's plan was to rent the space out to a small law firm or accounting firm, and then renovate it once a lease was signed, but so far, this office was part of a glut of open commercial office space in Washington D.C. El Faya had told the commercial real estate agent that he was planning on establishing his own law practice. The real estate agent was more than eager to show the space to this lawyer. The agent bragged about the beautiful view from the southern wall, and western wall, which was all glass, from floor to ceiling. The agent has assured El Faya that their architect was very easy to work with and the building owner could provide a substantial contribution towards renovation of the space. At the end of the meeting, El Faya had asked the agent for an extra key to be able to come back with his law partner and his decorator to inspect the space. The agent probably shouldn't have done it, but this had been a very lean year, and he was desperate for a commission, so he gave the extra key to El Faya.

The view from this office provided a perfect view of the target. El Faya was dressed in jeans, tennis shoes, a black turtleneck and black knit cap. He took off his tan jacket and laid it on the floor. Out of his black Nike canvas bag he took out the same type of Arctic Warfare sniper rifle he had used unsuccessfully against Saddam Husein in Iraq thirty years ago. He was certain that his time he would not miss his target. He set up the tripod and mounted the rifle. Then he unscrewed the scope from the rifle, and, standing in front of the wall of glass, put the scope to his eye like a pirate captain surveying the ocean, and surveyed the scene while he held a hot mug of coffee in the other hand. His sight line was perfect. There was no way he could miss. And this time he would not be battling a kidney stone.

El Faya sat against the wall, drinking his coffee and reflecting on the last thirty years. It was strange how he had arrived at this point in his life and in history. He had never had any grudge against America, never had a reason to kill one of America's favorite sons. But that was before his incarceration. He would never forgive those bastards for how he was treated. He had done nothing wrong. In fact, he was on their side. Yet these Americans had just decided he was the enemy merely because he was an Iraqi. They deserved every bit of suffering he would give them.

After his unsuccessful attempt on Saddam's life, El Faya had fled Dujail, humiliated that his failure had brought about all the suffering in his village. He had wandered around Iraq for a good year after that, never staying in any one place for very long. Eventually, he settled in Fallujah, where he got a job with the local police department. Over the next year, he heard about the executions of his friends and family in Dujail and it took every bit of composure he had to control his rage against Saddam. But he could not let anyone know who he was or the city he hailed from. Any suspicion that he was involved in the assassination attempt would result in his execution. The murders of his friends by Saddam and the burning of their orchards infuriated El Faya. If El Faya wanted to kill Saddam before, he wanted to kill him ten times more now. He never shared his thoughts with anyone, however, and mainly kept to himself.

After a few months, as a Fallujah police officer, he was assigned to investigate the theft of a local grocer. He tracked the thief down to a small house and found the thief, a young eighteen year-old, huddling in a corner, grasping a paper grocery bag filled with the stolen money. He arrested the boy, and put him in jail, but before the prosecutor arrived, he was paid a visit from a Major in Saddam Hussein's Republican Guard. The boy was his son. The Guardsman wanted Officer El Faya to release the boy. Sensing his advantage, El Faya promised to release the boy in exchange for an appointment in Saddam's Republican Guard. The Guardsman agreed, and soon El Faya found himself working for Saddam in Baghdad.

El Faya had been elated. It would only be a matter of time before he had access to Hussein, and when he encountered him, El Faya would kill him. Then he could gain justice for his little brother and the other members of his village. Unfortunately, his plan took significantly longer than he thought. He was initially assigned to a remote village in the northern part of Iraq where his responsibility included repressing the local Kurds. He thought he would never be re-assigned to the palace in Baghdad until finally, in the early 1990s, he was recalled to Baghdad. But instead of being assigned to the palace, he was enrolled in the effort to attack Kuwait. This was a miserable assignment, and one which could very easily get him killed. However, he knew he had to keep his eyes on the prize, so he did his best. As a sniper in the Republican Guard, he was quite successful in the Kuwaiti operation. Although Iraqi forces eventually had to surrender and retreat, he himself had performed admirably, and had killed a great many Americans. He felt a little bad about that, but if he refused to fight the Americans, he knew Saddam would kill him for sure. When he returned from Kuwait, his commanding officer filed a report confirming El Faya's valor in the operation. El Faya was promoted to Lieutenant, and assigned to guard a group of buildings on the southeast corner of Baghdad.

Unfortunately, even though he was in Baghdad, he still lacked access to Saddam. Saddam stayed mainly in the palace, and he had no reasonable excuse for entering the palace. There was one day in 1997 when Saddam had made a surprise inspection of his buildings. Saddam had actually saluted him and stood no more than three feet from him. But on the day Saddam arrived, El Faya did not have his weapon. Before he could even react, Saddam had left. He had blown his second opportunity.

His life settled into monotony for the next six years. One night in March 2003, however, he was called into a meeting in one of the palace conference rooms. The Head of the Republican Guard was in attendance and was warning them that the Americans were going to attack Baghdad. El Faya could not believe it. On one hand, he thought the invasion might give him an opportunity to kill Saddam. On the other hand, he would be pressed into military service against the Americans again, and he was lucky to escape alive the first time. He was not afraid to die, but he did not want to die before getting his final vengeance. In addition, as much as he hated Saddam, there was a certain amount of national pride in his own country, and he resented these Americans for attacking his country without provocation. The military men looked on the large flat screen on the wall. George Bush was announcing to the world that his forces had already begun the attack of Iraq.

As the sniper, El Faya was assigned to the fourth floor of the White Tower of Baghdad, near the southern edge of the city. His job would be to try and kill as many Americans as he could when the Americans rolled into the city.

El Faya knew this was a ridiculously dangerous assignment. He was not about to embark on a suicide mission for Saddam. The Americans certainly would figure out he was shooting at them from the tower. One Hellfire missile into the White Tower and he would be dead within minutes. So as the Americans stormed their tanks northward on the road to Baghdad, El Faya left the tower, snuck outside the city, hid his sniper rifle bag under a pile of rocks out in the desert, and then walked down the road toward the approaching American tanks with his hands held high. Not a proud moment for El Faya, but it kept him alive. The American soldiers saw him on the road and screamed at him to get on his belly in the dirt. The soldiers searched him, bound his hands and feet, blindfolded him, and threw him in the back of a transport truck. A few days later, after being processed as a prisoner by the Americans, he found himself in a prison called Abu Ghraib.

7:00 a.m.

Secret Service Officer Jim Butler escorted President-Elect Woodson and his wife into the Lincoln Towncar and then instructed the driver which route to take to Pennsylvania Avenue. "We're going to take GAMBLER down Route Charlie-5," said Butler.

"Will-do," said the driver.

"Mr. President-Elect, when we get to the destination, do not get out of the car until I get out and we clear you to exit, OK?"

"I've been through the drill before, Jim. Thanks."

Woodson's wife rested her head on her husband's arm and rubbed his bicep. "I am so excited, Tim. I know you're going to do great."

"When we get to the White House, Mr. President-Elect, we are going to bring you to the Roosevelt Room, where President Obama will be waiting to meet to pass you final transition information, such as the N-Codes."

Tim Woodson nodded somberly. The nuclear codes entrusted to the President of the United States would be an awesome responsibility.

7:00 a.m.

Anna Scall was the happiest person in the world today. She could not wait to be Vice President. And if anything happened to Tim Woodson, God forbid, she would be there to be the Leader of the Free World, the First Woman President of the United States. She fantasized about sitting behind the desk of the Oval Office. Today, she was wearing her skinny red jacket and skirt, with her hair pulled back in a bun. She was staying at the Marriott at the Metro Center. The White House was only six blocks away. Anna Scall loved to be out with the people. Ever since Cincinnati, she had been adored by crowds wherever she went. Today would be no different. She would walk the six blocks to the White House down E Street NW. She did not care what her Secret Service detail or Matt said. This was her day, and she was going to be a rock star.

7:50 a.m.

Supreme Court Chief Justice Dan Perkins greeted several Senators and other parishioners in the vestibule after 7:00 a.m. mass. Senator Ben Schaefer from Nebraska, a Republican, shook hands with the Chief Justice. Schaefer knew that Justice Perkins was the most liberal member of the Supreme Court, and shared a philosophy very different from his own.

"So are you excited about swearing in a Republican today?" jabbed Schaefer.

"Now, come on, Ben, you know we judges have to be fair. We cannot take sides between Republicans and Democrats. We have to treat everyone the same."

"Well, I guess I will have to wait and see what you boys in black are going to do with all the legislation we are going to pass over the next four years." Perkins laughed. The Senator shook the hand of the Chief Justice and then walked out of the Church. Just then, Father Rourke came back into the vestibule, wearing his white flowing alb, tied at the waist with a gold cincture, and a red scarf-like stole.

"It was good to see you in mass this morning, Dan," said the priest. "We are going to need lots of level-headedness the next four years."

"Yes, I look forward to a challenging host of new issues, Father. Please pray for me." Perkins looked at the priest, who clearly wanted to say something else.

"Father, you are not going to give me a lecture about abortion again, are you? I know how you feel and I told you I cannot speak about that."

"No, it's not that. I have prayed as hard as I can for you on that issue. But Dan, might I have a word with you on this whole issue of gay marriage? You have a case coming up this term on the whole gay marriage issue. Dan, it is specifically forbidden right in the Bible. Leviticus 18:22—'Thou shall not lie with mankind as with womankind—it is an abomination.'"

"Father, that passage comes directly after a discussion about idolatrous behavior in pagan temples, and the ritual sacrifice of children to the Pagan god Molech. Read in context, it is referring to homosexual activity in pagan temples, not homosexuality generally. But while we are on the subject of Leviticus, Leviticus also says you cannot have sex with a menstruating woman, you can't ever eat fat, you cannot round the corners of your beard, you cannot approach God if you have a flat nose, you cannot touch a dead pig, and you cannot, on pain of death, cuss out your mother or father."

"But Dan, the prohibition on homosexuality is not just in Leviticus. There is the Sodom and Gomorrah story, of course, and in Romans 1:26-27, Paul tells us: 'For this cause God gave them up unto vile affections: for even their women did change the natural use into that which is against nature: And likewise also the men, leaving the natural use of the woman, burned in their lust one toward another; men with men working that which is unseemly, and receiving in themselves that recompense of their error which was meet.' Dan, the Bible is very clear on this."

"But Father, you cannot take one thing Paul says and then ignore everything else he said. In Paul's letter to Timothy, he said women cannot braid their hair or wear pearls. Half the women in your congregation today were wearing pearls. And in Paul's letter to the Corinthians, he says you cannot have long hair. Paul also said you can get into heaven without performing any good deeds. Meanwhile, Paul was perfectly fine with slavery. In the Bible, slavery, polygamy, concubines, and prostitutes are all fair game. In Deuteronomy, stubborn children are to be stoned, rape victims must marry the rapist, and those with only one testicle cannot gain entry into the Assembly of the Lord. I guess what I am saying, Father, is that you cannot take all these Biblical passages literally and use them as a statutory code."

"But, Dan, don't you see that if homosexuals are allowed to marry, it will undermine the very sanctity of existing marriage between a man and a woman, which is a Sacrament in the Catholic Church."

"Father, we have people marrying because they are drunk in Las Vegas, marrying to get a green card, marrying a mail order bride, marrying an octogenarian to get his money, and marrying people they do not love out of shame for their sexuality. If all those people can marry, I do not see why two loving individuals cannot marry."

"But Dan, this is official Church doctrine, and you are a Catholic."

"Father, I am a Catholic, but I am also a judge. And when I put on the black robe, I have to do what is right under the law, irrespective of my own personal beliefs. But as I say, I really cannot debate any specific cases with you which might be pending before the Court. But I do find our discussions of Church doctrine interesting. You always make me think, Father. Now I really have to get moving, because I have to swear in the new President today."

"Well, thank the Lord for that, at least. What time do you have to be at the White House?"

"Around ten, so we can do a dry-run. Secret Service will be picking me up. But it's such a beautiful day out, I think I might take a run first."

"I wish I had your stamina, Dan," said the priest. "These old bones gave out long ago."

"Well, maybe we can get together in a week or two for a beer at O'Malley's, and we can exercise our drinking arm!"

"Ha! That sounds splendid! Now you have a nice day, Dan. God bless you!"

"Thank you, Father."

What the priest did not know was that Chief Justice Dan Perkins' brother Seamus Perkins was gay, very much in love, and living in a State which did not allow gay marriage. There was no way in the world he was going to vote against gay marriage when the Daltry v. Schwartzenegger gay marriage case came up for a vote this year. Perkins got in his Lincoln Town car, and the Secret Service drove him to his house, where he quickly changed into running clothes. Today's run was going to be invigorating and fun. Swearing in another Republican as President, however, was going to be dreadful. The country was going to need a lot of prayers.

8:00 a.m.

Mohammed El Faya still had a little more time to kill before the kill shot. The irony of all this was that at one time, he was on America's side. His whole life was about killing Saddam Hussein for what he did to Mohammed's brother. When the Americans took care of Hussein, he did not have much to live for. He had tried to tell the American pigs that he was on their side, not Saddam's side, but they wouldn't listen. He rubbed his ankle and remembered where the sadistic American guard had slammed the butt of his rifle against el Faya's ankle breaking it in two places. He had walked ever since with a limp.

The first night in Abu Graib in 2003 was terrible. He had been in his small cell only a few hours when the three Americans came in, and took him into a holding room, throwing him into a metal folding chair. One was in plain clothes, jeans and a tan jacket, and wearing sunglasses. The other two were in green Army fatigues. The one with the sunglasses seemed to be in charge. He set a tape recorder down on the metal table.

"Do you speak English or do we need a translator?" asked the sunglasses man.

"I speak English."

"Good. What is your name, son?"

"Mohammed El Faya."

"Where were you born?"

"Dujail."

"How old are you?"

"41."

It took about another ten minutes to get all his biographical information, and to explain how he came to work for Saddam in the Republican Guard. In order to curry favor, El Faya quickly confessed his plot to kill Saddam Hussein. The Americans were skeptical. How was it that he was the only one to escape from Dujail? El Faya explained his shame at missing his target.

"So let me see if I have this straight. You have been a member of the Republican Guard for almost twenty years, you fought and killed American soldiers in the Gulf War, and you had almost twenty years to kill Saddam Hussein, yet somehow, you managed to never even get a shot off on him. Expert marksman like you, I find that hard to believe."

"I was never stationed anywhere where I could get access. It would look too suspicious. So I waited for the opportunity. I never got the chance."

"Mohammed, do you think we're stupid?"

"No, not at all."

Sunglasses-man took out a ziploc bag and a paper plate from his briefcase, Out of the Ziploc bag, he dumped what appeared to be human feces onto the plate.

"See that, Mohammed? That's what I think of your story. It's shit. You are shit. That's what I think. Now either you start telling us where the weapons of mass destruction are, or what terrorist plots your friends are hatching, or you are going to be eating that shit."

El Faya looked down. This American was purposely trying to offend his Muslim faith. "I am not aware of any weapons of mass destruction or any plots. I am just a guard at a post, that's it."

Just then, one of the Army men went behind El Faya and slammed his face into the plate, soiling his face and breaking his nose.

"I don't think you heard my friend here, Mister." The three men laughed.

Sunglasses man talked again. "I am going to give you another chance. Start talking."

El Faya was horrified and his nose hurt terribly. He racked his brain for anything to say. He could not come up with anything.

The interrogator took out a small book and put it on the table. "We recovered this from your pants pocket when we put you in your cell. This is your copy of the Qur'an, correct?"

"Yes, it is."

"It always disturbs me up how you terrorists think. You walk around all day with this Qur'an in your pocket, which tells you to be a good person, and then you fly airplanes into buildings, killing thousands of people."

"Our people did not attack you on 9/11. Those were Saudi Arabians."

"Really? And how is it that you know that, mother-fucker?"

"Because it was printed in just about every newspaper on the planet."

"Oh," said sunglasses-man. "I see. We have a smartass. Well you know what I think of your little Muslim book, smart ass? I think it's shit." With that, he rubbed the holy book all over the excrement and then put it back in the captive's pocket. "There, now the little shit-eater can have his shit book back."

El Faya was angry and spit at the sunglasses man, calling him a filthy pig.

"I'm a pig?" said the sunglasses man. "Interesting." With that, sunglasses man slammed the prisoner down onto the floor and with the butt of a rifle, pile drove it into El Faya's ankle, causing him to wince in pain. Then he took out a plastic paper bag out of his briefcase and violently put it over the captive's head, strangling him. "Please! NO!! I cannot breathe!" The other two Army men helped the interrogator manhandle the man with the bag on his head down the hall to a room marked "Wetroom." "Come with us, you little shit!" As El Faya entered the room, he saw a horse's trough filled with water. The three men placed him roughly on a backboard and then duct-taped him to the board at his chest, his mid-section and his ankles. The three men then lifted the prisoner up, placing the top of the board on the rim of the water trough. Sunglasses man took off the bag.

"You have exactly three seconds to start talking, and to tell us where the weapons are and what terrorist plots against Americans are being planned."

"Fuck you!"

"Dunk him!" the sunglasses-man ordered. The two Army soldiers slid the water board into the trough. El Faya was thrashing wildly, afraid he was going to drown. After what seemed like an eternity, he was raised out of the trough.

"Please!" said El Faya, sputtering water and coughing. "Tell me what you want me to say and I will say it."

"It's not what we want you to say. We want the truth. Where are Saddam's weapons of mass destruction?"

El Faya hesitated. He had no idea what they were talking about. The three men dunked him again. El Faya looked through the waving water at the evil faces of his captors above him. He was in all-out panic mode, sure that this was going to be his last minute on Earth. Suddenly, he was removed from the water. He coughed again on his removal.

"Tikrit! Tikrit! They are in Tikrit! I swear it! I saw them, lots of these weapons you seek, in a large factory building in Tikrit. There, I have helped you, please release me!"

The three men took El Faya down, untaped him, and returned him to his cell. One of the Army men shoved him against the metal bunk, smashing his head. "Have a nice sleep, shit!" The three men talked out in the hall. The sunglasses man, a CIA operative, said there was nothing in Tikrit. They had already searched every building there. The three concluded the man knew nothing.

That did not stop the torture, however. Over the next three months, angry black dogs were let into El Faya's cell to scare him to death. They turned on the lights and blared loud sirens every hour or so to prevent him from sleeping. On one particular night, some sadistic guards made each of the prisoners on his floor strip bare, and then led the men into the hall, instructing them, at gunpoint, to jump on each other in a pile up of flesh, while the guards laughed. He was interrogated ten more times, with the same result. Each time he made up a fantastic story, and convinced his interrogators he knew nothing. In 2006, some of the prisoners, including El Faya, were released in the middle of the night into Jordan. As the American soldier roughly threw him out of the truck into the cold night air onto the desert sand, El Faya decided that his vengeance for Saddam had suddenly faded and he would now fight a new enemy—the evil imperialists from the United States of America.

8:30 a.m. Washington, D.C.

Tim Woodson and his wife got in the limousine for their ride from the Watergate Hotel to the White House. As the car traveled slowly down the streets of Washington on Virginia Avenue, Woodson looked out at the droves of well-wishers and fans in winter coats and parkas lining the route from the Watergate to the White House. They all looked so happy to have him there. When the limousine was almost to E Street, Woodson lowered his window. The Secret Service agents in the car went ballistic. "Sir, do not do that!" and they raised the window again. Woodson was annoyed. Who was the President here, after all? What he needed to do was to get out among the people.

"Driver, I would like you to stop up here. I would like to step out for a few minutes and say hello to my constituents."

Mike Green, one of the Secret Service agents in the car, said, "Sir, I want to strongly recommend that you not do that. Every crazy and their brother is out today. If you get out of the car, sir, we cannot guarantee your safety in this crowd."

"Mike, I appreciate your dedication. But one of the things you guys are going to have to learn about me is that when I give an order, I expect it to be followed. Now stop the car and open the door!"

Reluctantly, the driver stopped the car, and Mike Green exited the vehicle first, talking into his sleeve and coordinating the move with all the other agents. He did not like this at all.

Across town, Anna Scall was giving her Secret Service detail even bigger fits, because she wanted to walk all the way from her hotel to the White House. Eight agents in black trench coats formed a phalanx around her, as she made her way down E Street toward the White House in her smart red coat and skirt, waving like a beauty queen to the adoring fans.

Meanwhile, in Georgetown, Chief Justice Dan Perkins was running along Canal Street, finishing off his morning run. The air was so crisp this morning. He felt great. After a quick shower, he would take the limousine to the White House for the inauguration. He stopped for a moment to check his pulse and adjust his iPod, and then continued his run. The three Secret Service agents running with him were darting their eyes out in all directions, looking for potential bad guys.

Mohammed El Faya took out a glass cutter and cut the pane of glass from the floor to a point about three feet up. He removed the glass he had cut and slid it across the carpet. He laid out his rubber mat on the carpet and got back into position. His sniper rifle was loaded with ammunition. He would only need one or two shots. He looked through his scope. The target had not come within the killing field yet. Soon America would pay for what they had done to him.

CHAPTER 12. ASTROLABE

January 20, 2013. 8:30 a.m. Paris time.
Salon-de-Provence France. Beneath L'Ecole St. Michel.

Professor John Morse studied the notes he had made. Somehow these clues must together form a word to open the vault door. The answer, he thought, must lie in the astrolabe. Morse studied the astrolabe on the podium. The astrolabe was round, about a foot in diameter, and made entirely of brass. There were markings around the edge of the astrolabe in concentric circles. There was a small brass ring at the top about as big as a thumb. Morse held up the instrument to Father du Bois and his children, holding it by the ring. "This is an astrolabe. It is used for determining the altitude of the stars." Morse thought of how best to explain the intricate markings and moving parts on the medieval astrolabe, and decided it would be best to use a simple analogy they could understand. He took out his notepad and drew a drinking straw, with a piece of arcing cardboard attached. He made notches on the drawing for the different degrees, and then drew in a string attached to one end of the straw, anchored at the end by a washer. His drawing looked like this:

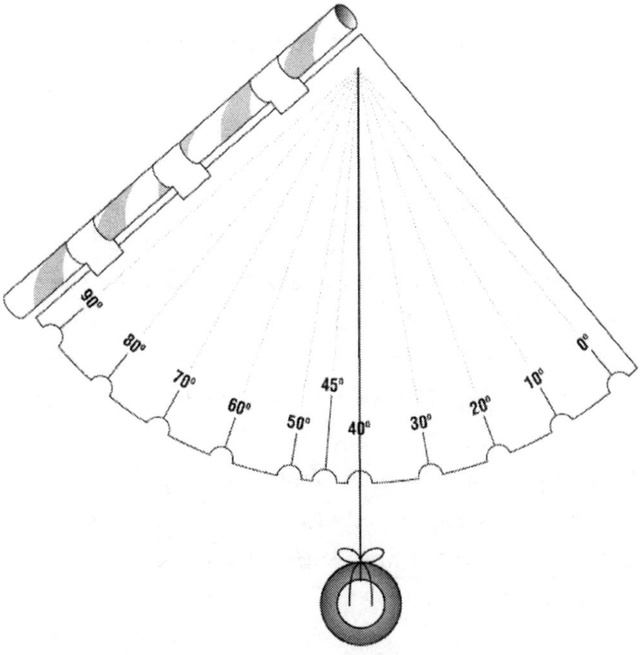

This is a drawing of a very crude astrolabe. Picture yourself trying to figure out how far Venus is above the horizon on a particular night. You see Venus in the night sky, but you do not know exactly how far above the horizon it is. The Earth's horizon is zero degrees. If you crane your neck back like this, and look directly straight above you into the sky, that's 90 degrees. So any star or planet you look at will be between 0 degrees—the horizon— and 90 degrees—straight above you. But how do we know what the exact altitude is? You look through the bottom end of the straw, and tilt the straw upward at an angle until you can see Venus through the other end of the straw. Now you can see that as you tilt the straw upward, the washer on the string is going to swing back towards you, from 0 degrees to 90 degrees. When you find Venus through the straw, you merely look at the number of degrees marked by the string and the washer, and you have your answer.

A medieval astrolabe works in much the same way. Morse showed his children the astrolabe. "This ring at the top is called the 'armilla.' That is the Latin word for 'ring.' That is what you hold onto when you are measuring with the astrolabe. Screwed into the center of the astrolabe is this movable lever called the 'alidade.' It looks kind of like a spinner in a board game. Attached to the ends of the alidade are little raised pieces of metal with holes in them. You put your eye up to the sighting vane and look through the holes at the planet or star you are trying to find. The sighting vane acts just like the straw. You spin the alidade around to the point where you can see the star or the planet through the holes on the sighting vane, and then the alidade, like the string and the washer, will point to the correct number of degrees. And then you have your altitude.

Zoey was unimpressed. "And I care about this—why?"

"There are many uses of the astrolabe, but one of the most common uses was to determine the location of one's ship while at sea," said Morse.

Zoey was still bored to death. "So this will come in real handy when I am on a pirate ship in the ocean," she said sarcastically.

"Well, for right now, I am hoping this astrolabe can help us unlock this door and learn the mysteries which lay on the other side."

"Professor, this astrolabe must have something to do with constellations, right?"

Professor Morse studied the astrolabe in thought. He inspected the "mater." The "mater" was the entire round, immovable portion of the astrolabe, which was hollowed out in the middle. This hollowed portion, called the "womb," in turn housed several movable plates. Around the edge of the raised outer ring of the mater were certain letters.

"Take a look at this," said Morse. "On some astrolabes," he explained, "The numbers 1 through 24 run around the outer edge of this circle, with each number corresponding to an hour of the day. On some astrolabes, however, like this one, they also use letters, but they omit the letters 'J,' 'U,' and 'W.' That leaves 23 letters, plus a cross symbol at the very top, for a total of 24. Don't ask me why they omit, J, U, and W. I have no idea—they just do. The cross at the top of the circle denotes noon and South. The letter F denotes 6 a.m. and West. The letter M denotes midnight and North. The letter S denotes 6 p.m. and East. We have ourselves an alphabet—or close to one—right here on this astrolabe. Perhaps we can use this to chart our constellations and we will get our word."

Zach was getting lost. "Pops, you are totally losing me. How do we get the constellations on the astrolabe?"

"For that," said Morse, "We will need a star chart. Fortunately, I brought one with me in my bag." The square piece of blue cardboard had a circle in the middle, with a movable wheel. When the wheel was rotated, different constellations appeared. Entitled, "The Sky at Night," the planisphere showed the main stars visible in the heavens for every night of the year.

Morse took out his notes listing the constellations from their last set of clues:

CASSIOPEIA
CETUS
URSA MINOR
GEMINI
SCORPIO
URSA MAJOR
PERSEUS
CANCER
CYGNUS
ORION

"Now," said Morse, "If you use this planisphere, and search for Cassiopeia, which looks like a small letter 'W' near the middle of the circle, you can see that the stars forming her constellation lie between 0 hours and 2 hours. Running those out on to the edge of the mater on our astrolabe, we see that 0 hours is the cross symbol, 1 hour is "A," and 2 hours is "B." So that means that for Cassiopeia, the letter must be the cross symbol (a blank), an A, or a B.

Morse showed them on the ancient astrolabe:

So Cassiopeia has three possibilities— +, A, or B. Morse wrote on his notebook: Cassiopeia = + , A, or B.

"Cetus is much bigger, and runs between 1 and 3 hours. So Cetus = A, B, or C.

"Ursa Minor is between 15 and 19 hours. So on our astrolabe, that equates to P, Q, R, S, T. Ursa Minor = P, Q, R, S, or T.

"Gemini is between 6 hours and 8 hours, so that's F, G, H. Gemini = F, G, H."

Morse continued to make notes from the planisphere and the astrolabe, until he had summarized his notes as follows:

	Between Hours	**Letter from Astrolabe**
CASSIOPEIA	0, 1, 2	+, A, B
CETUS	1, 2, 3	A, B, C
URSA MINOR	15, 16, 17, 18, 19	P, Q, R, S, T
GEMINI	6, 7, 8	F, G, H
SCORPIO	16, 17, 18	Q, R, S
URSA MAJOR	8, 9, 10, 11, 12, 13, 14	L, M, N, O
PERSEUS	3, 4, 5	C, D, E
CANCER	8, 9	H, I
CYGNUS	19, 20, 21	T, V, X
ORION	5, 6, 7	E, F, G

"Now all we have to do," said Morse, "is to pick one letter from our choices for each constellation and we will have our ten-letter word to open the vault!"

Morse put his pencil in his mouth, and began chewing on the eraser.

"Well, for Scorpio, we can probably get rid of the 'Q,' because there is no 'U,' and only a handful of words have a Q without a U. And under Orion, we can certainly eliminate 'F,' because no word that I know of ends with 'TF,' 'VF,' or 'XF.' We can probably eliminate the 'G', because no word ends in 'TG,' 'VG,' or 'XG.' That means the last letter is almost certainly 'E.'"

Father du Bois followed along. "Under Cygnus, we can get rid of the 'X,' because I cannot think of any words ending in 'XE.' And under Cancer, we can get rid of the 'H,' because no word ends in 'HTE' or

'HVE.' That means the letter for Cancer must be an 'I.'" Father du Bois summarized what they had so far:

Letter from Astrolabe

CASSIOPEIA ————	+, A, B
CETUS ————	A, B, C
URSA MINOR ————	P, R, S, T
GEMINI ————	F, G, H
SCORPIO ————	R, S
URSA MAJOR ————	H, I, K, L, M, N, O
PERSEUS ————	B, C, D
CANCER ————	I
CYGNUS ————	T,V
ORION ————	E

Morse looked at the letters and was having trouble definitively ruling out any other letter. He focused on what they did know. If one assumed that the "+" symbol could act as a blank, then the word they were seeking was either 9 or 10 letters long and it ended in either "BITE," "BIVE," "CITE," "CIVE," "DITE" or "DIVE." He tried to come up with as many combinations as he could think of but nothing sounded right.

Zach looked over his father's shoulder. "Maybe you have to do something with those letters over the top of the door, the thing about love in your heart," Zach suggested. Morse was irritated his son was interrupting his train of thought, but then he stopped. He looked over the doorway again. *"Seuls peuvent entrer ceux qui ont le coeur plein d'amour."* "Love," thought Morse. "What does love have to do with it?" Then he remembered that many of the clues related to Greek gods. Perhaps the Greek goddess of love….. Of course!

"Oh, my goodness," said Professor Morse. "It is much easier than I thought. It has been staring us in the face the entire time. He showed the notepad to Father du Bois and the children. He put the correct letters in bold print, and lined out the incorrect letters:

Letter from Astrolabe

CASSIOPEIA ————	**+**, A, B
CETUS ————	+, **A**, B, C
URSA MINOR ————	O, **P**
GEMINI ————	F, G, **H**
SCORPIO ————	**R**, S
URSA MAJOR ————	H, I, K, L, M, N, **O**
PERSEUS ————	B, C, **D**
CANCER ————	**I**
CYGNUS ————	**T**, V
ORION ————	**E**

"+APHRODITE," said Morse. "The Greek goddess of love! Only those with love in their heart may enter." Morse quickly turned the first dial on the left to the "cross" symbol, and then turned the rest of the dials so that they spelled out "APHRODITE." Morse turned the handle. The lock on the vault clicked open. Morse smiled broadly and opened the vault door, peering inside into the cold blackness.

CHAPTER 13. SCHOLARS

March 1538. Agen, France.

Julius Caesar Scaliger was the most noted scholar in Agen, and, indeed, most of Southern France. He was a poet, grammarian, author, orator, physician, soldier, scientist, botanist, and astrologer. He had a monstrously large wrinkled forehead and a receding hairline of curly brown hair which met in the middle in a pronounced widow's peak. His eyebrows were pencil-thin and seemed too long for his popping, frog-like eyes, and the gray bags underneath his eyes were earned from too much reading. His most prominent feature, however, was his moustache and beard. His thick, twisted moustache was no match for the bushy, tumbleweed of a beard which went down to the top of his chest. Despite his unkept beard, however, he was a meticulous dresser, and was often seen strutting down the limestone streets of Agen with his walnut walking stick. Scaliger, a confirmed egomaniac, had an opinion about everything, and whatever the opinion was, he was sure to share it with as large an audience as he could find. He loved the scholarly debate with other brilliant minds, but truly felt that no one was his intellectual equal in the end. A friendly debate would often end with Scaliger sighing and feeling sorry for his opponent, who just could not seem to grasp why Scaliger's own position was the superior one.

Scaliger had come to Agen in 1525 as the personal physician and good friend of Antonio della Rovero, the Archbishop of Agen. Scaliger liked to tell that he was born at Castle La Rocca and was a scion of the House of La Scala, a prestigious family of nobles who had ruled Verona, Italy for 150 years. He claimed to be related to Emperor Maximilian. A page at the age of 12, he fought as a soldier for the Emperor for seventeen years. At the Battle of Ravena, his father and brother were killed. Scaliger claimed that he performed dozens of acts of valor during the battle and, in reward, the Emperor had bestowed upon him the highest honors of chivalry, including the Order of the Golden Spur. Injuries during the war ended his prestigious military career, so Scaliger took up the study of medicine at the University of Bologna, where he excelled. Scaliger's critics later claimed that much of this history was a web of lies; that he was really the son of Benedetto Bordone, a Verona map maker; and that he had not been educated in Bologna, but at a less prestigious university in Padua. In any event, no one in Agen assumed he was anything less than the genuine article, and the local politicians warmly welcomed and respected him.

Shortly after arriving in Agen, Scaliger had met a beautiful thirteen year-old Agen girl named Andiette de Roques Lobejac, who had never told Scaliger that she had fled to Agen as a young girl and had been adopted by a local family. Even though she was thirty years his junior, he found her absolutely delightful and, after overcoming some objections from the girl's father due to their age disparity, the two were quickly wed. His wife Andiette went on to have sixteen children, the oldest of which was Henriette. Henriette was a perfect child—intellectually and physically brilliant, obedient, hard-working, honest and loyal. Scaliger, who could find faults with everyone, nevertheless could find no fault with his eldest daughter, and saw her as a miniature version of himself. He loved teaching her fractions, puzzles, anagrams, and astrology. The child just absorbed knowledge like a sponge. In 1531, when Henriette was five, Scaliger sent an invitation to a wandering physician named Michele de Nostradame, who had been reputed to have had some success curing plague victims. Scaliger, a doctor himself, could not wait to hear Nostradamus tell how he had discovered a cure for diseases which had ravaged the French countryside.

Nostradamus, for his part, was excited to meet Scaliger. Nostradamus' career so far had not been as illustrious. On October 3, 1529, Nostradamus enrolled in medical school at the Medical Faculty at Montpellier to study for his medical doctorate. On the liber scolasticorum where Nostradamus had written his name for admission, the Student Registrar, Guillame Rondelet, scratched out Nostradamus' entry, noting in the margin:

He whom you here see crossed out—mark well, reader—has been an apothecary or quack. We have established through Chante, an apothecary of this city, and through students, who have heard him speak ill of doctors. Wherefore as laid down by statute I have been enjoined to strike him out from the book of students.

Nostradamus had been expelled both for being an apothecary and for making obnoxious jokes about medical doctors. Booted out of medical school before he could even crack a book, Nostradamus went on the road, like a carnival doctor, traveling from town to town, seeking out medical cures, learning about plants and remedies, and hoping to make money curing the strangers that he met on his way. It was reported in some parts that Nostradamus actually cured certain plague victims. It is difficult to know whether these cures in fact occurred, and, if they did, whether Nostradamus' cures were accidental, but whichever the case, his reputation as a healer began to spread through southern France. The invitation from Scaliger was a Godsend for Nostradamus. Nostradamus viewed Scaliger as an intellectual giant, stating that he was the "father to the eloquence of Cicero, in his perfect and supreme poetry another Virgil, in his medical teaching worth any two to Galen, and to whom I remain more indebted than to anybody else in this world." In fact, Nostradamus would later name his eldest son César in honor of Scaliger. Surely, Nostradamus thought, he could pick up substantial knowledge living in the orbit of this famous doctor and philosopher. And so it was that Nostradamus made his way across Southern France to the small town of Agen.

When Nostradamus arrived in Agen in 1531, the two men spent hours each day on Scaliger's porch debating botany or astrology or grammar, and each enjoyed the other's company immensely. Nostradamus was as impressed as Scaliger was with the quickness of his eldest daughter Henriette, and Nostradamus developed a true fondness for the girl. Seven years after Nostradamus arrived in Agen, the two doctors were sharing a smoke on Scaliger's porch, when Scaliger brought up the subject of Nostradamus' love interests. Scaliger had noticed that Nostradamus had turned down most of the invitations to fêtes and galas thrown by neighborhood Agen women who were hoping to rope this eligible bachelor for their daughters. Wasn't Nostradamus interested in love? And that's when Nostradamus confessed to Scaliger that the only female he found interesting at all was Scaliger's now-twelve year-old daughter Henriette. At first, this was somewhat repulsive to Scaliger. After all, Nostradamus had met the girl when Henriette was only five. Was this man some kind of pervert? But in 1538, a girl who was twelve was eligible to marry, and Scaliger could not deny that his own wife was some thirty years younger than he. Scaliger, too, had married a woman at a very young age. It was an awkward moment for the two scholars, but Scaliger quickly applied his keen logical mind to the problem. Suitors would begin coming for his daughter soon, that much was certain. There were not that many men of means or, more importantly, wit in the town of Agen. Surely, this doctor had the means to make a good living for his daughter. And the man was his friend, after all. Surely, he would not mistreat her. At least he knew Nostradamus well. He would not be able to say that about many of the other suitors who would come to call. And this girl was special. Most men would not appreciate her intellect. He knew that Nostradamus appreciated her for her mind as well as her other features. A brain like hers would be wasted on most of these Agen apes. When one analyzed the situation dispassionately with the cool lens of logic, the union made sense. So, after discussion of appropriate dowry, in January 1538, Scaliger gave his consent to Nostradamus to marry his eldest daughter.

Antonio Della Rovere, also called Marc-Antoine Della Rovere, was the Archbishop of Agen. The Della Rovere family came from modest roots in Savona, Liguira. However, two of the Della Roveres worked their way through the ranks to become Pope: Francesco della Rovere, who ruled as Pope Sixtus IV and his nephew Giuliano della Rovere, who ruled as Pope Julius II from 1503 to 1513. Pope Sixtus IV is known for having built the Sistine Chapel, which is named for him. After two members of the family became popes, the family's wealth increased dramatically. The Della Roveres became patrons to the arts and sciences. Antonio Della Rovere became the Archbishop of Agen rather easily due to his family's connections. Short, stout, and bald, with a friendly fat face and big cheeks, the Archbishop enjoyed both a good intellectual discussion and a good bottle of wine. The Della Rovere family had long been friends with Scaliger and had served as the doctor's patron. For this reason, the Archbishop and Scaliger were quite close, and it was with no reluctance at all that Scaliger uprooted all of his belongings to become the Archbishop's personal physician here in Agen. The Archbishop, too, also took a liking to Nostradamus, and often joined the philosophical discussions with the two men.

Today, the subject was Henriette's vision of the future from the previous evening. Scaliger and Nostradamus had summoned the Archbishop, as a vision from God was certainly something within the Archbishop's bailiwick, and he may have some keen insights on the subject.

Scaliger took out the small Bible which Henriette had used to write her verses and laid it on the table before the other two men.

"In analyzing this matter," said Scaliger, "I think we should begin with what we know for certain. I can assure both of you gentlemen, without equivocation, that the girl is not fabricating. She is as innocent as a lamb and as certain as Polaris. She would no more concoct this story than the Archbishop would convert to Judaism."

The Archbishop laughed, sipping on his red wine. "Now that would be something for the Cardinal to see."

"I agree," said Nostradamus. "Henriette is beyond reproach. However, while I believe that it may be possible, using certain scientific methods, to look through the mists, as it were, and divine certain happenings in the future, it is only with a rigorous scientific approach or natural divine skills that this can be accomplished. Merely daydreaming in the almond fields will not suffice."

"I have heard you claim this before, Michel," said Scaliger. "How exactly do you claim to know future events through a 'scientific method,' as you say? I am most interested in these theories, for they seem wild and preposterous to me. But if you are correct, and a man could truly read the future, that would be a significant power indeed, and that power should be used only by intellectuals to promote the common good."

"I have done such a thing myself several times," said Nostradamus. "All of you may recall the Great Scare of 1524. You may remember in that time, between February 13 and 25, 1524, every planet in the universe was in perfect alignment in the sign of Pisces, and 16 of 20 conjunctions were occupying Water signs. And every noted astrologer at that time predicted a great flood the likes of which were not seen since Noah. On January 24, 1524, when Mars had already joined Jupiter and Saturn in Pisces, thousands of people headed out of the cities, looking for higher ground. You may have heard of Count von Igelheim of Germany who commissioned the building of an ark for the occasion. The Elector of Brandenburg also made for the mountaintops."

"I remember it well," said the Archbishop. "I myself packed up my belongings and headed for the Franciscan Monastery just north of here, for it sits on high ground."

"Quite so," said Nostradamus. "And yet, in the eye of this hurricane of frenzied astrologers, I alone remained calm. And that is because I had rigorously applied a scientific method to the problem, and learned, from a review of various astrological texts, that the exact same alignment of planets had occurred in Libra in 1186! Absolutely nothing of significance happened on that day in 1186. Therefore, I concluded with great confidence that there would be no flood, and no cause for panic. And, as I successfully predicted, no such flood occurred."

"Wait," said the Archbishop incredulously, "You are claiming that when the planets are aligned in a particular way in one age of time, similar events will occur in history at a later point in time when the planets are arranged again identically?"

"Precisely!" said Nostradamus.

"That sounds like a very questionable theory," scoffed Scaliger.

"It is not theory at all, gentlemen, but proven fact. For example, if one looks at the assassination of Julius Caesar, which occurred on the Ides of March—March 15, in 44 B.C. and if one looks to the nearest alignment of at least four planets immediately preceding that date, at latitude 41 degrees 54'N, which is Rome, we see that Mars, Venus, Mercury, and the Sun were all aligned in the tenth house on that date and time, with the Moon in the twelfth house. The next time that alignment of planets will occur again is at geographical latitude 32 degrees to 33 degrees, between November 22, 1963 and November 29, 1963. Therefore, it is my prediction that a significant political assassination, on the order of the assassination of Julius Caesar, will occur between those dates at that latitude. In addition, this later alignment occurs in Sagittarius, the sign of the Archer, so I might also speculate that the victim is killed either by an arrow or projectile of some kind."

"That is all well and good, man," said Scaliger. "But I can just as well predict that 200 years from today, a man will have green beans explode from his nose. Since we will never live that long, we will never be able to verify if your prediction or my prediction is correct."

"I agree," said the Archbishop. "One could make that claim about anything."

"But Julius," protested Nostradamus, "You have heard my account of the two pigs, have you not? Surely, that event convinces you that the prediction of future events is possible?"

"Oh, stars above! We are not going to hear about the pigs again, are we?"

"What pigs?" asked the Archbishop.

"Archbishop, have you never heard me tell of my famous encounter with the two pigs? Well, I shall tell the story again, although Jules has heard it many times. I was once the guest of the Lord of Florinville at the Castle of Faim, because I happened to be treating the Lord's mother of a bad case of gout. As the Lord and I crossed the yard, there were two pigs, a white pig and a black pig, running about. The Lord had heard it tell before that I had a gift of foresight. He asked me, 'Doctor, since you can foretell the future, tell me, which of the pigs shall we eat tonight, the white one or the black one?' When I responded 'the black one,' my host went into the kitchen and instructed the cook to prepare the white one, so that he would prove me wrong. When the meal was served, my host asked me which pig was served, and again I answered the black one. Chuckling with delight, my host revealed that he had instructed the cook to prepare the white one instead. When I insisted that in fact we had eaten the black pig, my host summoned the cook, who confessed that while he was preparing the white pig, and left the kitchen momentarily, a tame wolf came into the kitchen and devoured the white pig. Having no choice, the cook prepared the black pig for the meal. This astounded one and all, and resulted, by the way, in an excellent additional compensation for me as well as one very fine meal!"

"Michel, my first response is that you had an even chance of guessing the right one either way, much as if I asked you to guess whether I am holding one finger or two fingers behind my back. Achieving success when you have a 50% chance of arriving at the conclusion by guessing is not that incredible. But Michel, even if we assume you had the gift of foresight to predict the correct pig, and you are a gentleman, so I take you at your word, you did not arrive at your conclusion for the pigs by looking at stars," said Scaliger. "So how does the pig story support your scientific-method thesis?"

"Yes," said Nostradamus. "You are correct. However, when events are closer in time to the prediction, they may be foretold by sensing the vibrations of the matter. Julius, in the same way that I move my arm as if I am throwing a ball to you, you will instinctively move your hands to catch it, you are predicting what will happen in the future because you are in tune with how balls move through air. Some people possess this same gift of foresight with respect to the actions of humans, and how one human will kinetically interact with another human. The rare few of us who possess this ability can see matters which will occur close in time. It is my intention to test my theories out in the future using a combination of techniques, both astrological and vibrational."

"Well then, can you please predict for me where Doctor Scaliger's finest bottle of Bordeaux is in this house, because I am in bad need of a refurbishment!" The Archbishop laughed like a jolly elf and excused himself to go into the house to look for more wine.

"So what do you make of this girl's verses, Michel? She is an extremely bright girl, but I have never seen her write poetry before. These verses are all rhyming, and the meter of the rhyme seems fairly good. Do you think she could do this all by herself?"

"No, I don't. And if she says she wrote these in a dream, I believe her, because she is a good Christian girl and God is with her. These things she writes of, however, are horrible, Jules. I fear we must not show these to anyone, at least in our lifetimes, as they may evoke horrible fears in people and they may seek to punish us—especially with the Inquisition constantly pestering us."

Scaliger reviewed some of the passages in the Bible written in India ink. "Mass murders, savagery, wars— this list is terrible. At the end of the verses there is reference to rams and hawks and eagles all attacking a great leader. Do you see that? What do you make of that?"

"I must confess, Jules, I do not know. These are probably references to great events in history which will only be understood after they occur. The thing I am most concerned about are these references to evil Popes. One of those appears to be Pope Julius II, who is related to our good friend the Archbishop. Do not mention those verses to him, or he will take great offense. You and I know Julius was a wicked man, but we must not offend our good friend."

"Yes, I am concerned about those passages as well. The last thing we need is to anger the Inquisition. Although I must say, I am absolutely fascinated by this reference to the man Copernicus, who claims the Earth moves around the sun. I, too, have always hypothesized such an orbit."

"Do not speak too loudly, Jules, for I am sure the Church would disagree with you there, too."

"Quite so, Michel."

"I think the best thing for us to do, Julius, is for me to safeguard this Bible and hide its contents from prying eyes. In the meantime, I will consult my astrological texts to see if anything written here can be verified through a logical scientific methodology. I will also meditate to see if I can sense any vibrations here which line up with what is predicted by

Henriette in her Bible."

"Very well," said Scaliger. "She is your wife, after all."

Nostradamus put the bible away. With that, Andiette Scaliger, Julius' wife, came out with the Archbishop and an opened new bottle of wine. "What are you kind gentlemen discussing, Jules?"

"Oh, these verses written by Henriette the other day out in the field. Michel here was just explaining his theories on the prediction of future events."

"Oh, I am most confident that certain people can predict future events," said Andiette.

Nostradamus looked at her. "How do you know that?"

Andiette looked down at her apron silently. She did not want to re-live the shameful night she received her vision about Petit Paul and murdered another soul. "I don't know. I just assume that God speaks to certain people. Like Joan of Arc, for example."

"Yes," said the Archbishop. "God most certainly speaks to people from time to time. He did it to Joan and to Daniel and to David and to many people in the Bible. This child of yours, in my opinion, probably speaks the truth. I have not read any of her prophecies, but she seems to be a genuinely innocent child. But the problem is, with the Inquisition everywhere, you just do not know how other people might interpret this. What we see as words from God may be interpreted as words from the Devil. So you need to be careful with this."

"I agree," said Scaliger. "Michel's idea to safeguard the Bible is a good one. But before we put the book away, I would make one interesting observation. These 58 four-lined verses—we shall call them 'quatrains' for lack of a better term—include a prediction here written on top of Corinthians: II which contains one foot dragging its toe in our past, and one foot kicking into our possible future. Let me read it to you:

Suprême au pape lui-même, c'est le huitième,
Ceux qui protestent sont traités comme traîtres et assassiné.
Bouffi d'orgueil, il s'est marié avec la crème,
Des belles femmes: une morte, une survécu, deux divorcées, deux décapitées

Supreme to the pope himself, he is the eighth,
Those who protest are murdered and treated as traitors.

Fat with pride, he married the cream of the crop,
Beautiful women: one died, one survived, two divorced, two beheaded

"The eighth" is obviously a reference to Henry VIII of England. "Supreme to the pope himself" is straightforward. We all know that Henry declared himself to be supreme to the pope. I am sure both of you are aware of the Act of Supremacy of 1534 and the Treasons Act of 1534, passed some four years ago. Although we would not say it publicly, as frank men standing on a porch, I think we can all agree amongst ourselves that 'fat with pride' is a moniker which some would give Henry. But note the last line, referencing six wives. Henry has only had three wives that I know of: Catherine of Aragon, Anne Boleyn, and Jane Seymour. Henry divorced Catherine and beheaded Anne Boleyn. Nothing to date has happened with Jane Seymour. I think all we need to do to verify the accuracy and reliability of these quatrains is to wait and see what happens to the wives of King Henry VIII!"

"Why, that is fascinating!" exclaimed the Archbishop. "You are exactly right!"

Nostradamus was not as jubilant at Scaliger's observation as the Archbishop. Frankly, he was somewhat peeved that these men failed to understand that Nostradamus was a man of science, with innate gifts plainly recognized by whomever he met. Why were these men falling all over themselves about the prattling of a twelve year-old girl? Well, he would keep this Bible hidden, lest others start believing that his true psychic gifts came from his wife. If that happened, he would become the laughing stock of France.

"I agree, it is most interesting," said Nostradamus as fair-mindedly as he could. "I shall safeguard the Bible, and we shall see what happens to Henry." Nostradamus raised his glass, trying to muster up cheeriness: "To the future wives of Henry VIII— may they be prepared to lose their head for love!"

The three men laughed and drained their wine glasses.

"Now, Michel, pass me that wine bottle and let me explain to you both again why Vergil is so much better than Homer."

The three men laughed and Nostradamus groaned. He hated Vergil. Nostradamus tucked Henriette's Bible into his jacket for another day.

CHAPTER 14. ALAMO

January 20, 2013. FBI Headquarters. 10 a.m. EST. Washington, D.C.

"Boss, I think we have a hot one," said Ahmad Mahmood, a tall, India-born FBI analyst who had been assigned to assist Lead Investigator Ruddy Montana.

Montana came across the room to Mahmood's desk, and looked over his shoulder at the computer screen. Montana was handsome for his fifty years, with a square jaw and friendly brown eyes, gray buzz cut and tan complexion. But he was only 5 foot 4 inches tall. And for most people he met, that was all they needed to know—he was short. It made no difference that Montana had been a cum laude graduate of Yale, a decorated Army Ranger, a municipal police captain cited multiple times for valor during duty, or a former Olympic fencing champion. All most people saw was his height. But what he lacked in stature, he more than made up for in an uncanny ability to close cases. Montana held the record for closing more cases than any other FBI Detective, which was the reason he was assigned the Cincinnati case. Unfortunately, however, this case was proving difficult to crack. Most big cases would have broken by now, and it was irritating Montana that the Cincinnati massacre was largely still a question mark.

The FBI investigators were able to find the detonator in the rubble, of course. Nothing special about its origin. The materials could have been purchased at any Home Depot. The RDX from the C-4 explosives, however, was unique. The RDX came from a Defentris, Inc. chemical plant in Alexandria, Virginia, but unfortunately the Defentris security tapes did not reveal the thief. All current and former employees of Defentris were interviewed, but nothing looked like a promising lead. There were no prints on the white trash barrel other than students and teachers from the school. A full twenty-block canvas of neighbors by the FBI and local police turned up no witnesses who had seen the bomber. The school had no video cameras. There were no cameras on the graveyard across the street or on any of the intersections. The 1-800 number established by the FBI for hot tips came up with nothing but junk and false leads. Because the fire department had responded so quickly, firemen and paramedics ran all over the crime scene before the FBI could get there, so no shoe imprints were available.

Montana had been focusing on the janitor's uniform. Montana reasoned that an adult could not just wander into the elementary school carrying a heavy trash barrel without looking strange. He must have worn Mills Janitorial coveralls, and probably a red Mills Janitorial hat to cover his face. In order to get that, he probably stole either a hat or coveralls or both from Mills Janitorial. Montana's team had poured over the security tapes at Mills looking for anything strange and had found nothing. No one remembered losing their uniform. No one remembered any stranger asking about coveralls or hats. The other option was to hire a seamstress to make the Mills Janitorial patch, and then sew it on a cap and coveralls. A telephone canvas of forty seamstresses and sewing companies in Cincinnati came up with nothing. Montana tried dozens of other ideas, but so far the well was dry, until now.

"Two days ago," said Mahmood, "we received an anonymous tip about the bombing which later proved to be interesting. I will tell you the tip in a minute. Anyway, we traced the tipster's call to a payphone in downtown D.C. We pulled up satellite images from two days ago, and here he is. You can see that the caller is a medium to heavy set male, wearing a brown winter jacket, no markings, jeans, white Nike shoes, and a cowboy hat which covers his entire head and face. Nothing much we can go by there." Montana looked at the satellite images of the caller.

"We followed the caller on the satellite images, and he quickly ducks into the subway at Chinatown, and then we lose him. I have ordered the Transit Authority tapes to see if we can identify him when he is in the subway. That's it for the caller so far. On the 911 call, the caller says we should check out the Store-a-Lot Facility in downtown Cincinnati."

"Did you send the 911 audio to the voiceprint guys?"

"Already done," said Mahmood.

"What's with the Store-a-Lot?"

"Yesterday, we sent some agents down there. We could not get a warrant to search the garages there because all we had was the word of an anonymous tipster. But we were able to secure all of the Store-a-Lot security tapes. Fortunately for us, they keep the tapes for six months. I have been going through these for the last hour. Take a look at this. It is from the morning of the bombing, at about 6 a.m."

The tape showed a man driving a 1998 white Mazda hatchback up to a storage unit, parking his car, and, after looking around, opening the door with his key. About three minutes later, the video showed the garage door opening and the man peering out of the garage. The man then exited the garage, this time dressed in a set of dark coveralls and a baseball cap. He dragged a heavy white trash barrel into the back of his Nissan and closed the hatchback.

"Did you zoom on his coveralls or his hat?" asked Montana.

"Yep." Mahmood pressed a button and the computer zoomed in on the hat. "Cannot say for certain but it could say 'Mills Janitorial' on it."

"That is definitely our man," Montana said quietly, and with far less enthusiasm than Mahmood would have expected to see under the circumstances.

"Watch this," said Mahmood.

Just as the man in the hat and coveralls pulled out of his parking space, a man on a motorcycle came speeding around the corner. The cyclist was not expecting the car to pull out in front of him. The cyclist skidded out and the bike went crashing into the bomber's car. The long-haired man on the motorcycle, smarting from the fall, got up and limped toward the bomber's car. He was visibly upset. The video showed the motorcycle driver banging on the window angrily, waiving his hands, and pointing to his damaged motorcycle. The video next showed a wisp of smoke from the bomber's car window, and the motorcycle driver recoiled, holding his chest. It appeared that the bomber had shot the motorcycle driver through the open window. The video then showed the bomber exiting his vehicle, standing over the motorcycle driver, and shooting him two more times.

"Looks like he has a silencer," remarked Montana.

"Yep. Right again." The computer then zoomed in on what appeared to be a silencer.

In the video, the bomber then re-opened the storage unit, lifted up the metal garage door, and went back to his victim. Holding the man by the wrists, making sure none of the victim's blood got on his uniform, he dragged the motorcycle rider into the storage room and dumped him. Then he rolled the man's motorcycle into the storage unit and closed the door behind him. Before getting back in his car, the bomber then looked at the ground where the motorcycle rider had been lying, and paused.

"He is trying to figure out what to do with all that blood," said Montana.

"Think so," said Mahmood.

"Look, he's looking for a hose, see.... No, there's no hose. What are you going to do now, punk?"

The video then showed the bomber lifting the hood of his car and taking out a plastic bottle.

"He's taking out the washer fluid."

The video then showed the bomber pouring the blue wiper fluid on the ground where the blood was, and watching the liquid run in a small rivulet toward the drain a few stalls away. The bomber then replaced the wiper fluid container and closed his hood. Then he calmly drove away.

"Did you get the plate?"

Mahmood closed in on the plate. "DFE-778, from Virginia. Registered to a Alonso S. Vasquez, Virginia DMV lists a dummy driver's license for him, what they call a 'MA' or 'Master Add' listing, meaning the DMV created a license number for him so they could attach the tickets he kept getting. He has two tickets for driving without a license. No show on each one. Warrant out for his arrest in Virginia. On each of the tickets, he told the police he lived at 1916 Castleberry, but near as I can tell that is a warehouse in the produce district of Virginia Beach. No one lives there. He has all the classic signs of an illegal Mexican alien. But we have his picture...." Mahmood pulled off the sheet coming off the laser printer from the Virginia DMV database and handed it to Montana. "He's 5' 7" tall, medium build, no facial hair, scar on his left cheek."

"Put an APB out for this guy and his car and get this photo on every news channel in the next fifteen minutes. We will have everyone in the country looking for this guy. We should have him by lunch. Also call our Virginia branch office and have a TAC-team execute a search warrant for the Castleberry address just in case."

Montana did not show it, but he was quite satisfied. He would close this case today.

January 20, 2013. 10:15 a.m. San Antonio Riverwalk

So far, Mash'al had stuck to the plan by staying on his anti-psychotic medicine, and had made it as far as San Antonio. Unfortunately, however, he had gone through all the money the Planner had given him for the medicine. Soon the voices would return. He was wearing an Army surplus jacket and underneath the jacket, a black and orange Cincinnati Bengals jersey. He had no money left, and for the last week had been begging tourists on the San Antonio Riverwalk for change. Today, his voices had returned for the first time in months and they were not happy. They were screaming at him, telling him he was running out of blood, running out of skin. He needed more blood and skin to complete the tapestry. Yes, complete the tapestry, that's what he must do. He went up to a bunch of men in suits and asked them for change. They quickly ignored him and moved on. "The Americans have taken my skin," he mumbled angrily.

Police Officer Ray Gallagos had been on the San Antonio Police Force for only six months. His job was to make sure the pan-handlers and homeless people stayed away from the Riverwalk, which was San Antonio's primary tourist draw. From his perch on the bridge on Presa Street, he saw the man in the Army jacket hassling tourists. He quickly went down the stone steps from the bridge and went up to the man in the coat.

"Sir, I am going to have to ask you to leave this area. Come with me."

"Oh, OK, sorry," the man mumbled. The police officer followed the man in the Army jacket up the stone steps onto Presa Street. As Masha'al walked up the steps, the voices descended on his brain. "He knows! He knows! He is the man who took the blood and the skin! He wants more!" Mash'al looked back at the police officer and his face looked like a jackal with blood on his mouth. "He is the one," thought Mash'al. Suddenly, Mash'al wheeled around, grabbed the officer's gun out of his holster and shoved him back down the steps. Mash'al ran onto the street yelling, "They will not get me! I have the tapestry!"

Gallagos was angry and worried. The man had stolen his revolver, and that would get him in trouble. If he hurt anyone with that gun, it would be on Gallagos' head. He sternly announced into his shoulder mike. "This is 517 to all units. We have a vagrant, 5' 7" tall, medium build, no facial hair, scar on his left cheek, wearing an Army surplus jacket, Cincinnati Bengals football jersey, and jeans. He just assaulted me, threw me down a flight of stairs, and stole my firearm by the bridge overpass on Presa Street." Gallagos ran up the stairs and looked for the man in the Army jacket. "Suspect has a loaded firearm and is running down Crockett toward the Alamo!" Gallagos dashed down Crocker Street toward the Alamo. "He is waiving the gun, and he is going straight toward the Alamo. There are kids in there!"

Within five minutes, ten police cars had surrounded the Alamo. Police sergeant Will Ramirez heard the officer's callout at the precinct. "Did he just say Cincinnati Bengals?" He raced back to his desk, and pulled up the FBI photo of the Cincinnati bombing suspect. It said he was 5' 7" tall, no facial hair, scar on his left cheek. Holy Christ. He called Officer Gallagos on his shoulder mike.

"517, where are you right now?"

Gallagos said, "Outside the Alamo, I am standing on Crocker Street near one of the police cars. I did not go in there because the guy has my weapon. Look, I am really sorry, Sarge."

"Ray, do not worry about that right now. Get to a squad car and turn on the video monitor. I am sending you a photo. I want you to tell me if this is the guy who assaulted you."

Officer Gallagos jumped into a nearby squad car and turned on the video monitor. A few moments later, the face of the vagrant flashed on his screen. He radioed the Sergeant. "That's him, Sarge."

"Are you positive, Ray? I need you to be 100% positive."

"I am positive, Sarge. I looked him right in the eye. I will never forget that face."

"Ray, that's the Cincinnati Bomber you have there. I want your men to proceed with extreme caution. Find Captain Trudeau immediately and let him know."

Sergeant Ramirez went to the central dispatcher down the hall. "Wanda, I want all cars to know that the suspect in the Alamo is, in all likelihood, the Cincinnati Bomber. Proceed with extreme caution. We need all units to go to the Alamo. What's happening down there? Do they have him or has he taken any hostages?"

The dispatcher immediately relayed the message. "All units respond to the Alamo. Suspect may be the Cincinnati Bomber. I repeat: all units, this may be the Cincinnati Bomber. Proceed with caution. Suspect is 5' 7" tall, medium build, no facial hair, scar on left cheek, Army jacket, Cincinnati Bengals jersey, jeans. He has a loaded firearm stolen from a police officer. He is armed and dangerous. Unknown where he is in the Alamo or if he has taken hostages. Last seen running into the Alamo."

The vaulted stone shrine room of the Alamo has two large brown doors, several purple funeral wreaths on metal stands, and a series of tablets around the room listing the names of the brave soldiers who died in the

1836 battle. Near the ceiling are six flags. On this day in particular, a local Cub Scout troop was visiting the Alamo. A Mexican illegal alien, Rosa Trujeo, and her three daughters, Eva, Esperanza, and "Cat" (short for Catarina) were visiting the Alamo that day. Rosa was a maid at the Marriott Riverwalk downtown. She was interested in showing the children the monument because one of Rosa's ancestors was a Tejano volunteer who had fought in the first battle to capture the Alamo for the Texans in 1835. She was on crutches today because she had sprained her ankle at work slipping on liquid detergent in the hotel laundry room. Also present was Tommy Dickerson, a 60 year-old stocky Vietnam vet with a receding head of gray hair, worn long to his shoulders, who enjoyed visiting war memorials. He was on a cross-country trip to visit places like Gettysburg, the 9-11 Memorial, and the Vietnam Memorial Wall in Washington, D.C.

The Mexican woman, her three daughters, the twelve first-graders and their two Den Leaders were reading the names of Davy Crockett, Jim Bowie and others listed on the memorial tablets when the crazed madman in the Army jacket came running in.

"Everyone on the ground!" Mash'al shot a round in the air at the flags on the wall, and everyone in the room screamed and ducked to the floor.

"You, cell phone!" He pointed his gun at one of the terrified female den leaders, who handed over the phone. Mash'al called 911 and spoke to the dispatcher.

"I have a gun inside the Alamo. I have fifteen children in here. You get all the police out of here immediately or I will start killing children one by one. And I am going to need you to bring me blood. Lots of blood. And skin for the tapestry." Mash'al's voices began screaming at him again. "Quiet!" He yelled to no one in particular. The petrified girls huddled against their mother and the scouts did the same to the den leaders.

Mash'al began pacing the floor, mumbling angrily. He was distracted by the voices, and not paying very close attention to the hostages. Rosa Trujeo was not a timid person. She had not traveled in the back of a poultry truck thousands of miles to have her children killed by a maniac. As soon as the gunman turned his back to pace in the opposite direction, Trujeo crushed the terrorist's head with a roundhouse swing of her crutch, knocking him to the floor. That was all the opening the Vietnam veteran needed. With his wartime instincts from forty years ago kicking in, he dove on the terrorist, putting his hand on the gun and trying to dislodge the gun from the terrorist's hand. Rosa Trujeo was not finished. She ran to the terrorist's outstretched hand and stepped on it as hard as she could, crushing his finger bones, while Dickerson kept the terrorist pinned. The gun went off into the wall, firing wildly. Trujeo stomped again, and this time the gun became dislodged. Trujeo kicked it against the far wall. Dickerson yelled to one of the scouts. "You there! Take off your belt and throw it to me." The boy did as he was told. Dickerson used the belt to tie the terrorist's hands behind his back. Meanwhile, one of the den leaders had picked up the gun from the floor and trained it on the terrorist's face. "Don't move!" the den leader yelled, with suddenly much more courage than she had a moment ago. Dickerson yanked the terrorist up, who was now yelling in Arabic. Dickerson kicked open the door to the hall to see twenty police officer's revolvers trained on him. "Don't shoot!" he yelled. "We've got him!" Dickerson threw the terrorist down to the ground of the hall in disgust, and the police officers pounced on him, handcuffing him and leading him out of the Alamo. The other cops started back-slapping Dickerson and giving him high-fives.

Dickerson turned to the Rosa, her children, and the cub scouts and said, "Now that was fun!" They all laughed. They stayed behind in the shrine room a few more minutes to speak to police officers. After the brief interviews were complete, the group of brave tourists headed out of the Alamo, where they were greeted with wild applause from dozens of police officers and a newly-formed crowd of onlookers. The crowd died down after a few seconds. Dickerson proudly came forward, holding Rosa's hand in triumph with one hand and a cub scout's hand in the other. "All I have to say is it's finally nice to win one at the Alamo!" The crowd erupted into more cheers.

Thousands of miles away, Ruddy Montana heard the news coming in from San Antonio Police. He quickly called the FBI Director, who was at the White House this morning. If they hurried, they just might be able to get this into the Inauguration Speech.

It was time. Mohammed el Faya put the bullets into his long-range sniper rifle. The target had come into the kill zone.

CHAPTER 15. PROPHET

January 20, 2013. 11:00 a.m. Paris time.
Salon-de-Provence, France. Beneath l'Eglise de St. Michel

Professor John Morse shined his flashlight into the Nostradamus Vault. The only things in the stone room were two walnut chests. Could these be the famous chests Nostradamus willed to his eldest daughter Madeleine in his codicil? The wood appeared very old and was covered in dust. Morse took out a rag and wiped the dust from the top of both chests. Each had a painted lid which read in black ink "M. Nostradamus." A key stuck out from the keyhole on each chest.

"Pops! This is tight! Can I open them?" asked Zach"No," said Morse. "Zach, these are artifacts, centuries old. We have to be very delicate with them. You two kids stay back a little bit. Father du Bois watched on with the teenagers as Morse gingerly turned the key on the chest on the left and opened the lid. Inside, wrapped in black velvet, were stacks and stacks of vellum paper. Each page contained handwriting. Morse inspected the papers. There were ten neat, banded stacks of paper. It did not take Morse long to figure out what the papers were.

"These are the original Nostradamus 'Propheties!' If these are genuine, this will be one of the greatest finds of the century!" Careful not to damage the paper, Morse gently removed some of the bands.

"This is very interesting. I notice that Centuries I through IX have 100 quatrains each, and the last century, Century X, only has 42 quatrains. But in all the published versions we have on file, the century with 42 quatrains is Century VII, not X. It is possible that Nostradamus intended his final 58 quatrains to be the final chapter of his book, ending his work on a high dramatic note, but when the 58 verses could not be produced by Nostradamus before his death, the publisher made an editorial decision to bury the 'defective' century into the middle of the text, so it would be less obvious to the reader. It makes us wonder more about those missing 58."

"This is lame," said Zoey. "We go through all this and the only treasure is a bunch of stupid books. I thought there was going to be gold or jewels or something." Zoey strummed her guitar. "Lame-o, lame-o," she sang. "This trip is Lame-o."

"What's in the other box, Pops?" asked Zach.

Morse lifted up the lid of the second chest. There was one small item in the bottom of the chest. Morse removed the black velvet case. Inside was a rectangular piece of red wax, about an inch thick. As Morse examined the side of the wax tablet, he could see there was a piece of metal in between two rectangular slabs of wax. He took out of his black nylon bag of tools a small chisel and hammer, and making very delicate strikes, managed to separate the top piece of wax from the metal. Removing the wax, he peered at the rectangular piece of metal underneath. Buried just beneath the metal was a handwritten letter, signed "Michel de Nostradame." The document read:

Aux bonnes gens de la Terre et aux futures générations de croyants:

En écrivant cette lettre, je suis à quelques jours de la morgue. Le temps que vous lisiez ceci, je serai mort et enterré depuis lontemps. Mais pendant mes derniers jours, comme je réfléchis à mon séjour sur la Terre, j'aime penser que j'ai fait une contribution sérieuse pour améliorer l'humanité. A partir de mon début à la Faculté de Médecine à l'Université de Montpellier, à ma formation chez Julius Scaliger à Agen, à ma réussite à guérir les pestiférés d'Aix-en-Provence, jusqu'à ma construction des canaux de Salon, j'ai toujours placé les intérêts de mes semblables avant les miens. J'ai fait aussi un effort pour aider le monde en utilisant mes divins talents mystiques. Les plumes blanches dans mon bureau sont couvertes d'encre noir, suites de mes écrits prolifiques des dix dernières années. J'ai donné des tuyaux au Roi lui-même aussi bienqu'à beaucoup de gens de la cour. J'ai publié des Almanachs annuels pour les citoyens de la France pour les aider à se débrouiller et à faire des projets pour l'année qui vient. Et, bien sûr, j'ai écrit mes Prophéties. Sans aucun doute vous avez vu maintes prédictions dans mes Prophéties qui se sont réalisées au cours des siècles. Pourtant je crois que je dois donner un dernier petit tuyau, un avertissement terrible auquel tous ceux qui cherchent la bonté et la bienveillance dans le monde devraient faire attention.

Le vent du changement souffle sur nous. Le monde et l'Eglise catholique se trouvent devant de véritables forces du mal, et moi, Michel de Nostradamus, je vais les arrêter court. Comme vous savez peut-être, il manquait dans mes Prophéties, la plus grande prédiction d'événements futurs qu'un seul homme ait jamais assemblée, 58 sur les 1000 quatrains originaux. Ces 58 derniers quatrains que j'ai présagés par la pitié de Dieu se sont perdus mais se sont retrouvés juste avant ma mort. Ces 58 strophes que j'ai écrites sont contenues à l'intérieur d'une minuscule Bible, que j'ai écrite, inspiré par Dieu Lui-même. Tenir ces 58 strophes est dangereux, car de sinistres forces cherchent à empêcher l'humanité de faire un changement en mieux pour l'avenir. Pourtant, comme deux boeufs rétifs tirant une charrue à travers un champ rocailleux, vous devez persévérer pour trouver ces 58 dernières strophes.

J'ai établi un chemin d'indices pour vous, les vrais croyants, pour que vous puissiez trouver la Bible. Le chemin ne va pas être facile, mais il faut être inébranlables. Car ces 58 derniers quatrains sont mon chef d'oeuvre,et font connaître en détail incroyable le mal qui attend la terre et ses peuples. J'ai attendu jusqu'à présent pour révéler ces 58 strophes de peur d'être persécutés, moi et ma famille. Et bien que je ne sois qu'une seule et frêle voix humaine, je serai ici à travers les âges pour m'assurer qu'on tient compte de mes mots prophétiques afin de sauver le monde.

Beaucoup d'entre vous vont peut-être vous demander pourquoi j'ai créé ce grand jeu, au lieu de vous expliquer plus précisément où se trouve la Bible. La réponse c'est que le mal a beaucoup d'oreilles, et ces mots doivent être cryptés pour vous protéger et pour protéger l'humanité. Mais dépêchez-vous! Il reste peu de temps au monde. Comme toujours, laissez-vous guider par la sagesse.

Par rapport à la compensation pour mes efforts pour sauver l'humanité, je ne fais qu'une demande modeste, celle-ci - au moment donné où mes mots ont aidé l'humanité à échapper à l'heure la plus noire, publiez mes oeuvres s'il vous plaît pour que tout le monde puisse savoir que c'était moi, Michel de Nostradamus, qui a protégé toute l'humanité de la déstruction.

Michel de Nostradamus
Salon-de-Provence
le 18 juin, 1556

Professor Morse quickly made an English translation onto his notebook:

To the good people of the Earth and future generations of believers:

As I write this letter, I am only days away from the morgue. By the time you read this, I will be long dead and buried. But in my last dying days, as I reflect upon my time on this Earth, I would like to think that I have made an earnest contribution toward the betterment of mankind. From my start at the University of Montpellier Medical School, to my training with Julius Scaliger in Agen, to my curing of the plague in Aix-en-Provence, to my building of the canals of Salon, I have always put the interests of my fellow man before my own. So, too, have I endeavored to help the world with my God-given mystical gifts. The white quills in my study are covered in black ink from my prolific writing over the last ten years. I have provided advice to the King himself as well as many members of the royal court. I have published yearly Almanacs for the citizens of France to help them cope and plan for the calamities of the coming year. And, of course, I have written my Propheties. No doubt you have seen the many predictions in my Propheties which have come true over the centuries of time. Yet I feel I must provide one last small piece of advice, one dire warning to be heeded by all those who strive for goodness and kindness in the world.

The wind of change is upon us. The world and the Catholic Church face true evil ahead and I, Michel de Nostradame, will put a stop to it. As you may be aware, my Propheties, the greatest prediction of future events ever assembled by one man, was missing 58 quatrains from the original 1000. These last 58 quatrains which I have divined through God's mercy were lost to me until shortly before my death. These 58 verses which I have written are contained on the interior of a miniscule Bible, written by me with inspiration from God Himself. To hold these 58 verses is dangerous, for sinister forces seek to prevent mankind from changing the future for the better. Yet, like two oxen stubbornly pulling a plow through a rocky field, you must persevere and find these lost 58 verses.

I have set up a path of clues for you, the true believers, to find the Bible. The path will not be easy, but you must be steadfast. For these last 58 quatrains are my masterpiece, and set forth in astonishing detail the evil which awaits the earth and its peoples. I have waited until now to reveal these 58 verses for fear of persecution of myself and my family. And even though I am only one frail human voice, I will be here through the ages to ensure that my prophetic words are heeded so the world may be saved.

Many of you may wonder why I have created this big game, instead of speaking to you more directly about the Bible's whereabouts. The answer is that evil has many ears, and these words must be encrypted for your protection and the protection of humanity. But be quick about it! The world does not have much time left. As always, let wisdom be your guide. My only modest request of compensation for my labors to save humanity is this—when the time comes, and my words have helped humanity avoid its darkest hour, please publish my works so that all the world may know it was I, Michel de Nostradame, who hath protected all of humanity from destruction.

Michel de Nostradame
Salon-de-Provence
June 18, 1556

"Fascinating," said Morse.

"More dumb letters," said Zoey. "Yeah, this is a real funhouse."

"What do you make of it?" asked Father du Bois.

"I don't know," said Morse. "Nostradamus clearly wants us to go on this treasure hunt to find the missing Bible, but he has not given us the clues. Perhaps there is a hidden compartment in the chests."

Morse, the teenagers, and the priest searched both chests for any sign of a hidden compartment, and could find none.

"The clues must come from the letter itself," suggested Father du Bois.

"Yes, I think you are correct," said Morse, puzzling. "But if this treasure was so important to mankind, why hide it away to begin with? Why not give us the Bible now? It does not make sense."

"Perhaps Nostradamus believes that only the truly worthy may inherit his prophecies, Professor. Why create this ridiculous door to the vault? He obviously wants to test our wits. The reason is clear—only the worthy can learn the wisdom Nostradamus wishes to give us."

"Let's start with words that look out of place," suggested Professor

Morse. "If a word does not look like it is a part of normal conversation, then it was probably put there for a reason. For example, this business about the white quills seems out of place to me, as well as the part about oxen pulling a plow." Professor Morse wrote down "white quills" followed by "oxen/plow." "The business about building canals seems a far stretch to go to make a point," said the professor, writing down "canal."

"Frail human voice," said the priest. "That seemed out of place to me when I read it."

"I agree," said the Professor, writing down "frail human voice."

Meanwhile, Zoey found the red wax tablet very interesting. It reminded her of the time she and Zach had taken one of their mother's candles and made wax castles. They had made a big mess on the kitchen table and scratched the table getting the wax off. Their mother had been really mad that day. Zoey thought about her mother again. She missed her so much. Zoey returned her thoughts to the wax. She thought she could cut a little message into the wax like "Zach stinks" and show it to her brother. As she pressed her hands into the wax, a circular hole inadvertently popped out. Uh oh. Her dad would be mad. She probably wasn't supposed to be playing with the wax tablet. She looked over at her father. He wasn't paying attention. Maybe if she just popped the oval piece back in, no one would notice. As she prepared to put the piece back in, she looked at the tablet closer. There appeared to be little lines in the wax, barely visible unless you looked really closely. She traced the outline of another oval and then pushed her finger. Just as before, a little oval of wax popped out of the tablet.

"Dad, I think I found something," said Zoey. "I was looking at this wax tablet, and if you look closely, there's like these little lines and if you put your finger on there, a little piece of wax pops out."

Morse was frustrated. Couldn't his daughter keep her hands off the artifacts? He took the wax tablet from his daughter and looked at the hole. It was perfectly oval. He noticed similar cookie-cutter cuts at different places on the tablet. The light quickly dawned on him. He pushed his finger through the places where the little cuts formed perforated ovals in the wax until he had a tablet with numerous cut out oval holes. He returned the wax tablet to the letter of Nostradamus and, sure enough, the holes pointed to particular words in the text:

Aux bonnes gens de la Terre et aux futures générations de croyants:

En écrivant cette lettre, je suis à quelques jours de la m**orgue**. Le temps que vous lisiez ceci, je serai mort et enterré depuis lontemps. Mais pendant mes derniers jours, comme je réfléchis à mon séjour sur la Terre, j'aime penser que j'ai fait une contribution sérieuse pour améliorer l'humanité. A partir de mon début à la Faculté de Médecine à l'Université de Montpellier, à ma formation chez Julius Scaliger à **Agen**, à ma réussite à guérir les pestiférés d'Aix-en-Provence, jusqu'à ma construction des canaux de Salon, j'ai toujours placé les intérêts de mes semblables avant les miens. J'ai fait aussi un effort pour aider le monde en utilisant mes divins talents mystiques. Les plumes bl**anches** dans mon bureau sont couvertes d'encre noir, suites de mes écrits prolifiques des dix dernières années. J'ai donné des tuyaux au Roi lui-même aussi bienqu'à beaucoup de gens de la cour. J'ai publié des Almanachs annuels pour les citoyens de la France pour les aider à se débrouiller et à faire des projets pour l'année qui vient. Et, bien sûr, j'ai écrit mes Prophéties. Sans aucun doute vous avez vu maintes prédictions dans mes Prophéties qui se sont réalisées au cours des siècles. Pourtant je crois que je dois donner un dernier **petit tuyau**, un avertissement terrible auquel tous ceux qui cherchent la bonté et la bienveillance dans le monde devraient faire attention.

Le **vent** du changement souffle sur nous. Le monde et l'**Eglise** catholique se trouvent devant de véritables forces du mal, et moi, Michel de Nostradamus, je vais les arrêter court. Comme vous savez peut-être, il manquait dans mes Prophéties, la plus grande prédiction d'événements futurs qu'un seul homme ait jamais assemblée, 58 sur les 1000 quatrains originaux. Ces 58 derniers quatrains que j'ai présagés par la pitié de Dieu se sont perdus mais se sont retrouvés juste avant ma mort. Ces 58 strophes que j'ai écrites sont contenues à l'**intérieur** d'une **minuscule** Bible, que j'ai écrite, inspiré par Dieu Lui-même. **Tenir** ces 58 strophes est dangereux, car de sinistres forces cherchent à empêcher l'humanité de faire un changement en mieux pour l'avenir. Pourtant, comme deux boeufs rétifs **tirant** une charrue à travers un champ rocailleux, vous devez persévérer pour trouver ces 58 dernières strophes.

J'ai établi un chemin d'indices pour vous, les vrais croyants, pour que vous puissiez trouver la Bible. Le chemin ne va pas être facile, mais il faut être inébranlables. Car ces 58 derniers quatrains sont mon chef d'oeuvre,et font connaître en détail incroyable le mal qui attend la terre et ses peuples. J'ai attendu jusqu'à présent pour révéler ces 58 strophes de peur d'être persécutés, moi et ma famille. Et bien que je ne sois qu'une seule et frêle **voix humaine**, je serai ici à travers les âges pour m'assurer qu'on tient compte de mes mots prophétiques afin de sauver le monde.

Beaucoup d'entre vous vont peut-être vous demander pourquoi j'ai créé ce **grand jeu**, au lieu de vous expliquer plus précisément où se trouve la Bible. La réponse c'est que le mal a beaucoup d'oreilles, et ces mots doivent être cryptés pour vous protéger et pour protéger l'humanité. Mais dépêchez-vous! Il reste peu de temps au monde. Comme toujours, laissez-vous guider par la sagesse.

Par rapport à la compensation pour mes efforts pour sauver l'humanité, je ne fais qu'une demande modeste, celle-ci - au moment donné où mes mots ont aidé l'humanité à échapper à l'heure la plus noire, publiez mes oeuvres s'il vous plaît pour que tout le monde puisse savoir que c'était moi, Michel de Nostradame, qui a protégé toute l'humanité de la déstruction.

Michel de Nostradame
Salon-de-Provence
le 18 juin, 1556

"Zoey, you've done it!"

"See, Pops," said Zach. "Without us, you would have never figured out this thing."

"You are right, Zach. You guys have been a great help to me. Thank you!" Morse rearranged the French words on his notepad:

Agen	Agen
Morgue	morgue
Tirant	pulling
Intérieur	interior
Voix humaine	human voice
Petit	small
Vent	wind
Blanches	white
Minuscule	miniscule
Tuyau	piece of advice; tip
Grand jeu	big game
Eglise	church
Tenir	to hold

Morse was pleased with daughter. "Now what do these words all mean?"

The group of four studied the notepad, trying to make sense of the words.

"Perhaps there is something hidden in the morgue in Agen," suggested Morse, although he doubted his own words. "But all these other words do not seem to follow."

"Well, we do have a city," suggested the priest. "Whatever we are looking for is probably in Agen."

"That's true," said Morse.

"Maybe it is something in one of the churches in Agen," said Zach. "They do have the word 'church' in there.

"Yes," said Zach's father. "But what is this business about something white in the morgue?"

Zoey was still looking at the words through the wax holes.

"Dad, where do you see 'morgue?' I don't see that on here."

Morse looked at the letter again through the wax holes. "Why, it's right here, pointing to the hole." But then Morse studied the hole again. The wax tablet had cut off the "M" in "Morgue." The word which actually showed through was "ORGUE."

"Oh, good heavens! I missed it again. You are quite right, Zoey. The 'M' has been cut off. The word is not 'MORGUE,' it is 'ORGUE,' which means a musical organ, like the one in a church! And this word down here

'BLANCHES,' the feminine plural for the English word 'white,' actually has the 'B' and 'L' chopped off, leaving the word 'ANCHES.' And that word means a reed pipe or reed instrument in music." Morse sketched out the new word list on his pad:

Agen	Agen
Orgue	organ (music)
Tirant	pulling
Intérieur	interior
Voix humaine	human voice
Petit	small
Vent	wind
Anches	reeds (music)
Minuscule	miniscule
Tuyau	piece of advice; tip
Grand jeu	big game
Eglise	church
Tenir	to hold

For Zoey, the musician in the group, it seemed pretty obvious.

"Dad, it has something to do with music. You have 'organ' and 'reeds' and 'Church.' That means the reed pipes of an organ in a Church."

"Yes," said Father du Bois, catching on. "And if I recall correctly, the reed pipes are the smaller ones, so that takes care of 'small' and 'miniscule.'"

Morse agreed. "'VENT' or 'wind' refers to the air that is constantly being pumped into the organ, which allows for the sound to come out through the opening in the pipes. 'AGEN' obviously means the city of Agen, so the Church in Agen probably means the Cathedral of Saint-Caprais in Agen. So Nostradamus is telling us that the clue lies in the 'interior' of one of the 'small' 'reed pipes' of the pipe 'organ' in the cathedral! That's it!"

"Yes, Dad," said Zach. "But what does the 'big game' mean? And what does 'pulling' mean? And what does the 'human voice' mean? And I still do not see how the 'piece of advice' means anything."

"Well, I think I have the answer to one of those," said Morse. "The word 'TUYAU' in French can mean a piece of advice or a tip, but it can also mean a pipe, like a water pipe, or the pipe of a musical instrument, like a pipe on a pipe organ. So in this context, 'tuyau' must mean 'pipe.'"

"And what about 'to hold?'" asked Zach.

"Now that I see this all relates to music, I do not think the word really means 'to hold' in this context. The word 'TENIR' can mean 'to hold' but in this context I think it means 'to play,' as in 'to play a musical instrument.'"

"Well, that solves most of it," said the priest.

"Yes," said Morse, "I do not know what the rest means, but I suspect we shall find out when we get to Agen! This is very exciting! But first, we must photograph everything we have found here with the correct photography equipment and then make arrangements for the artifacts to be catalogued, preserved, and dated. I can have a team here in a day or two, Father, to make all the arrangements, if that is satisfactory to you."

"No, Professor, that will not be necessary."

"Pardon me?"

"I said, that will not be necessary."

"What do you mean?"

Father du Bois pulled out a revolver with a silencer and pointed it at the Professor.

"I regret to say, Professor, that this is the end of the line, as you say, for you and your family."

"Wait! Before you shoot," said Morse. "You should know that Zach here has already alerted the French authorities on his phone."

"I sincerely doubt that, Professor."

"You may recall when I sent him out to the wine cellar to do our research, claiming that we could not get a signal here. Do you think I would honestly do scientific research over a child's telephone? I have a laptop right in my bag with a state-of-the-art 5G Microwave Repeater. I have obtained a signal inside the Pyramids at Giza and in a Indian copper mine 2,000 feet beneath the earth."

"I don't believe you, Professor," said the priest. "If you had called the authorities, they would be here by now."

"Sir, it was readily apparent to me that you were not a Catholic priest the moment we passed the altar upstairs. Any good Catholic priest genuflects when passing in front of the altar, and you did not. In addition, I told you that the three wise men were Balthazar, Gaspar and Abednego, and you did not correct me. The third wise man was Melchior, not Abednego, as any good Catholic priest celebrating the Epiphany two weeks ago would know.

So that is why I sent my son outside, to call the police without raising your suspicion. Zach was supposed to leave the church and run outside, but he was too worried about me and came back."

Father du Bois turned his gun and pointed it at Zach's head. "Is that true, Zach? Is your father telling the truth? Why, you don't even speak French. What would you say if the police answered?" Zach racked his brain to remember anything from his French class.

"Aide!" said Zach.

The gunman considered. "That was pretty fast thinking, kid. That was pretty close. Tell me, what numbers did you call for the police?"

"Uhh, my dad had the number programmed in. I just hit Send."

"Really? Then why don't you pull out your iPhone and let's check who you've called." Zach looked at the gun pointed at his forehead and, for the first time on this trip, couldn't speak.

Zoey, who was standing to the side and behind the priest, looked in her father's eyes. She could see a flash of panic. He was lying about the phone. When the priest pulled out the phone, he would know. In a wave of desperation and adrenaline, Zoey took her acoustic guitar and, with a strength she was unaware she had until now, slammed the instrument as hard as she could into the back of the gunman's head. The gunman went to the floor and Zoey stood over him, violently pounding the guitar into his face again and again. When the gun hit the floor, Zach grabbed it and, without the slightest hesitation, shot the gunman once in the chest. Zoey stopped her assault with the guitar, staring at the fallen priest. Then Zach stood over the priest's body and pointed the gun downward.

"No, Zach!" said Morse. "That's enough, son. You did great. Just give me the gun." Morse was petrified and thankful for the quick action of his children but nevertheless surprised at their rage.

"It's over, guys. You are safe now." Zach was shaking and catatonic, the smoke from the revolver wafting upward from the silencer.

Zach handed his father the gun, who put it in his bag. Morse put his arms around his children.

"Daddy?" said Zoey, hugging her father tight. "Will you buy me a new guitar?"

"Sure," said Morse. "Whatever kind of guitar you want."

Morse considered his next move. The killer had been right. He had not given Zach instruction to call the authorities. He thought the priest might have been a conman, but he never thought in a million years he would try to kill them. If Morse called the authorities now, they would find a murder weapon with his fingerprints, his son's fingerprints, a dead body, gun powder residue on his son's hands, a bloody guitar, and the victim's blood all over their clothes. How could he possibly explain all this? And what were the criminal laws for juveniles in France? Could his son go to jail? He had no idea. It was highly unlikely that the priest impostor had told French authorities about the presence of the vault. That would mean that if they left the body here and closed the vault, the only ones who might find the body would be the killer's employer. But they would require time to realize that the killer had failed in his mission. And even if they sent someone new to search the church, they would not be able to open the vault door as easily as he had. Morse put the writings of Nostradamus, Nostradamus' ring and astrolabe, the wax tablets, and a wooden piece of one of the walnut chests into his nylon bag. He hated to take antiquities, but he could not leave them here with whoever was following Father du Bois. He took out a cotton rag he used for dusting off archaeological artifacts and wiped down the pieces of the guitar, the revolver and silencer, and the walnut chests. Then he closed the vault door with the priest assassin inside. He took the rag and wiped down the vault handle, the vault door, and the stand where the astrolabe had stood. Then he took the letters on the door, and rearranged them so that instead of reading "+Aphrodite," they spelled "ENCULEZ TOI."

Pleased with himself, he quickly led the teenagers back through the stone hallway and up through the trapdoor in the wine cask. As he got on top of the cask with the children, he opened his nylon bag, shining his flashlight inside. He found what he was looking for—a small tube of Crazy Glue. He found that it was often a valuable thing to bring on archaelogical digs. He applied the Crazy Glue to the seams of the trap door, letting the glue drip into the cracks. That should seal the cask up pretty good, he thought. The trio then left the Church, and quickly ran next door to the Nostradamus Museum, where Morse bought t-shirts which read, "*Nostradamus a Prédit que J'Achèterais ce Tee-Shirt,*" or "Nostradamus Predicted I'd Buy this T-Shirt" for his son and daughter to wear over their existing shirts, to make sure that no one saw the bloodstains underneath.

Meanwhile, back in the vault, there was a low groan, and a man in black priest's clothes struggled in agony to find his phone.

Back at the hotel, Morse and his children took off all their bloody clothing and put it in a trash bag. Then each took a hot shower. Morse instructed Zach to take extra care to wash his hands thoroughly to remove any gunpowder residue. After they changed into new clothes, Morse arranged for an Audi rental car to be sent to the hotel. They put the bag of bloody clothes with the gun in the trunk. Morse would later deposit the bag in a filling station dumpster. Morse took off, with Zach in the front seat and Zoey in the back. Both children fell asleep within minutes. They were emotionally exhausted from the traumatic attack in the vault. Morse looked at Zach sleeping and then in the rear view mirror at Zoey. These kids had been through so much. He hoped they were all going to be okay. He glanced at his odometer. He had a four hour drive along Route Nationale 113 to Agen.

Hours later, Morse was a few miles from the City of Agen when his son Zach woke up.

"Where are we?"

"We are just outside of Agen."

Zach was distracted. "Tight. Hey, Dad, were you scared today?"

"I have never been more scared in my life, Zach."

"Me, too."

Zach didn't say anything for another minute.

"Do you believe in Heaven?" asked Zach.

"Sure, I do, Zach."

"You think Mom's there?"

"I know she's there, waiting for all of us. And if I know her, she's probably running the place by now."

Zach's eyes were red and he looked like he was going to cry. His voice quivered in a high pitch. "Dad, you think if I killed that guy, I can still get into Heaven?"

"Of course you can, Zach. You are a very good person."

"But I murdered that guy," Zach said, crying. "I didn't even think twice about it." Zach sobbed and his nose was running. "First, I thought he was going to kill you. And I thought about how those terrorists killed Mom, and I thought it was going to happen all over again. And then when he pointed the gun at my head...." Zach started sobbing, and his father pulled the car over to the side of the road and hugged him.

"It's OK, Zach."

"I really thought I was going to die today. I was so scared." Zach buried his head into his father's shoulder, crying.

"If Zoey hadn't hit him with the guitar, I was a second or two from dying."

Morse started crying, too. "I know. I know. I love you and Zoey so much. I am not going to let anyone else hurt you."

"Dad, why do they do it?"

"Do what?"

"Why do they blow up little kids' schools and fly planes into buildings and shoot people?"

"I don't know, Zach. When your Mom died, I thought about that for a long time. But I finally realized, if I spend my whole time getting angry about what they did to us, then I am going to miss the life that I have left. I want to be there to listen to your rap songs, and hear Zoey play her guitar, and see you laugh and make jokes and live your life. I don't want to miss any of it. And when I thought I was going to lose you today, all I could think of is what a terrible father I have been to you since Mom died, and how I want to be better, and support you more, and love you more..." Morse was crying now.

"You're a great father, Pops."

"Thanks, Zach. You're a great son. By the way, where on earth did you come up with 'Aide?' I did not think you knew any French."

"In French class, the teacher won't let us say anything but French in the class. So if you want to go to the bathroom, you have to ask in French. So all I know is 'Aide!'

"Well, it sure came in handy today."

"Hey, Pops. What was that thing you spelled on the wall? ENCULEZ TOI?"

"I cannot tell you that. It is an expletive."

"A what?"

"I was basically cussing them out."

"So what does it mean?" asked Zach.

"I will have to tell you another time."

Zach did not press his father further, but he would definitely be

Googling "Enculez-toi" when he got home to America. In the distance, they could see the quaint city of Agen, France.

Back in Salon-de-Provence, two men placed small wads of plastic explosives in the middle of the vault door underneath the Eglise St. Michel. They had no concern whatsoever that there may be ancient artifacts behind the door. Within seconds they had blown the vault door. When they cleared the smoke and rubble with leaf blowers they found their comrade lying in a pool of blood on the floor of the interior of the vault. They felt his pulse. He was definitely dead. They searched his pockets and found his Blackberry. On the phone, he had typed, "Missed them. They have gone to the Cathedral in Agen. The prophecy is in a Bible."

CHAPTER 16. ORGAN

January 20, 2013. 3:30 p.m. Paris time. Agen, France.

Morse negotiated the Audi through the streets of the French city of Agen until he arrived at the old center of the town. Standing in a grove of trees was the twelfth century Agen Cathedral, known as the Cathedrale Saint-Caprais. Built in the form of a Latin cross, its white and gray stone walls surrounded a huge bell tower.

Morse parked the car and walked with his children into the inside of the Church. Zach and Zoey gaped upward, amazed at how tall the walls were inside. The interior of the Church was a wild crazy quilt of images and colors. Pictures of saints were painted on the walls in sky blue, orange, and avocado green. The vaulted ceilings were colored in alternating patches of midnight blue and gold. A religious figure or busy pattern adorned every inch of wall space. Ten golden, ornamental disks ringed with white candles dangled from overhead on gold chains, five on each side of the long rows of pews. To Morse, the church decor looked like a mess, like someone had taken out the wallpaper pattern book and, waffling on which pattern to choose, decided instead to choose them all.

Morse and the children proceeded down the main aisle between the pews, facing the altar ahead. When they got to the center of the rectangular cross in the cathedral, they turned north and went to the end of the giant hall. There, against the back wall, some fifty feet in the air, were the towering metal pipes of the Cathedral's pipe organ. Morse took out his camera and took some pictures. There was an oak-colored wooden spire in the middle, with a tripod of ornate, wooden crosses at the top. Two slightly smaller identical spires sat as bookends on the right and left. In the middle of each spire were a group of metal pipes.

"Quite amazing, isn't it?" said a voice behind them.

Morse and the children turned around to see a short, incredibly obese priest, with a bald head, unshaven chin, and thick black glasses. Zoey had her fair share of killer priests for one day, and was not about to trust this one. She grabbed her father's arm tightly and eyed the priest suspiciously.

"Yes," said Morse. "We were just admiring it."

"This organ was a gift from the Empress Eugenie, Napoleon's wife, in 1858."

"Oh, really? 1858, you say? Hmm, I was wondering, is this the only organ in the cathedral? I had been told that there might be an organ dating from earlier times."

"Oh, you must mean the chancel organ. That is much smaller. It is on the other side of the church. Follow me."

Morse and his children followed the fat priest, who waddled to and fro like a penguin who had eaten too many squid. He continued to mop his brow with his handkerchief as he escorted them to the opposite side of the church, to an organ about twenty feet tall. The sides and top of the organ were mahogany, and it was shaped in the form of a very skinny house, generally tall and rectangular, with a pointed top. Some twenty large silver pipes, with their points pointed downward, were fastened to the middle of the organ. On either side of the organ was a red pillar, again with the wild decorations of a lunatic wall-paperer. There was a walking space on either side of the organ, and it appeared that one could walk behind the organ to a small space behind it, where other organ pipes lined the wall.

"This is the original organ, which dates all the way to the sixteenth century. The only French organ older than this is in the Basilica of St. Navaire in Carcassonne. With some exceptions where we have made repairs and replacements, these are the same pipes that existed centuries ago. We do not use this much anymore because we have the big organ and this one is in pretty bad shape. Sometimes, though, on Easter, if we have a priest who is visiting us who is also an organist, we may play both organs during services, but usually we use the big one. May I ask what your interest is in medieval organs? Are you a music historian? I am Father Gerard, by the way." The priest extended his hand.

"I am John Morse, and these are my children Zach and Zoey. We are doing some sight-seeing. I have what you might call a hobby. I enjoy looking at old artifacts in buildings. I am a professor at UCLA."

"Oh, how nice." Father Gerard eyed Morse for a moment, considering his words. "Mr. Morse, pardon me, and I know this may sound somewhat strange, but I must tell you about the dream I had last night. I have never had one like it before. In the dream, there was a man in my church, with two children— a boy and a girl, much like yourself, and the man was on a most dire mission—a spiritual mission, for God himself. And in my dream, I felt an overwhelming need to help this man and his children, in whatever way I could. And then I woke up. I thought it was most unusual, and somewhat disturbing if you want to know the truth, but I did not give it much thought until just now, as I was praying in front of the Intentions Altar for our Blessed Virgin, I turned around and there you were, just like in my dream."

"That is most unusual," remarked Morse.

"I must know if there is any meaning to this. Are you really just sight-seeing, or is there more to it than that?" The priest smiled, his rubbery red cheeks blushing.

Morse looked into the brown eyes of the pudgy priest. There was something to this man, a kindness about him. Zoey seemed to sense it too, and eased the grip on her father's arm.

"As a matter of fact, we are on a quest of sorts, Father." Morse relayed to the priest their experiences from the morning involving Nostradamus' vault, leaving out the part about killing the priest. "And so the words of Nostradamus himself have led us here to your pipe organ," concluded Morse.

"May I see Nostradamus' letter?" The priest asked.

"Certainly," said Morse, pulling out the letter and showing the priest the notes Morse had made.

"Ahh, he is most certainly speaking of our organ here. The 'big game!' Fantastic! You are right, it is all right there."

"Actually," said Morse, "That was one of the things we did not understand. The words that we could not find a meaning for were 'big game,' 'human voice,' and 'pulling.'"

"That is because you do not play the pipe organ," said Father Gerard, chuckling. "I would be happy to translate for you."

Father Gerard took them over to an instrument that looked like a piano, but had dozens of strange-looking knobs and levers. "This is the keyboard for the pipe organ. A pipe organ makes music when wind passes over the hole in a pipe, much the same as if you take an empty glass soda bottle and lightly blow over the top of it. Pressurized air is constantly being pumped through the organ when the organist plays. The organist then pulls on a tab or knob on this keyboard and a valve is opened or closed, either letting wind in or closing the wind out. Obviously, if the wind passed through all the pipes at once, we would have an ugly mess of sound. So the organist closes a lot of the valves and only opens up certain ones to provide a certain sound or note. These knobs which let air in or close air out are called '*les tirants de jeux*.' In English, you would call these knobs 'organ stops.' So when our friend Nostradamus referred to 'tirant,' he did not really mean the present participle of the French verb 'tirer,' to pull. Instead, he was referring to these pull-knobs, the *tirants de jeux*."

"Can I try it?" asked Zoey fascinated by another musical instrument.

"Certainly," the priest said, scooting over on the bench and allowing Zoey to open and close some of the stops. Zoey played with some of the stops and made a very loud, obnoxious sound come from the organ. She giggled and looked at her dad.

"OK, that is one mystery solved," said Morse. "But what is the 'big game'?"

"Ahh, in order to understand that, you have to know that there are two main types of organ pipes, the 'flues,' and the 'reeds.' With a 'flue' pipe, near the foot of the pipe, the pressurized air is released in a flat stream, through a narrow slot. The longer the pipe, the lower the sound. Flue pipes are generally flatter and fatter. Reed pipes look very different. They are fatter at the top, and then taper down into a very narrow bottom. Near the foot of the pipe, the pressurized air must escape through two brass parts called a shallot and a tongue. Generally, reed pipes have a brighter sound than a flue pipe. When you allow several pipes to play at once, you get a mixture of sound. One of the beautiful, rich mixtures of reed pipes is called a '*grand-jeu*,' or, in English, the 'big game.' In the context of playing an organ, it really means 'the great play,' or the 'grand play.'" "I see," said Morse. "What about the 'human voice?' What does that mean?"

"The '*voix humaine*,' or 'human voice,' is one of the smallest of the reed pipes, with a short cylindrical resonator, partially stopped. It is this pipe here. We distinguish that from some of the big pipes in the middle, which some like to refer to as the 'Voice of God.'" The priest played the pipe. Father Gerard then grabbed a long stick with a light blue dust ruffle on the end, and raised it up to the pipes on the wall. The '*voix humaine*' is that pipe there."

"Father, I know this is a lot to ask, but this letter seems to be saying that there is a hidden message in that little organ pipe. Would it be possible for us to remove that pipe and examine it?"

"Well, I would normally say no, but given my dream from last night, and your incredible tale of Nostradamus, I am as interested as you in solving the riddle. We normally take the pipes down for cleaning once a year, so I know how to do it. Let me get my ladder and tool box, and we will see what we can see."

A few minutes later, Father Gerard came over to their position pushing a large inclined metal stairway on wheels, and holding a red tool box. He pushed the stairway next to the organ on the left side, secured the wheel brackets to the floor and mounted the stairway. This took some time due to Father Girard's girth and obvious lack of exercise. However, after a few moments he had scaled to the stair in front of the voix humaine. Unscrewing the supporting screws, he gently brought the tiny pipe down to Professor Morse for examination.

Morse looked on the outside of the pipe. He did not see anything jump out at him upon visual examination. He pulled out his magnifying glass from his nylon bag and set the pipe down on one of the stairs. Peering through the glass, he cleared off the dust on the pipe with a wet rag and looked for any markings. At first he did not see it. But after a few minutes of inspection, near the very bottom of the resonator, he could barely make out one French word in script:

Montre.

"Montre," said Morse. "That means 'show.' Show what?"

"Let me see that," said the priest, inspecting the pipe. "Incredible. All this time, and I have never seen that before. I guess I did not know to be looking for a secret message!"

"What does 'show' mean?" repeated Morse.

"Ah. This Nostradamus knew his organs," said Father Gerard. "If you look at the organ, you can see that the pipes are encased in a brown wooden enclosure or casement called a 'buffet.' What you don't know is that there are dozens of pipes behind the ones you see here that you cannot see unless you completely remove the pipes from the casement. These twenty or so huge flue pipes in the very front and center are the ones which 'show' the most, so for French organs, we call these big showy pipes in the front the '*montre*.'"

"Yes! That's it!" said Morse. "So it appears that your message is inside one of these big flue pipes in the middle. Could you remove those for us?"

"I can, Mr. Morse," said the cleric, "but I would think it highly doubtful that a message written hundreds of years ago would survive inside one of these pipes. These are cleaned once a year. If there were a scroll or something in one of the pipes, we would have either found it on cleaning or it would have made the pipe sound wrong. But I will check it for you anyway just in case."

This project took considerably longer, because the pipes were large and towered very high in the air. The priest handed down the organ pipes one by one to Professor John Morse and his children.

Morse examined each of the organ pipes on the ground with his magnifying glass. His examination was quite thorough but failed to reveal any script or writing on the outside of the pipe. It must be on the inside, he thought. He looked through the pipe. There was nothing visible. He put two fingers inside the top of the pipe, searching for anything unusual. What he felt was strange. He expected the pipe to be smooth on the inside. But it felt rougher than he expected. He definitely thought he felt a small groove. He looked at the end of the pipe again, this time shining his penlight at the opening. He put his finger back inside several inches and felt again. He felt a small circle, with a line through the middle of it, almost like....the head of a screw!

"Zoey, come over here. I need someone with smaller hands." Zoey came over to the pipe.

"Put your fingers inside there, and a few inches in, you should feel the head of a screw. Do you feel it?"

Zoey felt it. Morse handed her a small French coin. "Use this coin and see if you can undo the screw." Zoey tried for a few minutes but did not have much luck.

"It might be a little rusted. Father, do you have any WD-40?" The priest looked through his tool box and produced a small blue bottle. Morse squirted gray liquid into the pipe from the red straw at the top of the WD-40 bottle.

"Now, try it." Zoey tried for a few minutes but only budged it a little.

"Bounce, shorty," said Zach. He knocked her out of the way, took the coin from Zoey and put his fingers in the top of the pipe. After a few minutes, Zach closed his eyes and bit on his lip. He just about had it.

"I think I turned it!" he said. Just then he dropped the coin in his greasy hands and the coin slid and clinked all the way to the bottom of the pipe. Morse handed him another coin.

Zach fiddled with the new coin for another minute or two, and soon felt the coin turning the screw inside the pipe. After a few seconds, the small screw fell into Zach's fingers. "I did it."

Zach reached back in and felt the sharp edge of thin metal which had been screwed into the top of the big pipe. The metal ribbon was about a half inch wide, and coiled twice along the inner walls of the top of the pipe. Zach pulled on the tape with his fingernails and soon yanked it out the top. It looked like a brass bracelet.

"Incroyable!" the priest exclaimed. "I cannot believe that tape was inside this pipe all these years."

Morse put the small brass collar on the ground and gently unwound it, pressing down at the edges to make the brass ribbon flat. Holding the ends down with his fingers, he examined the metal tape with his magnifying glass.

"There are words on here!" Morse exclaimed. "It says:

A ma belle femme Henriette: Mille Regretz de vous abandonner

Or in English: "To my beautiful wife Henriette: A thousand regrets for abandoning you."

"Is that it?" asked Zach.

"Who's Henriette?" asked Zoey.

"Henriette," said Morse, "is probably a reference to Nostradamus' first wife, Henriette d'Encausse. While here in Agen, he married his first wife, Henriette, and had two small children. Then, later in life, he moved to Salon."

"Why did he move to Salon?" asked the priest.

"Well, his wife and children died of some form of the plague. Shortly after that, Nostradamus had a falling out with his friend Scaliger. With his wife and children dead and his best friend mad at him, there was no reason for Nostradamus to stay, so he moved on to Salon-de-Provence."

"Why did his friend get mad at him?" asked Zoey.

"No one really knows, Zoey. Most of the speculation is professional jealousy. Each of the men was a bit of an egomaniac. They probably got tired sharing the spotlight."

Zoey looked thoroughly confused. "Huh? What spotlight? What do you mean?"

Morse tried to put his thoughts into musical terms. "It would be like if Madonna and Lady Gaga shared the same apartment. After a while, they are going to get tired of each other."

"Oh," said Zoey, smiling. "I get it. So this Nostradamus and this other Caesar guy were kind of like Divas?"

"Yes, in a sense. I think that is a very good description of them"

"So what about this thing about abandoning Henriette?" asked Zach. "You think that means he feels bad he abandoned the old lady and let her croak from the plague?"

"Probably so. There is some discussion in the books on Nostradamus that when his wife died, Nostradamus was away from home, traveling the countryside. Nostradamus had developed a special pill made from rose petals which he believed could cure the plague. We still have his recipe for the pills, because he wrote it in some of his almanacs. And if you concocted a batch of it today, I assure you, it would not cure anything. But Nostradamus and half the villagers in France believed his rose pill could cure the plague, so Nostradamus was summoned far and wide whenever there was an epidemic to cure the plague. Indeed, Nostradamus, who was convinced of his own skills as a doctor, probably felt a duty as a doctor to leave his wife and children and cure whomever he could. The horrible irony, however, is that Nostradamus, the one person who was reputed to be able to cure the plague, was not present to cure his own wife and children. He must have felt very guilty when he returned home and found them dead, believing that he might have been able to cure them."

"But Pops," said Zach. "Where do we go from here? How does this help us find the little Bible with the prophecy?"

Morse shook his head. "I confess I do not know where to go from here.... Hmmm. It says '1000 regrets.' Father, is there anything about an organ relating to the number 1,000?"

"No, not that I can think of," said the priest.

"How many pipes are there in an organ?"

"It all depends. The largest organ in the world is in Atlantic City, New Jersey and has 33,000 pipes. The organ at Notre Dame has 7,800 pipes. This organ has less than 1,000 pipes."

"The number 1,000 must mean something," Morse speculated. "What about the Roman numeral 'M' which represents 1,000. Is there a capital M written anywhere on the organ?"

"No," said the priest. "Not that I know of." The priest laughed. "But then again, I never knew these secret messages you found were on there, either."

The professor walked up the ladder, looking at the pipes on the wall.

He also inspected the wood casement. He could see no letter 'M' or anything looking like the number 1,000.

"The message talks about Nostradamus having regrets about his wife. Maybe the clue is telling you to go to the graveyard where Nostradamus' wife was buried," suggested Father Gerard, looking up at Morse on the ladder.

Morse replied, "I have no idea where she was buried. In all the books I have read on Nostradamus, I have not heard anything about Henriette's final resting place. Father, I assume that there are not burial crypts underneath this cathedral, are there?"

"No, all we have down in the basement is folding chairs and dirt!"

Morse came down from the ladder and took out his notebook. In silence, he studied the words some more, biting his lip. This was a tough one. Abandonment. What if that was the key? Judas Iscariot had abandoned Christ.

"Father, in all these paintings on the wall, is there a painting of Judas Iscariot?"

"No, the Betrayer is not on the walls of our Church."

"Not even in some kind of Last Supper drawing?"

"No, I have seen these walls many times. Judas is not pictured."

"One of the gospels says that Jesus, just before dying, cried out, 'My God, My God, why have you abandoned me?' Is there anything painted on the walls of the Church which might show Jesus' last words to God before he died on the cross?"

"Well, we have many crucifixes in the cathedral, of course, and many paintings on the walls of Jesus on the cross, but nothing that jumps out at me for that quote."

"Perhaps the number 1,000, though, has something to do with the Bible. Father, do you have a Bible here?"

"Why of course, my son, I keep it with me always."

He pulled a small black Bible from his pocket and gave it to Morse.

Morse looked up John, Chapter 3 in the Bible.

"Have you ever read the book 'The Bible Code,' Father?"

"No, I cannot say I have."

"Well, there are some crackpots who claim that there is a hidden code in the Bible. Some of these people point out that John Chapter 3 is the 1,000th verse of the Bible, and 1,000 is supposed to be some kind of perfect number. It sounds silly, I know, but I wonder if that is what Nostradamus meant."

"Pops, isn't John Chapter 3 the sign that the crazy guys hold up at baseball games?"

"Very good, Zach. Yes, John 3:16 is the quote that says that God so loved the world that he sent his only Son to save our sins. Many people think that John 3:16 is one of the most important passages in the Bible, and yes, sometimes true believers hold up a sign that says John 3:16 at public events like baseball games. But let me see what else is in John Chapter 3."

Morse read the passage and then became excited. "Father, where is your baptismal font?"

Father Gerard pointed to a triangular-shaped stone podium near the cathedral's altar. Morse ran over to the baptismal font. "In John 3, a man named Nicodemus questions Jesus how a man can be born again, thinking Jesus meant it literally. Jesus explains things to Nicodemus, and then he goes to Judea, where he spends the rest of his time baptizing people. Perhaps Nostradamus wants us to look in the baptismal font."

Morse began crawling all over the stone podium, feeling for some kind of hidden latch or key.

Father Gerard was skeptical. "I do not think that is going to help you, Professor. That font was installed in 1956. I doubt that Nostradamus could have left a message in a font that was not installed until 1956!"

Morse was discouraged, and gave up his search. "I see your point."

Zoey was studying Morse's notes and the metal band taken from the organ pipe. "Hey, Daddy, you are not a very good speller."

"What do you mean?" asked Morse.

"This piece of metal spelled the word 'Regretz' with a 'Z,' and you spelled it on your pad with an 'S.'"

Morse looked at his notes and the metal band again. Zoey was right. The metal strip used a "Z" in the word "regretz." Morse pondered that. The French word for "regrets" was spelled the same way as its English counterpart, with an "S," not a "Z," on the end. Perhaps that was how the word was spelled in old French, in the sixteenth century, he thought. Hmmm. He took out his laptop computer and juiced it up. After a few minutes, he had the Windows 7 screen up. He clicked in Internet Explorer and typed in "mille regretz," and got this from Wikipedia:

Mille Regretz is a French chanson which in its 4 part setting is usually credited to the fifteenth-century musician Josquin des Prez....

Morse scanned down further.

Translations of the song differ in their interpretation of the words 'fache/face amoureuse' in line 2 (variously 'amorous anger' or 'loving face'):

"Mille regretz de vous abandonner
Et d'eslonger vostre fache amoureuse,
Jay si grand dueil et paine douloureuse,
Quon me verra brief mes jours definer."

"A thousand regrets at deserting you
And leaving behind your loving face,
I feel so much sadness and such painful distress
That it seems to me my days will soon dwindle away."

"That's it!" Morse exclaimed. "Zoey, you are genius! He was obviously referring to a song which was popular at the time called Mille Regretz, about a man who is deeply regretful about the loss of his wife. The first line of the song is a direct quote from the line on the metal strip. So the clue must somehow relate to the song."

Zach was not enjoying the praise being heaped on his stupid sister. "Oh, yeah, she is a real genius. Mrs. Straight C-Minus. OK, Genius, what are we supposed to do with this stupid song now that we have it?"

Zoey thought for a second. "Maybe we should just play the song?"

Morse stared at Zoey. Then he stared at Zach. Then he stared at the priest. Could it be that simple? Quickly, he began searching on his computer for free sheet music to the Josquin song Mille Regretz. On a Hartford University site, he found the music.

"Father, if I prop up my laptop over here where you normally keep your sheet music, do you think you would be able to play this song?"

"Is the Pope Catholic?" the priest laughed and settled himself on the bench before the three rows of piano-like keys. He put on his reading glasses, cracked his knuckles, looked at the laptop, and began playing.

The song was very mournful and slow. It was quite fitting for a song about deep regrets and the loss of a loved one.

“That song is so sad,” said Zoey. The song went on for about a minute. When it got to the end, the priest pulled out a few organ stops and hit the last melancholy notes. As the last note was played, the priest heard a small click down by his feet. He bent down on his knees, and noticed that the mahogany panel just above the foot pedals had opened on the right side three inches, like a small door.

“Your not going to believe this,” said the priest, “but a door just opened down here!” Morse got down with the priest, pulled open the panel all the way and shined his penlight into the hollow chamber beyond. He reached in his hand and pulled out a stack of several time-worn parchment scrolls, tied together with twine. Morse could barely breathe, he was so excited.

CHAPTER 17. QUATRAINS

January 20, 2013. 4:00 p.m. Paris time. Agen, France.

Morse unrolled the first of the scrolls on the organist's bench. The scroll contained handwriting in black India ink.

La Première Confession de Michel de Nostradamus:
L'Abandon

Moi, Michel de Nostradame, avoue solennellement avoir abandonné ma femme Henriette et mes deux petits enfants et avoir causé leur mort. Malgré le fait que le seul talent de ma vie a été la guérison fortuite de la maladie du charbon par mes propres remèdes à base de plantes, j'ai négligé ma femme et mes enfants, choisissant au contraire de parcourir la campagne de la France, allant de maison en maison en demandant s'il y avait des habitants qui avaient besoin d'être guéris. Pendant ce temps, ma femme, qui était plus belle que les déesses d'Olympe, avec mes deux enfants, innocents et sans défense, ont contracté la maladie du charbon en mon absence. Chaque jour ils ont prié les saints que je revienne pour les guérir, et chaque jour leurs prières.étaient inexaucées. Dans l'intervalle, je voyageais cavalièrement comme un gitan, en cherchant la gloire et la fortune et l'assouvissement de mon amour-propre. Et ce grand péché de l'Abandon, je l'avoue.

Veuillez agréer l'expression de mes salutations distinguées,
Michel de Nostradame

Morse made a translation on his notepad:

The First Confession of Michel de Nostradame: Abandonment

I, Michel de Nostradame, do solemnly confess that I abandoned my wife Henriette and my two small children, causing their deaths. Despite the fact that my only documented skill in life has been the fortuitous curing of le charbon with my home-made herbal remedies, I neglected my wife and children, deciding instead to tromp all over the French countryside, going from house to house, inquiring as to whether any of the inhabitants needed curing. In the meantime, my wife, who was more beautiful than the goddesses of Olympus, along with my two helpless innocent children, contracted le charbon in my absence. Each day, they prayed to the saints that I would come home and cure them, and each day, their prayers were unanswered. Meanwhile, I cavalierly traveled about like a gypsy, seeking fame and fortune and a gratification of my own ego. And for this great sin of Abandonment, I confess.

Sincerely,
Michel de Nostradame

Morse took out the first letter written by Nostradamus that they had found in the vault. The handwriting did not match.

"Well, we know one thing for certain," said Morse. "Whoever wrote the first letter we found in the vault did not write this letter. I wonder what is going on here. This letter from the organ seems very sarcastic and angry. From what I know of Nostradamus from books, he was a very proud man, very convinced of his own abilities, and very blind to his own short-comings. I frankly cannot see him writing anything like this. On the other hand, he must have known about this letter, because his letter from the vault pointed us here. It is puzzling."

Morse unrolled the second scroll on the piano bench. Glued with wax into the middle of the scroll were twelve smaller pieces of parchment, which appeared to have been ripped from a book. Closer inspection revealed that the pages were ripped from a King James Bible. Across the twelve pages of Corinthians were twelve handwritten quatrains, one per page, scrawled in India ink. Morse wrote the French words down in his notebook, along with his English translations:

1.
Suprême au pape lui-même, c'est le huitième,
Ceux qui protestent sont traités comme traîtres et assassiné.
Bouffi d'orgueil, il s'est marié avec la crème,
Des belles femmes: une morte, une survécu, deux divorcées, deux capitées

Supreme to the pope himself, he is the eighth,
Those who protest are murdered and treated as traitors.
Fat with pride, he married the cream of the crop,
Beautiful women: one died, one survived, two divorced, two beheaded
2.

Le Monstre de Valachie est le diable.
Il empale ses victimes avec un bâton trenchant.
Sa cruauté et son caractère impitoyables sont abominables.
Il écorche tout vif des hommes implorants.

The Monster of Wallachia is the devil.
He impales his victims with a sharp stick.
His cruelty and ruthlessness are abominable.
He skins alive pleading men.

3.
Un loup déguisé en prêtre, il achètera la papauté.
Son avidité est insatiable, rien ne lui suffit.
Il engendra six enfants illégitimes avec ses prostiuées.
Même le meurtre de ses propres enfants ne satisfait pas son appétit.

A wolf in priest's clothing, he shall buy the papacy.
His greed is insatiable, nothing is enough for him.
He will father six illegitimate children with his whores.
Even the murder of his own children does not satisfy his appetite.

4.
Après Pius, le prochain pape connaît la guerre, pas la paix.
Il est méchant et boit sans cesse.
Il attrapera la maladie de ses prostituées.
Et il vendra des billets au salut après la messe.

After Pius, the next pope knows war, not peace.
He is wicked and drinks all the time.
He will get disease from his whores
Then he will sell tickets to salvation after mass.

5.
Le prochain pape est aussi perdu.
L'argent destiné aux pauvres va aux corridas et aux banquets.
Il coupe les mains et les pieds aux intrus.
Leurs enfants sont esclaves, leurs maisons brûlées.

The next pope is also lost.
Money for the poor goes to bull-fights and banquets.
He cuts off the hands and feet of trespassers.
Their children are slaves, their houses are burned.

6.
Sur la porte il clouera sa protestation,
Quatre-vingt- quinze plaintes contre le château.
Ils exigeront son excommunication.
Il refuse de désavouer ses mots.

On the door he will nail his protest,
95 complaints on the castle.
They will demand his excommunication.
He will refuse to recant his words.

7.
Après encore un, le prochain pape ordonne que 8.000 soient tués.
Il croit aussi que la papauté est à vendre.
Refusant de croire en Dieu Lui-même, il est athée.
L'argent de l'Eglise, il se gêne pas de le prendre.

After another one, the next pope orders 8,000 killed
He also believes the papacy is for sale
Disbelieving in God Himself, he is an atheist
The money of the Church he feels free to take.

8.
Le prochain pape garde 45.000 prostituées.
Il est coupable de l'inceste avec sa fille et ses soeurs.
Son gendre est empoisonné.
Le meurtre et le mal noircissent son coeur.

The next pope keeps 45,000 prostitutes.
He has incest with his daughter and his sisters.
His son-in-law is poisoned.
Murder and evil blacken his heart.

9.
Pendant un temps d'obscurité, une lumière.
Le savant de Cracovie cherche les cieux.
Sa théorie est tout à fait contraire,
Le soleil, pas la terre, est au milieu.

In an age of darkness, a light.
The scientist from Krakow searches the heavens.
His theory is quite contrary,
The sun, not the earth, is in the middle.

10.
Le prochain pape n'est pas beaucoup meilleur.
Il va adopter un innocent, et après lui fera subir la sodomie.
Comme une maladie répugnante sur une belle fleur,
Son désir dégoûtant est une anomalie.

The next Pope is no better.
He will adopt an innocent, and then subject him to sodomy.
Like filthy disease on a beautiful flower,
His disgusting lust is abnormal.

11.
Après encore un, le prochain pape s'amuse à torturer.
Il aime la vierge de fer et le chevalet.
La douleur incroyable que ses victimes doivent endurer.
Leurs cris de douleur vous font trembler.

After another one, the next pope takes joy in torturing.
He loves the iron-maiden and the rack.
Incredible pain his victims must endure.
Their cries of anguish make you tremble.

12.
A Novgorod 50.000 seront tués.
Il battra sa belle-fille enceinte, en causant une fausse couche.
Puis, en colère, son fils sera empalé.
Après le viol, il prend du poison par la bouche.

In Novgorod, 50,000 will be slain.
He will beat his pregnant daughter-in-law, causing her miscarriage.
Then, in anger, his son will be impaled.
After rape, he takes poison in his mouth.

"Dad, I think this is from that Bible Nostradamus was talking about," said Zach.

His father agreed. "These appear to be twelve of the missing 58 quatrains! These quatrains are specific, and appear to relate to real people and real events in history. Take this first one:

> *1.*
> *Supreme to the pope himself, he is the eighth,*
> *Those who protest are murdered and treated as traitors.*
> *Fat with pride, he married the cream of the crop,*
> *Beautiful women: one died, one survived, two divorced, two beheaded*

That obviously is a reference to Henry VIII, who declared himself to be supreme to the Pope. Anyone who protested, for example Sir Thomas More, was murdered and treated as a traitor. And he most certainly had six wives—one who died, one who survived, two who were divorced, and two who were beheaded."

Morse scanned the next quatrain. "The 'Monster of Wallachia' who impales people is obviously Vlad the Impaler, the ruler of what is now modern-day Romania, whose cruel punishments are legendary. In fact, his name Vlad Dracul, is where we get the character Dracula."

The next seven quatrains appeared to have something to do with popes. Morse typed in "lives of early popes" into a search engine in his computer and came up with several hits. "The next quatrain talks about a man who bribed his way into the papacy and was the father of illegitimate children. I cannot speak to the reliability of this website, but it says here that Pope Alexander VI, also called the 'anti-pope,' held the papacy from 1492 to 1503. It was well known, according to this website, that he bribed his way into the papacy. It also says that he was quite a fornicator and fathered six illegitimate children. It also says Pope Leo X later referred to him as a 'the most savage wolf the world has ever seen.' So that certainly fits the wolf reference. I am not sure about murdering his own children, but the rest fits." Morse wrote "Henry VIII" next to the number "1," "Vlad the Impaler" next to the number "2," and "Pope Alexander VI" next to the number "3" on his notepad.

Zach shook his head in disgust. "Man, that pope's worse than that Zeus dude."

"Eww," said Zoey. "Dad, this is gross. You guys are so disgusting. When are you going to stop talking about you-know-what? Can I go over there and play music on that other big pipe organ?"

"Sure," said Morse. "If it is OK with Father Gerard, here."

"Of course it is," says Father Gerard. "Here, I will teach you how to play some songs. I don't think I can stand listening to libelous statements about the behavior of popes." The priest walked across the cathedral to the larger organ on the opposite wall. Within a few minutes, Catholic hymns resounded from the large organ pipes.

"Hey, Dad, look at how the prophecies all rhyme in French. This Nostradamus dude was like a French rapper."

"In a way, I guess that's true."

"Is this right what it says here about all these popes? I never knew any popes were bad."

"I am not certain. I had heard before that some of the medieval popes were not upstanding citizens, but I confess I had not read any of this before." said Morse. "Look at the next one here:

After Pius, the next pope knows war, not peace.
He is wicked and drinks all the time.
He will get disease from his whores
Then he will sell tickets to salvation after mass.

The next pope after Alexander VI and after Pope Pius was Pope Julius II. According to this website, the pope donned full armor and rode off to battle with the papal army. In fact, Julius liked soldiers so much that he hired the Swiss troops which still guard the Vatican today. It is believed that Julius II contracted syphilis from one of his many lovers, so the reference to disease matches. And it was Julius II who first came up with the idea of papal indulgences, which can certainly be described as 'tickets to salvation after mass.' So Quatrain No. 4 must mean Julius II." Morse wrote "Julius II" after No. 4 in his notebook.

"What's this thing about cutting off peoples' hands and feet?" asked Zach. Morse looked at the website about the lives of the popes. "It says here that the next pope was Leo X, who indeed indulged in papal extravagance, attending banquets and carnivals and bull-fights. He created a private game reserve where he went hunting with his cardinals. And if anyone dared to trespass on the reserve, he had their hands and feet cut off, sold their children into slavery and burned their houses to the ground. I don't know if that's true, but it is a perfect fit."

"Man, that is whack! How did those dudes get to be pope? Once the guy started cutting people's hands and feet off, why didn't they just fire him?" asked Zach.

"I don't know. Things were obviously very different back then." Morse continued to work through the quatrains. Quatrain 6 obviously referred to Martin Luther. Quatrain 7 referred to Clement VII, the Atheist Pope. Quatrain 8 referred to Paul III, the Incestuous Pope who poisoned his son-in-law, mother and niece to obtain the family fortune, and then had incest with his sisters and daughter. Quatrain 9 referred to Copernicus, the man who first theorized that the Earth moved around the Sun. Quatrain 10 referred to Julius III, the Pedophile Pope, who adopted a young orphan named Innocenzo, made him a cardinal, and then sodomized him, in addition to several other young boys. Quatrain 11 referred to Paul IV, the Torturer Pope, a former Grand Inquisitor who paid for new torture machines out of his own pocket.

"Finally," said Morse, "That brings us to Quatrain 12, which is a clear reference to Ivan the Terrible, who massacred 50,000 in Novgorod, Russia, beat his own daughter for wearing flashy clothing, causing her miscarriage, and then, in a rage, impaled his own son. He is also said to have raped a woman named Irina Godounov, which angered his brother Boris Godounov, who probably poisoned him to death."

Morse studied the list with his son. "It appears to be some kind of cataloguing of evil men throughout the century, although Copernicus and Luther would probably not be categorized as evil. The first eleven I do not find particularly incredible, because all of the events listed occurred prior to Nostradamus' death. So the first eleven we cannot even credibly call prophecies. But the twelfth quatrain, which refers to Ivan the Terrible, is different. The Massacre of Novgorod occurred in 1570, four years after Nostradamus died. The beating of the daughter occurred in 1581. And Ivan was not killed until 1584, long after Nostradamus died. And this business about poisoning was not really known until the 1960s, when Ivan's body was removed from his tomb by archaeologists, who found high levels of mercury in his remains, and speculated that he was poisoned. I see no way Nostradamus could have known all of that. So maybe we have a true prophet here after all. Of course, these quatrains on the Bible pages do not appear to be written in Nostradamus' handwriting. Judging by the curvature of the writing, I would almost hazard a guess that they were written by a woman. We will not really know for sure until we date the documents and have the handwriting and ink analyzed by experts."

Morse unrolled the third scroll.

K R S L
Quand les gros cochons volent,
Les rois tremblent,
Les cloches sonnent,
Et les gens réjouissent!

Morse Translated the text:

When fat pigs fly
Kings tremble
Bells ring
And the people rejoice.

"Fat pigs fly," said Morse. "I have no idea what that means." Morse did a number of computer searches and came up with nothing. "This drawing, I cannot make out anything from that, either. K, R, S, L. I do not know what that means. And the chessboard is not doing anything for me, either. There's nothing more here on these scrolls."

Morse took some photos of the pipe organ and its secret door, and placed the scrolls in his nylon bag. He shut down his laptop and called for Zoey and Father Gerard.

"Father, I cannot thank you enough for your help. I think we are at a roadblock right now, and the kids need to get some food. Can you point us to a good café?"

"Why, of course. Guillame's is right around the corner and their bread is fatanstique. You cannot go wrong. I must confess this has been very exciting this morning. Can you do me a favor? Take my phone number and put it into your cell phone. If you get a chance later, I would love to hear how this mystery of Nostradamus ends."

"We will definitely do that," said Morse. The priest gave him the telephone number and Morse entered it accordingly. "I cannot thank you enough for your help. And I assure you, I will make sure these historical artifacts are examined and then returned to a French museum. I will probably return with a team in a few weeks to take some samples from the organ so we can document everything, so I will see you again."

"Wonderful, well, it was very nice meeting your lovely children, and if Zoey is ever interested, I would be happy to give her pipe organ lessons. She looks like she has the musical ear, as we say."

Zoey smiled. "Thank you, Father."

Morse escorted his two children out of the church and waved goodbye to Father Gerard.

"*Bon chance*!" said the priest, smiling happily.

Morse led his children across the street to Guillame's, an outdoor café with an orange awning. The group was famished. Everything on the menu looked appetizing. Zoey ordered a croque madame, a French sandwich with ham, cheese, and a poached egg. The ham sandwich was the safest thing on the menu. She was strictly a peanut better and jelly gal. She was not going to start eating snails or something. Zach was the health nut, and ordered fresh fruit and "*l'eau du robinet*," the French equivalent of tap water. Zach was on his high school cross country team and ran about eight miles each day. After every meal, he would stretch and do pushups. Professor Morse was not a health nut. Since his wife died, he had not cared how far his waist line expanded. He ordered a chicken crepe with a cream sauce, which was sure to put on a few pounds.

"Pops, you have gotta stop eating that garbage. You are going to turn into Jabba the Hut."

"You're right, Zach. I wish I had your willpower. But I love to eat."

About ten minutes later, their food came.

"Daddy, do you think there are more bad guys coming after us?"

"Oh, Zoey, I don't think so. No one saw us leaving Salon. And I cannot imagine anyone is going to find that body for a long time."

"Why did that bad priest want to kill us?"

"I don't know. It must have something to do with these prophecies. Whoever it is does not want us to find all the prophecies."

"Then why did they call you over to France in the first place?" asked Zach. "Why not just leave all that stuff there in the vault? You would have never known about it if they had not called you."

"I suspect that the real Father du Bois summoned me to France after he found the underground vault. Somehow, some other third party found out about it, eliminated Father du Bois and then posed as him when we arrived."

"Well, if they cared that much about these dumb prophecies to send a killer to come after us, don't you think they are going to just send another killer after us?" asked Zach.

"I suppose it's possible, assuming they could figure out where we are."

"Dad, these boys ain't no dummies. They figured out how to find Father du Bois, got some priest clothes and hired a guy to kill us all within a matter of days. They have probably checked in with that guy we left in the vault. When he doesn't answer, they will send a backup team after him. And when they see he is dead, they'll start looking for us. You rented a car with your VISA card, and you filled it up with gas along the way. I saw you. If they can track that stuff, they are going to find us in no time. Why are we still here playing detective? Why don't we bail outa here and get back to America where it's safe?"

Zach raised a good point. Morse had been so intrigued by the ancient puzzle of Nostradamus that he ignored the obvious danger signs for his family. Zach was right. They had to get a plane back to America quickly. He could return to France when it was safe at a later time. Morse asked the waiter to put their food in to-go bags. He paid the bill with cash. Morse asked the waiter for directions to the airport, but the waiter, miffed that he had not gotten a bigger tip, feigned ignorance. Morse decided to go back across the street to the cathedral and ask Father Gerard for directions to the Agen airport. When the three entered the church, Zoey ran ahead down the aisle to find her musician friend. When she got to the ancient pipe organ, she did not see the priest. Curious, she went to the left edge of the pipe organ and went through the passage behind the organ to the small pipe room behind it. As Morse and Zach came down the aisle at a slower pace, they heard Zoey scream. They ran to the pipe room.

"Dad! He's dead!" screamed Zoey. Zoey ran and grabbed her father.

When Morse and Zach entered the pipe room, they saw Father Gerard, lying face down, with a pool of dark red blood around his head. Morse examined his pulse. He was definitely dead. It appeared that he had been shot in the head. There was only one reason someone would murder this nice priest. The killers were here, and they were after Morse and his family. A moment of dread and panic gripped him. Morse cursed himself for not getting to an airport earlier when they had the chance. Morse quickly peeked around the corner of the pipe room and looked into the cathedral. He did not see anyone lurking in the church. But they must be very close. How would they get out of here safely?

Morse asked himself what he would do if he was tracking a man and his two children. He would pass their pictures around. He would look for the license plate of the Audi, and watch the car. And he would watch all roads to the airport. Morse went to the window on the south side of the church and looked out. He saw the Audi parked in one of the spaces on the street. There was a tall man in a gray suit and sunglasses leaning against the car. They would have to take different transportation. Morse looked out the window on the north side. There was a street with parked cars, a bus stop, and a small park. That would have to be their way out.

"Daddy, I'm scared!" whined Zoey.

"Dad, we gotta get outa here. We are sitting ducks in here."

"Come with me," said Morse. Morse ran to the center of the church, and then into a small side door next to the altar. Inside the door was a small dressing room, with a long closet. This was where the priests donned their vestments before beginning mass. Morse slid open the door and pulled out a black priest's collar, shirt and robe. The robe belonged to

Father Gerard. Due to the priest's girth, this robe was very large. Morse handed another smaller priest's collar, shirt, and robe to Zach.

"They are going to be expecting a man and two teenagers. They are not going to be expecting two priests. Zoey, I want you to get on my back like you are doing a piggyback ride, but under my robe. You are going to have to hang down low so you stay under the robe. When I say go, we are going to walk calmly to the next bus that comes in and get on wherever it's going." Zach thought the plan sounded better than anything he could think of. Near the closet of priest's vestments was a small bathroom. Morse looked inside the bathroom to see if there was anything they could use to disguise their faces or make themselves look different. As he looked down, he saw a set of electric clippers. Morse recalled that Father Gerard had a buzz cut. Morse looked at his son's long, beautiful Zac Efron hair. Zach Morse saw the clippers and then looked at his father with more trepidation than he felt when the killer's gun was pointed at him.

"No way! Shut up! I am not cutting my hair!"

"Zach, you have to. They have your picture, with your long hair. That will give us away in a minute. They will not be expecting two bald priests."

"No way! This hair gives me my swagga. I am not cutting my hair for anything!"

"Zach, I am sorry, but you and your sister could be killed. Your hair will grow back. We have to get out of here alive!"

Zach looked back at the clippers. He was filled with panic at the thought of cutting his hair, but he realized that his hair could give them away.

"OK, but be gentle. Just so you know, if we get killed anyway, and I die bald, I will never forgive you."

Morse took the clippers and buzzed off all of his son's beautiful hair. Then he turned the clippers on himself. The sink was filled with clumps of Zach's blondish-brown hair and Morse's gray hair. Morse and his son looked at themselves in the mirror. They did not look anything like their former selves. Morse felt good. Zach did not.

Zoey jumped on the back of her father, and then Zach put Father Gerard's fat robe over him. Then Zach put on his own robe. Morse peeked out the door of the small dressing room. No one was there. He and Zach walked to the north door, with Zoey clinging on underneath the robe.

They looked out the door for a few minutes, and then saw a bus heading their way.

"Go!" said Morse. Two bald priests, one looking slightly like a hunchback, walked out the north door of the cathedral and headed towards the bus stop. About a block away, a man in jeans and a gray t-shirt was holding a picture of a UCLA professor and his two children. As he scanned the block or two around the Agen cathedral, he paid no attention to the two bald priests heading for the bus stop. A minute later, Morse and his children were safely on board the bus, which was headed out of town. They walked to the very back of the bus, where Zoey crawled out from the robe. They looked out the back window of the bus. They could not see any pursuers, but they knew they were back in the town somewhere. Zach looked at his light reflection in the window of the bus. He was bald. He could not believe he was bald. He was thoroughly depressed. He took off his priest's robe and wadded it up in a ball as a pillow.

"I can't believe I even came on this stupid French trip. I am going to sleep. Wake me up when we get there. This blows." He was not happy about his hair. He was going to be crabby for a very long time.

Morse walked up the aisle and talked to another passenger.

"*Excusez-moi,*" Morse spoke in French. "I am concerned I got on the wrong bus. Can you tell me where this bus is heading?"

"Carcassonne, Father."

"Ah, Carcassonne, thank you very much."

Morse returned to his children. "We are on our way to Carcassonne."

"Where is that?" asked Zoey.

"It's about two hours east of here. We passed it on the way here while you were sleeping before. We are going back in the direction we came."

"Can we go home when we get there?" asked Zoey.

"Yes, absolutely."

"Good," said Zoey. "I don't like France." She went to sleep next to her brother. Morse regretted bringing these children along. It was hard being a single father. He hoped they would not be pursued to Carcassonne. Perhaps they could get a flight from there. Morse stayed awake for another thirty minutes, constantly looking out the bus' back window to make sure they were not being followed. Then Morse took off his own priest's robe and fell asleep, exhausted from the day's events.

CHAPTER 18. BUS

January 20, 2010. 5:45 p.m. Paris time. 11:45 EST.
Ten miles south of Toulouse.

Almost two hours into the bus trip, the bus hit a pot hole and John Morse woke up, startled. He quickly looked around the bus in panic, and then out the back window. Everything seemed safe.

"What kind of cancer does your son have?" A good looking man in his late thirties with a tan face, blue eyes, and a strong chin poked his head out towards Morse. He spoke in English. He was seated one row up and across the aisle from Morse and his children. He was had a friendly, almost mischievous grin, and a large gap between his teeth. He was wearing a Harvard sweatshirt.

"I'm sorry, what?"

"Your son, he has lost his hair. I just assumed maybe he had cancer."

Morse caught on. "Oh, I see, no, he does not have cancer. He just recently shaved his head."

The man looked puzzled. "And you shaved your head, too? Is that for some religious purpose?"

A handsome, broad-shouldered 6 foot, 3 inch blonde man with sunglasses and a gray shirt reading "Brown Hockey" nudged his friend in the Harvard sweatshirt.

"Doug, stop bothering them!" He leaned across his friend's lap and spoke to Morse in a deep voice. "I am sorry, sir. My partner here really enjoys butting into other people's business."

"No, it's quite all right," said Morse. "Umm, we just uh, well…" Morse stammered, unable to quickly think up a lie to explain their shaven heads.

"Look," said the man known as Doug. "I am sorry to intrude. We are not judging you or anything. I just thought you might be in trouble. I saw you three come on the bus in priest's outfits and then your daughter did that little Houdini number under the robe. I have been sitting here like the Curious Cat for an hour now trying to get up the nerve to ask you what this is all about. If you and your family are in trouble, we would be happy to help."

The bigger man rolled his eyes. "Doug, I am sure they don't need our help. We are really sorry to bother you." The big man gave his partner another withering glance.

Morse thought for a moment. At this point, they probably could use all the help they could get.

"Actually, we are in a spot of trouble. My name is John Morse."

"Doug Bushnell," he said warmly, shaking Morse's hand, his eyes lighting up, knowing that whatever the story was he was going to get it.

"I'm Ray Lardiggio," said the bigger man. Morse felt every bone in his hand turn to dust in the big man's vice-like handshake.

Morse addressed the couple. "I am a Professor at UCLA. I came here with my family on a scholarly trip to find certain ancient artifacts. Along the way, for some reason I do not yet know, we have incurred the wrath of some sinister forces, who have tried to kill us. They trailed us to Agen, and before we could get to the airport, they pinned us down in the Agen Cathedral. The only way to escape was to change our appearance, dress like priests and get on this bus. Our plan is to get to the airport in Carcassonne as soon as possible and get home to safety. "

The big man's protective instincts kicked in. "Who is chasing you? What do they look like?"

"I don't know," said Morse. "I saw one man in a gray suit and another in a t-shirt and jeans. They were kind of non-descript and I was looking through a window quite some distance away."

"You're coming with us," said Ray. "We will keep you safe."

Doug looked miffed at his partner. "Excuse me a sec," he said to Morse and then had a private conversation with Ray in a very quiet voice. "Umm, ix-nay on the otection-pray, Batman. I don't mind being friendly, but you just signed us up to protect them for the rest of our trip. I have buildings to photograph, you know, and we only have one more day."

Ray looked at his partner in disappointment. "I do not care what our vacation plans are. These people are in trouble. We are going to give them our help."

"You are always doing this, making plans without me. We've paid a lot of money for this trip. Your Hockey Gene is coming out again. You see a potential to bang someone's head, and your Testosterone Meter shoots to the moon."

"Doug, it is not about banging heads. They have little kids there."

Doug looked disgusted. "I hate it when you go into super-hero mode.

OK, fine, but let's save mankind quickly, OK, Ray, because I still haven't eaten an escargot yet."

Ray moved across his partner, crushing his shoulder as he leaned. "Professor Morse, we are going to do everything we can to help you."

"That is so nice of you," said Morse. "I will definitely take you up on that. Do you know the best way to get to the Carcassonne Airport?"

"As I understand it," said Doug. "It is on the west side of the city. When we get off the bus, we will walk you to a cab so you can get to the airport."

"We will go with you in the cab to make sure you're safe," corrected Ray.

"Right. That's what I meant," said Doug, frowning.

"What brings the two of you to Carcassonne?" asked Morse.

"Sight-seeing," said Doug. "I teach architecture at Harvard. I convinced Ray to go with me to photograph a lot of the ancient castles in France. The architecture is really quite amazing. Ray is a high school hockey and football coach, so castles are not really up his alley, but he is so crazy about me he will follow me anywhere."

Ray thought Doug was trying to slight his intelligence with the crack about the castles. "I am also the coach of the Science Olympiad Team, Mr. Architectural Genius. I may not have spent two thousand hours in the library researching castle moat irrigation or drawbridge gears, like some people we know, but I do like the stories about the battles in these old castles. Those are cool. Like the siege of the Foix Castle or the story about the pig flying over the Walls of Carcassonne. And by the way, it is he who follows me everywhere."

"Yeah," said Doug. "He was like a school girl in the third Lord of the Rings movie when the giant elephant thingies attacked the castle. I fell asleep in that movie."

"Yeah, he's got great movie taste. His favorite movie is Julie & Julia, for crying out loud."

"Meryl Streep is a goddess. She can do no wrong."

"Excuse me," said Morse. "What did you say about the pig flying over the Walls of Carcassonne?"

"You never heard that story?" asked Ray. "It's how the city got its name. It all started….."

"Well, not exactly," interrupted Doug.

"OK, you know the story better," conceded Ray. "You're the castle expert. You tell it."

"OK," said Doug. "Well, the City probably gets its name from a ruler in 118 B.C. named 'Julia Carcaso.' The fortifications for the City were built in the time of Roman Gaul, as early as the first century A.D. Later, the Roman name for the City became 'Carcasso,' and it eventually morphed into Carcassonne over the years. However, the locals tell a slightly different story, which is probably just a legend.

"In 795 A.D., five years before he became Holy Roman Emperor, Charlemagne tried to lay siege to the City. At the time, the city was ruled by a Saracen princess named Dame Carcas, who had stepped in to rule the city after her husband had passed away. After many months of battle, the villagers inside the castle had hardly any foodstuffs left. They were out of water and supplies. If they did not surrender soon, they would all starve. They were down to one pig and one bag of grain—some stories say it was a bag of corn. Dame Carcas got a clever idea. She took the last bag of grain and, as other townspeople looked on in bewilderment, fed the grain to the pig. Then she hoisted the pig to the top of the ramparts and heaved it down on the attacking army below. The pig exploded on impact, and the grain fed to the pig came pouring out.

"When Charlemagne saw the pig and its entrails, he became concerned. The townspeople apparently had enough supplies to use their food as weapons. Moreover, if even the town's pigs had enough to eat, surely they had many more months' worth of food inside the castle on which to survive. At this rate, Charlemagne believed he would not be able to take the castle, so he retreated. After Charlemagne's army left, Dame Carcas went to the Bell Tower of St. Nazaire and rang the bells, signaling victory. The townspeople erupted in joyous celebration, yelling 'Carcas sonne' or 'Carcas rings.' And that is how the city got the name 'Carcassonne.'"

"Oh my goodness," said Morse. He reached to his feet and pulled out the scroll taken from the Organ of Agen. "This is an ancient scroll I recovered in Agen, and may have been authored by Nostradamus or one of his contemporaries." Doug and Ray looked at the scroll.

When fat pigs fly
Kings tremble
Bells ring
And the people rejoice.

"The 'flying pig' is Dame Carcas' pig. The 'trembling king' is Charlemagne.' The bells ringing are the Bells of St. Nazaire. And the people rejoicing are the villagers of Carcassonne. This is obviously pointing me to go to Carcassonne! What luck!"

"Yes," said Doug, "And you even have Charlemagne the Great's monogram there."

"What?"

"Yes, that drawing there is the monogram of Charlemagne. Charlemagne was known by his German name 'Karls des Grossen, or Charles the Great. The Latin form was Carolus Magnus. When Pope Leo III made Charles the Holy Roman Emperor on Christmas Day in the year 800 A.D., the Pope gave him the name KAROLUS with a K. Charles thought he was hot stuff and decided to create his own official monogram for signing documents. The drawing shows a K on the left; an A in the middle—see the two lines going up with the little downward pointy thing between them, that's the 'A'—an R on the top; an O in the middle again, which looks kind of like a diamond; an L on the bottom; a U back in the middle again –the U kind of looks like a V, with two lines going downward—and an S on the right. KAROLUS, or Charlemagne the Great. So the drawing obviously goes with the verse about Carcassonne."

"How did you know that?" asked Morse.

"Don't ask," said Ray sarcastically. "He has become a regular encyclopedia of useless medieval knowledge. Hey, I notice the chess board on the bottom. What's that?"

"Oh," said Morse. "That's the rest of the clue. I don't play chess, so I do not have the foggiest notion what it means."

"Well you are in luck again," said Ray. "I happen to be a chess player. I can help you out with it."

Ray studied the chess board. "Well, I see at the top there is an arrow pointing downward. That probably means it is Black's turn to move. The scroll is asking you to figure out what Black's Best Next Move is."

"Oh, I see," said Morse. "Do you know what the best next move is?"

"Sure." Ray wrote letters A through H along the bottom and 1 through 8 on the left side of the board, like this:

Ray pointed to the Black Bishop in the middle of the board.

"This is a classic 'Discovered Check,' when one piece on a player's board screens another one of his pieces from a check of the opponent's king. By moving the blocking piece—the screen—out of the way, there is a 'Discovered Check.' Take a look at the board here. The Black Bishop is sitting on space E5. If he wasn't there, the Black Queen on E7 would have a direct beeline to the White King on E1. Moving the Black Bishop on E5 out of the way, then, causes the Black Queen to check the White King. The rule is you always have to get out of check after the other side checks your king. So what we need to do is move the Black Bishop to a place where he will threaten another valuable White piece. While White is tied up getting out of check, the Black Bishop moves in for the kill. Black's best move here is to play his Black Bishop on E5 toC3, and take the White Knight. That will result in a check—in fact, a double-check— on the White King. After White wastes a turn getting his King out of check, the Black Bishop then slides over and kills the White Queen on A5. A Black Bishop Screen and a Discovered Check."

“Very clever,” said Morse. “The Black Bishop. Doug, is there anything in the Town of Carcassonne relating to a Bishop?”

“Why, certainly there is. In the 11th century Basilica of St. Nazaire and St. Celse—that’s the one with the bell tower Dame Carcas was ringing—there are tombs of two bishops. That is where Ray and I are going. The Basilica is particularly fascinating because it represents a combination of Romance and Gothic styles. It started out as a Romance structure, but then as a result of the Cathars Wars, the city became controlled by the French. The French wanted the cathedral constructed in the new Gothic style; so much of the Basilica was demolished and replaced with a Gothic version. But they ran out of funds, and so they had to keep the old Romance nave. Therefore, they had to come up with a compromise between the Romance nave with its tight dimensions and the Gothic transept which was intended for a larger building. The result is a bizarre combination of Romance and Gothic styles. It is really interesting.”

“Doug, I don’t think he cares about your architecture styles,” said Ray. “He wants to know about the bishops.”

“Right, sorry,” said Doug. “It’s just that the architecture is so fascinating. Anyway, in the Basilica, there are two bishop’s tombs—the empty tomb of Saint Pierre de Rochefort, former Bishop of Carcassonne, and the Tomb of Bishop Radulphe. Both are absolutely beautiful.”

“If you had to categorize them, which of the bishops could you describe as a “black bishop?”

“Well, Saint Pierre is said to descend from a group of heretics living in the Black Mountains of Languedoc. Could that fit?”

“That must be it!” said Morse. “So the black bishop must mean the Tomb of St. Pierre in the Basilica of St. Nazaire. And the discovered check move must give us our last clue as to where to look by the tomb!”

“Makes sense to me,” said Doug. “Hey, this is kind of fun.”

Just then Zoey woke up. “Hey what is that thing up there?”

The bus travelers turned and looked out the window. Up ahead lay a beautiful city of castle walls and towers.

Carcassonne looked like something out of a Disney fairy tale. The city had two castle walls, an outer wall and an inner wall, complete with archer parapets. The double walls ran for two miles and surrounded a busy collection of medieval streets and museums. The city had over forty towers with light blue and red-brick colored spires.

As the bus passed across the ancient nine-arched Pont Vieux Bridge running over the River Aude into Carcassonne, Morse looked out his window in amazement. He had never seen such a beautiful city. Morse woke up his son Zach. Zach cleared his eyes and looked up at the huge medieval towers.

"Hey, this kind of looks like Disneyland," said Zoey. "Are we in Eurodisney?"

"No, Zoey."

"It is funny you should say that, though," said Doug, "Walt Disney came to the City of Carcassonne and drew his inspiration for Sleeping Beauty's Castle from the towers of this very city. So in a way, this is kind of like Disneyland."

"Are there roller coasters?"

Zach and the men laughed. "No," said her father. "No roller coasters." Morse introduced Doug and Ray to his two children. Then Morse told the children how he and his new friends had solved part of the riddle from the organ while they were sleeping. Zach especially liked the part about the flying pig.

"Welcome to the Medieval City of Carcassonne," said the bus driver.

The bus rumbled through the huge castle arch, past the first, and then the second towering stone wall of Carcassonne.

"Woa," said Zach, looking out the window. After thinking for a minute, he turned to his father. "Hey Pops, I got a new one:

Boyz in the village said, "This Charlie Dude's a pain,
He keeps on attackin' he's my boy Charlemagne
We just got a piggy and one bag 'a grain
Maybe we should bounce off and head to Spain."

Lady said, "Boyz, don't you all be afraid
I gotta big plan and I think we got it made.
Feed the food to the piggy, and shoot him off the wall
Like a three-point shot of a piggy basketball."

So they shot off the pig and the townies made a wish
Landed right on target, and it made a swish.
Charlie he was scared when the piggy made a splatter
"If the piggy is fat, then the people's even fatter"

So he packed up his homies and he bolted outa there
And the lady rang the church bells of St. Nazaire
So her peeps were all happy that the battle she done won
And that there's the Story of Carcassonne!"

Oonce, oonce, oonce, oonce....

The adults all laughed. "Your boy has a real talent there," said Ray. "I like the part about the piggy basketball."

Two rows ahead of them, a man speaking in French, wearing headphones attached to a laptop seemed to be very excited and was gesturing to some of the other passengers.

"What is he saying, Dad?" asked Zoey.

"He is saying that someone just tried to assassinate the Chief Justice of the Supreme Court."

The Morse family and their two new friends, intrigued by the story, walked up and looked over the shoulder of the man on the bus with the laptop, who had unplugged the earphones so that the words on the screen played out through the laptop's speakers.

CHAPTER 19. INAUGURATION

January 20, 2013, 12:15 p.m. EST. Washington, D.C.

President Tim Woodson had just taken the oath of office, but the speech was beginning fifteen minutes later than expected, because Supreme Court Justice Dan Perkins had never shown up. It took an extra ten minutes for the Secret Service to shuffle Justice Ginsburg up to the podium.

"My Fellow Americans," announced President Woodson. "What a beautiful day it is today. I want to thank all of you for your support during these troubled times. Now is the time to come together as Americans, to forge a new path, with renewed ideals, and a strengthened purpose.

"As I told you on the campaign trail, my Number 1 focus as President is going to be protecting all Americans from the senseless attacks of Al-Qaeda and other terrorists. We all remember the Cincinnati Massacre vividly. I have invited all the family members of those slain in that massacre to be present in the gallery below me today. Today we are all family, we all share your loss, and we all re-commit ourselves to stopping those evil individuals who would seek to weaken our resolve through violence and fear. Family members of the Cincinnati Massacre, I have some good news to share with you this afternoon. Early this morning, in San Antonio, Texas, the San Antonio Police arrested the terrorist responsible for the massacre in Cincinnati.

"I would like to tell you a little bit about that arrest, because it is a story of true American heroes. F.B.I. Lead Investigator Ruddy Montana and his team of investigators have been following up thousands of leads ever since the bombing occurred. They have fielded thousands of calls, investigated physical evidence, interviewed hundreds of witnesses, and tracked everything from fibers left at the scene to shoeprints in the mud. Their investigation ultimately led them to a storage lot in downtown Cincinnati. Surveillance tapes from that storage lot facility revealed the face of the bomber. The F.B.I. handed out that picture to law enforcement officials all over the country.

"This morning, an alert police officer named Ray Gallagos, with only six months experience on the police force, identified a vagrant wandering the streets of San Antonio and interrogated him, believing him to be suspicious. The police officer was quickly able to identify the man from the F.B.I. photo as the Cincinnati Bomber. The man panicked and ran into the Alamo, one of our country's most historic buildings, and a site where true Americans once fought for freedom against great odds.

"When the killer ran into the Alamo, he got more than he bargained for. He ran into some real American heroes. Rosa Trujeo, a maid working in a local hotel, was in the Alamo with her three small girls. She was on disability for a leg injury and carried a crutch. Ms. Trujeo pummeled the bomber with her crutch. At that point, Tommy Dickerson, a 60 year-old Vietnam veteran who was visiting the Alamo, tackled the bomber to the ground and tied his hands behind his back. He was assisted in tying the knots by a den of Cub Scouts who were visiting the Alamo with their den mothers. Truth is certainly stranger than fiction. A terrorist subdued by disabled mother of three, a 60 year-old veteran, and a bunch of children. It makes me proud to be an American, I can tell you that. After Dickerson hogtied the criminal, he called out to the police, who had just surrounded the building. He was handcuffed and is now in custody.

All of you may remember the story of the Alamo, where Jim Bowie and Davy Crockett and a band of other regular Americans held off a superior force for days until the last man gave his last breath for freedom. Well today, we will remember other great Americans at the Alamo, who, like their forefathers of old, faced great odds with bravery and courage and true grit. And this time, the Americans won!"

The crowd erupted with loud applause and cheers.

"Thank you. Now, as we applaud the Americans who were able to apprehend the Cincinnati terrorist, we must remind ourselves that the battle against terrorism continues every day. This morning, many of you may have wondered why Supreme Court Justice Dan Perkins did not swear me in this morning. I have just been informed by the Secret Service that during his morning jog, an assassin with a sniper rifle attempted to shoot and kill Chief Justice Perkins."

The crowd gasped and looked on with concern and open mouths.

"But the proponents of terrorism met another American hero this morning. Gil Johnston, one of the three Secret Service Agents guarding Chief Justice Perkins, bravely got between the assassin's gun and his intended target, saving Chief Justice Perkins' life. The Chief Justice was not injured, although he was obviously very shaken up. His Secret Service protector, unfortunately, was not so lucky. I am sorry to say that Agent Gil Johnston died at the scene from gunshot wounds. Agent Johnston was a veteran of the Gulf War, and the Wars in Iraq and Afghanistan. He leaves behind a wife Nancy and two small children, Ben and Teddy. He will be deeply missed. As my first act as President, I will be awarding the Congressional Medal of Honor to Agent Johnston, and the Medal of Freedom to the heroes of the Alamo."

"I am also proud to say that agents from the federal government caught this assassin shortly after the attack. He was killed in a shoot-out with law enforcement. What his intentions were I cannot say. Whether he was connected with the Cincinnati Bomber I cannot say. What I can say is that we will use every tool the federal government possesses to get to the bottom of these horrible crimes and find out how they occurred and how we can stop similar attacks from occurring again. We will find all the terrorists involved in these attacks, mark my word. We will hunt them, we will arrest them, and if they fight us back, we will most assuredly kill them. Because America does not give in to terrorists!"

The crowd erupted again in wild applause.

"This is a new day, America! A proud new day! This is the beginning of the end for the terrorists. There's a new sheriff in town!"

The Republicans in the crowd liked that comment and cheered; the Democrats not so much. Anna Scall stood next to and just behind the President, and on the "sheriff" comment, she came forward, and beamed from the podium, holding the President's hand upward in victory. Scall waved to the crowd like a beauty pageant winner. Woodson's wife was seated ten feet behind them. Mrs. Woodson looked radiant in her pearls, but she smiled stiffly as she looked at Scall holding her husband's hand. She could not wait to convince her husband to banish that woman from the wheels of power at the earliest opportunity.

"Now let me tell you, America, how we are going to get our economy moving again. My plan…" The President went on for another twenty minutes outlining his agenda.

Back at F.B.I. Headquarters, Ruddy Montana was in the conference room, getting briefed on both the Alamo situation and the events with the Chief Justice. A dozen men were around the table, each with his ear on a cell phone and his eye on a laptop. Agent Ahmad Mahmood came through the glass door of the conference room.

"Hey, Boss, I think you should see this."

Montana left the conference room and came down to Mahmood's office.

"I was running files to see what I could come up with on this Mohammed el Faya guy. Turns out he was in Abu Ghraib. He was in prison there about the same time that all those photos surfaced about abuse in the prison. His file says that he did not have any usable intel, so after a while, they let him go in Jordan."

"OK, so?"

"So guess who his military interrogator was at the time?"

"I give up," said Montana.

"Agent Gil Johnston."

"You have got to be kidding me. So it is possible the Supreme Court Justice was not the target after all. Jeez, I had thought this was a home-grown one. I figured maybe this had something to do with that opinion on gay marriage that is coming up this term. Guess I was wrong. This was plain old revenge."

"It looks that way," said Mahmood. "Also, from what I can tell from his files, this guy was like an expert marksman. If he wanted to take out the Supreme Court Justice, he could have done it easily in one shot. He would not have missed. Johnston was shot four times. That sounds like an angry guy to me."

"But one thing we don't know," said Montana. "How in the world did a guy with no money, left for dead in the streets of Jordan, manage to come to the United States, sneak through border patrol, obtain a sniper rifle, and figure out where to find his C.I.A. interrogator?"

"You raise a good point," said Mahmood. "I wondered that myself. It almost sounds like he had inside help."

"This was starting out as such a good day, Ahmad. Why did you have to ruin it for me?"

Back in the West Wing, the new staff had picked their new offices and were bringing in cardboard boxes, plants, and diplomas. Chance Bixby, the President's new Chief of Staff, Bill Dominic, the new President's foreign policy advisor, and Matt Suba, Vice President Scall's Chief of Staff, were in a huddled meeting in Bixby's office. Bixby had a cell phone cradled to his ear.

"I am hearing this Trujeo woman at the Alamo was a fucking illegal alien. Someone turn on CNN and see if they are saying anything about her. Jesus Fucking Christ, Woodson has probably done 100 speeches railing on illegal immigrants, and now he just announced he is going to pin the Medal of Freeedom on an illegal alien! God, how unlucky can you get!"

"That's easy," said Suba. "Call Immigration and tell them we are making her an American citizen as of last month. Someone lost her paperwork, whatever. We backdate the paperwork, talk to the lady, tell her this is a one-time deal making her a citizen, and to keep her mouth shut. She says nothing, and no one is the wiser. If we get it done fast, no one will ever know."

Bixby really hated Suba. That guy seemed like he never wanted to follow the rules. On the other hand, this was going to be a disaster if they did not do something fast. The Trujeo woman was half of his Inauguration Speech, for Christ's sake, he could not take that back!

"Listen," said Suba. "We have to get on the funeral arrangements for the Secret Service guy right away. I will call the widow and get it all planned out, full military thing with the gun salute, flag, the works. I'll see where she wants to do the funeral."

"That would be fine," said Bixby, barely listening. Bixby called a Deputy Director at Immigration to see if he could fix the Trujeo matter. Surely bumping up naturalization paperwork on one hotel maid could not be that difficult? The official was not in, so Bixby left an urgent message.

"Hey, Chance," said Dominic, "I have some new info on the Chief Justice assassination. I talked to the guys over at the C.I.A. and the Secret Service. They tell me that before coming to the Secret Service, Gil Johnston was an interrogator at Abu Ghraib."

"So?" said Bixby.

"So guess who was interrogated rather roughly at Abu Ghraib?" "You have got to be kidding me."

"Nope. Our shooter, Mohammed el Faya." Dominic shoved the top secret file across Bixby's desk. Bixby looked at it in disgust.

"Annie! Get the team in here now!"

Bixby scowled. If this was just a revenge killing for Abu Ghraib, Keith Olbermann was going to have a field day.

CHAPTER 20. CARCASSONNE

January 20, 2013. 6:15 Paris time, 12:15 p.m. EST. Carcassonne, France.

Doug and Ray were relieved when they heard the Chief Justice had not been killed. They had been following the gay marriage case, *Daltry v. Schwartzenegger*, which was pending before the Supreme Court. If gay marriage was going to be upheld by the Court, they would definitely need Chief Justice Perkins' vote. Ray actually knew someone who knew the Justice's brother Seamus, who was gay. Ray and Doug could not fathom that a judge would vote against gay marriage when his own brother was gay. Morse, his two children, and their new friends returned to their seats for the last few minutes of the bus ride.

The bus bounced its way through the cobblestone streets and dropped them off in the middle of a busy marketplace. Doug and Ray got off the bus first. Ray looked around for a cab, but saw none. He turned back to make sure Morse and his children got off the bus safely. When Morse got off the bus, a man in jeans, a cowboy hat, and a gray and black striped shirt walked up to him with a fold-out map. His olive complexion gave Morse the impression that he was either Arabian or Italian, which for some reason, seemed out of place with the cowboy hat.

"Excuse me, sir, do you speak English?"

Morse replied, "Yes, I do."

"I am trying to read this map here, and it's all in French…"

As the man brought the map closer to Morse, he stealthily pulled out a revolver with a silencer and pointed it at Morse under the map.

In a low voice the man said to Morse, "Easy now, Professor. I have a gun pointed right at you. I need you to bring your children and come with me."

Morse looked over the gunman's shoulder at Ray, who had seen the whole scene go down. Ray's football instincts kicked in when he saw the gunman. He powered his body directly at the man in the cowboy hat, pummeling him from behind into the side of the tour bus like an angry nose tackle. The man did not drop the gun as he fell, however. Ray grabbed the man's wrist before he could use the gun. The gun went off, shooting a bullet into the side of the bus. Concerned tourists started yelling and fled from the bus stop. Ray and the gunman were locked in a battle over the gun.

"RUN!" yelled Ray.

John, Zach, and Zoey Morse bolted away from the bus stop, down the street, weaving in and out of tourists and patio umbrellas. Zach, the cross-country star, quickly took the lead. Zoey, using her skills from soccer, had no problem keeping up. Morse, on the other hand, was slow and trailed behind as the three dodged around parked cars, in and out of market stalls, and down the ancient streets of Carcassonne. They never turned back, afraid of what lay behind them. After about eight blocks, Morse was cramping up and breathing heavily. The teenagers were frustrated with their father, who was clearly out of shape. They worried that he was going to get them killed.

"Come on, Dad! They're coming!" pleaded Zach.

"You run ahead and stay with Zoey. Leave me behind," he gasped. "I will be fine, I just need to rest for a minute," Morse panted.

"Dad, we are not leaving you." Zach and Zoey looked around, while their father caught his breath. Zach saw a large doorway to a castle tower directly to his left. Just then, the dark man in the gray and black shirt, sans his cowboy hat, came around the corner at full speed about two blocks away.

"Quick! In here!" yelled Zach, ushering his dad and sister through the door. They bolted up the steps as fast as they could. After about six stories Morse was exhausted, sweating profusely and slowing down. Down below, he could hear the sound of the gunman. Morse had to push on. His kids were already at the top of the tower. He sprinted up the last two flights, coming out on top of an ancient castle wall.

He was momentarily distracted by the brisk breeze and panoramic sights. The view up here was breathtaking. Straight ahead running in one direction was a long gray stone pathway, with gray castle walls on either side at shoulder height, and cutouts along the top of the wall for long-dead archers.

A moment later, the terror of the moment returned, and Morse ran forward along the top of the castle wall, his children far ahead of him. As he approached a corner of the ramparts, a bullet whizzed by his right arm, exploding into dust in the wall to his right. In sheer panic, he ran as fast as he could along the wall. He made it to the heavy oak door of the next tower. Once inside, he noted that there were no steps heading down. He was inside a small stone chamber. He had to continue through the door on the opposite side. As soon as he burst out the door on the back side, he almost fell across some kind of brown leather and wood contraption. He saw Zach up ahead holding a rope.

"Quick, Pops! Come towards us and get out of the way!"

Morse stepped across a semi-circular lattice cup of wood and leather, attached to a long beam. In a flash, he could see what his son was planning. He scrambled over another ten feet. He helped his son turn a large lever. Just then, the gunman in the gray shirt and jeans came barreling out the door and fell into the wooden cup.

"See ya!" yelled Zach. With that he and his father turned the lever, and the catapult which Zach had set up near the door flung their assailant and his weapon heavenward. The three watched as the gunman hit the wall, and then flew off the edge of the wall, hurtling towards the cobblestones below, where he landed violently.

"Great thinking, Zach!"

"They had this thing up here on the wall, so I figured it was worth a shot."

"I can't believe that worked," smiled Morse.

Down far below, the dark-skinned man in the gray Armani suit and aviator sunglasses suit saw his partner fly off the castle wall and land in a bloody splatter on the gray stones of the marketplace. The man in the suit was not happy. Those Americans would pay for this. He saw them run across the castle walls, and when they went through the door of a tower on the end of the walls, he judged where they would come out below. He would be waiting for them.

Fortunately, however, Zoey's sharp eyes spotted the man in the suit below. The three concocted a plan to avoid him. After running into the end tower, they would duck down below the castle walls where they could not be seen, and crouching, retrace their steps back the way they came. The three went as fast as they could in crouched position back across the ramparts. When they came down to the bottom of the stairs, Morse looked around the corner of the wall and saw no one suspicious. In the distance, they could hear sirens. Obviously, the police had made it to the scene, either in response to the gunshot or the dead man. The nearest cab would be out the front gate, but that was the obvious way out. The man in the gray suit would probably be waiting for them there. Morse decided to cut back across the village to the Basilica of St. Nazaire and wait it out there for a while.

They walked up the steps into the grand entrance on the north side of the church through the tall columns decorated with leaves, flowers, and demons. The basilica inside was dark and tall. The extended Romanesque vault was set on rows of towering columns, which alternated between circular and square. At the end of the great hall was a gigantic circular window of stained glass. Along the walls were smaller works of stained glass showing the lives of Jesus, St. Paul, and St. Celse. They quickly made their way down the great hall of the Basilica, looking for a good place to hide. As they got near the front, they happened to pass on their left the empty fourteenth century tomb of St. Pierre de Rochefort, the former Bishop of Carcassonne from 1300 to 1322, who was responsible for nearly all the Gothic work of the Basilica. The tomb was behind a tall, slender wall. On the wall were three figures carved into the stone. The middle figure was clearly the bishop, wearing his bishop's miter and staff. On either side were carvings of a deacon. A pointed triangle, like the roof of a house, was carved above each figure, and above the triangles was another circular window of stained glass.

This was clearly the "black bishop," Morse was sure of it. When he was on the bus, Morse had predicted that there might be tiles on the floor in front of the bishop set out in the form of a chessboard. Then all he would have to do is find the square on the board corresponding to the bishop's best move, and the clue would be behind that tile on the floor. But when Morse saw the real tomb of the bishop, he was disappointed. There were not tiles set forth like a chessboard. There were some bricks in the wall, but there was nothing that one would readily identify as looking like a chessboard. In any event, there was no place to hide here. They moved across the church and looked over on the right side, where there were more stone engravings, this time for the Tomb of Bishop Radulphe. Again, there was nothing resembling a chessboard. And once again, there was no place to hide. Just then, a man came running down the main aisle of the Basilica towards them. As he got closer, they could see it was Doug. He had his Nikon camera strapped across his shoulder.

"There you are. I am so glad I found you. Listen, Ray was shot in the arm. He is in an ambulance right now on his way to the hospital. He told me to protect you, but guys, I am just paralyzed with fear right now about Ray. That is all I can think about. I know what Ray said, but I really feel like my place is with him in the hospital. I hope you understand."

“Of course we do,” said Morse. “Go with Ray, and please thank him. He saved our lives.”

“Thank you so much for understanding.” Doug sprinted back down the aisle of the Basilica towards the entrance. As he got near the entrance, he almost collided with the man in the gray suit.

“Excuse me, sir,” said the dark-skinned man in the sunglasses, grabbing Doug’s arm. “I am looking for my friend and his two teenagers, a boy and a girl. He looks like this, except he is bald.” He handed Doug a photograph. Doug was scared to death.

“Um, yes, as a matter of fact, I did see them about five minutes ago in the Cathedral of St. Michel, over there. They were acting strange, and then I saw them hide behind the pipe organ. I guess they were playing some kind of game or something, I don’t know.”

“Thank you, you have been most helpful.”

The man in the glasses and gray suit turned and ran out of the church.

In the meantime, John Morse and his children were at the front of the church, and, from behind a statute of St. Celse, saw Doug talking to the gunman. He would find them in no time. They would have to hide. Looking around frantically, Zach Morse saw the church’s confessional, and alerted his father. The three bolted over to the confessional, pulled aside the purple velvet curtain, and went inside into the blackness. They never saw Doug direct the gunman to a different cathedral.

In a traditional Catholic confessional, the priest would slide open a small wooden slot about one foot square, revealing a mesh screen. The penitent would then confess his sins to the priest through the screen. Fortunately for the Morses, no priest was on duty in the confessional today, so no one knew they were in the dark room. They were quite cramped in the small box. They shifted positions a few times quietly to remain comfortable. Something was stabbing into Morse’s back. He wanted to get a look at it so he could figure out how the three of them could contort their bodies to fit in the confessional without cramping up. He pulled out his pen light and turned it on. A small wooden statue of Bishop Rochefort was attached to the wall inside the confessional. It was the statue which had been pressing into Morse’s back. He rearranged his position so that the statue was not pressing into his spinal column. He turned off his light.

“Daddy, it is really dark in here, I’m scared,” said Zoey.

Morse agreed it was dark.

Dark. Like the dark squares on a chessboard.

The bishop in the dark. The dark bishop!

Morse reached his fingers through the mesh screen and slid open the wooden window normally opened by the priest. In the darkness, he could make out the screen separating priest and penitent. The screen.

Wait a minute. What had Ray said about the chess move? The dark bishop was screening the queen from calling check. By moving the bishop out of the way, there was a discovered check. The dark bishop's screen. Morse looked at the wire mesh of the confessional and the bishop's statue on the wall. That was it!

Morse turned on his pen light again.

"Here, Zach, hold this," he whispered.

"Dad, you have to turn that light out, you are going to get us killed," whispered Zach.

"I will be quiet, I promise."

Morse took out his Swiss Army knife, pulled out the tiny slotted screwdriver and began undoing the screws on the four corners of the mesh screen. When he finished, he pulled on the screen. It still did not budge. It must be glued as well, Morse thought. He pushed back the screwdriver into the knife and pulled out the biggest blade. With his fingers, he gently cut away the glue on the side of the wood holding in the screen to the wall separating the priest's part of the confessional from that of the penitent. After about five minutes he had most of the glue cut away. He put his fingers into the mesh and yanked again and this time the screen, surrounded by a frame of wood on all sides, came out. He shined his penlight into the rectangular hole made from the missing screen. The wall panel separating the two parts of the confessional was made out of painted brown wood, and was about eight inches thick. When the screen was removed, however, Morse could tell that the panel was actually hollow on the bottom part of the panel. He shined the penlight downward toward the separating board into the hollow space between the wood. There was definitely something there. He reached his fingers in gingerly and pulled out a long cylindrical, rusted metal pipe, with a cap on the end. He twisted open the cap on the top. There were scrolls inside!

Meanwhile, the man in the dark suit had scurried over to the Cathedral of St. Michel, based upon the erroneous directions given to him by Doug. After fifteen minutes of searching, the man in the suit knew he had been duped. He sprinted back to the Basilica, in the hopes that his prey would still be there. When he dashed into the great hall of the Basilica, he checked every pew. They were nowhere to be found. He checked the left side and the right and could not find them anywhere. He figured they must have already left. Just as he was about to leave, he looked at the old confessional to the right of the altar. The confessional had been equipped with a small purple light over the top of the priest's door and a small green light over the penitent's section of the confessional. The light was electronically rigged to the priest's seat and the penitent's kneeler. In this way, anyone seeking confession could know immediately whether a priest was present and available for taking confession, and whether the stall for the penitent was already taken. He noticed something odd. The green light for the penitent's box was lit but the priest's purple light was not. That made no sense. Why would someone go into a confessional if no priest was there? Unless they were hiding. As he got closer, he noticed a small flicker of light under the penitent's curtain. They were definitely in there. He walked over to the curtain with his gun and silencer drawn.

He yanked open the curtain and was immediately hit with a metal pole to the face, slammed into his eye like a jousting sword. He fell back in pain, holding his eye, and losing the gun. Zach quickly kicked the gun across the floor, but the gunman grabbed his ankle, knocking him down. Zach tried to kick the man in the gray suit back with his free leg, but the man was fast, and soon had Zach in a headlock on the floor. Morse ran up to the assailant with his pipe again, hoping to free his son, but the man in the suit pulled out a stiletto from his pocket and put the blade to Zach's neck.

"Not another move, Professor, or I slit his throat right here."

Morse froze. The gunman stood up, holding Zach by the neck with his threatening blade, and moved backwards across the floor until he was within reach of his gun. Then he picked up the gun from the floor and released Zach, who moved back with his father and sister. The gunman pointed the gun at them.

"Put down the pipe." Morse did as he was instructed.

"Now, you are going to begin by telling me everything you know about the prophecy."

"What prophecy?" asked Morse.

"Come now, Professor, we are not stupid. We know you came to France to obtain an ancient prophecy. I know that you have parts of the prophecy already. I want to know what you know."

"I assume you are referring to the prophecy of Nostradamus," said the Professor. "We were able to retrieve some of his work from Salon and more from Agen. But I assure you, this has only academic interest. If you have read any of Nostradamus' other works, I am sure you will agree that he was not much of a prophet. His prophecies are vague and indecipherable, and could mean almost anything. It is certainly not worth killing someone over."

"Professor, one thing you do not want to do to a man who has a gun aimed at your head is to lie to him. You know as well as I do that the Missing 58 quatrains are the true prophecies. How many of them have you found?"

Morse considered a moment.

"Twelve."

"Give them to me now."

Morse paused, and then reached in his bag, pulling out the scroll with the twelve pages of the Bible containing the first twelve prophecies.

"Where are the rest of them?"

"I do not have them."

"Where are they?" The gunman put his revolver to Morse's head. "TELL ME!"

"I do not know," Morse stammered. "All I know is that they are somewhere in Carcassonne, and they have something to do with a bishop."

"And how do you know that?"

Morse reached in his bag and pulled out the scroll with the verse about the flying pig. He explained the story and then showed him the reference to the chessboard.

"And that is all you have?"

"Yes, I swear!"

"Very well, then, Professor, we will carry on the quest without you."

He aimed the gun at them.

"Wait! Why kill us? What is the point? These prophecies dealt with events in the fifteenth and sixteenth centuries. What could possibly be so important about them that you would need to kill an old man and two teenagers over? Your Qur'an teaches non-violence. Why go against the teachings of your holiest book?"

The gunman seemed very agitated.

"Do not lecture me about my religion, Professor Morse. Certain events are in motion right now that will change the course of history. You do not know of them now, but if you continue on this foolish quest for the prophecies, you will find them. And the man planning this course is not about to let that happen. Goodbye, Professor." The gunman leveled his gun again.

Just then, a man behind the gunman impaled him violently in the back of the head with a long, metal candelabrum, driving the middle post of the candelabra into the back of the gunman's skull. He fell forward, lifeless. Standing over the body, filled with adrenaline and shaking in fear, was their friend Doug from the bus.

"Oh my God, I cannot believe I just did that!" he said.

"Doug! Thank you so much!" cried the Professor. "You saved our lives again!"

The group looked down at the gunman. Blood was pouring from his head wound onto the stone floor of the Basilica. Morse took out a handkerchief, and wiped down the candelabra so that no one would find Doug's prints on it. They were careful not to step in the blood. Morse picked up the pipe from the floor and threw it in his bag and zipped it up.

"Why did you come back?" asked Morse.

"Well, I was half way to the front gate when I stopped. I figured my misdirection was probably going to hold him off for only about ten minutes, and Ray made me promise I would look after you. I cannot believe I did that." He stood motionless, staring at the dead body.

"Come on," said Morse. "We have to get going. We do not want to be at the scene when the police find this." They ran down the aisle to the front of the church and then walked calmly out the exit. It did not appear that anyone had seen them inside the church. They made their way through the crowds to the front gate of Carcassonne, and then walked down to one of the streets below, where there was a line of cabs. Doug was headed to the hospital to help Ray. Doug and Morse exchanged business cards.

"I cannot tell you how much you and Ray have done to help our family. We will forever be in your debt. Whatever you need at any time, you call me, and it's yours."

"Thanks, John. We will give you a call when we get back to the States."

Doug hugged the teenagers and Morse and got into his cab.

Morse took another cab with his children off to the Carcassonne Airport. During the cab ride, Morse unscrewed the cap on the metal pipe taken from the church.

Zach whispered to his father. "Dad, put that thing away, this treasure hunt has almost gotten us killed four times."

"Well, we won't be able to take a metal pipe on an airplane. It is a weapon. So we might as well get rid of the pipe now and take what is inside." Morse pulled out the scrolls that lie within and then set the pipe on the floorboards of the cab. He looked over at his son with a forlorn look. Zach knew his father could not resist looking what was inside.

"Oh, all right, go ahead. But you promised us, no matter what, we are going home."

Morse unrolled the first set of scrolls. Like the last time, pages of a Bible had been pasted onto the scroll, with prophetic quatrains written in India ink over the type. There were 37 additional quatrains in all. Morse looked at the first quatrain.

13.
Il écrit d'amants et de rois,
De fantômes et de monsters,
De faunes et de fées dans les bois,
Les pièces sont écrites par le Chantre.

He writes of lovers and of kings,
Of ghosts and monsters,
Of fauns and fairies in the woods,
The plays are written by the Bard.

The thirteenth quatrain obviously was referring to Shakespeare, who lived long after Nostradamus was alive. Morse scanned the remaining quatrains. He would have to translate the rest when they had more time. He rolled the scroll back up, and put it in his bag.

The second scroll contained another "confession" of Nostradamus.

La Deuxième Confession de Michel de Nostradamus:
La Fraude

Moi, Michel de Nostradame, avoue solennellement avoir commis de la fraude. J'ai fait semblant d'être docteur en médecine quand, à vrai dire, j'ai été renvoyé de la Faculté de Médecine et je n'ai aucune formation en médecine. A Lyon j'ai donné une ordonnance sans valeur à une femme, et je lui ai facturé dix couronnes. Quand elle a protesté que l'ordonnance ne valait rien, et qu'elle n'allait pas mieux, j'ai refusé de lui rendre l'argent. J'ai essayé de guérir la goutte en brûlant un trou dans la poitrine de mon patient en me servant d'in bouton ardent. Puis je l'ai couvert de jus de rose , de beurre et d'une perle d'argent et de cuivre. Il n'y a aucune justification pour ce traitement qui non seulement ne guérit point la patiente mais aussi lui cause une douleur insoutenable. Ma pillule de rose, que j'ai prétendu pouvoir guérir la Peste, est aussi frauduleuse. J'ai manqué de payer mes dettes. Quand Jean de Morel m'a prêté l'argent pour payer l'addition à mon hôtel à Paris, je ne lui ai pas rendu l'argent, et quand il m'a écrit six ans plus tard pour demander son argent , j'ai fait semblant de ne pas le connaître. J'ai déclaré que j'étais astrologue, capable de lire des diagrammes astrologiques de naisssances, mais ces interprétations sont pleines d'erreurs, car je ne sais pas du tout calculer avec justesse le mouvement des corps célestes à travers le ciel. Finalement, mes prophéties d'événements futurs sont des inventions pures et simples et sont rédigéesd'une telle manière qu'elles peuvent dire n'importe quoi ou rien du tout. Ce grand péché de la Fraude, je l'avoue.

Michel de Nostradame

Translated into English, it read:

The Second Confession of Michel de Nostradame:
Fraud

I, Michel de Nostradame, do solemnly confess that I have committed fraud. I have held myself out to be a medical doctor, when in fact I was expelled from medical school and have no medical training whatsoever. In Lyon, I gave a woman a worthless prescription, and charged her ten crowns. When she protested that the prescription was worthless, and she no better, I refused to give her the money back. I have attempted to cure gout by burning a hole in my patient's chest with a flaming hot knob, which I then covered with rose juice, butter, and a bead made of silver and copper. There is absolutely no medical justification for such a treatment, which not only fails to cure the patient, but causes the patient excruciating pain. My rose pill, which I claimed cured the Plague, is also a fraud. I have failed to repay my debts. When Jean de Morel lent me money to pay my hotel bill in Paris, I never paid him back, and when he wrote me six years later asking for his money, I pretended not to know him. I have held myself out as an astrologer able to give readings of astrological birth charts, yet my readings are replete with errors, as I haven't the foggiest idea how to correctly calculate the movements of the heavenly bodies across the sky. Finally, my prophecies of future events are complete fabrications, and are worded in such a way as to mean anything or nothing at all. For this great sin of Fraud, I confess.

Michel de Nostradame

Morse rolled the scroll back up and placed it inside his bag. Then he opened up the third scroll.

La page, le soldat, le héros,
Le defenseur de Cicéron,
L'astrologue, le médecin,
Le plus bien grammairien Latin
Della Rovere est son ami
Le botaniste, l'érudit, L'hérétique présumé
L'ennemi de Monsieur Dolet,
Le plus grand champion de Virgile
(le travail de Homer est infantile!)
L'historien, le professeur,
Dans la vie ultérieure un grand auteur
Que vous cherchez êtes peut-être
Dans le tombeau de son ancêtre
Consulter sa carte et vous verrez
L'avenir d'humanité révélé!

Morse translated the text into his notebook:

The page, the soldier, the hero,
The defender of Cicero,
The astrologer, the doctor,
The best Latin grammarian,
Della Rovere is his friend,
The botanist, the scholar,
The alleged heretic,
The enemy of Monsieur Dolet,
The greatest champion of Virgil
(the work of Homer is infantile)
The historian, the teacher,
In later life, the great author,
What you seek is, perhaps,
In the tomb of his ancestor
Look at this map and you will see
The future of the mankind revealed!

"What do you think it means?" asked Zach.

"I think this is an easy one," said Morse. "This is referring to Julius Caesar Scaliger, Nostradamus' one-time friend and mentor. In his early life, Scaliger was a page and a soldier and, he claimed, a war hero. He was an astrologer and a doctor and a Latin grammarian. He was the personal doctor to the Bishop Antonio della Rovere, who was his friend and patron. He wrote a great compendium of plants in which he catalogued hundreds of species of plants, so he could certainly be called a botanist. In 1538, he was accused of heresy, but later acquitted. He hated a man named Dolet, who was a contemporary of his at the time, and even wrote a poem vulgarly applauding his death. He was a historian, a teacher, and an author in later life. There is no question this refers to Julius Caesar Scaliger. So all we have to do is find the tomb of his ancestor, which is listed on the map. And I know exactly where that is!"

"Where is it?" asked Zach.

"In Verona, Italy. In the 1300s, the Scaliger family members were the Lords of Verona. Julius Caesar Scaliger always claimed to be a descendant of the royal family of Scaligers. In the ancient church of Santa Maria

Antica, which still exists today, there are a series of tombs, or 'tempietti,' enclosing the sarcophagi of the great Scaliger Lords of Verona, which must be what Julius Caesar Scaliger is referring to as the tomb of his ancestor."

"What about the picture of the horse at the bottom?" asked Zoey.

"The most spectacular of the Scaliger tombs is the tomb of Cangrande Scaliger, which is raised over the top of an archway leading into the Church. Directly on top of the sarcophagus is a huge equestrian statue. That is the horse. So the clue must be hidden inside the tomb of Cangrande Scaliger in Verona!"

Just then, the cab pulled up to the airport. Morse put the scrolls away in his bag. After paying the fare, the three rushed into the airport. Morse looked at the electronic screens for Air France showing outgoing flights. It was now 9 p.m. Paris time. Unfortunately, there were no further flights tonight going to Paris or London or anywhere in the United States. There was a 9:45 p.m. flight to Bordeaux; a 9:30 p.m. flight to Rome; a 9:30 p.m. flight to Verona; a 9:50 flight to Venice; a 10:00 p.m. flight to Monaco; and a 10:00 p.m. flight to Madrid.

Morse went up to the Air France counter. Are there any flights first thing in the morning leaving from Bordeaux, Rome, Verona, Venice, Monaco, or Madrid going directly to the United States? The agent spent a few minutes checking her screens.

"The earliest flight I have is Air France Flight 5377 leaving Verona, Italy, tomorrow at 10:50 a.m. arriving in New York, NY at 9:25 p.m. I also have an Alitalia flight leaving from Rome at 11:15 a.m., arriving in New York, NY at 10:30 p.m."

"We will take the Air France flight," said Morse.

His children looked at him suspiciously.

"What?"

"You promised us we are going to go home," said Zach.

"We are going home, first thing in the morning."

"But let me guess," said Zach, "When we get to Verona, we may do a little sight-seeing first?"

Morse shrugged. "Well, if we are just killing time, we might as well solve the final clues of the mystery, don't you think?"

"You are unbelievable," said Zach. "All I can say is, when we get home, my hair better grow back soon."

CHAPTER 21. VERONA

January 20, 2013, 11 p.m. Paris time. Somewhere over Northern Italy

As his children slept on the Ryan Air flight to Verona, Morse took out his notebook and the scroll containing the 37 new quatrains. He copied each of the quatrains into his notebook first in French, and then next to it, his English translation. When he was finished with the first six, his notebook looked like this:

13.
Il écrit d'amants et de rois,
De fantômes et de monstres,
De faunes et de fées dans les bois,
Les pièces sont écrites par le Chantre.

He writes of lovers and of kings,
Of ghosts and monsters,
Of fauns and fairies in the woods,
The plays are written by the Bard.

14.
Il maîtrise l'astrologie et la physique.
Il regarde les étoiles avec sa lunette.
"La terre tourne autour du soleil," dit-il à ses critiques,
Et pour cela, on l'arrête.

He masters astrology and physics.
He looks at the stars through his telescope.
"The earth revolves around the sun," he says to his critics,
And for that, he is arrested.

15.
Le plus grand savant qui soit jamais né.
Les lois du mouvement et de la terre,
Les lois des mathématiques et de la gravité.
Déguisé, il arrêtera les faussaires.

The greatest scientist ever born.
The laws of motion and of earth,
The laws of math and gravity.
Disguised, he will arrest the counterfeiters.

16.
Le four de Farriner causera un feu.
Bientôt tout Londres est englouti par les flames,
Le Maire ne fait pas ce qu'il peut,
La destruction pour tous les hommes et toutes les dames.

Farriner's oven will cause a fire.
Soon all of London is engulfed in flames,
The Mayor does not do what he can,
Destruction for all the men and ladies.

17.
Ces trois amènent le son de la musique.
Les anges sourient à leurs symphonies.
Chacun est doué et unique,
Les plus beaux sons jamais écrits.

These three bring the sound of music.
The angels smile at their symphonies.
Each is gifted and unique,
The most beautiful sounds ever written.

18.
Fâchés contre les impots et assoiffés de liberté,
Ils déchargeront leur thé dans la baie profonde.
Surpassés en nombre, ils battront les Anglais.
Leur drapeau aura des étoiles et des bandes.

Angry at taxes and thirsting for liberty
They will dump their tea in the deep bay.
Although outnumbered, they will defeat the English.
Their flag will have stars and stripes.

Morse wrote his solution for Quatrains 13 to 18:

13. WILLIAM SHAKESPEARE
14. GALILEO
15. ISCAAC NEWTON?
16. GREAT FIRE OF LONDON
17. BACH, BEETHOVEN, MOZART
18. THE AMERICAN REVOLUTION.

The scientist who discovered the laws of motion clearly sounded like Isaac Newton, but Morse was unsure about the part about arresting counterfeiters. He could not get an Internet signal on the plane, so he could not look up the question. He would later learn that Isaac Newton had once worked for the Mint, and had disguised himself in a sting operation to locate and arrest counterfeiters.

Morse went through the remaining quatrains (see Appendix) and provided similar solutions. He now had a total of 49 of the missing 58 quatrains. His finished list looked as follows:

1. KING HENRY VIII
2. VLAD THE IMPALER
3. POPE ALEXANDER VI
4. POPE JULIUS II
5. POPE LEO X
6. MARTIN LUTHER
7. POPE CLEMENT VII
8. POPE PAUL III
9. COPERNICUS
10. POPE PAUL IV
11. POPE JULIUS III
12. IVAN THE TERRIBLE
13. WILLIAM SHAKESPEARE
14. GALILEO
15. ISCAAC NEWTON?
16. GREAT FIRE OF LONDON
17. BACH, BEETHOVEN, MOZART
18. THE AMERICAN REVOLUTION.

19. THE FRENCH REVOLUTION
20. NAPOLEON BONAPARTE
21. CHARLES DARWIN
22. LOUIS PASTEUR
23. AMERICAN SLAVERY
24. ALEXANDER GRAHAM BELL AND THE TELEPHONE
25. THOMAS EDISON AND THE LIGHTBULB
26. ALBERT EINSTEIN
27. WRIGHT BROTHERS AND THE AIRPLANE
28. WORLD WAR I
29. HENRY FORD AND THE AUTOMOBILE
30. JOSEPH STALIN
31. ADOLF HITLER
32. JOSEF MENGELE
33. HIROSHIMA AND NAGASAKI
34. MOHATMA GHANDI
35. MOTHER THERESA OF CALCUTTA
36. WATSON AND CRICK, DNA
37. JOHN F. KENNEDY
38. MARTIN LUTHER KING
39. MOON LANDING
40. POL POT AND THE KHMER ROUGE
41. IDI AMIN
42. STEVE JOBS AND THE PERSONAL COMPUTER
43. AIDS
44. LADY DIANA
45. TIMOTHY MCVEIGH
46. SADDAM HUSSEIN
47. UDAY HUSSEIN
48. OSAMA BIN LADEN AND 9/11
49. DESERT STORM, IRAQ WAR, AFGHANISTAN WAR, ABU GHRAIB

Morse could not say, of course, whether these scrolls were the genuine article or forgeries. That would have to await carbon dating and a comparison of handwriting samples by experts. He was, of course, very skeptical by nature. But one thing was for sure. If these were forgeries, someone had gone to a significant amount of trouble for a hoax. The purpose of such a hoax he could not imagine. And why would anyone wishing to play a hoax involve gunmen with real guns? The man in the gray suit was definitely impaled by Doug's candelabra in the Basilica. Morse had checked the man's wounds immediately after the incident, just to make sure this was not some elaborate con game. He was definitely dead. Why would anyone get killed over a practical joke?

The man in the gray suit had said just before he died that events were in motion and that the prophecies would give away the hand of the killers. These prophecies went all the way up through 2010 at least. If there were nine more prophecies, could the new quatrains in Verona actually predict their own futures?

Morse put away the scroll in his bag, which had gotten considerably bulkier since Zach had placed his longboard in it. When he got to their hotel, he would need to immediately obtain a map of Verona. They had very little time to look for the last set of scrolls, and Morse was determined to use what little time they had efficiently. Fortunately, Morse had a good friend and colleague, Benito Parducci, who was Director of Antiquities for the City of Verona. He was hoping his friend would give him a peek into the Scaliger sarcophagus first thing in the morning.

A few hours later, the Air France 747 touched down in Verona International Airport. As they got off the plane, Morse and his children crouched down low behind other passengers, worried that more gunmen might be waiting for them here in Verona, as they had been in Carcassonne. However, once they passed into the general terminal area, they saw no one who looked suspicious, and they were able to breathe a little easier. They caught a quick cab to the five-star Due Torri Hotel Baglioni, in the heart of the historic center of Verona. The tangerine and cream colored tiles, fresh white roses, and ornate columns in the bright lobby welcomed them. Morse paid in cash, for fear someone could be tracking his credit card and learn their location. He asked for a wakeup call at 5 a.m. Zach and Zoey groaned when they heard that, but were otherwise too tired to complain. He obtained a map of Verona from the hotel clerk. When he got to the room, it was after 1 a.m. Morse looked up Benito Parducci in the Verona phone book on the night stand. Fortunately, Parducci was listed. Morse made a note of his phone and address. Then they hit the blue and butter striped super king bed like bricks and fell asleep within a matter of minutes.

When the alarm went off at 5 a.m., Morse jumped out of bed in the dark.

"Come on guys, we have to get going. Who wants the first shower?"

"Dad, you have got to be joking," moaned Zach, crouching in a ball under the soft covers. "It's still dark out."

"Dad, we haven't slept in a week," complained Zoey, also burying herself under the covers in the darkness. "Can't we sleep a little while longer?"

"Guys we only have a couple hours here and then we can go home. We have one more riddle to solve, and we know where it is. Come on!"

Neither teenager moved from the bed.

"OK, I will take the first shower, but I want you two up after that."

Morse took a hot shower. He stayed in until the entire bathroom was fogged up, letting the hot water pulsate his sore muscles. He was so out of shape. He definitely needed to hit the gym when he got home.

He called down to room service for a fresh pot of black coffee and some fresh fruit for the kids. At 6 a.m., Morse called his friend Benito Parducci, waking him up from a dead sleep.

"*Buon giorno, il mio amico, questo è John Morse da UCLA.*"

"John Morse? "*Ah, sì, Professore Morse. Così buono di sentire da lei. Ma è molto presto qui*"!

"Yes, my friend, I know it is early. I am here in Verona."

Parducci spoke English better than Morse spoke Italian, so they switched languages.

"Ah, fantastic! Well, we must have the lunch then. What brings you to Verona?"

"You are not going to believe this, but I am on a treasure hunt of sorts."

"*Una caccia al tesoro.* A treasure hunt, you say?"

"Yes, I was summoned to France last week because a local priest there found an ancient manuscript of the prophet Nostradamus from the sixteenth century. At first I thought it was all a hoax, but Benito, I tell you, the manuscript I found looks quite genuine. At any event, the manuscript sent me looking for a final clue, which appears to be hidden in the sarcophagus of our good friend Cangrande della Scalla."

"The Big Dog?"

Morse laughed "Cane grande" in Italian means "big dog." "Yes, the very one."

"Are you putting me on? Is this a practical joke?"

"I assure you it is not. I can show you the manuscripts if you like. It is most intriguing."

"Well, I remember you always liked adventure. You Americans all think you are Indiana Jones."

"Yes, well, I have been feeling like that these past few days. Do you think you could meet me over at the Scaliger Tombs this morning? I have a flight which leaves in just a few hours."

"Well, normally, I would say no, but now you have me intrigued. In addition, it will be funny to see the look on your face when you see there is nothing in the sarcophagus but a very ugly mummified body."

"Are you certain?"

"Quite certain. In February 2004, we took the lid off the sarcophagus and removed the body, because historians wanted to try to determine Cangrande's cause of death. His mummified body was actually quite well preserved, and they were able to detect significant amounts of digitalis in his body, suggesting that he was poisoned. The local theory here is that Cangrande was murdered by his ambitious nephew. I will let you look inside, but I have seen the inside of the sarcophagus several times, and there is nothing in there but a body."

"Perhaps it is hidden inside the handle or in a secret panel or something?"

"Well, we shall have fun finding out. How about I meet you in one hour at the Arch and we shall go on your—how do you say it—'crazy chase of gooses.'"

"Very funny, Benito. OK, I will see you then."

Morse corralled his children out of bed and by 6:30 they were ready to explore beautiful Verona. When they left the hotel, they had a beautiful three block walk to the Tombs of the Scaligeri. In the distance, they could see the tall, red brick Lamberti Clock Tower, the hallmark of the city, standing guard since 1172 over the snaking and curving River Adige and the red-roofed buildings of the city. The clock tower's top had fallen off in 1403 when it was hit by lighting, but in the 1400s, the resourceful Veronians had built the tower higher still. Another ten blocks away was the ancient Roman Arena, carved out of pure marble, which could seat

20,000 people. And looming in the distance near the Arena, on the banks of the Adige, was the beautiful red brick Castelvecchio, the ancient castle built by the della Scalas, with its strange turrets that were curved rather than squared off. The Ponte Scaligero, or Bridge of the Scaligeris, ran away from, and could only be accessed from, the castle, and ran across the Adige. The bridge was said to be the escape route for the della Scalas if they needed to leave the city.

The city was filled with piazzas, or large plazas, carpeted with gray stone, ancient buildings, and lots of pigeons. Zach was excited when he saw the wide-open piazzas, and grabbed his longboard with the green wheels out of Morse's zippered bag. At last, some fun! Zach rolled down the piazza on his skateboard, and Zoey ran after him asking for a turn. The two jumped off small staircases and ramps and hurtled towards unsuspecting pigeons, which were not used to fleeing from longboarding American teenagers. There was not a cloud in the sky this morning. The air was crisp and cool. It was a wonderful day to hunt for buried treasure.

After a few blocks they arrived at the famous archway to the Scaligeri Tombs. Over the top of the Arch was an ancient sarcophagus. In stone directly above the sarcophagus, was a stone statue of a man lying on a bed with a sheet. Directly above that was a small pointed roof, and above that, a statue of a man riding a horse. In the courtyard near the arch was a black iron fence, with sharp-pointed tops. Inside the area enclosed by the fence were several platforms five or six feet off the ground, which rose on the corners on columns to exquisitely ornate Gothic roofs. Under each roof, on a platform, was another Scaliger tomb.

After waiting about twenty minutes, Benito Parducci arrived. He was a happy fat man who looked like Stromboli the Puppetmaster from Disney's Pinocchio, bald with the exception of bushy brown hair over his ears, and a full brown beard. He was wearing a white linen shirt, a blue vest with a loud zigzag pattern, and black pants.

"Hello, Mr. Indiana Jones!" laughed Parducci. "So good to see you." He gave Morse a big bear hug.

"And who are these children?"

"These are my children, Zach and Zoey. Kids, say hello to Dr. Parducci."

"Oh my goodness, they have gotten so big! Last time I saw you in California, they were no bigger than my knee. You are very lucky, Professor!"

The teenagers shook Parducci's hand, and then, growing weary of adult talk, went back into the piazza to skateboard some more.

"Come, let us sit down over here and look at these manuscripts over some nice black coffee."

Parducci motioned him over to a small café in the Piazza. Morse sat down and unzipped his bag, removing all the manuscripts taken from the journeys. He quickly recounted their tale from Salon de Provence to Agen, back to Carcassonne, and finally to Verona. Parducci was quite concerned over the part of the story relating to the gunmen.

"My friend, I am so sorry. I cannot imagine who would want to kill someone over an old manuscript. No one followed you here, did they?" Parducci looked around nervously.

"No, we made quite sure of that. I think they have lost the trail for now anyway. So what do you think, could we get a look at the sarcophagus?

"Of course, I will take you there now."

Parducci walked over to the Church of Santa Maria Antica, and Parducci unlocked a non-descript doorway inside one of the arches. He led Morse up a very narrow and steep staircase two stories up. At the top of the staircase was another door, which Parducci unlocked. When the door opened, Morse could see that he was standing on top of the archway, right next to the sarcophagus of Cangrande della Scala. To the left was the open air of the piazza and the front of the sarcophagus. To Morse's right was to the dark back wall behind the sarcophagus. Parducci directed Morse to the opposite side of the sarcophagus and explained that they would both need to lift the cover off together and place it to the side. Morse did as he was directed. Inside was a mummy, with tattered remnants of clothing. Parducci would not let Morse touch anything inside the tomb.

"I will search. What is it exactly we are looking for?"

"A set of scrolls, probably wrapped up inside some type of tube, if it is similar to the last two we have seen." Parducci gingerly searched all around the mummy, looking for anything matching that description. He also searched for secret panels inside the sarcophagus and found none. Morse was disappointed. Parducci and Morse then returned the cover of the sarcophagus to its original position. Upon Morse's urging, Parducci continued to look all around the sarcophagus, hoping to find a hidden panel or a hollow handle, but he could find none. Morse was sure this was the place. Where could it be? Morse checked all along the stone walls around the sarcophagus and could not find any hidden compartment in the stone.

"Perhaps it is in the equestrian statue up on the roof. The scroll did contain a picture of a horse."

"My friend, I sincerely doubt it. In 2003, we performed restoration on the equestrian statue. I am confident one of the workers would have found a hidden scroll if there was such a thing. I have probably gone too far in letting you up here already. I cannot possibly let you go climbing along the roof, where you could fall off. I am sorry; I wish I had more answers for you."

"Can I see that last scroll again?" asked Parducci. Parducci looked at the scroll over Morse's shoulder, as Morse read the translation.

Le page, le soldat, le héros
Le défenseur de Cicéron
L'astrologue, le médecin,
Le meilleur grammmairien du latin,
Son ami est Della Rovere,
Le botaniste, l'érudit,
L'hérétique présumé,
L'ennemi de Monsieur Dolet,
Le plus grand champion de Virgile
(L'oeuvre d'Homère est infantile)
L'historien, le professeur,
Plus tard, le grand auteur.
Ce que vous cherchez est, peut-être,
Dans le tombeau de son ancêtre.
Regardez sa carte et vous verrez
L'avenir de l'humanité révélé!

The page, the soldier, the hero,
The defender of Cicero,
The astrologer, the doctor,
The best Latin grammarian,
Della Rovere is his friend,
The botanist, the scholar,
The alleged heretic,
The enemy of Monsieur Dolet,

The greatest champion of Virgil
(the work of Homer is infantile)
The historian, the teacher,
In later life, the great author,
What you seek is, perhaps,
In the tomb of his ancestor
Look at this map and you will see
The future of the mankind revealed!

"You said, 'Look at THIS map and you will see…,'" said Parducci.

"Yes, so?" asked Morse.

"In French 'CETTE' is 'this.' 'SA' is 'his.' It says 'SA CARTE' on your scroll. The correct translation is: 'Look at HIS map.'"

Morse looked at the words again. What a stupid blunder! Of course, Parducci was right.

"HIS map….I wonder what that means."

"I think I know what it means," said Parducci. "I agree this first part refers to Julius Caesar Scaliger. But Julius Caesar Scaliger's account of his family heritage was largely a fabrication. He was not, as he claimed, a descendant of the royal Scaligers. Quite to the contrary. His father was from Verona, but he was no nobleman. He was a manuscript editor and cartographer. His name was Benedetto Bordone. He made maps. So 'HIS' map means the map drawn by Benedetto Bordone, his father. Unless I am badly mistaken, this map you have here on the scroll was probably a copy of one drawn by Julius Caesar Scaliger's father, Benedetto Bordone."

"So that means," said Morse, "that the final clue is not in the sarcophagus of Cangrande della Scala, but rather in the sarcophagus of Benedetto Bordone."

"Ha ha! I have solved the puzzle! You may call me Indiana Parducci!"

"I will call Steven Spielberg and make sure you get the next part. Benito, do you have any idea where I could find the tomb of Benedetto Bordone?"

"No, but the answer could be in the City Archives. It is right by the Arena. I will take you there!"

Morse and Parducci ran down the stairs, excited about their new discovery. They alerted the teenagers and the four hopped into a cab and rode ten blocks over to the City Archives. Parducci and Morse approached the clerk. Parducci explained what they needed and the clerk directed them to long rows of fat, dusty tomes that were probably over a hundred years old.

They were called the Grave Directories. Anytime someone in Verona was buried, they were required to obtain a permit from the city graveyard director. By searching through these books, they should theoretically be able to pinpoint the final resting place of anyone who had died in Verona within the last 100 years. Parducci was concerned when he looked at the books, however, as Bordone would have died much longer than 100 years ago. He pointed this out to the clerk, who then directed him to a three volume set of ancient books, showing an obviously incomplete list of some famous people of Verona from centuries gone by who were buried somewhere in Verona. These included Dante Alighieri, the thirteenth century poet and author who wrote the Divine Comedy, describing his journey through Hell, Purgatory and Paradise. Parducci looked through the Italian books quickly, and, incredibly, found an entry for Benedetto Bordone. He started laughing. "What is so funny?" asked Morse.

"You will never guess where he is buried!"

"Where?"

"In a vault beneath the thirteenth century Capuchin monastery San Francesco al Corso!" Parducci was smiling devilishly.

"I am sorry. I am not following you. Am I supposed to know that monastery?"

"Well, of course you should. It is where they have the famous tomb of Guilietta Capulet!"

"You mean from Romeo and Juliet?"

"The very one!"

"But she is just a character in a Shakespeare play, not a real person."

"Well, we don't know that for sure. Shakespeare based his story on a book called The Tragical History of Romeus and Juliet by Arthur Brooke written in 1562. Brooke, in turn, got the story by translating into English an Italian fable about the same lovers written by Matteo Bandello in his Novelle in 1559. Many believe that Bandello is the true author of Romeo and Juliet, but that is not the case. Bandello actually copied much of the story from an Italian author named Luigi da Porto, who first told the story in 1530. Da Porto claimed that he did not make the story up, that in fact it was based on a true story of real families in Verona. In support of his claim, he noted that the early fourteenth century historical chronicles from Bartolomes Della Scala recounted the events of the star-crossed lovers as if it was a true historical event. So far all we know, Romeo and Juliet and their families may have been real people."

"So tell me about this tomb."

"There is an open marble tomb in a dark crypt in the basement of the Capuchin monastery. Both the crypt and the monastery date from the thirteenth century. I think even the tour guide operators admit that the bodily remains of Juliet were never contained in the tomb, but that does not stop hundreds of people every year from getting married in the crypt. Why anyone would want to get married in a funeral crypt is beyond me."

"Where is the monastery?" asked Morse.

"It is just outside the borders of the City of Verona, on the Via del Ponteire, and is a five minute cab ride from here."

"Well, let's go!"

Five minutes later, the two scholars and the two teenagers were on the Via Del Pontiere, in front of the old Capuchin monastery. There was a line of tourists waiting to get in. Parducci used his credentials to get beyond the queue of onlookers. As they went inside, Morse asked, "Where would Bordone's crypt be?"

"I have no idea. I suppose there must be a vault underneath the crypt of Juliet's tomb. We will have to ask the proprietors. They run a little business out of the monastery."

A few minutes later, Parducci had a lengthy conversation in Italian with a skinny woman with red hair in the manager's office. As they talked, she continually looked over Parducci's shoulder with suspicion. Finally, it appeared that the woman was relenting. She grabbed a brass key ring from the wall and introduced herself to Morse and the teenagers.

"Hello," she said in English. "I am Therese Signorelli. I manage this place. I understand you want to see the Monk's Crypt."

"Yes, I suppose we do," said Morse.

"No one has been down there in fifty years. It is locked up. It is probably filled with cobwebs and rats."

"Oh, we don't mind," said Morse. "Anything in the pursuit of history, you know."

"Rats?" said Zoey, grabbing her dad's arm. I am not going down there if there are rats."

"Yeah, Pops, how 'bout I wait up here too. I am not so keen on rats myself," said Zach.

"Perhaps your children would like to take a look at Juliet's tomb? There is a tour leaving in a few minutes." The proprietor looked at Morse. Morse was at first confused, and then realized she wanted money for their tickets.

"Yes, of course, here are some Euros. That would be splendid. You kids go on the tour and we will meet you back here in a few minutes."

The red-headed woman took the money, gave the teenagers their tickets, and then escorted Morse and Parducci down a long hallway, in the direction away from the tomb. She unlocked a doorway, went down three flights of steps, and reached a small brick room with a door at the bottom. She gave both Parducci and Morse a onceover, and rolled her eyes, signaling that they were crazy. She unlocked the door. They went onto a small platform, and saw a stone stairway descending into darkness another two floors. There were inches of dust all over the platform.

"I do not have insurance for this if you fall, so don't fall," she said.

Morse took out two flashlights from his nylon zippered bag and proceeded down the stairway, pushing huge cobwebs out of his way as he descended the stairway. At the bottom of the stairs was a long wall. At regular intervals along the wall were iron doors, a total of twelve in all, with a metal pull ring on each. There were no names on the doors signaling what might lie beyond. Pictures were engraved in metal on each door, however. Morse searched for a horse but could find none. The pictures included a knight in full armour, a poet, a poor friar, a blacksmith, a bishop, a scientist, several men looking over a document, a weaver, and another bishop.

Morse looked at the pictures. Only the one on the end seemed to match. It looked like men looking over a document. That could be a map. But Morse rejected that idea quickly. The scroll had a horse on it. There must be some connection to a horse. None of the engravings appeared to show a horse. But then Morse remembered the second scroll's chess drawing. Chess....

"The horse represents a 'knight' on the chessboard!" exclaimed Morse. "It must be the first door here, with the picture of the knight."

"Ah, my friend, this time I think you have solved it!" said Parducci, smiling.

Parducci used the key ring given to him by the proprietor and opened the lock on the first door. Inside was a small stone room, covered in cobwebs. In the middle was a covered stone sarcophagus. There was a large stone slab over the top. Morse shone his flashlight at the foot of the sarcophagus. In large letters etched on the stone, it read "BENEDETTO BORDONE, IL CARTOGRAFO DI VERONA 1460- 1531."

"This is it!" Morse exclaimed, more excited than a five year-old on Christmas morning. Morse and Parducci took opposite sides on the sarcophagus lid as they had done before. With a herculean effort they managed to budge the stone slab off to the side a little bit. It was enough to look in the tomb. In the tomb was a skeleton, obviously very old. In the skeleton's hand bones, draped across the rib cage, was a huge scroll, as big as an architect's rendering of a new house.

Morse gently removed the huge ancient scroll and laid it on top of the stone lid. When he unrolled it, he could see it was an ancient map of the city of Verona, probably drawn by Bordone. But curled inside the huge scroll were three smaller scrolls, which looked strikingly similar to the ones Morse had found before. Morse peeked inside one and saw the familiar handwriting.

"These are the ones, Benito!"

"Well, let's get them upstairs where we can have a look at them!"

They put the sarcophagus back where it belonged and trudged up the stairs. A rat scampered across the stairway as Morse went up the stairway. When they reached the top, they went into the office and returned the proprietor's set of keys. Then they proceeded into the grassy courtyard outside the monastery. Several "picnic tables" made of stone were in the courtyard. Morse and Parducci sat on a stone bench and laid out the scrolls on the table.

The first scroll contained another Confession of Nostradamus.

La Troisième Confession de Michel de Nostradamus:
Le Plagiat

Moi, Michel de Nostradame, avoue solennellement être plagiaire. Mes "prédictions" sont en grande partie copiées, souvent mot pour mot du Mirabilis Liber de 1522. En plus, j'ai volé des passages à La Sibylle Tiburtine, St. Augustin d' Hippone, St. Sever, Johann Lichtenberger, Ste. Brigitte de Suède, Joachim de Flore, Merlin, l'Evêque Bèmechobus, Pline l'Ancien, Strabon, Pétrone, Suétone, Lucien, Eusèbe, Julius Obsequens, Villehardouin, Joinville, Froissart, Commynes, Claude Ptolémée, Abraham Ibn Ezra, et Richard Roussat. J'avais même l'effronterie de voler à Virgile, le plus grand écrivain qui ait jamais vécu. Que je dérobe le langage des Bucoliques, Géorgiques, et l'Enéide est absolument incroyable. Mais mon plus grand péché était d'essayer de voler, et de déclarer qu'elles étaient à moi tout seul, les 58 strophes divinement inspirées, écrites par Henriette Scalinger Nostradamus, ma belle femme et fille de mon ami Jules-César Scalinger, et descendante directe de la soeur de la Pucelle d'Orléans. Ce grand péché du Plagiat, je l'avoue.

Michel de Nostradame

Morse translated from French to English:

The Third Confession of Michele de Nostradame:
Plagiarism

I, Michele de Nostradame do solemnly confess that I am a plagiarist. My "predictions" are largely copied, many times word for word from the Mirabilis Liber of 1522. In addition, I have stolen passages from The Tritburtine Sybil, St. Augustine of Hippo, St. Severus, Johann Lichtenberger, St. Brigid of Sweden, Joachim of Fiore, Merlin, Bishop Bemechobus, Pliny the Elder, Strabo, Petronius, Seutonius, Luciuan, Eusebius, Julius Obsequens, Villehardouin, Joinville, Froissart, Commynes, Claudius Ptolemy, Abraham Ibn Ezra, and Richard Roussat. I have even had the gall to steal from Virgil, the greatest writer to have ever lived. That I would purloin the language of the Ecologues, Georgics, and the Aeneid is simply unthinkable. But my greatest sin was my attempt to steal, and claim as my own, the 58 divinely-inspired verses written by Henriette Scaliger de Nostradame, my beautiful wife and the daughter of my friend Julius Caesar Scaliger, and direct descendant of the sister of the Maid of Orleans. For this great sin of Plagiarism, I confess.

Michel de Nostradame

Morse opened the second scroll, which read as follows:

Michel:

Si vous avez suivi la piste jusqu'à ce point, vous saurez alors que c'est moi, Jules-César Scalinger, qui vous a mené ici. Je ne pouvais pas vous donner ces grandes prophéties d'Henriette, écrites avec l'aide de la Main de Dieu Lui-même, avant que vous n'ayez fait pénitence, en vous confessant de vos péchés devant Dieu. J'ai confiance que maintenant vous pourrez publier ces 58 prophéties au nom d'Henriette, pas du vôtre, et que vous pourrez réprimer votre amour-propre. Seul un homme repentant, véritable et honorable est digne de partager l'héritage d'Henriette avec le monde. Suivez votre conscience, Michel. Le monde a besoin de vous.

Jules-César Scalinger

Morse translated*:*

Michel:

If you have followed the trail to this point, then you know that it is I, Julius Caesar Scaliger, who has led you here. I could not give you these great prophecies of Henriette, written with the help of the Hand of God Himself, until you had performed your penance, confessing your sins before God. I trust that now you will be able to publish these 58 prophecies in Henriette's name, not in your own, and to stifle your own pride. Only a penitent, true and honorable man is worthy of sharing my Henriette's legacy with the world. Follow your conscience, Michel. The world needs you.

Julius Caesar Scaliger

Morse was absolutely flabbergasted. Julius Caesar Scaliger was Nostradamus' father-in-law! And the prophetic 58 verses were written by Nostradamus' wife—a descendant of Joan of Arc's sister! Morse's head was exploding from all of the implications from this last scroll. This would be one of the most significant finds of all time! He was going to be famous!

There was one scroll left. Morse and Parducci eyed it together. The last quatrains!

Just then Zach and Zoey came out into the courtyard.

"Pops, it is after 10:00 a.m. Our flight leaves in 45 minutes! Shouldn't we get to the airport?"

Morse looked at his watch. Zach was right.

"Maybe we should get a later flight."

Zach exploded. "Dad, we are not getting a later flight! We have almost been killed four different times! I am not sitting around here and waiting for another killer to find us! Get your scrolls and let's go!"

Morse looked at Parducci. Unfortunately, he had a feeling that his friend was not going to let him keep the scrolls.

"John, I am sorry. But you know I must keep these scrolls. I am the Veronian Director of Antiquities. These are Veronian antiquities, found in a Veronian tomb. They must be kept here in Verona, in a museum. Surely you must see that. These scrolls from the tomb are the property of Verona."

"Yes, of course, my friend, of course you are right. If it had not been for you, we would never have found them"

"But of course, when the world learns of our discovery here, I will certainly give you all the credit…." Parducci smiled. "Well, most of the credit! Surely, there is a place in the spotlight for Old Benito!"

Morse laughed and patted his old friend on the back. "Of course, we shall share the discovery together, Benito. But I have to get copies of these immediately. Is there somewhere we can get copies?"

"Dad!" said Zach. "There isn't time. We are not going to truck all over Verona trying to find a frickin' Kinko's! We are leaving. He can fax the things to you!"

"Your son is wise, John. I will have these scanned back at my office immediately and will e-mail them to you. You will have photographic copies you can download from your laptop as soon as you arrive in the United States."

Morse trusted his friend not to break the story and claim all the credit. There simply was not enough time to write all the French down in his notebook. He would have to wait.

"OK, you win. Let's get a cab." They called a cab and Morse quickly jotted down the cell number of his Veronian friend.

"I will call you from the cab," said Morse.

"Very well," said Parducci, closing their cab door with a smile.

During the five minute cab ride to the airport, Morse got out his notebook and cell phone. He simply had to know what was in those last quatrains. As the cab bobbled its way through the piazzas toward the Verona Airport, Morse was trying to write furiously as his friend dictated the words from the scrolls. As he wrote the words down, he became concerned and then alarmed. The taxi landed at the curb. Morse folded the notebook and put it into his pocket. They dashed to the ticket gate and picked up their boarding passes. Luckily, the lines through security were not long. Unfortunately, however, when they got to the electronic scanner, Zach's longboard set off alarms. Morse had forgotten it was in there. On the way to France, it had been in their packed luggage. All of that was gone now. He had thrown the longboard in his carry-on. The security officer would not allow him to bring the longboard through.

"They let it through security when we flew here from Carcassonne," Morse said in Italian. The security man did not care. In his view it was a weapon. It was not going on the plane.

Zach was overwhelmed with anger. First, he was shot at and almost killed, then he had to cut his hair, and now he was losing the longboard with the green wheels. He hated his father right now.

"I promise, Zach, we will get you a new one back in Los Angeles." They left the longboard with security, took off their shoes and went through the gate. They had five minutes to get to the gate. They sprinted as fast as they could, Zach and Zoey arriving at the gate in plenty of time, with their father panting and pulling up the rear. They made it just in time as the door closed. Morse had sweat all over him.

They got in their seats and buckled up. Zach gave Morse one more angry look and went to sleep. Zoey was happy no killers had followed them to the plane. She went to sleep as well.

Morse took out his notebook with concern. There was something on there about bombings and nuclear war. He needed to translate those final quatrains immediately.

Morse looked at his notebook when he was finished:

50.

Le père du grand orateur vient d'Afrique.
Enfant il habite une île tropicale, considérant son sort.
D'abord, on pense qu'il est magnifique,
Ensuite son soutien est au point mort.

The great orator's father is from Africa.
As a child he lives on a tropical island, contemplating his future.
At first they think he is magnificent,
Then support for him stalls.

51.
Les Guerriers de la Foi déclencheront la Guerre Finale.
La Torche, Le Jeune Faucon, Le Constructeur,
L'Aigle, Les Deux Béliers—
Ils sont tous sous l'autorité du Projeteur.

The Warriors of the Faith will commence the Final War
The Torch, the Young Hawk, the Builder,
The Eagle, The Two Rams—
They all report to the Planner.

52.
La Torche est en colère et derange.
Les enfants dans l'école mourront.
Leurs parents pleurent quand ils sont tués.
Dans la forteresse ils le trouveront.

The Torch is angry and deranged.
The children in the school will die.
Their parents grieve when they are killed.
In the fortress, they will find him.

53.
Le Faucon s'est battu une fois pour son frère.
Il a visé le tyrant mais son coup n'était pas bien calculé.
Maltraité par l'investigateur militaire.
Il le tuera pour se venger.

The Hawk once fought for his brother.
He aimed for the tyrant but his move wasn't well-planned.
Mistreated by the military investigator.
He will kill him in vengeance.

54.
Le Chef assistera aux obsèques du garde.
Le Constructeur cache une bombe dans la statue.
La Dame Puissante, quelque chose la retarde.
Dans l'église tous sont perdus.

The Leader will attend the funeral of the guard.
The Builder hides a bomb in the statue.
As for the Powerful Lady, something delays her.
Inside the church, all are lost.

55.
Les remplacements sont choisis trop rapidement
Le Projeteur, MABUS , est progéniture du Diable
Il complote sa prise de pouvoir méchamment
Une fois au pouvoir, il est redoutable.

The replacements are chosen too swiftly.
The Planner, MABUS, is the spawn of the Devil.
He plots his takeover wickedly.
Once in power, he is formidable.

56.
Ils attaquent le stade quand on va jouer, pendant le jour.
L'Aigle s'approche de l'air.
Les gens fuient chercher le secours.
Les Béliers attaquent de la terre.

They attack the stadium when they are about to play, during the day,
The Eagle approaches from the air.
The people flee to seek help.
The Rams attack from the ground.

57.
MABUS gouverne par la mort ou le chantage.
Il se venge avec des nuages de la mort.
Le meurtre de millions cause de grand ombrage.
Une Guerre de Haine pendant deux siècles, alors...

MABUS governs by death or blackmail
He retaliates with clouds of death
His murder of millions causes great offense
A War of Hate for two centuries, then…

58.
Des cendres, il y a une renaissance,
Une paix finale et une durable trêve.
Il y a une nouvelle alliance
Et du bonheur comme dans un rêve.

From the ashes, there is rebirth,
A final peace and lasting truce.
There is a new alliance
And happiness as in a dream.

Morse was dumbfounded. "Holy Mother of God!"

CHAPTER 22. CHURCH

January 21, 2013. 10 p.m. Washington, D.C.

The four men finished a late meal of hummus, halabi kebabs, string bean soup and melon. They were in good spirits. Ammar, the Builder, known to the world as Hector Santiago, poured some ginger tea for his three friends, all of whom were sons of Osama bin Laden. The three brothers had been schooled by their father from the time they were born to be "Abisali," or "Warriors of the Faith." All three traveled from Pakistan to Jordan to Morocco and finally to Mexico. They adopted Mexican names, and with their olive skin and dark curly hair, could pass well enough for Mexicans. In their early twenties, the three had entered America under F-1 visas as visiting engineering students, a skill they had picked up from their father, but they never even arrived on campus at the University of Albuquerque. They went underground, later obtaining fake social security numbers and driver's licenses. Ultimately, they landed in Miami.

The older brother, known to the world as Francisco Perez, went to flight school, and after several years of training, obtained a job as a pilot for Corporate Jet Express in 2010. He acted as co-pilot during his probationary period for the first year, but six months ago, was being assigned his own flights as the pilot. According to his friends and neighbors, he was a devout Catholic, going to Catholic mass in Miami every Sunday. But secretly, he kept his Muslim faith and the religious rituals learned from his father long ago. The two twins, known to the world as Diego and Antonio Sanchez, went to trucking school, and after a year of training, had received their Commercial Driver's Licenses. Each worked as an over-the-road eighteen-wheel truck driver for Fleet Trucking. They had been proud to receive their Arabic code names for this mission for the faith. The older brother, Francisco, was given the name "Altair," Arabic for "Flying Eagle." The twins were each known as "Al Hamal," or "the Rams." Earlier today, they had each received a text message from Mudabbir, the Planner. Their phase of the operation was ready. Tomorrow would be a great day for the Prophet. Ammar regretted that he would not be able to detonate the bomb in the statue from within the church, for he longed to die as a martyr for the faith. But Mudabbir had told him detonation must be accomplished a safe distance away. Ammar had signed a lease for this house over a year ago. The house was two blocks away from St. Anthony of Padua, which was certainly within range for adequate detonation. When the detonation occurred, the Americans would not know what hit them. Their President and Vice President, all of their Supreme Court Justices, the Speaker of the House, the Majority Leader of the Senate, and half the government would be blown away in one mighty blast. The Americans' government would be in shambles. And just then, when the imperialists were at their weakest, the three brothers would deal the death blow for Islam on the stadium in New Orleans.

On the wall behind the four men were several maps, including an architectural map of the Louisiana Superdome, showing the primary beams holding up the stadium and the walkways leading from the Superdome to the Hornets Basketball Arena. Another map showed detailed information about Highway 10, Poydras Street, and the roads and exits leading into the stadium. A third map showed a detailed map of the parking lots around the stadium. Their plan was for Altair to fly his Delta plane directly into the top of the stadium, taking out as many of the people in the stands as possible. When the survivors fled out of the stadium, the Al-Hamal brothers would be ready to ram them with trucks filled with C4. The twins had rigged special machine guns which, at a moment's notice, could be fitted onto the front of their trucks. Any guards who tried to stop them outside the stadium would be gunned down in a hail of gunfire. The hardest part of this mission was the waiting. They had waited their whole lives for this moment.

Ammar, the Builder, raised his mug of ginger tea. "My friends," he said in Arabic. "Tomorrow is a great day. We shall cut the head off the Americans' government tomorrow, leaving them as helpless as children. And then you three will finish what your father, our Master, started. God is great."

"God is great!" said all three brothers, raising their mugs as well.

"I am sorry, Ammar, that we will find the virgins before you. It is a shame that you cannot die in the explosion."

"Yes, it is a great sacrifice," lamented Ammar. "But I am certain that the Americans will find me eventually and torture and kill me, so I will join you eventually. Just save some virgins for me!" he smiled. The four men laughed.

"The Superbowl is on February 3," said one of the twins. "Just five days after Milad un Nabi, the Prophet's birthday. What a fitting birthday present this will be, don't you think?"

"Yes!" the three exclaimed. "A great birthday present indeed!"

"Who do you think Mudabbir is?" asked Altair.

"I do not know, but I get the impression that he is not Muslim," said one of the brothers.

"Why do you say that?"

"We had our first meeting this past year at the end of July, in the middle of Ramadan, and he mentioned nothing about fasting or the holiday."

"You may be right," said Altair. "I get the impression he is high in their government, because he seems to know everything. For example, he told Ammar that the Secret Service did not detect the statues in their security sweep of the church. How would he know that?"

"It does not matter to me," said Ammar. "I would take directions from the Devil himself to take out those American dogs. They wiped out my whole family, and they are going to pay for that."

Altair patted his friend's back in comfort. They finished their tea in quiet. After some brief discussion about what the news media would say the next day, Ammar decided he needed to get some sleep. The three brothers bid farewell to their friend. It would be the last time they would see him.

The Al Hamal brothers were driving their trucks to New York City tonight. Mudabbir had sent them a text message about an hour ago. Three Americans were arriving on a flight from Italy tonight. They would be staying at the Marriott in Times Square tonight before their scheduled flight to Los Angeles tomorrow. The Mudabbir said they needed to be killed. Apparently, they had information about their plans and may decide to go to the authorities. The Al Hamal brothers were not going to allow that. Mudabbir had sent them a photo on their phones with the text message. A middle-aged professor and two teenagers. The job should be very easy.

La Guardia Airport. New York City, NY

John Morse and his two children were to arrive at La Guardia Airport from Verona, Italy at 9:55 p.m. Their connecting flight was scheduled to go to Los Angeles the next morning, so Morse had made a reservation for the Marriott in Times Square. But the more he thought about it on the plane, the more he thought it was a bad idea to stay overnight in New York. Having read the final quatrains, he now knew why assassins had chased them in France. If terrorists really were planning to kill the President and bomb the Superdome, they would not hesitate to kill someone who was in a position to stop their plot. Surely, the assassins would find them in New York. The only smart play was surprise. As the plane got close to New York City, Morse looked at his notebook and read Quatrain 54:

Le Chef assistera aux obsèques du garde.
Le Constructeur cache une bombe dans la statue.
La Dame Puissante, quelque chose la retarde.
Dans l'église tous sont perdus.

The Leader will attend the funeral of the guard.
The Builder hides a bomb in the statue.
As for the Powerful Lady, something delays her.
Inside the church, all are lost.

During their long flight from Verona, Morse had been catching up on all the news in America. He learned that there would be a funeral mass tomorrow for Gil Johnston, the Secret Service agent who was assassinated on Inauguration Day at St. Anthony of Padua Church in Washington, D.C. The President and Vice President and all the Justices of the Supreme Court were scheduled to attend. He only had about twelve hours to warn them.

When they disembarked from the plane in New York, Morse led his sleepy teenagers to the Airport Gift Shop, where he bought New York Yankees hats for all of them, which they kept down low over their eyes. They huddled on the inside of a crowd making its way to the baggage area, and then quickly dashed from the crowd into the street, where they hopped on the nearest Avis bus. Morse and the teenagers looked out the windows of the bus nervously, sure that someone was coming after them, but they saw no one suspicious. Morse rented a tan Toyota Camry from the agent. He knew he would have to use a credit card, which would leave a trail, but if no one here was following them now, they could quickly disappear in the rental car. They took the keys from the Avis counter and went out to the parking lot. Morse started the engine, showed his paperwork to the Avis guard, and they gunned it out of the parking lot. Zach and Zoey looked out the back window. No one was following them.

Morse quickly turned on the car's navigator and pointed it north towards Providence, Rhode Island, where his mother lived. He needed to get these kids out of danger immediately. The trip took a little over three hours. He filled his mother in on all the details when he arrived in Providence. He told her to go to a particular hotel and to refrain from using credit cards for now. He told his mother he would be in contact with her in a few days. The kids were sad to see their father go, but were happy to be temporarily out of danger. As Zach went down the hall of his grandmother's house, he passed a mirror, and groaned when he saw his bald head.

At 2 a.m., Morse started the rental car up and headed back towards Washington, D.C. The navigator said the trip should take about seven hours if he drove the speed limit. That would get them in about 9 a.m. He hoped that would be enough time to stop the assassination. The Al Hamal brothers would never know that their trucks would pass within fifty feet of Morse's rental car later that night just south of Philadelphia.

Morse pulled onto I-95. With his children now safe with their grandmother, he could turn to his next job of protecting the President. He took out his cell phone and dialed 911.

"911."

"Yes, I have an emergency to report."

"What is the nature of your emergency, sir?"

"I have information that there will be an assassination attempt on the President tomorrow morning."

"Who is this, please?"

"I would rather not say."

"And where are you calling from?"

"I would rather not say. All I can tell you is that I have credible information that assassins will attempt to kill the President tomorrow morning."

"Sir, please hold the line. Let me speak to my supervisor."

A few second later, a man's voice came on the line. "

"This is Sergeant Bill Guest from the Providence Police Department. Who is this, please?"

"I would rather not say. I live in Los Angeles."

"What are you doing in Providence, sir?"

"I am returning from a trip to Italy."

"You were sight-seeing in Italy?"

"Yes. And while I was there, I uncovered information that there is going to be an attempt on the President's life tomorrow."

"And where did you obtain this information from?"

"In Italy, from an ancient manuscript." As soon as he said it, Morse regretted it. No one would ever believe him that a young girl living in the sixteenth century had predicted an assassination attempt tomorrow.

"Did you say a manuscript?"

"That's not really important right now," said Morse. "But you need to have the Secret Service do a security sweep of all the statues in St. Anthony's church. I believe a bomb may be planted in one of the statues."

"OK, sir, you need to tell me exactly where you are right this minute."

"I cannot tell you that."

"And why is that?"

"Because they are chasing us and are trying to kill us, and if I tell anyone where we are, they might try and kill me or my family."

"And exactly who is 'they'?"

"Why the killers, of course!"

"And do these killers have names?"

"I have no idea what their names are."

"Then how do you know they are plotting to kill the President?"

"I just do."

"You just do?"

"Are you part of the plot, sir?"

"No, of course not! I am trying to prevent it!"

"Look, why don't you just come down to our station house. You will be completely safe here, and then we can talk about it."

"I am sorry, I cannot do that."

"OK, here is what we are going to do. I am going to refer you to Homeland Security. This may take a few minutes. Do not hang up the line, do you understand?"

Morse held on the line for about thirty seconds, but then he became worried they were somehow tracing the call and triangulating his location. He didn't know why, but out of a concern for the safety of himself and his family, he hung up. That call would simply have to do. They should be able to follow up from the information he gave them. He grimly looked down I-95 through the car window. He hoped he was doing the right thing.

Sergeant Guest was disgusted when he learned that the caller had hung up. The guy sounded like a crackpot, but you never know. He contacted Homeland Security.

"Homeland Security."

"Yes, this is Sergeant Bill Guest from the Providence Police Department. We just got an emergency 911 call from an unidentified gentleman who says there is going to be an assassination attempt on the President's life tomorrow."

"Did he say where this would occur?"

"No he did not." This was Guest's first call to Homeland Security. Guest had momentarily forgotten about the reference to bombs in statues at a church. That omission would later prove to be critical.

"Did he say how he knew about this plot?"

"Yes, I think he said he learned it in Italy from an ancient manuscript, so I naturally thought he was a crackpot, but you never know."

"Did he give his current location?"

"No, he did not."

"Did you get a phone number from him?"

"Yes, we have a phone number 210-555-2478, but we could not get a location on him. Not enough time. But if he hit our dispatch center, he is somewhere in the Providence area."

"OK, we will try and contact him. Thank you, Sergeant, for the information."

"No problem."

The Homeland Security operator called back Morse's cell phone number, but Morse's cell battery had run out. The Homeland Security operator left a message for him to call. Then the operator typed the message "CALLER FROM R.I. CLAIMS THREAT ON PRESIDENT'S LIFE TOMORROW, CLAIMS TO HAVE OBTAINED INFROMATION ON THREAT FROM ITALIAN MANUSCRIPT, PROBABLE CRAZY. NO OTHER SPECIFICS."

Washington, D.C. 7 a.m.

At 7 a.m., Vice President Anna Scall was in her office in the White House, ready to attend the funeral of the fallen Secret Service Agent. This was a true blue American patriotic day, and not a single politician in Washington was going to miss this funeral. The Majority Leader of the Senate and the Speaker of the House, as well as all nine Supreme Court Justices, would be there. Her husband was taking her children on a ski trip to Colorado this week, so he would not be attending, however. Scall looked at herself in the mirror of the bathroom which was directly off her office. She was wearing black designer suede boots, a black pencil skirt, a white ruffled blouse, and a black Chanel jacket, with sea water gray pearls. Her long brown hair was sleekly coiffed in a low ponytail. As usual, she looked fantastic and she knew it. God, she loved being the Vice President. She applied a healthy dose of Matte No. 23 authentic MAC lipstick to her plump lips and was about to leave the bathroom when her Chief of Staff, Matt Suba, appeared in the doorway, his barrel chest blocking her exit. He was wearing a $2,000 charcoal gray Armani suit, a white shirt, and red tie. He had obviously hit the tanning booth recently, for he looked much tanner than he should for January. He smiled his player smile.

"Morning, hot pants."

"Hey, you can't be in here," she said coyly.

He walked towards her until he was inches away. "Oh yeah, who's gonna make me?"

Scall put her hands on his chest. "Matt, stop. You are going to get me in trouble."

Suba closed the bathroom door. "Nobody saw me come in and there are no cameras in here. You are the Vice President, you can do whatever you want."

He pressed himself back against her, grabbing her by the waist and lifting her up on the vanity.

"Ichabod Crane is gone this weekend and I have not had you in two weeks," he said. He started undoing her blouse.

"Matt, I can't, you are going to mess me all up before the funeral."

"Look, we will just be late for the funeral. The guy's dead. He is not going anywhere."

Suba took off his coat, and then his tie and undershirt, and hung them all on the door hook. He went back to Scall, who spread her legs on the vanity. Suba went between her legs and started kissing her. He knew she would not be able to resist him. After they kissed for about a minute, Suba picked up his cell phone and called Scall's Secret Service agent.

"Bobby, this is Matt. Look, CHICKEN FRIED is tied up with some Vice Presidential business, and is going to be late for the funeral. Why don't you guys come down and get her at around 8, OK?"

"Roger that," said the agent.

Suba finished the call and then took off Scall's bra and skirt, leaving her boots and thong underwear. He took off the rest of his clothes and then entered the Vice President, slamming her against the bathroom floor. None of the agents down the hall heard her moans of rapture as her Chief of Staff took her again and again. By 7:45 a.m., both the Vice President and her lover were finished and primping in the mirror, trying to make sure they each looked as polished as they had before their lovemaking session. The Secret Service agents met them at her door by 8 a.m.

"CHICKEN FRIED is en route to the driveway," said the Secret Service Agent into his wrist. Have the car ready."

7:22 a.m. was sunrise. Ammar, the Builder, began his last Al Fajr, the dawn prayer ritual. On his prayer rug, he prayed in the direction of Mecca, asking Allah to give him the strength to carry out his holy mission. Then he went into the bathroom and engaged in the cleansing ritual of the martyr. By 7:45 a.m., he was seated by the window with binoculars, looking out at the circus that had gathered outside St. Anthony's church. His detonator, made out of a crude prepaid cell phone, was ready to go.

By 7:30 a.m., President Woodson and the other dignitaries were already at the church, each one trying to summon the most somber face for the deluge of cameras set up outside the small Catholic Church in Georgetown. The President and the First Lady had the front row, and behind them was the pew for the Vice President and her Chief of Staff. The next row contained the nine Supreme Court Justices, and behind them, dozens of legislators. A phalanx of uniformed Secret Service pallbearers, in uniform, proceeded solemnly across the parking lot with the coffin draped in the American flag. The coffin was brought near the altar of the church and the Secret Service agents took their seats. The pastor of St. Anthony of Padua took the lectern, ready to give comforting words to those in attendance. Behind him, the eyes of the statue of St. Anthony looked on, hiding a coat of dangerous explosives.

At 8 a.m., Morse's rental car was barreling down the streets of Georgetown towards the church. Unfortunately, however, the police had barricaded everything within a ten-block radius. Morse drove up to the barricade and jumped out of his car. "You have to let me through. There is going to be an attack on the President's life! They have hidden bombs in one of the statues of the church!"

The police officer at the barricade stopped him.

"Whoa. Wait a second. Let me see some ID."

Morse hesitated, but gave him the ID.

"And how do you know there is going to be an attack on the President?"

"Trust me, I just do."

"OK, hold on right here. Do not move."

The policeman radioed into his shoulder mike. "Dispatch, I have a gentleman here with a California Driver's license, name John Morse, M-O-R-S-E, license number 637488889, and he claims there is going to be an attack on the President's life. He says there are bombs in the statues in the church. What do you want me to do?"

The dispatcher said, "Hold him there and we will investigate."

The dispatcher then radioed one of the Metro Police officers in the parking lot of St. Anthony's. The officer then ran over to Agent Pete Williams with the Secret Service and told him he had a man at the barricades frantically saying that the President's life is in danger. "He says there are bombs in one of the statues of the church."

By 7 a.m., an alert FBI agent named Jim Duncan had picked up the Homeland Security operator's description of Morse's message from earlier that morning, along with thirty other death threats on the President from crazies. It took about 45 minutes for the Providence Police Department to send the actual tape of the call by e-mail to the FBI agent in Washington. When Duncan listened to the tape he became concerned. Sure, the part about the manuscript sounded crazy, but he did not like the reference to bombs in statues. That sounded very specific. He picked up the phone and called his contact at Secret Service. It was 8 a.m. The funeral mass had just begun.

At 8 a.m., Secret Service Sergeant at the White House Bill Thomas got a call from Agent Duncan. He explained the tape.

"Did you guys X-ray the statues in your security sweep?"

"They must have. I am sure they had dogs in there. We also checked with the priest, and there had been no recent contractor working in there or anything."

"Well, Bill, it is your call, but this caller is making a specific warning about bombs in statues. If it were me, I would pull everybody out of there."

Thomas thought about it a second. The President would be mad. This was going to be a great photo op for a lot of politicians. But marketing was not his job. His job was to protect the President. He knew what he had to do. He hung up with the FBI agent. Thomas radioed the Secret Service Agent in charge of the President, Pete Williams.

"Agent Williams, this is Sergeant Thomas at the White House. I think you need to get GAMBLER and everyone out of that church NOW! We have a credible report there could be a bomb in one of the statues." Seconds later, a Metro Police Officer ran up to Williams and told him the exact same thing. Williams jumped into action and radioed Stark Johnston, the Agent in the church protecting the President.

"Stark, get GAMBLER out of there NOW! There is a bomb in the church! Repeat, bomb in the church!"

Stark Johnston heard the words being piped into his earpiece. Johnston grabbed the startled President by the arm and he and two other agents, ran him down the main aisle of the church.

At 8:05 a.m., Vice President Anna Scall and her Chief of Staff Matt Suba arrived by limousine at one of the police barricades. They showed ID and the officer opened the barricade for them. When they were fifty feet from the driveway entrance of the Church, there was a gigantic explosive fireball emanating from St. Anthony of Padua Catholic Church. A smoke storm of bricks and wood and human flesh erupted in all directions. The Secret Service Agent driving the car did not need to be told what to do. He hit the gas and bolted away from the church, in an effort to make sure the terrorists did not get the Vice President.

"Mayday! The church where the President is has just blown up! I have CHICKEN FRIED. She is not injured. I am taking her to location Delta Bravo Charlie 773. Repeat Delta Bravo Charlie 773." The police officer at the barricade, stunned by the smoke cloud in the distance, took a few seconds to move the barricade. The limousine powered through the space and screamed down the streets of Georgetown. Several police cars met them two blocks later and gave them safe escort to the safe location for the Vice President.

Few people know that the President, the Vice President, the Speaker of the House, the Senate Majority Leader, and the nine Justices of the Supreme Court, wear pulse monitors, either in the form of a wristband or ankle band so that Homeland Security and the Secret Service will always know if the important members of the government are alive or dead. An agent at Homeland Security's offices in Virginia is always watching the pulse monitors. A large panel board shows a green light if the pulse is still detected and a red light if it is not. Malfunctions in the monitors, which are occasional, are always a cause of momentary panic. Agent Carvel Tefft was the agent on call this morning in charge of watching the pulse monitors. At 8:05 a.m., the green lights for everyone except the Vice President of the United States suddenly went from green to red. Agent Tefft was dumbfounded. He had never seen anything like that before. He hoped this was another system malfunction. He called his boss' cell phone.

"Boss, we have a situation here," he dead-panned.

Half an hour later, the Attorney General of the United States, received an urgent phone call from the Secret Service. They wanted to know if it was constitutionally required for a Supreme Court Justice to swear in the President of the United States. The Attorney General was confused why they were asking this question.

"No," he said. "The President is just required to take an oath. Any judge, even a justice of the peace, can administer the oath. Why do you ask?"

"Turn on your TV," said the Agent.

Vice President of the United States Anna Scall was waiting patiently in the mock courtroom of the Georgetown University Law School. A television had been wheeled into the room. They were watching the news about the explosion unfold on the television. A few minutes later, ten Secret Service agents entered the courtroom, accompanied by the Chief Justice of the United States Court of Appeals for the D.C. Circuit.

"Vice President Scall," said the agent. "I regret to inform you that the President of the United States, Tim Woodson, is dead. The Chief Justice from the appellate court is here to swear you in as the next President of the United States."

Anna Scall was speechless. The appellate judge brought a Bible over and asked her to place her hand on the holy book.

"Repeat after me," said the justice, reading from a hastily prepared index card.

"I, Anna Scall…."

"I, Anna Scall…" she repeated. Anna Scall was about to become the first female President of the United States.

As a crestfallen John Morse stared at the black clouds in the distance, Morse recalled the prophetic words of Henriette de Nostradame:

The Leader will attend the funeral of the guard.
The Builder hides a bomb in the statue.
As for the Powerful Lady, something delays her.
Inside the church, all are lost.

Tens of thousands of miles away, in a cave in Pakistan, a young man ran with excitement with a laptop computer down the hall. "It has happened! The President is dead!" he exclaimed. "The final attack of America has begun!"

The Master looked at the laptop and, for the first time in many months, cackled loudly.

CHAPTER 23. INVESTIGATION

January 22, 2013. Washington, D.C.

Secret Service Detective Tom Jensen heard about the explosion seconds after it occurred. He figured the explosion was either set on a timer or was remotely detonated from someone nearby. Most bombers like to see their work in action, so there was a high likelihood the bomber was still within the area, and probably within sight distance of the church. He ordered an immediate ten-city block cordon around the bomb site, with no one except paramedics, police and the injured getting in or out. All paramedics would need to present identification to get through the road blocks. He called Ruddy Montana, and asked him to send his best 100 agents out into the field immediately to begin canvassing every house within the cordon, starting with the houses closest to the bomb site. He also called the FBI explosives experts, ordering them to the scene immediately. Then he got in his Lincoln town car and headed down to the church. He still couldn't believe the bomber had been successful. How had his agents missed the bombs in their security sweeps of the church? Someone's head was going to roll.

The D.C. police officer at the barricade with Morse, after hearing the explosion and seeing the fireball several blocks away, was filled with adrenaline. This man here knew about the explosion before it occurred. He could be a terrorist. The officer drew his revolver and pointed it at Morse.

"Sir, I need you to turn around slowly and put your hands on the hood of your car."

"What?" Morse asked, confused.

"SIR!" the officer yelled, aiming the gun. "I am not going to ask you again! Turn around and put your hands on the hood."

Morse did as he was told.

The officer radioed for backup into his shoulder mike. "This is DSN 176, I am at the Southwest Alpha barricade at St. Anthony's. I need two backup cars here immediately. I have a possible suspect for the church bombing."

The officer placed Morse in the back of his squad car and shut the door. Moments later, five more police cars came screaming up to the barricade, lights blaring. The D.C. cops poured out of the cars with their guns drawn, filled with testosterone. Another officer obtained Morse's nylon zippered bag from the front seat of his car and seized his Avis rental contract, as well as his map of D.C., which he bagged as potential evidence. The officers apparently decided to take him down to the precinct, figuring they could interrogate Morse before Homeland Security took over. Every officer there wanted a crack at Morse, and they fought over who should get to interrogate him. Each hoped they could get an admission from Morse and be the hero of this thing. Two officers hopped in each of the three police cars and they drove down to the station.

"Officer, can I ask where you are putting my bag?"

The officer ignored him.

"Officer, can I ask you…

"Sir, you have the right to remain silent, and I suggest you use it right now!" yelled the cop in the front seat.

Morse remained quiet.

After a few minutes, he said. "Officer, in my bag, you are going to find several ancient scrolls, which are over five hundred years old. They are one of the greatest finds in history, and if you are rough with them, you are going to forever damage or destroy them. So could I ask you to please treat the items in the bag carefully?"

The officer turned back to Morse with a grimace. "Sir, maybe you did not hear me. I need you to shut your pie-hole NOW, do you understand?"

Morse rolled his eyes. Ignorant people really irritated him. He certainly appreciated their bravery in keeping the peace, but why did so many of these officers always have to act like ignorant apes?

Vail, Colorado.

In Vail, Colorado, 7' 2" Tim Scall and his three children were skiing down Adventure Ridge. Their favorite trails were Cheetah and Simbah, big wide-open intermediate trails. His kids waited for him at the bottom, for they were faster than he was. He loved this trip. The campaign had been excruciatingly difficult for everyone in the family, and wreaked absolute havoc on his dental practice. He was not ready to adjust to his new life as the husband of the Vice President. He was going to have nothing to do each day. Also, the assassination of the agent on Inauguration Day had worried him. He did not want his wife or kids taken out by some crazy. They badly needed a vacation. He was absolutely savoring this time on the mountain with his children. They had gone inner tubing at night and visited a natural hot spring. And even though it was January, the weather was in the 30s and the sky was clear and blue. He was so happy to be here. All his children were good snowboarders. He had tried it once, but preferred skiing. With his height, he felt like you needed a lower center of gravity to snowboard. The only bad time they had so far was this morning, when they took a wrong turn and went down "Cub's Way," a beginner trail which was very flat. Flat trails are terrible for snowboards, and result in long walks. Scall had tried to pull his snowboarding daughter with his ski pole, but had thrown out his shoulder pulling her. But now they were having loads of fun.

As he got near the end of Simba, he stopped with his kids to take a breather. They were waiting with a big guy named Don, who was skiing with them. He was their Secret Service escort while they were on the hill. Tim Scall took off his snow goggles to clear the fog on the glass. The sun reflected off the white snow, so it was hard to see. He squinted up the hill, but it looked like a lot of skiers were coming down the hill quickly. Scall put his goggles back on. Five members of the Vail Ski Patrol in red parkas with a big Red Cross on the front came whizzing down Simba, and hockey-stopped in front of them in a spray of snow.

"Are you Tim Scall?" asked one of the leaders.

"Yes, I am."

"We have received an urgent call from the Secret Service to get you off the mountain now."

"What is happening?" asked Don. "I have not heard anything." Don checked his earpiece.

"Sometimes the reception up here on the hill is bad," said the man from the Ski Patrol.

"Can I see your IDs?" asked Don.

The Vail employees quickly showed them their IDs and Don patted them down the best he could. They looked legit.

"OK, you ski up ahead and show us the way and we will follow you," said Don.

"What is it?" asked Tim Scall. "Is my wife OK?"

"Yes," said one of the members of the Ski Patrol. "According to what

I just saw on CNN, your wife is the new President of the United States. The President has just been killed."

Tim Scall was flabbergasted. Suddenly, all thoughts of skiing went out of his head. He wanted to get back to Washington as soon as possible and talk to his wife.

"Let's go!" he said. They skied as fast as they could down to Vail Village, where a limousine filled with hot chocolate was waiting for them.

Agent Gonzalo Fender was one of the brightest FBI agents in the field. Originally from Mexico City, he spoke fluent Spanish. He also impressed the FBI with a PhD in Psychology and his fluency in Arabic, French, German, and Farsi. He was a devout Catholic, but he also had a brother-in-law who was Muslim, so he was very familiar with the prayer rituals and practices of Muslims. He was one of the agents tasked to speak with the residents who lived around St. Anthony's Church. He had already interviewed fourteen residents so far, with no luck. Then he rang the doorbell of Hector Santiago.

"Hello, sir, my name is Gonzalo Fender of the FBI. I guess you may have noticed the bombing incident we had down the street, and I am wondering if I could ask you a few questions."

"I didn't see anything," the man said quickly.

"Oh, I am sure you didn't. But this is just routine, you know, we have to question everyone. Is it OK if I come in?"

"I guess so," said Santiago, inviting him in.

They sat on the couch.

"Can I get you some coffee or something?" asked Santiago.

"No, that's fine." Fender pulled out a notebook. "What is your name, sir?

"Hector Santiago."

"Can I see your ID?"

Santiago showed him his driver's license, and Fender took note of his Date of Birth and Social Security number.

"Crazy morning, heh?" asked Fender.

"Yeah, I have been watching it on the news. It looks terrible."

"Did you see the bomb go off? You have a real good view from your window here." Fender took a look out the window.

"No, I was sleeping, but I heard it though. Shook the whole house."

Fender looked around. There were a lot of crucifixes. Almost too many crucifixes. "You a religious man?"

"Very much so, Officer. I am the maintenance man for St. Anthony's."

"Ah, the maintenance man." Fender wrote that down. Now that was interesting.

"What are your hours over there at the church?

"Mostly, I clean up every morning, after the mass for the school children. And then I clean up after 5 p.m. mass on Saturday, and on Sunday afternoons after the masses then. And then at night, I buff all the floors, and polish all the pews, and vacuum the carpeting."

Fender thought. The maintenance man would have access at night, with no one watching.

"How long have you had this job?"

"A couple years."

"Really? Where you from originally?"

"Mexico."

"Really? What part of Mexico?

"Guadalajara."

"Really? El Zorro del Desierto, heh?" ["the Desert Fox"]

Santiago smiled, but it did not seem to Fender like the comment registered. One of the greatest soccer players on the Mexican national team was Jared Borgetti, known to everyone in Mexico as the Desert Fox. He played on the Guadalajaran team for seven months in 2009. Any self-respecting Mexican from Guadalajara would know about the Desert Fox. Fender decided to test the man further. He smiled warmly to keep the maintenance man unsuspecting.

"¿Estas mirando el Mundial? [Have you been following the World Cup?"]

"Si."[Yes.]

"¿Quién te gusta mas, Jared Borgetti o Diego Maradona?" [Who do you like better, Jared Borgetti or Diego Maradona?]

"Los dos son bueno." [They are both good.] Santiago smiled nervously. He blew that one. Maradona was one of the greatest soccer players in the world, but he played for Argentina, and he retired in 1997. He was now coach of the Argentinian team. Anyone who followed the World Cup would know that. The man could have just said he did not know much about soccer, but instead, he decided to lie. Fender decided to poke around.

"Listen, you are like the fifteenth house I have visited and I have to use the restroom. Do you mind if I borrow your bathroom?

"Sure," said Santiago, pointing the way.

When Fender got into the bedroom, he noticed two more crucifixes on the wall, and then something strange. Rolled up in a corner, behind a potted plant, was a small rug. He pulled it out. It was definitely a Muslim prayer rug. It looked just like the one his brother-in-law owned. What is a Catholic doing with a Muslim prayer rug?

He went into the bathroom, and flushed the toilet. As he got ready to wash his hands, he looked at the stopper in the sink. On the inner rim of the stopper, there was a tiny bit of a gray clay-like substance. Fender scraped it off, put it in a Ziploc bag from his pocket, and pocketed the sample.

He went back into the main room.

"Did you have a good holiday?"

"Yes."

"Now, do you celebrate Milad un Nabi on the 24th or the 29th?"

"The… I'm sorry, what did you say?"

"Milad un Nabi, the Prophet's birthday. Sunnis celebrate it on the 24th, but Shia celebrate it on the 29th. I wondered which one you were?"

"Officer, I am not Muslim."

"Sure you are," said Fender.

"Officer, as you can see by all the crucifixes on my walls, I am a Catholic."

"Then why do you have a sajjada in your bedroom?"

"A sajjada? What is that?"

"It is a Muslim prayer rug, as you well know."

"That is just a rug, not a prayer rug."

"Then why does it have a Mihrab on it?"

"A what?"

"A Mihrab—an arch-shaped design at the top of the carpet which allows you to orient the rug towards Mecca?"

"I don't know what you are talking about."

"Mr. Santiago, I think we need to take a drive down to the station house."

"Am I under arrest?"

"Mr. Santiago, we can do this the easy way or the hard way. You can come downtown with me voluntarily, or I can arrest you for conspiracy to murder the President of the United States and cuff you right now. Which is it going to be?"

"I will come with you, but I have done nothing wrong." Agent Fender put the suspect in the back of his car, but did not cuff him. He was not worried the suspect would escape, as his car had no interior door handles and there was a glass partition between the front seat and the back seat.

"Dispatch, This is Agent Fender, Agent 6497," he said into his radio mike on his belt. "I am at 1417 Agnes, home of a Hector Santiago. He is the maintenance man for St. Anthony's. I have a strong suspicion that this gentleman is our bomber. I have him in the back of my car and I am bringing him downtown for questioning. I would like a DC Metro escort, please. I would like someone from the U.S. Attorney's Office to meet us because we are going to need search warrants for this guy's house."

"Roger that, 6497," said Dispatch.

"This is Wolf Blitzer in the CNN Situation Room. If you are just turning in, tragedy struck this morning as a bomb decimated St. Anthony's Catholic Church in Georgetown, where the President and numerous politicians were attending a funeral. We have confirmed from the Department of Homeland Security that President Tim Woodson is dead. I repeat, the President of the United States is dead. The blast also killed all nine Supreme Court Justices, the Senate Majority Leader, the Speaker of the House, and at least thirty other senators and congressmen. This is the worst attack on the American government in our nation's history. Anna Scall, the Vice President, was running ten minutes late for the funeral due to some last minute business, and was fortunate enough to avoid being caught in the blast. We are being told that a half hour ago, Anna Scall was sworn in by an appellate judge as the new President of the Untied States. By that action, Anna Scall becomes the first female U.S. President in American history, obviously a milestone in itself, but something we all wish would not have occurred under these tragic circumstances. The Secret Service has confirmed that they have secured the families of both President Woodson and President Scall. We are being told by the White House Press Corps that Anna Scall, our new President, will address the nation in a press conference momentarily. We turn now to CNN's political correspondent Candy Crowley, who is on the scene in Georgetown. Candy, what can you tell us?"

"Well, Wolf, as you know, the tragic bomb blast occurred at about 8:05 a.m. this morning. The priest had just walked to the microphone to begin the funeral ceremony of the Secret Service Agent who was gunned down by terrorists on Inauguration Day. We are being told by the Secret Service that a tipster had notified police only moments before the blast that bombs were hidden inside statues in the church, and that an attempt was being made on the President's life. The Secret Service agents guarding the President were notified via their earpieces, but apparently, Wolf, the warning came just moments too late, for it was at that point that the entire church exploded. Witnesses in the parking lot described it as a giant fireball. We had one of our crews covering the funeral. One of our cameramen was running what we refer to as B-roll, or background footage for later use, of the outside of the church, when he caught the explosion on film. At this point, Wolf, we would like to warn our viewers that this is tragic and graphic footage, so if they have little ones there, they may want to have those viewers not look at this footage." With that, the television screen showed a calm-looking exterior of St. Anthony's of Padua. At 8:05 on the film, the church suddenly exploded, the camera appeared to fall off its tripod, for the next few seconds of film showed the blacktop of the parking lot. People were screaming. Then it appeared that the cameraman picked up the camera and started filming. There were clouds of dark black smoke everywhere, and the cameraman was heard exclaiming, "Oh my God! Oh my God!" Then the film went dead.

"Candy, that is horrible indeed. Has Homeland Security given you any information on who was killed in the blast?"

"Yes, right now, they believe they have 62 confirmed dead. That includes the President of the United States, Tim Woodson, his wife, the First Lady, all nine justices of the Supreme Court, the Senate Majority Leader, the Speaker of the House, and at least twelve Secret Service agents. In addition, we have 31 legislators confirmed dead. We are going to post their names on cnn.com, but they include nine Democratic Senators, three Republican Senators, fourteen Democratic members of the House of Representatives, six Republican members, and the Mayor of the District of Columbia."

"Is it possible that there are other Senators or Representatives who are killed or injured?"

"It is possible, Wolf. We do not yet have a list from the Secret Service as to who was supposed to be in the church for this funeral, and we are making calls to each of the offices of those legislators to find out if they are present or missing."

"Do they have a suspect yet?"

"We have no word of a suspect yet, Wolf. I have been told by the Fire Marshall that this was an explosive device, not an accidental thing. This was an act of terrorism, that is certain, but just who the perpetrator or perpetrators are at this point, we cannot say."

"Is there any suggestion this was Al Qaeda?"

"Again, no word from Homeland Security whether this was an act of Al Qaeda or a home grown terrorist. We will just have to wait and see."

"Is there anyone who may still be alive under all that rubble?"

"Wolf, firefighters are working tirelessly with cranes and backhoes to remove the debris in an attempt to rescue anyone who may still be in the church, but the Fire Marshall told me moments ago that due to the power of the explosives used, the chances of anyone surviving are slim."

"Candy, do we have any idea where the new President, President Scall, is right now?"

"She is at an undisclosed location somewhere in Georgetown, Wolf. Apparently, her limousine was just seconds from pulling into the parking lot when the blast occurred. She is expected to address the nation in a press conference momentarily."

"Candy, you mentioned something about a tipster. Any idea who that tipster was?"

"No, the police have informed me that the tipster is at FBI Headquarters now and is being questioned as a 'Person of Interest.' That is what they are calling him. They took great pains to tell me he is not a suspect at this time, but merely a 'person of interest.'"

"Any idea how he could have known the blast was going to occur?"

"We asked the FBI that, but as you can imagine, Wolf, they are being very tight-lipped about their investigation right now."

"Candy, I am sure many of our viewers are wondering how the Secret Service could allow bombs to remain in the church before a Presidential visit. Was there a security sweep of the church done before the funeral and, if so, how did they miss what were clearly explosive bombs?"

"I do not know that, either, Wolf, but we will certainly be staying on the story to get those answers. Reporting live from Georgetown, this is Candy Crowley, CNN News."

"We turn now to one of our experts, retired Secret Service Sergeant William Insell, Sergeant Insell, what type of security sweep would normally be made for a church site like this before a President arrives?"

"Well, Wolf, what normally happens is…"

"I am sorry, Sergeant, I am going to have to interrupt you. I am being told that our new President, Anna Scall, is at the microphone from an undisclosed location in Georgetown, and is about to address the nation." The camera cut away to the screen, where Anna Scall somberly approached the microphone. Chief of Staff Matt Suba was standing tall just over her right shoulder on the platform.

"My fellow Americans. Today, we face another great tragedy, as terrorists have murdered most of the leading members of our American government. As you may have heard, we lost many great Americans today, including President Woodson, the First Lady, the Majority Leader, the Speaker of the House, all nine Justices of the Supreme Court, over two dozen legislators, and some of the best and brightest from the Secret Service. It was only through the grace of God and sheer happenstance that I arrived ten minutes late and missed being killed in the blast, literally by seconds. It is with a heavy but a proud heart that I take up the mantle of the United States of America for my country. As your new President, here is what I intend to do:

"First, we must find and bury our dead, and remember each and every one of them for the wonderful human beings they were. Every single person lost in this tragedy helped millions of everyday Americans in their own way, and we will not rest until every one of the fallen is honored. Nearly every person lost was a personal friend or colleague of mine, so I share the pain many of you must feel today.

"Second, we will treat the injured. The firefighters here will not rest, will not sleep, until all of the rubble is cleared, and we rescue anyone at all who could still be alive after this tragedy. And they will receive the best medical care that money can buy. We have dedicated surgeons and health care professionals ready both here in Washington DC and around the country. As a former nurse myself, I can assure you that the injured will be cared for.

"Third, we will find these murderers. They will not be able to hide in caves; they will not be able to hide behind their religion or their cause.

Whatever rock they are hiding under, we will find these cowardly worms. And we will crush them with an iron boot and the full wrath of the American people; I can assure you of that. And if any country is found to have harbored them, assisted them, comforted them, schooled them, funded them, or taken any action to assist them in committing these violent acts, that country will be an enemy of the Untied States, and our military will take swift and decisive action against them.

"Fourth, we will investigate how this security breach occurred, so that it cannot happen again. Of course, at a moment like this, when so many Secret Service agents have fallen, it is tough to try and cast blame on the noble professionals who work tirelessly to try and prevent catastrophes like this every day. But the stark fact remains that terrorists were able to sneak into a church in the dead of night, plant bombs inside the church, and escape without detection. None of the security sweeps uncovered the bombs. That is simply unacceptable. We will have a top to bottom investigation—not for casting blame, but for the purpose of ensuring that these terrorists cannot make similar attacks in the future.

"Fifth, we need to immediately reconstitute our government. The obvious intention of these terrorists was to knock out our government in one fell swoop, thereby making us powerless for whatever ensuing attacks are coming in the days and weeks ahead. We will not allow terrorists to weaken our government. Here is what I intend to do to reconstitute the government.

"My first act, pursuant to Section 2 of the Twenty-Fifth Amendment, will be to appoint a new Vice President. My choice is Matt Suba, my Chief of Staff for the last three and a half years. This is Matt here. Matt is a true American, not a partisan. He has helped me through all of my campaigns, and he has been an inspiration for me, providing sound advice and good counsel. I need him in the White House. I will be asking the members who remain in the Senate and House to immediately hold hearings and confirm Matt within the week. And I say to my friends in Congress: this is NOT the time to bicker and fight in a partisan manner. This is the time to act like grownups and do what is best for America. I urge Congress to trust my judgment on this, and not second-guess me. Matt is the right man for the job.

"Lest anyone accuse me of being anything less than non-partisan, I also offer the following proposal regarding replacements for our Supreme

Court. I do not intend to appoint nine conservative Republicans to the Court, as some of you may have feared. That would not be fair. That would not be just. And that would play right into the hands of our enemies, who seek to change our government through violence. The Court was previously composed of five conservatives and four liberals. I intend to appoint precisely five conservatives and four liberals, and I would ask Congress to immediately confirm all nine choices together as a panel at its earliest opportunity, so that the Court can continue with its important work.

"In terms of replacing the remainder of Congress, I would ask each Governor— and if replacements are made in a special election, then the voters of that particular state—whether you are a Republican or Democrat, conservative or liberal, to choose your replacement in the following manner. If a Republican was lost, then appoint a Republican for the replacement. If a Democrat was lost, appoint a Democrat for the replacement. In this way, our enemies cannot succeed in changing the fabric and composition of our government through cowardly acts of violence and terrorism.

"Finally, let me say something to the American people who have lost so much today. St. Anthony of Padua is the Catholic patron saint for the recovery of things which are lost. That is quite appropriate today, because our country has lost much, and we are in desperate need of assistance with our recovery. In the days and weeks ahead, I would ask you to honor each of the fallen for their great contributions in this life, and to put aside partisanship and political rhetoric in an effort to restore this great American government. I regret that it is under these circumstances that I have come to lead you. Nevertheless, I am proud to lead you out of this crisis. And today, in the shadow of our loss, I am more proud than ever to be an American. Thank you."

Thousands of miles away, on Air Force One flying over Colorado, Tim Scall watched the television coverage. He could not believe his wife was going to appoint Matt Suba as Vice President without even discussing it with him. He hated that thick-necked oaf. There were dozens of politicians more qualified. Well, at least she was safe. He would discuss it with her when they returned to the White House. It was just hitting him that he was now officially the First Gentleman of the United States. He popped some Presidential M&M's into his mouth. He left his seat in front of the television to see how his kids were doing. This was going to be an even bigger change in their lives.

John Morse was seated in a small, windowless interrogation room. An investigator from the FBI, wearing a white shirt, rolled up sleeves, khaki pants, and a firearm strapped over his shoulder, entered the room carrying Morse's nylon bag and a manila folder. Morse learned that his children had been picked up by the FBI in Providence and were being flown to the FBI Field Office in Washington, D.C. for interrogation.

"Hello, Professor Morse, my name is Detective Tom Jenson with the Secret Service, and I have been assigned to your case. How are you doing, do you need a soda or coffee or anything?"

"Bottled water would be great, if you have it."

"Sure." He opened the door and yelled for someone to get him a bottle of water for the prisoner.

"Detective, are my children OK?"

"Yes, Professor Morse, they are fine. No need to worry about them. How old are your children, by the way?"

"Zach is fifteen and Zoey is fourteen."

"OK, would you have any problems if we asked them some questions?"

"As long as I am present."

"Is that so you can get your story straight?"

"No, Detective, I am a father, probably like you, and I do not want my children being mistreated."

"Don't worry, we will not mistreat them. So is it OK?" He pushed a consent form across to Morse. Morse pushed it back.

"As I said, you can feel free to question them if I am present."

"Do the children have a mother?"

"No. She died in the 9/11 tragedy."

"Really? That's too bad. I guess that must have been hard on you, seeing as the government employees at the airport screwed up and let those terrorists on the plane with box cutters. Must be tough to think how much the government let you down."

"As I understand it, airport personnel at that time were not employed by the government, so no, I do not blame the government for that."

"But you probably tried to get answers from the government after 9/11, right? I know that was tough for a lot of families."

"Detective, one thing you should know about me is that I am an educated man. I am not stupid. I can see where you are going with these questions, so let me jump to the finish line here so we can all stop wasting our time. I did not have a grudge against my own government as a result of the death of my wife in the 9/11 tragedy. If anything, I blame myself for not going on the trip with her and for failing to tell her to get off the plane when she had a premonition that something bad was going to happen."

"Is that why you decided to bomb the church today, because you are angry at yourself?"

"Detective, I did not bomb anything today. I tried to prevent the bombing from occurring."

"Really? Is that why you wouldn't give us your name when you made the 911 call?"

"Huh?"

The detective pulled out a laptop and played the 911 call Morse had made.

"Why wouldn't you give us your name?"

"I was afraid they would find me and kill my family."

"Who is 'they'?"

"The terrorists."

"Your partners, you mean?"

"No, not my partners. I do not even know who they were. They were trying to kill me."

"And how do you know that?"

"Because they sent an armed gunman to kill us in the town of Salon-de-Provence France and we barely escaped with our lives; then they sent two hired gunmen tried to kill us in the town of Agen and then in Carcassonne, France, and again, we barely escaped with our lives. I had every reason to suspect they would trail me back to America, so I did not want to tell anyone where I was."

"We tracked your flight itinerary and figured out you went to Carcassonne. We just got off the phone with the Police Department in Carcassonne. They have two murders they are investigating there, one in which an individual was thrown off the top of the castle walls and killed, and a second in which someone was bludgeoned to death in the church there. The police say several witnesses remember seeing a bald man, a bald teenager, and a teenage girl running around at the time of the murder. I suppose that was you?"

"Yes, that was us. The men who were killed were hired assassins sent to murder us."

"So you killed them, then?"

"The first man was thrown over the wall by my son during a struggle in which he was chasing us along the castle walls with a gun. The second man was killed by a friend that we met in Carcassonne, an American. At the time, the man in the church had a gun leveled at our heads and announced he was right about to kill us. Our friend bludgeoned him with a candelabrum in the nick of time and saved our lives."

"So you are saying your skinny little fifteen year-old son managed to overpower a 220-pound assailant wielding a gun, and throw him over the castle walls?"

"No, he rigged a catapult and the killer fell into it."

"A catapult, you say?" The detective started laughing. "Really? This sounds like an episode of Wile E. Coyote and the Roadrunner. You said you are not stupid, Professor. Do you think I am stupid?"

"No."

"Well, you must think I am stupid if I am going to believe a story like that."

"It is very easy to corroborate, Detective. If you contact the police in Carcassonne, I am sure they will tell you that they found an ancient catapult on the castle walls. And I would venture to guess that there might be blood stains on the catapult, because just before chasing us up in the castle, he shot a friend of ours named Ray in the arm and they struggled, and my recollection is that the killer had some of Ray's blood on him when he was chasing us."

"And does this Ray have a last name?"

"I am sure he does, but I do not remember it. It was Italian, as I recall. But if you survey hospitals in Carcassonne near La Cité, I am sure you will find him recuperating there, with a gunshot wound to the arm, along with his boyfriend Doug, who was the one who rescued us in the church. Wait, now that I think about it, I have Doug's business card. Here it is."

"And why would assassins want to kill an old professor, his teenagers, and a couple of gay guys?"

Morse shifted in his chair, uncomfortable for the first time. The Detective could see he had hit a soft spot.

"What is it, Professor, finally run out of answers?"

"No, it is just that the answer is somewhat hard for even me to believe, so I am sure you will have a hard time believing me."

"Try me."

"I was initially summoned to France because I am somewhat of an expert on the ancient sixteenth century prophet Nostradamus. In Salon-de-Provence, beneath an ancient church, a priest had made quite a remarkable discovery—an ancient vault, hundreds of years old, which had artifacts from Nostradamus himself. These artifacts sent me and my children on a cross-country treasure hunt of sorts, from Salon to Agen to Carcassonne and finally to the Italian city of Verona. And what we found was as intriguing as it was difficult to believe. According to the ancient scrolls that we found on our journey, Nostradamus' first wife Henriette, believed to be a descendant from Joan of Arc herself, predicted with incredible accuracy every major historical event and character from the sixteenth century until the present day. And the last set of prophecies actually predicted the assassination of President Woodson today. Initially, I thought the whole thing a giant hoax, until assassins started trying to kill us, and then I wondered if the prophecies could possibly be real. And although it pains me as a man of science to say this, I believe in my heart of hearts that these prophecies are genuine."

"Professor Morse, I am not a man of science. I am a simple detective. And I have been doing this job a long time. But I have to tell you, from my heart of hearts, that that is the biggest load of festering bullshit that I have ever heard uttered from the mouth of a suspect."

"I told you that you were not going to like it. But it can all be corroborated. Bring my children into the room here and question them all you want. They will tell you the same thing. Question Doug and Ray in Carcassonne, and they will tell you the same thing. And you have my bag, so you have all the scrolls. If you do not believe me, there is an easy way to verify if they are genuine. You have experts here at the FBI. Carbon date the scrolls and the ink, and see if they date to the sixteenth century. That should be easy enough to do. There is also a known copy of Nostradamus' writing. It is his will. The original is in a French museum, but I am sure you can pull a copy off the Internet. The first scroll obtained from the vault is believed to be written by Nostradamus. You should get a match. The later scrolls are believed to be authored by Julius Caesar Scaliger. If you can find a copy of his handwriting online, your handwriting experts can match that handwriting to the other scrolls."

"Oh, and while we are at it, we can write you a poem and knit you a sweater. I have a better idea. It involves you telling me the truth."

"I have told you the truth!"

"Professor, I had a colleague of mine do some digging on you. He found a little TV show you did on Nostradamus earlier this year. I think you will find it interesting." He showed the video of Morse's debate, in which Morse argued that Nostradamus was a liar and a fake.

"So here you are on TV saying this Nostradamus guy is a quack and a liar, and now you are telling us he is sending you messages from the grave. That is a little inconsistent, don't you think?"

"That debate was before I went on this trip and uncovered all these artifacts."

"You know what I think, Professor? I think you concocted this whole thing about the treasure hunt to make yourself sound like Indiana Jones. Then you recruited some Muslim fanatics, got them to bomb the church, so that you can say 'I told you so,' and make a lot of money on your next Nostradamus book. What do you think about that theory?"

"I think it is ludicrously stupid."

"Really? Well answer me this. According to your Avis rental contract, you left New York at around 10:30 p.m. It takes about four and a half hours to drive to Washington, DC. That should put you in DC at around 3 a.m. That was plenty of time for you to get to a police station, tell them this crazy theory about Nostradamus, and warn the President in time. We may not have believed you, but we certainly would have looked at those statues in the church. Where were you between 3 a.m. and 8 a.m.?"

"Dropping off my children at their grandmother's house in Providence, Rhode Island, and then driving to Washington, D.C."

"Why didn't you call the police while you were driving to Rhode Island?"

"I don't know. I probably should have. I wanted to get my kids safe first."

"You probably should have? That's it? You are afraid the President and every major leader of our Government were going to be killed, and you are waiting to call police for three hours? You have got to be kidding me!"

"I wish I was, but that is the truth."

"I am going to leave you now, Professor, and while I am gone, I am going to ask you to think about your country, and your duties as an American citizen, and when I come back in here, you are going to tell me the truth." With that, the Detective headed towards the door. Just before leaving, he turned around.

"By the way, who is Hector Santiago?"

"I have no idea."

"I thought you would say that."

The Detective walked out with the bag and the manila folder.

CHAPTER 24. MABUS

January 24, 2013. Washington, DC

It was Tom Benjamin's last season in professional football. He had not been back to the Superbowl since his last Superbowl win with the Giants. He had been traded to the Carolina Panthers at the beginning of the season. But the 2012 season had been fantastic, with Benjamin grabbing the last bit of the old magic, completing an incredible record-breaking 72% of passes in a single season. Steve Shane, Benjamin's number one passing target, had 1,912 passing yards, breaking Jerry Rice's single season yardage record. In the NFC Playoff Game against the Seattle Seahawks, with four seconds left on the clock, Benjamin lobbed a beautiful spiral to Shane in the corner of the end zone for the winning touchdown. The final score was 28 to 26. The Carolina Panthers, the home team of President Anna Scall, would be going to New Orleans for the Superbowl against the Miami Dolphins. It was hard to see how the President, a diehard football fan, could miss going to that game. The Secret Service Agents watching the game in the White House groaned when they saw the result. The logistics for security at the Superdome just became more complicated.

When the dead had been counted two days after the blast, political junkies across the country quickly did the math. The Democrats had a four-vote majority, 52 to 48, in the Senate before the explosion. But after the explosion, seven Democratic Senators and three Republican Senators had perished. That brought the tally to 45 Democrats and 45 Republicans, a tie. Normally the sitting Vice President would cast the deciding vote, but now there was no Vice President, resulting in a deadlock. Because the majority party in the Senate gets to control the agenda of the Senate, each party wanted to make sure they had the control. In order to do that, they needed their state Governors to appoint replacements immediately. On the morning of January 24, 2013, at 10 a.m., the Republican Governor from Nebraska, ignoring the President's plea to pick replacements according to the party of the fallen Senator, appointed a Republican to replace the Democrat from his state who had perished. This gave the Republicans a temporary 46 to 45 lead. An hour later, Republicans in the Senate voted a Senator from Kentucky as their Majority Leader, who immediately called for a vote on Matt Suba's nomination for Vice President. The Democratic

Minority Leader said they would be ready for debate at about 2 p.m. that day. At 1 p.m., the Governors from Arkansas and Oregon appointed Democrats to replace their fallen comrades, giving the Democrats a 47 to 46 lead. The Democrats met at 1:30 p.m. and elected a Senator from Pennsylvania as their new Majority Leader. Having gained control of the agenda, the new Majority Leader canceled the vote on Matt Suba. This game of musical chairs happened three more times that afternoon, with Republican Governors from Missouri, Wyoming, and Montana sending three more Republicans to the Senate, and Democratic Governors from Texas, New Jersey, and Maine sending three more Democrats. When the dust settled at the end of the day, the Democrats were barely in charge, 50 to 49, with a special election scheduled for Arizona, one of the few states that do not allow the Governor to fill the Senator's seat.

That night, Fox News commentators were in frenzy. Glazing over the fact that the Republican Governors had also ignored President Scall's plan of replacement, the commentators excoriated the Democrats, accusing them of playing games in a time of national crisis. The government had to be restored, they said, and only a vote on Matt Suba, up or down, immediately would restore order from the chaos. The tea-baggers were outraged, and the next morning, on January 25, 2013, all hell broke loose. Citizens drove to Washington. Republican think tank organizations bused in people from all over the country to demonstrate in front of the Senate.

The new Democratic Majority Leader from Pennsylvania was in a tight spot. She was in a state which used to lean Democratic, but which started to migrate to the Republicans in the last election. Her state was almost evenly split, and so she had to make sure she kept all of the electorate happy. On January 25, 2013, her exhausted staff advised her that the calls were coming in 20 to 1 in favor of giving an immediate vote to Matt Suba. Most of the calls involved people cussing or screaming. Her staff said they had never heard anything quite like that. However, the other members of her Party were insistent. Do not schedule a vote for this man. We do not even know who he is yet. He has not been vetted. He could be Charles Manson for all they knew. They had to have time to investigate Suba. The Democratic Majority Leader held on until Sunday, January 27, 2013, when she was ambushed with a pile-on during Meet the Press. Even David Gregory, always known for his even-handedness, seemed testier than usual with his questions. Her pollster told her that night that her favorability ratings were plummeting. She could not stand the heat anymore. On Monday, January 28, 2013, the Majority Leader announced that debate would begin on the Suba appointment, with a vote scheduled for Friday, February 1, 2013. The House announced a similar schedule, with their vote to occur on Thursday, January 31, 2013. Journalists from around the country went in to hyperdrive over the next four days, interviewing everyone they could from South Carolina who had ever met Matt Suba, the country's proposed Vice President.

Meanwhile, FBI agents had spent the last week combing over every inch of the homes of Hector Santiago and John Morse. The lab technicians analyzed the small gray clay material found in Santiago's sink. It was C-4 explosive all right, and it matched the RDX stolen from the Alexandria, Virginia chemical plant, as well as remnants of the explosive found at the church. The apartment also had paint and brushes. The FBI Agents noticed that the color brown was in short supply. Photos taken of the church before the blast showed the statue of St. Anthony wearing a brown monk's robe. Under the mattress, they found a Qur'an, which was obviously inconsistent with someone claiming to be a devout Catholic. Analysis of Santiago's background uncovered that he had entered the country illegally. Agents traveled to Mexico and spoke with friends who had known him years ago. Unfortunately, however, Santiago had not cracked in any of the interviews, and just kept saying he was not saying anything. FBI investigators, however, were encouraged by the fact that he had yet to ask for an attorney, despite being given his Miranda rights. The Assistant U.S. Attorney in charge of the case said he thought the case against Santiago was pretty thin. Santiago could say he picked up the remnants of the explosive cleaning the church. It was questionable whether the lies about his religion would come into evidence. He asked the investigators to dig for more.

They had still not let Morse or his children go. They had given Morse two polygraphs, and a polygraph to each of his children, and they had passed. Zach had shown some nervousness on the questions about killing the assassins, which was certainly understandable; as the teenager was probably worried he could be charged with a crime. On January 27, 2013, they decided to get serious with Morse. They put him in a chamber for over 36 hours with no light and then woke him up violently and started peppering him with questions. But the severe techniques only served to disorient him and get him angry, nothing more. In the meantime, Detective Tom Jensen decided for the sake of being thorough to check on the items in Morse's bag. He had his lab technicians carbon date both the scrolls and the ink. The results were conclusive: both came from the early sixteenth century, as Morse had claimed. Investigators in Verona, Italy had picked up Parducci for questioning and had seized the final scrolls. The Verona Police confirmed that the scrolls found there also dated from the sixteenth century. And Jensen found an expert on Nostradamus from a French museum who was kind enough to e-mail a sample of the handwriting of both Nostradamus and Julius Caesar Scaliger. Again, the results were conclusive. The first scroll found in the vault matched known handwriting exemplars of Nostradamus; the other scrolls' handwriting matched known handwriting exemplars of the sixteenth century scholar Julius Caesar Scaliger.

Jensen had also tracked down "Doug and Ray" in Carcassonne. As Morse claimed, Ray Lardiggio, an American tourist, had received a gunshot wound to the arm during a recent visit to Carcassonne. When interviewed, he confirmed Morse's account of the events at Carcassonne. His friend Doug Bushnell had been initially hesitant to talk, but when he heard that Morse had explained everything about what had occurred in the church, he felt there was no point in being quiet about it. He was sure he would be exonerated. He had saved three people's lives, after all. Police detectives in Carcassonne confirmed that the ancient confessional in the Basilica was missing its screen. And the dead priest in Agen was consistent with Morse's story as well. Large clumps of hair had been found in the priest's dressing room. The French detectives had overnighted the hair samples to the FBI. Sure enough, it matched underarm hair samples taken from Morse and his son. In short, their story, as strange as it was, completely checked out.

Jensen was ultimately able to obtain identification from the French authorities as to the assassins found in Salon and Carcassonne. Each was a Muslim radical whose name was on the Homeland Security Watch List. Two of the three were suspected in a number of killings and bombings in southern Europe.

Jensen could find no record that Morse ever possessed a firearm of any kind. He had no criminal record. He had no history of violence, no history of psychological illness or disturbance. The teenagers' school records also looked pretty good. Zach was an A student, Zoey was a C student. Both were active in school activities and had no history of drugs, no history of school suspensions. On Thursday, January 31, 2013, Jensen brought the scrolls to one of their linguists, and had him translate everything on the parchment, to make sure that Morse's translations were correct. The linguist confirmed that the translations were correct. He finally realized Morse and his kids were probably legit, and not involved in any terror plot. Jensen talked to Ruddy Montana from the FBI, who agreed. Morse just did not seem like the type. Jensen had nothing to hold Morse on except for violating French laws against stealing antiquities, so on Saturday morning, the day before the Superbowl, he had Morse and his children released, upon Morse's agreement to return all scrolls found in France to the French government within thirty days. He returned to Morse his notebook, bag and other personal items.

"Stay in Washington for the next few days, Mr. Morse, we may want to talk to you again."

Morse was angered by his treatment, but delighted to be released. He asked if they could have police protection for a few days, in case someone was still following them. Jensen said he could not spare the manpower. When Morse was released, he drove the children to a café in Georgetown to get something to eat. While he was eating a turkey sandwich, Morse was momentarily distracted by the television over the café's bar. He had not seen the news in ten days and wondered what had happened in the bombing investigation. The television journalist on the TV over the bar was in front of the Capitol explaining a historic vote:

"This is Andrea Mitchell with CNN News. History was made just a few moments ago, when the Majority Leader crossed her own party and voted in favor of the nomination of Matt Suba, casting the deciding vote in Suba's favor, after a heated debate this week in the Senate. Many in her party whispered that she was a traitor to the party, but the Majority Leader from Pennsylvania explained at a press conference in the Rotunda that she agreed with the President that the President's judgment had to be trusted in this time of crisis so that the American government could be restored. Republicans cheered the Majority Leader's non-partisan vote, but other critics complained that it was a vote cast for expediency, as the Majority Leader is in a state which is almost evenly split between conservative Republicans and liberal Democrats."

Morse's blood ran cold. He quickly pulled out his notebook with the final quatrains taken from Verona:

55.
Les remplacements sont choisis trop rapidement
Le Projeteur, MABUS , est progéniture du Diable
Il complote sa prise de pouvoir méchamment
Une fois au pouvoir, il est redoutable.

The replacements are chosen too swiftly.
The Planner, MABUS, is the spawn of the Devil.
He plots his takeover wickedly.
Once in power, he is formidable.

MABUS. Morse wrote the words "M. SUBA" on his notebook. He reversed the name "Suba" and got "M. ABUS"—MABUS! He recalled his debate with Erika Flynn in December, when he mocked her for switching the letters of a prophecy around. But this was simply too great a coincidence!

If the prophet Henriette de Nostradame was correct, the Americans had just voted into power the Devil Himself, the one who had planned the Cincinnati Massacre, the Inauguration Day Shooting, and the St. Anthony's Bombing, and who still had more attacks to come! He scanned down to the final quatrains:

56.
Ils attaquent le stade quand on va jouer, pendant le jour.
L'Aigle s'approche de l'air.
Les gens fuient chercher le secours.
Les Béliers attaquent de la terre.

They attack the stadium when they are about to play, during the day,
The Eagle approaches from the air.
The people flee to seek help.
The Rams attack from the ground.

The stadium—that had to mean the Louisiana Superdome in New Orleans, where the Superbowl was scheduled for the following day. The "Eagle approaches from the air" has to mean an airplane flying into the Louisiana Superdome. "The Rams attacking from the ground" has to mean attacking the panicked fans when they attempt to leave the stadium. Morse then thought of something else. He went up to the bartender.

"Who is playing in the Superbowl this weekend?"

"Carolina Panthers and the Miami Dolphins."

The Carolina Panthers. Anna Scall was from South Carolina. She would certainly be at the game. If the terrorists were successful, Matt Suba would become President of the United States. Morse looked at the next chilling quatrain:

57.
MABUS gouverne par la mort ou le chantage.
Il se venge avec des nuages de la mort.
Le meurtre de millions cause de grand ombrage.
Une Guerre de Haine pendant deux siècles, alors...

MABUS governs by death or blackmail
He retaliates with clouds of death
His murder of millions causes great offense
A War of Hate for two centuries, then...

A mass murder at the Superbowl followed by a nuclear and religious war for two hundred years. Morse had to stop this!

Agen, France. 1539.

The Grand Inquisitor snarled behind his hooded, black robe. Henri had lasted two days through the inquisitor's tortures, but he was exhausted. He could not last much longer. Henri was chained to a stone wall in a prison cell beneath a Franciscan Abbey in Southern Spain. The Grand Inquisitor, in a sham of a trial, had found him guilty last week of witchcraft and heresy. He had been transported to the abbey's prison quarters several days ago. The Inquisitor stirred the iron poker into the hot embers again, heating up the sharp end until it was molten red. He removed the poker from the fire and surgically jammed it into Henri's shoulder. The poker smoked and sizzled as it burned through the flesh. Henri screamed in agony.

"Stop, please!"

"Talk!" screamed the Grand Inquisitor menacingly. "Where is your sister Andiette?"

"I don't know! I swear to you! I have not seen her in years."

The Inquisitor put the poker back into the pot of embers again.

"Where is she?!" He stabbed the poker into Henri's leg, putting a burning black hole into his thigh.

"Aaaaaagh!" Henri screamed. His face was covered with sweat. He had burn marks, whip lashes and scars all over his body.

The Inquisitor put the poker in the embers a third time.

"This one," he growled, "is going in your eye if you do not talk." He put the red hot end of the poker an inch from Henri's face. As the Inquisitor started to put the poker to the skin, Henri screamed.

"She is in Agen! Her name is Andiette Scaliger now."

"Does she have the prophecy?"

"I don't know about a prophecy."

The Inquisitor heated the poker again.

"I do not know about a prophecy. I swear! But I have heard her daughter has the gift of sight like her mother. That's all I know. I PROMISE!" Henri began weeping, ashamed of his confession.

The Grand Inquisitor patted Henri on the back as he cried.

"There, there. It is all right, my son. Confession is good for the soul. I absolve you of your sins." With that, the Grand Inquisitor slammed the red hot poker with all his might through Henri's neck, impaling him against the wall.

In Agen, France, at 3 in the morning, Andiette Scaliger was sleeping peacefully with her husband Julius until she was interrupted by a horrible nightmare. She bolted out of bed and threw on a dress and shoes. Her husband was awakened by the noise and groggily stared at his wife.

"Andiette, what are you doing, it is the middle of the night!" "Julius, we are all in terrible danger! I can feel it! I have seen the face of the Devil!

He is coming for us!"

"The face of the Devil? What on earth are you talking about? You just had a nightmare! Go back to bed this instant."

"Julius, you know about the vision I had as a youth of the boy being attacked by his father? You remember that? This dream was just like that! I must trust my visions."

"Andiette, please, get back in bed. You are being silly and narcissistic."

"I do not know what that means, Julius, but I must go. I am going to get Henriette and the children. If you want to get us later, we will be at the Cathedral. It is the only place which is safe." Henriette, their daughter, had been living with them while her husband Michel was out of town curing victims of the plague. Andiette banged on her daughter's door. She was surprised to see when she opened her door that she was already dressed. The two babies were crying, having been awakened from a sound sleep. The mother and grandmother quickly dressed the children.

"Henriette, it is your Bible he is after. You must fetch it quickly."

Henriette went to her dresser and retrieved the small Bible and gave it to her mother. Then she and the children and her mother went into the cold night air of Agen. Andiette opened her mouth in surprise when she looked down the street. In front of the temporarily vacated home of Michel and Henriette de Nostradame, a coach was stopped. They could see the breath from the black horse's nostrils in the distance. A tall, hooded figure was knocking at Henriette's door.

"Quickly," whispered Andiette, "We can make it to the Cathedral if we don't make any noise."

Swaddling the children tightly, Henriette followed Andiette around the back of the Scaliger house and across an alley, on their way to the Cathedral. They crossed over three streets. They could see the lights of the Agen Cathedral about 100 yards away, but the sprint would be out in the open, where anyone could see them. Just then, one of the infants began screaming.

"GO!" yelled Andiette. The two women burst from their hiding place and ran as quickly as they could across the dark cobblestone street to the entrance of the Agen Cathedral. Andiette, holding the Bible, got to the door of the Cathedral first. Henriette was carrying the infants and was about twenty feet behind her mother. Just as Henriette got to the steps of the Cathedral, a big, dark hand grabbed her arm like a vice. Henriette let out a scream.

Henriette whirled and saw a huge big-chested figure, over six feet tall, wearing a dark monk's robe.

"Henriette de Nostradame, you must come with me. You are charged with witchcraft and heresy."

"Let her go!" Andiette yelled from the Cathedral.

"I would be happy to let her go," the Inquisitor smiled darkly. "On one condition. There is a prophecy hidden somewhere in Agen. Give it to me now, and your lives and the lives of your children will be spared."

Henriette looked at Andiette, silently shaking her head giving her the "NO" sign. Andiette hid the Bible in a pocket of her dress.

Henriette said, "There is no prophecy."

The Inquisitor grabbed both of her children from her arms

"DO NOT TOY WITH ME, GIRL!" Then he smiled.

"You have a simple choice. You give me the prophecy or your children will die."

Henriette thought for a moment.

"All right. There is a prophecy."

"No," yelled Andiette.

"QUIET, WOMAN!" yelled the Inquisitor.

"But it is not written down. It is in my head. Spare my children and I will give it to you."

"I have a better idea," said the Inquisitor. "You and your children will come with me." The Inquisitor grabbed the children from their mother's arms and placed them into the seat of his coach. Then he returned to Henriette. "And when I am satisfied that you have given me the prophecy, then I will decide whether you are a witch or a heretic or simply a stupid little girl. And you will tell me the truth, or you and your children will die."

The Inquisitor grabbed her arm and threw her into the coach as well.

"No! Henriette!" Andiette screamed. But she knew she could not try to rescue her. The prophecy was too important. Andiette knew the prophecy would be safe in the church.

The Grand Inquisitor instructed his driver to proceed. The driver snapped the reins, and the horses took off with a gallop. On the coach ride, Henriette recounted to the Grand Inquisitor as much as she could remember about the prophecy. Twenty minutes later, the coach stopped.

They were in the woods, somewhere south of Agen. The Grand Inquisitor led Henriette and her children through the wet leaves of the forest to an old graveyard. The stench was overwhelming. There were flies buzzing everywhere. Something did not look right about this place. As Henriette adjusted her eyes in the darkness, she saw a horrible sight: piles of dead human bodies. She was petrified, and began to move to retreat back to the coach, but the Inquisitor grabbed her arm and pushed her forward. The Inquisitor took her past the bodies to a huge stone vault set into the ground. The door to the vault was open. As she peered inside, there appeared to be rotting dead bodies inside.

"Henriette, have you told me everything you know about this prophecy?"

"Yes, I have, I swear!"

"You said if I told you, you would spare me."

"NO, I said then I would determine if you are a witch or a heretic or a stupid girl. Henriette, only a witch marked by the Devil could know these things you know. You speak ill of our Popes. You talk about murder and horrible crimes of nature. I can only conclude you are a witch. I am sorry."

The Grand Inquisitor threw Henriette and her children violently into the vault and closed the vault door.

Henriette could see nothing but blackness around her, but the stench of the bodies infected with plague was overwhelming.

"NO!" she screamed, banging on the stone. "Let us out! Please!"

"Henriette," said the Inquisitor through the door. "What else is there concerning this prophecy you have not told me? Tell me now and your soul may be saved."

"There is nothing! I swear!"

Satisfied, the Inquisitor said, "Good, then this dies with you here." The Inquisitor stomped away, his black boots pressing into the soft mud and leaves of the forest.

Inside the vault, Henriette could hear the sound of rats. She screamed the loudest scream she had ever screamed. But no one could hear her.

As the Inquisitor returned back to his Coach, he pulled back the hood of his robe. His face bore a striking resemblance to someone born over 400 years later—the forty-ninth Vice President of the United States.

The next day, Andiette and Julius Scaliger led a search party, which tracked the wheel tracks and hoof prints of the Inquisitor's coach to the site in the woods where the Inquisitor had left them. Scaliger himself, unconcerned for his own safety or worry that he might contract the plague, followed the Inquisitor's boot prints to the vault and removed the stone. He cried out in anguish and horror when he saw his daughter and grandchildren. Incredibly, his daughter and one of the grandchildren were still alive, barely so. Scaliger wrapped them in blankets and put them in a coach, where they were brought back to his house. He put salves on the wounds she suffered from rat bites and sores which had begun to break out across her body. He fed her and the baby warm soup. Each day, he consulted his text books and tried every conceivable remedy he could find. Unfortunately, even Galen's texts were no use. They were simply too far gone. As the next three weeks dragged on, Scaliger became concerned that there was no hope left. The only one Scaliger knew who had ever been reputed to be able to cure the plague was his daughter's husband. But where was he? He had been gone now for months with no letter, no indication of a date of return. Scaliger, despite being a man of science, began praying every day in the Church that Michel de Nostradame would return. But he did not return in time, and Henriette and the second child died of plague and infection.

After their funerals, Scaliger became a different man, quick to anger and accusation, brooding in his house, failing to bathe. He was filled with his own guilt for not going out with his wife and trusting her instincts on the night Henriette disappeared. But he turned that guilt into anger, a seething, and festering anger for his son-in-law, who he felt had abandoned his wife and caused her death, as well as the death of his grandchildren. On the day Michel de Nostradame finally returned, Scaliger and Nostradamus had a tremendous fight, with Scaliger turning red in the face, demanding a return of his dowry and insisting that he leave town at once. Scaliger also went to his friend, the village clerk, and had him purge all records of Nostradamus' marriage to his daughter, explaining that Nostradamus was not worthy to be related to him. Henriette's name was changed in the village records to d'Encausse, Andiette's maiden name. When Nostradamus had the gall to ask Scaliger for a return of his wife's prophetic Bible, Scaliger went through the roof. He filed a lawsuit against Nostradamus, seeking the return of his dowry, and had the town constable arrest him for family abandonment. Nostradamus, worried that the lawsuit and arrest could ruin his reputation, sent word to Scaliger that if he dropped the lawsuit and criminal charges, he would gladly leave Agen, no questions asked. Scaliger relented, and Nostradamus was released. On the day Nostradamus left town, Scaliger stood in the street and clapped. Scaliger would hate Nostradamus until the day he died.

Andiette Scaliger could see that the anger was consuming her husband's heart. Only the joy of more children could possibly soothe his soul. So Andiette convinced her husband to have more children, and they went on to have over a dozen children as the years went on. The children filled Scaliger with joy and helped him return to a normal life. His son Joseph was a particular source of pride for him, more brilliant even than Henriette. Scaliger poured his energies into educating his son, who would grow up to be quite a scholar in his own right. Only in the last few years of his life, with the help of his wife Andiette, his children, and the Catholic faith, did Scaliger finally come to peace with the events which involved his daughter.

In the last year of his life, he decided on how best to warn the world of his daughter's prophecies without endangering them or bringing shame onto his own family. His wife told him that the pages of the Bible must be kept in a church. That was the only place where they were safe from the Devil. Scaliger decided on three churches. He would hide the Bible pages in three churches for future generations to find. As his final act of charity, he would give Nostradamus a chance to publish the prophecies, as long as he could unscramble Scaliger's riddles and at the same time confess his horrible sins. A battle of wits and a church confession. He loved his idea.

Washington, D.C. Saturday, February 2, 2013.

"I have spotted them," the first Al Hamal brother said into his cell phone.

"I am right around the corner from you, on P Street. The truck is ready."

The non-descript black van with stolen Maryland license plates rolled up to the edge of the curb. Altair, the older brother, jumped out of the van, wearing an Army surplus jacket and sunglasses, and carrying a .38 Smith and Wesson. He went up to Morse's table at the café, grabbed him roughly by the arm, and before Morse knew what was going on, threw him into the sliding door of the black van. Zach and Zoey looked on in horror as the black van with their father peeled off around the corner in a squeal of tires. Neither Zach nor Zoey got the license plate.

"NO!" Zoey yelled. "Daddy! Come back!"

Zach's self-preservation and protective instincts kicked in. There was nothing they could do about their father now. But killers could be coming for himself and his sister. They had to get out of here quickly.

"Come with me!" Zach said to his sister urgently. "I will protect us." Zoey grabbed her father's bag and the two ran through a door in the kitchen, through the kitchen, and out the back door into an alley. They dodged and darted down the streets of Washington. After about twenty blocks, they ducked into a hotel. Zach looked around. He was confident they were not trailed. He took his sister into the hotel restaurant. He would regroup here and decide what to do. Zach was terrified. His father was gone, probably dead, and he was all alone in a strange city with no money, and terrorists after him and his sister. He hoped everything would be okay.

CHAPTER 25. CAPTIVITY

FBI Headquarters, Washnington, D.C.

"Detective Jensen, this is Agent Bertrand. You told me to tail the Professor and his kids. He went with the kids to the Island Café on O Street. Nothing unusual for the first few minutes. Then a black van with white plates pulled up to the curb. We did not get a license number. An Arab looking man, about 5' 8", Army surplus jacket, jeans, sunglasses, black hair slicked back, no facial hair or tattoos we could see, jumped out with what appeared to be a gun, grabbed the professor right in front of his kids, threw him into the sliding door of the van, and peeled out. We were two blocks away at the time, watching through binoculars, keeping a safe distance from the subject. We immediately tailed the van, it went down P Street and under an overpass and by the time we caught up, it was gone. Can you guys pull satellite and find it? It is a non-descript black van, conversion van not a minivan, I think possibly Maryland plates. Sorry we lost 'em, Detective, but if you can track them by air, we will pursue."

"Where are the kids?"

"We don't know because we went after the van. But we are going back to the café and see if we can find them."

"Roger that, keep me posted."

The detective was disgusted. How easy was it to tail a professor and two children?

"Christine, I need you to pull satellite or aerial drone photos from O and P Street, about three to five minutes ago. We are looking for a black van that pulled up to the side of the Island Café and grabbed our witness and threw him into the van."

Within one minute, the big board in the room showed a satellite photo of Washington, DC. The computer operator, Christine, zoomed in on the location.

"There it is."

They followed the black van on the screen as it left the café, pulled under an overpass, and came out the other side. It weaved its way through traffic for the next ten minutes and then pulled onto I-95 South. Jensen called the Metro DC Police and the County Sheriff's Office and explained the situation to the officers there. Then he put calls in to his FBI field operatives in the area.

"All units," Jensen called out. "We have a non-descript black conversion van which seconds ago left the Washington DC area and pulled south onto I-95. We believe there is a hostage on board."

Jensen considered his next move. If one of the police officers turned on his lights and tried to arrest the driver, the driver could shoot the hostage or crash the van. Better to wait until the van was stopped, and the suspect was not expecting them. Then they could move on the suspect and save the hostage.

"Do not arrest the suspect at this time and do not let him know you are following him. Keep a safe distance away and keep me advised. Our plan is to wait until he stops for gas and then we can grab him and save the hostage."

The FBI field operatives did as they were told. The black van continued driving south for several hours on Highway 95 without stopping. When the van got to Charleston, South Carolina, it pulled off the highway, and quickly drove downtown. Jensen could see the whole thing from the satellite.

"OK, everybody, he is probably going to stop soon. When he does, and when he appears to be clear of the hostage, take down the driver with whatever force you need, although try and keep the driver alive if you can."

The black van pulled into the parking lot of the Charleston Marriott Hotel. The front drive contained an overhead structure, blocking the aerial satellite view from above.

"Chance," said Jensen to the driver of the lead FBI car. "I have no eyes, what do you see?"

"We are three cars behind them. He is getting out now. Baseball cap, jeans, white t-shirt. Cannot see his face. About 5 foot, ten inches. It looks like he is valeting the van. We will get him, boss."

The FBI operatives, wearing black outfits and Kevlar vests, dove out of the three Ford Explorers and converged on the hotel. Ten FBI agents dashed into the hotel lobby. Five other operatives ran down the ramp yelling at the valet driver to stop. They grabbed the valet driver from the van, got him out of the car and searched the van. There was nothing inside the van. One of the agents confirmed with the valet that only one man had gotten out of the car.

The agents in the lobby found no one matching the driver's description.

"Sir, he is not in the lobby."

"Lock down that whole hotel! No one gets in or out!"

The FBI agent asked the hotel agent at the front counter where the exits were for the hotel. The agent explained where all the emergency doors were, and said you could also leave by the doors downstairs. The FBI agent dashed down the stairs into another smaller lobby on the Parking Level. A glass revolving door led out to a circular driveway and a line of cabs.

"Sir, there is another driveway down here on the parking level so he might have gotten out in a cab. My men have all the other exits secured and we will do a room by room search in case he is still here. Do we have a physical description for this guy at all?"

"Unfortunately, no."

"OK, we will look for the baseball cap, jeans, and white t-shirt. That doesn't exactly narrow it down. Boss, didn't you say this guy had a hostage?"

"Yes, we thought so."

"Well, only one guy got out of the car. And nobody is in the van. So where did the hostage go?"

Jensen thought about that. They had watched him the entire time from the café, under the overpass, onto Highway 95, onto the ext ramp, through the streets of Charleston, and then here to the hotel. Where could he have dumped the hostage?

"Christine, pull up the satellite images again from the beginning of the abduction."

Jensen looked at the tape. When the van got to the overpass, Jensen ordered her to run the tape slowly.

"Look at that right there," said Jensen.

"What am I looking at?" asked Christine.

"Look over the left wheel, do you see the dirt?"

"OK, so there's some dirt."

Jensen instructed her to close in on a shot of the van taken after it left from underneath the overpass.

"Zoom in right near the tire."

"There's no dirt."

"There is no dirt," concluded Jensen. "They switched vans under the underpass. And that means that the van had to either leave the underpass later, or it went into a truck."

Jensen looked at the tape, and sure enough, a large tractor trailer pulled under the overpass ten seconds or so before the van did, and then, perhaps a little bit longer than it should have, pulled out from underneath the overpass on the opposite side.

"He is in the truck," Jensen concluded.

Jensen ordered Christine to pull the DMV information for the truck from the license plate number obtained by satellite. It was registered to Fleet Trucking. Calls to the company revealed that the driver in charge of that particular truck was Antonio Sanchez.

"I need everything we have got on this guy immediately."

Christine looked at the Detective.

"Why would bad guys go to such trouble to kidnap this professor, unless he knew something they didn't want him to tell? What if all this mumbo jumbo about the Nostradamus prophecy is true? What if they really are going to attack the Superdome on Sunday, and Morse knows about it? These guys know Morse was picked up by the FBI. Wouldn't they kidnap him to find out what he has told us?"

"I see your point. But a prophecy from the sixteenth century? Come on!""I have this cousin, and her husband died. And she couldn't find her life insurance policy anywhere, and she and her kids had no food, no money, nothing. She went to this séance where this guy said he could talk to the dead, and the guy told her where the policy was kept in the house. Weird things can happen."

"Christine, in an investigation, you have to investigate facts. You can't go off and say the Boogeyman did it. I am not aware of any scientific basis for a claim that someone can predict events hundreds of years in the future. If we have free will, and we do, we can decide to do any particular thing on any particular day. There is no way someone could predict that."

"Well, these scrolls seem to have accurately predicted the Cincinnati Massacre, and the scroll even said the killer would be found in a fortress. The Alamo is definitely a fortress. Then it said that they will hide a bomb in a statute. We know that occurred. And it said the Great Lady will be late, which she was. And then it said that the legislators would quickly vote in replacements. Well that certainly happened with Matt Suba. Oh, and by the way, in case you had not noticed, the name 'SUBA' backwards is 'ABUS.' 'M. ABUS' is 'MABUS.' And I could believe he was the spawn of the Devil because all Republicans, in my opinion, are the spawn of

Satan. Why couldn't the Superdome thing be true? And if it is true, then this guy with the truck and his pals are planning on a mass murder of thousands of people by air and land at the Superdome."

Jensen shook his head. "I suppose it is theoretically possible. I think it is more likely Morse is somehow connected with these terrorists." Christine punched some buttons on her keyboard. The satellite photos tracking the truck had just started to load. They watched the progress of the truck for several hours. In Alabama, the truck went into a dead zone where there were no satellite images. They could try and track every truck coming out of the dead zone but that would take a considerable amount of time. They were stymied for right now.

Hours later, his field detectives called from the Marriott Hotel in Charleston. There were a lot of names on the list, but they were not able to find anyone matching the van driver's description. They had also traced the cabs leaving the hotel from the lower level at about the same time the driver entered the lobby. There were four such cabs, and all four had gone to the Charleston Airport. They made lists of every passenger on every commercial airliner leaving Charleston that day. They would find the driver eventually. But would it be in time to stop the attack?

Later in the afternoon, Detective Jensen spoke on the telephone with President Scall at the White House. Jensen said there was a credible threat that terrorists would attack the Superdome, and he urged her not to attend. Jensen explained all the facts that he had so far, although he was a bit nervous telling the President about the sixteenth century prophecy.

"Let me get this straight, Detective," said the President, who was holding in her hand five field box tickets at the fifty yard-line for the game in New Orleans. "You are telling me that Nostradamus has predicted I will be attacked at the Superdome?"

Matt Suba was with her in the Oval Office and laughed when he heard the description, rolling his eyes.

"Well, not exactly, Madame President. All I am saying is that this gentleman John Morse, who is a respected professor, no criminal record, warned the police before the bombing at St. Anthony's that there was a bomb in one of the statues in the church set to explode. It was too late to stop the bombing, but his warning was accurate and precise. This scroll that he had with him also predicted that you would be late for the event, and you were. I do not know how he could have known that. Morse also claims—and you can laugh at his sources all you want—but he claims that there is going to be an attack by land and air on the Superdome—and shortly after telling us that, he is kidnapped in a very intricately designed kidnapping plot. We have not yet located the kidnappers who took him, although we are getting close. This football game is tomorrow. If it were me, I would play it safe and stay home, Madame President."

"Did you ever think this Morse might be a partner with these terrorists, Detective?" asked Suba.

"Of course we did, and that still is a possibility. If he was a partner with them, though, why would he warn us of the church bombing?"

"Maybe he got cold feet right before the attack," said the President.

"That is certainly a possibility."

"Maybe he staged this to look like a kidnapping, when in fact, his friends were the ones who took him?" asked Suba.

"That is also possible, although our agents said the abduction did not look fake at all. Plus, the kids were not taken. I doubt any father would leave his fifteen and fourteen year-old alone in a strange city to fend for themselves. In any event, he was right about his last warning. I would just not be able to sleep at night if I did not inform you of his next prediction."

Suba laughed. "Thank you for the head's up, Detective. But I think the President will wait until you get us something a little bit more solid than the ravings of a college professor and predictions from 500 years ago."

"Very well, Madame President. Thank you for your time."

Jensen felt hot under the collar and stupid. His credibility was hanging by a thread. He needed something solid. He went back into the control room and pushed his people to dig for more.

Morse woke up inside the van, his head throbbing. They must have knocked him out with a punch to the face. It was hard to focus in the dark with his head hurting so badly. He looked around. They were clearly moving, but something did not feel right. The van seemed like it was stationary. When his eyes became focused in the darkness he figured it out. He was inside the van, but the van was inside the back of a large eighteen wheel truck. He looked around quickly inside the van for his kids. Where were they? Now, he remembered. When they took him, they had left the children.

His mouth was covered in duct tape. His hands were tied behind his back with a clear plastic zip tie and his ankles were bound together with rope. He needed something sharp. He thought of everything he was wearing. Nothing was really sharp. Well, there was one thing. His shirt collar strips. He was wearing an Oxford business shirt. Instead of buttons at the collar, the shirt had small metal strips that inserted in his collar to keep it straight and firm. Perhaps if he could get those strips out, they would be sharp enough to cut the plastic. But hard as he tried, he could not think of a way with his hands bound to unfasten the strips from his collar.

He racked his brain, which hurt. "Think," he told himself. He sat in the darkness of the van for another half hour until he got it. The cigarette lighter. If he couldn't cut the plastic, maybe he could melt it. H scooted on his rear into the front seat and, with his hands towards the steering console, reached for the cigarette lighter and pressed it in. After a few minutes he felt his way for the lighter and removed it. It was hot. He carefully placed the hot cigarette lighter against the plastic.

"Ow!" he said. Doing it this way would also burn his wrist, but there was no other way. He kept doing this, burning the plastic, and then removing it seconds later. After a few minutes, he could feel some give in the plastic. It was weakening. He put the lighter back in and re-charged it. When it was hot again, he kept burning his way through. Eventually, the plastic gave way and his hands were free. He used his free hands to untie the ropes around his feet.

He searched in his pocket for his cell phone to call his kids. His phone, his keys, his ID, his money—everything was gone. He tried to open the doors of the van but they wouldn't budge. He wondered how they locked the doors from the outside. He tried to smash through the window of the van with his hand several times but he wasn't strong enough. He needed something hard and heavy. The tire jack, that should work. He climbed his way into the back of the car and tried to open the plastic panel holding the spare and the jack, but he could not find where it opened. Perhaps the user's manual would say where the jack was located.

He climbed into the front seat and opened the glove compartment. Inside the glove compartment was a user's manual for the Chevy conversion van. When he took out the user's manual, a folded, two-page piece of paper fell out. Morse inspected the paper. It was directions to a street address in Miami, Florida. 14780 Hibernia Lane, Miami Florida. The "FROM" address was Miami-Dade International Airport. Morse pocketed the two-page paper and then looked up the location of the tire jack. There was a black knob he had missed which he needed to turn to take the panel off. Morse jumped back into the rear of the van and found the knob, and the plastic panel came off.

He unscrewed the nut on the threaded post holding in the tire jack. He took it out and felt it in his hand. It seemed sturdy enough. He slammed the tire jack with full force into the side window and it cracked. After two more smashes, the glass shattered into thousands of pieces. He climbed out the window of the van and stood on the floor of the truck. He looked at the outside of the van. Some type of metal device was wedged into the doors, holding them shut from the outside. He looked around. The kidnappers had not heard him yet. He went to the front of the truck and listened. He was hoping he could hear where the kidnappers were taking him, but he could hear nothing but the sound of wheels hitting pavement. He walked to the back of the truck, hoping to try and pry loose the back latch, but he could not get it to open. It was locked from the outside.

Then he looked back to the van. If he could get the van to drive out the back he could smash the doors open. The van wheels were resting inside wedges cut into a raised wooden platform. He would need to lift up the van off the platform. The jack could work again for him.

Morse first put the gear shift into Neutral. Then he took all three parts of the jack and assembled them together. Acting just as if he were changing a spare tire, Morse jacked up the rear of the van. After a few minutes, he had the back of the van lifted up. Now he needed something to plug the wedge holes with. He looked around. Near the back of the truck saw two long and wide metal boards which had obviously been used as a ramp to drive the van into the truck. Morse took the first metal board and laid it sideways across the wooden platform so that the metal covered the two rear holes in the wooden platform. Then he let the jack down. When the van came down, the back tires rested on the metal board, not inside the holes of the wooden platform. Morse then went to the front end of the van and used the jack to raise the front tires. When the van was raised again from the front, he took the second metal board and laid it across the holes in the front and gently lowered the car on the jack. When the front wheels touched, the van started to slowly roll back and forth. Suddenly, the van started to roll very slowly backward on the platform. When it got to the back of the wooden platform, the back tires came down on the floor of the truck with a thud and the van stayed there, half on and half off the platform. Morse quickly jumped to the top of the platform and put all his weight into pushing the front of the van off the platform. Nothing happened at first, but then the truck accelerated, and the van came rolling off the platform, where, at very low speed it contacted the rear door of the truck. "Perfect!" thought Morse.

Then Morse took the wooden platform where the van had been resting, and the two metal boards and pushed them all the way on their side at the very edge of the side of the truck. This way the van would have a clear path to roll backwards and forwards unimpeded inside the truck. Now all he would have to do is wait for one good stop for the van to go crashing into the front of the truck, and one good acceleration to send the van hurtling to the back of the truck. Morse dove back in through the window of the van and buckled himself into the middle seat. He chose the middle seat because he figured that if the van made it out on to the highway, he would probably get creamed by an oncoming vehicle driving behind the truck. The middle was the safest place in the car. He waited. After about three minutes, the truck driver suddenly put on the brakes, and the van went rolling towards the front of the truck, smashing into the front wall.

One minute earlier, Antonio Sanchez, one of the three sons of Osama Bin Laden tasked to blow up the Superdome, drove his large truck past Highway Exit 9. He had made it all the way to Alabama, and no one had stopped his truck. Allah be praised. Things were going well. Surely, if Ammar or the American told the authorities anything, he would be caught by now. He had not heard any noise from the back of the truck so he assumed the American was still sleeping. Just then, a woman suddenly cut in front of him. He slammed on his brakes. These American women did not know how to drive. As soon as he hit the brakes, he heard a huge crash from behind him. What could that be? He saw another exit 2/10 of a mile to the right. He needed to get off the highway immediately and figure out what Morse had done back there. He hit the accelerator, heading for the exit.

As soon as he hit the accelerator on the truck, the van went hurtling to the back of the truck where it smashed through the door and went flying out onto the highway. Cars slammed on their brakes and swerved out of the way to avoid the oncoming van. The van fishtailed when it hit the highway. Morse looked out the front window as scores of cars came at him at high speed, honking, swerving and skidding. The van quickly decelerated. Morse was slowly heading the wrong way down the highway. Morse unbuckled and dove into the driver's seat where he was able to slowly steer the van, rolling in neutral, onto the shoulder. He dove out of the window of the van and ran down the shoulder, waving his arms for help.

Sanchez looked out his rear window and saw what had happened. This was not good. He wanted to pull over and go kill Morse, but he couldn't risk it. Police would be swarming here in a minute. He had to get off the highway and get a new truck. He saw that this exit, Exit 10, had a truck stop. He swerved toward the exit and got to the ramp just in time. He pulled around a grove of trees into the truck lot. There were dozens of tractor trailers parked on the lot. Across the lot was a small diner. He parked his truck. He quickly duct taped the back doors so they would not arouse suspicion and headed toward the diner. When he went through the door, he pulled up a chair next to a Hispanic man.

"Crazy out there today, isn't it?" Sanchez asked.

"You're tellin' me. I have been driving for sixteen hours straight, I'm over my hours, but my boss says I will be fired if I don't get to New Orleans by tonight." He pulled out his Hours of Service Logs. "They don't call these 'funny papers' for nothing.' I guess I will say I drove for eight hours today, that sound about right?"

"Sanchez laughed. Sounds right to me. Hey, listen, I have one load of apples, it weighs practically nothing, and I have to get to New Orleans tonight, but if I stop here, I can see my kids tonight. My bitch of an ex-wife hardly ever lets me see them. If I paid you $50, do you think you could take 'em for me?"

The other driver considered. "Let me see how big the load is." As they walked out of the diner, Sanchez said, "Antonio Sanchez. What's your name?"

"Manny Davis. That's my truck over there." He pointed to a large green truck that said "BFS."

When they got out to Sanchez's truck, Manny saw the duct tape and said, "Hey, what happened to your truck?"

Sanchez pulled out a gun with a silencer. "Give me your keys."

Davis has a second of panic on his face. "Hey, mister, I don't mean any trouble, you can have the truck, just let me go, I have three kids." He handed Sanchez the keys to his truck.

"They will miss you." Sanchez shot Davis in the head. Moments later, Sanchez pulled the green truck onto the interstate heading south towards New Orleans. The whole pit stop had only taken three or four minutes. There were no police yet. That was good.

Morse was able to flag down a man in a blue pickup. "You OK, mister?"

"I am in terrible danger! Can you take me to the next exit?"

"Sure," said the man. "Hop in." Morse jumped in the front seat, his eyes darting around to see if the gunman was coming after him.

"I was kidnapped and I escaped. I need to call the police. Can I borrow your cell phone?"

"Sure, no problem." The man handed him his phone.

"What highway are we on? Where are we?"

"You are on Highway 59, five miles south of Montgomery, Alabama."

Morse dialed 911. "Yes, my name is John Morse. I am on Highway 59, five miles south of Montgomery. I was kidnapped in Washington DC in a black van and the black van was put inside the belly of a tractor trailer. One minute ago I just escaped by ramming the black van out through the doors of the tractor trailer and onto the highway. If you come to the scene out here, you should find the black van. A nice driver on the road driving a blue pickup, license number…." Morse looked at the driver.

"EBT-657" said the man.

"EBT-657 just picked me up and is taking me to the next exit. I request police assistance at Exit…uh, let's see, where are we? Exit 11, I think. Also, Detective Jenson at the Secret Service needs to be aware of this. I have a lead for him to follow that is a matter of national security involving a potential terrorist attack. Can you call him?"

"Sure, where is your kidnapper now and what does he look like?"

"Hispanic or Arab is all I can tell you. Medium build, that's all I know. I only got a quick look at him. I don't know where he is, I think he kept driving."

"OK, Mr. Morse, when you get off at Exit 10 there is a McDonalds right there. Just stay in the McDonald's and we will come and get you. What is this terrorist plot you are referring to?"

"I will tell the Secret Service Detective all that."

"Is the plot here in Montgomery, sir?"

"No, I do not believe so."

"OK, will be right over to get you."

"Great, thank you." Morse hung up and turned to the driver. "Can I make one more call to my kids?"

"Sure, no problem. Hey, I hope you are OK."

Morse dialed Zach's cell phone. He answered on the third ring.

"Zach?"

"DAD! Where are you? Are you OK?"

"Yes, Zach, I escaped. I am OK. I am in Montgomery, Alabama. Where are you and Zoey?"

"We are in the Capitol Plaza Hotel in Washington DC hanging around the lobby. We did not know where to go."

"Thank God you are OK. Did any one follow you?"

"No, I don't think so."

"OK, here is what you need to do. I do not have any credit cards on me, so you are going to have to call Grandma. You have her number, don't you?"

"Yes."

"OK, tell her what's happened, and Grandma can call the hotel and get you a room with her credit card. Then tell Grandma to fly to Washington, DC as soon as she can and get you two. I will be home as soon as I can."

"Why don't you come home now?"

"I will. I just need to meet with the FBI and Secret Service and warn them about this attack on the Superdome. I have a lead for them to follow. It's an address in Miami. Then I will be home."

"Dad, don't try to be a hero, just come home."

"I will, very soon. It's all going to be OK."

Zoey grabbed the phone. "Hey, Dad."

"Hi Zoey!"

"I have the bag with the Nostradamus stuff."

"You do? Oh, Zoey, you are wonderful! Here is what you need to do. Go to the hotel clerk and tell them you need to keep the bag in the hotel safe. They will give you a key. Then you can give me the key later. I don't want you to have to worry about that bag on the flight home. It has caused us enough trouble already."

"Hey Dad? Did they hurt you?" asked Zoey.

"Not at all, Zoey. I am fit as a fiddle."

"OK, good. Be careful Dad. We love you."

"I love you, too."

The man in the blue pickup dropped Morse off at the McDonald's where Morse waited for the police to arrive.

Antonio Sanchez was driving out of the truck stop onto the highway when he saw the truck had a police scanner. Hmm, he thought. That is helpful. He turned on the police scanner and started monitoring the emergency band. The Dispatcher was talking about the black van on the highway.

"Also, Unit 12, can you pick up the kidnap victim, Mr. Morse, at the McDonald's on Exit 11 and take him to the station. He says he has an important lead for the FBI on a major terrorist plot."

Sanchez sighed. He could not let Morse give them whatever lead they were talking about. Exit 11 was just ahead. If he got there quickly....

Sanchez pulled the green truck off Exit 11. Just past the McDonald's was a Shell Station with a big parking lot. That would have to do. He pulled the green truck into the back of the parking lot, hopped out and ran back to the street. He ran as quickly as he could back toward the ramp coming from the highway and waited for the first police car to come. About a minute later, a lone police car, Unit 12 of the Montgomery Police Department, came down the ramp from the highway and turned right, heading towards the McDonalds. Sanchez ran into the street waving his arms, his gun tucked into the back of his pants.

"Officer! Officer! Help!" The police car pulled over. There was only one officer in the car. That was good.

The officer rolled down his window and leaned over. "Are you John Morse?"

Sanchez leaned in the window and pulled out his gun with the silencer. Before the officer could react, he shot him in the face. Then he ran to the driver's side of the police car. Shoving the officer over into the driver's seat, he got in the police car and turned on the lights. He took the officer's hat and glasses and put them on. Then he quickly pulled into the McDonald's parking lot, where he saw Morse waiting. He rolled down the window half way.

"You John Morse?"

"Yes," said Morse. "Thank God you're here."

"Get in the back," said the officer.

Morse got in the back of the car. There were no interior locks and no way to open the police car from the inside. There was a mesh screen between the officer's compartment and the back seat.

"Are you with the Montgomery P.D.?" asked Morse.

It was then that Morse noticed the slumped officer in the passenger seat with the blood stained head.

"NO! Help!" He tried to open the doors but was unsuccessful. "Help! Let me out!" he yelled, banging the windows.

Sanchez pulled out of the McDonald's lot and quickly made his way back to the highway, where he headed south to New Orleans, with Morse still screaming from the back seat. Twenty miles down the road, Sanchez found a rest stop on the side of the highway. He pulled off and drove over to the edge of the lot, near a clump of bushes. He quickly undressed the police officer, who was about his own size. He changed in the car, swapping his outfit for the police officer's. He put his jeans and shirt on the officer's body. Then he walked around to the passenger's side and opened the door. He dragged the officer's body out and dumped it in the bushes, out of sight. Then he got back in the car and headed back onto the highway. Just then there was an announcement over the police radio.

"Unit 12. What's your status? Did you find the kidnap victim?" Sanchez picked up the radio.

"That's affirmative. En route to the station with the victim. 12 out."

"10-4."

The Montgomery Police Department would not realize for another 45 minutes that Unit 12 had been taken. By that time, the police car had pulled off the interstate and was taking the back roads into New Orleans.

The body of the dead trucker, Manny Davis, was found at about 6 p.m. by a trucker pulling into a spot near the place where Manny had been killed.

Later that night, at 10 p.m., two local teenagers who used the rest stop on Highway 59 as a lover's lane found the police officer's dead body in the bushes. By midnight, there was a nationwide manhunt for the killer/kidnapper Antonio Sanchez. No one knew he was actually one of the young sons of Osama Bin Laden.

CHAPTER 26. SUPERBOWL

Miami, Florida. February 3, 2013. 2 a.m.

Lou Caradanno was tired. He had been piloting Delta planes all week to Los Angeles and back and had seen his wife very little. He was really mad he had to take the 2 p.m. flight to Los Angeles tomorrow and miss the Superbowl. He had promised his wife he would watch it with her, but he was one of the lowest in seniority at Delta, so he always got the crummy routes nobody wanted. It was a good paying job, though, and that was tough to come by these days. His wife rustled him at 2 a.m.

"Honey, I thought I heard a noise."

Uggh. "Are you sure?"

"I am pretty sure."

Caradanno sat in bed for another minute. His wife nudged him again.

"Lou, go check it out, OK?"

"Uh, OK honey."

He rolled out of bed, slowly looking for the light switch.

A dark shadow silently came into the doorway. There were two quick pings and it was all over. Mr. and Mrs. Lou Caradanno were dead. The gunman turned the light on. He rolled each body into a long canvas bag and zipped them up. Then he took each body down into the family's basement, and hid them behind some old paint cans. Then the killer went upstairs and mopped the hardwood floor of the bedroom with cleanser and a mop so there would be no blood residue.

The killer looked into the pilot's closet. His Delta Uniform was there, pressed and ready to go. He put that and the pilot's shoes into a third bag. He also checked the nightstand, and took the pilot's Delta ID, his car keys, his wallet, and his cell phone. The man known to the world as Francisco Perez, known to his master as an Abisali, known to the team as Altair, known to his father Osama Bin Laden as son, would now have a new identity—Lou Caradonna, Delta Pilot.

Perez went into Caradonna's garage and opened the door with the garage opener. He pulled Caradonna's 4x4 out of the driveway. Perez's wife Feyza and his sister-in-law Saieed, driving the minivan, followed him to the next location, the home of Delta Flight Attendant Nancy Eli on Hibernia Lane. Perez, his wife, and his sister-in-law would have two more stops after that. By 4 a.m., the bodies of one pilot, one co-pilot, two flight attendants, and four spouses, were in canvas bags. By 6 a.m., the terrorist team was back at the safe house in Miami, where they met Tikah, the man who would act as co-pilot. Tikah took the Delta IDs from his friend. The Delta IDs would have new faces within the hour.

New Orleans. Warehouse District. February 3, 2013. 6 a.m.

By 6 a.m., both Al Hamal brothers were back at the truck garage in the warehouse district of New Orleans. One of the brothers, the one known as Antonio, finished packing the last box of C4 explosives. His little brother was finishing the rigging of the special machine guns to the front of the truck. The guns folded into sleeves on the side of the truck hood so that when the truck drove down the road, no one would notice the guns. A remote control pressed from a handheld device would pivot the machine guns out of their sleeves. Morse was handcuffed in the back of the police car, which was parked next to the truck.

"It is a shame we have to give up one of the trucks," said Antonio. "The explosions would be better with two trucks."

"Yes, but we have the police car," said his brother.

Morse was listening through the slightly open window of the back of the police car, where he was bound and gagged. The brothers had only questioned him for about ten minutes about an hour ago, asking him what "lead" he was going to give to police. Morse said there was no lead. The brothers seemed to shrug it off, as if they were not very interested. Morse considered this. It was probably because they figured their plan was so far advanced now, it could not be stopped.

Miami, Florida, 8 a.m.

That morning, at 8 a.m., Francisco Perez was scheduled to fly a group of corporate executives in the company Lear jet from Miami to New Orleans for the big game. He called in sick at the last minute, asking a fellow pilot named Tim Welsch to take his shift. Perez asked Welsch to punch in Perez's time card when he started and ended the shift. Perez said he was on probation for attendance right now and didn't want to get in trouble. Perez promised Welsch that he would pay him for the flight out of his next paycheck, and would give him $100 as a bonus. Welsch agreed. He had spiraling credit card bills and needed money. For anyone in the control tower, it would look like Perez was piloting the jet.

Washington, DC, 8:45 a.m.

President Anna Scall was excited about her first trip on Air Force One. She was dressed in black pants, a black and blue Panthers jersey with "Benjamin" written on the back, and a blue and black ponytail. Matt Suba told the President that he had to stay back and attend to the bombing investigation and other matters, but that he would watch the game on TV. The President's husband and children would be joining her on Air Force One to go to the big game. As Scall and her husband got to the top of the steps to board the plane, Stephen Colbert from The Colbert Report suddenly jumped out from inside the plane, growling like a panther, acting as if his hands were cat's paws. Colbert was a native of South Carolina and had been invited by the President to join her family on the plane. His entire face looked like a blue cat. She laughed and took a photo with Colbert and her husband and then hopped inside the plane, excited about attending the Superbowl.

At 10 a.m., Matt Suba left the White House and went into a small coffee shop across the street. He took out his untraceable cell phone with prepaid minutes and sent a text message to his pilots. Moments later, he received a text message back. Everything was in place and ready to go. He made a similar text to his ground team. The message back was: "Dinner party ready to go. Our good friend John is with us and has promised he will not spoil the party." Suba smiled. There was a reason he called himself Mudabbir. He was an excellent planner. By the end of today, he would be President of the Untied States, and the world would be a different place.

Miami Dade International Airport. 1:30 p.m.

The terrorist flight team approached the TSA security gate. Francisco Perez, wearing his captain flight outfit and his ID badge bearing the name of Louis Caradonno, strolled confidently to the X-ray machine. He took off Caradonno's wristwatch, wallet, cell phone, and keys, and placed them in the plastic holder. He walked through the metal detector without a hitch. The TSA guard reviewed his credentials and flight information and passed him through. Tikah was next, and also made it through without a hitch. Then came the two women, posing as the flight attendants. The guard looked at their IDs for a few second longer, but passed them through.

As they started to walk away, one of the TSA guards said, "Captain!"

Perez calmly turned around slowly. "Yes?"

"Dolphins or Panthers?"

"Why, the Dolphins, of course!" He smiled warmly, flashing his white teeth. Then they made their way to the gate. They passed through the gate checkpoint and boarded the Delta plane, Flight 16 to Los Angeles. The flight was full this afternoon. Perez made his pre-flight checks, and Tikah fiddled around in the cockpit pretending he knew what he was doing. They closed and locked the cockpit door, while Perez's wife and his sister-in-law helped usher passengers to their seats. After twenty minutes, all the passengers were in and the tower cleared him for takeoff. By 2:05 p.m., Flight 16 was in the air, and headed toward the Gulf of Mexico

Washington, DC. Office of Homeland Security. 3 p.m.

Detective Ruddy Montana and Detective Tom Jensen were nervous. Morse had been right about the church bombing. He had been right about the Vice President being late. He had been right about a legislative appointment which was rushed. His last prediction was that there would be an attack on the Superbowl from the land and air. And now he was kidnapped. Montana and Jensen had been in touch with the Montgomery Police Department and knew that the kidnappers had killed a police officer, stolen his car, grabbed Morse while police were swarming everywhere, and then escaped into the backwoods. Why would anyone risk all that to kidnap an egghead professor, unless he was either part of the plot or knew about the plot? In both detectives' minds, that did not smell good. They feared there would be another attack on the Superbowl, and they only had a few hours to stop it.

Just to see what would happen, Jensen had hooked up Hector Santiago to pulse and skin monitors and then questioned him about references in the prophecy Morse had provided. Santiago said nothing, but his pulse started racing and he looked nervous when Jensen referenced "Abisali," "the Eagle," "the Rams," "the Builder," or "the Planner." References to "MABUS" and to "the spawn of the Devil" had no reaction. The accuracy of the prophecy was sending a chill up Jensen's spine. He had to crack this plot before it was too late.

The interviews of guests at the Charleston Marriott revealed no pilots or truck drivers, as Jensen had hoped. That probably meant that the driver of the black van escaped into one of the taxis going to the Charleston Airport. They checked the flights leaving Charleston but there were flights going everywhere. The list was huge.

Montana had put out an APB on Morse's children, and this morning, they got a hit from Morse's mother's credit card at a hotel in Washington, D.C. Two agents went over to pick the kids up and bring them in. They were due any minute.

The TSA was instructed to be extra vigilant today, and to call in anything even remotely suspicious. The FBI had ordered extra security at the Superdome. Snipers were on the roof of the Dome. Concrete barriers were set up at various points along the parking lot of the Superdome. An Apache helicopter was ordered to maintain surveillance from the air over the Dome.

Montana and Jensen turned to the elevator and saw Zach and Zoey Morse walking in with two agents. He brought them in a conference room.

"Hi, kids. Thanks for coming in again," said Montana, patting Zach on the back with a fatherly tone. Montana was chosen to do the interview, because Zach did not like how he had been previously treated by Jensen.

"I guess you heard your father escaped and then was re-kidnapped," said Montana.

Zach's face was blanched. This whole ordeal had completely exhausted him. "Yeah, we heard. Have you heard anything from him?"

"No. But we hoped you could help us. We checked the cell phone records of the gentleman who rescued your father in Alabama and it says that right after he made the 911 call to the Montgomery Police, he called you, Zach, on your cell phone."

"Yeah, that's right."

"What did he say?"

"He said he was OK, that he was fit as a fiddle, that they had not hurt him. He asked if we were OK and we said yes. Zoey told him she still had his bag with the Nostradamus stuff in it, and he told her to lock it in the hotel safe."

"Anything else?" asked Montana.

"Yeah, he said that we should call our Grandma, get her credit card number and stay in the hotel. He said Grandma would come for us sometime today."

"OK. And when your Grandma gets in town, we will tell her where you are so that she can come down here with you."

"Whatever," said Zach.

"Anything else?"

"No."

"Are you sure? Take a moment and think about it. Go through each thing he said in your mind. Anything he said might be able to help us find him."

Zach thought a minute. "There was something else. I asked him why he couldn't just come home now, and he said he wanted to talk to you guys because he had some kind of lead."

"A lead? What kind of lead?"

Zach thought for a minute. "I'm not sure, he said something about an address in Miami he wanted you to check out."

"Did he say what the address was?"

"No," he didn't."

"OK, that is very helpful. Anything else you can think of?"

"Nope."

The detectives asked Zoey if she could remember anything.

"Daddy just told me where to put his bag and I told him to be safe and that I loved him." Zoey's eyes started to water. "Is he going to be OK?"

"We are going to do our best," said Montana.

The two Detectives ran out of the conference room and went to one of their computer analysts.

"OK, Christine, we have something. Miami. Check all flights leaving Charleston yesterday and going to Miami or Fort Lauderdale. Then cross-check that against the FAA for any known pilots or flight attendants and then check with the USDOT for truck drivers." Ten minutes later, Christine called them back to her station. She had three matches.

"I have a Timothy O'Rourke who is a truck driver for Allied Van Lines, left Charleston on a 3:00 p.m. flight yesterday for Fort Lauderdale."

Christine pulled up his photo. He was a large white man with red hair.

"O'Rourke," said Montana. "Irishman. That doesn't fit. The guy at the Cincinnati Bombing was Mexican or Arab. So was the guy who we suspect for the church bombing. And near as we can tell, so was the guy who grabbed Morse. I do not think the guy is Irish. Who's next?"

"We have a Francisco Perez. Left on a 2:30 flight from Charleston to Miami. Works for a private jetliner giving Lear jet rides to corporate executives."

"He sounds interesting. Photo?"

Christine pulled up the photograph. The detectives stared at the screen.

"What do you think, Tom? He look Mexican to you?"

Jensen squinted at the photo. "He looks Arab if you ask me."

"I agree. Is he scheduled to fly today?"

"Yes, he is flying to New Orleans at 2:00 p.m. CJE Flight 2417."

Montana and Jensen looked at their watches. It was 3:05 p.m. Montana yelled for another agent to come over to the station. "We need a conference call with the Regional Director of the FAA and the pilot of CJE Flight 2417, immediately! There could be a terrorist flying that plane!"

"Tell me about the third guy, Christine."

"It's a woman. Betty Islington. Flight attendant for TWA, left from Charleston to Miami at 5 p.m. yesterday, lives in Miami. Here is her photo."

The woman was an African American, 52 years old.

"Doesn't look right. I think this Perez is our guy. Team meeting in the conference room, people, three minutes!"

Somewhere in the air over the Gulf of Mexico 3:30 p.m.

"Flight 2417, this is Mike Peterson, Regional Director of the FAA. I also have two detectives with me from Homeland Security on the line. I need to speak to the captain."

"Uh, this is the captain."

"Is this Captain Francisco Perez?" asked Peterson.

Tim Welsch thought for a moment. He had clocked in under Perez's name. If they knew he had done that, he could get fired. He would have to hope the tower didn't know. "Yes, it is."

"Captain Perez, I need you to turn your plane north and head to Destin Airfield."

"Sir, I am supposed to be going to New Orleans. These guys have tickets to the Superbowl."

"Captain, I do not care who has tickets to the Superdome! Please look out over your left wing."

The pilot looked out his window. There was an F-16 fighter jet just off his wing. Another fighter jet was on the other side of his plane. "Do you see those jets, Captain?"

"Yes, I do."

"If you do not turn your plane immediately north this instant, and head to Destin Airfield with a vector Zero, Niner, Seven, I have authorization from the Chairman of the Joint Chiefs to have those fighters shoot your plane out of the sky."

"Whoa! Hold on a minute! I'll turn this thing wherever you want. Don't shoot, please! Look, I'm turning, I'm turning." He turned the plane to the north. The fighters trailed him.

"Keep your present course, Captain."

"No problem. Please, don't shoot! I have two kids!"

"Keep your present course and nothing bad will happen."

The plane continued north for another forty five minutes. When the plane started to fly over the land instead of the water, one of the corporate executives knocked on the pilot's cabin door. The pilot opened the door. The executive and his friends were completely drunk, and were wearing Dolphins jerseys.

"Hey, there, Commander, I was just noticing we were flying over land now, are we almost there?"

"No, we had to take a detour. We are flying into Destin Airfield."

"Destin Airfield? What are you talking about? We are going to miss the game!" The other Miami executives heard their friend's discussion and came up to the pilot's door. "It's almost 4! The game is going to start soon! I didn't pay $4,000 a ticket and $1,000 for this flight so you can dump me off in Destin! Now you turn this goddamn plane to New Orleans or I am going to have your job!"

"I cannot do that sir! I was ordered by the FAA to land there?"

"Well, why would they say that?"

"I don't know. But they said they would blow us out of the sky if we didn't go to Destin."

The drunk executive looked out the window. He didn't see anything.

"Who is going to shoot us?"

"The F-16s that were there a minute ago."

"Well, I don't see 'em now. Look, you just fly us to New Orleans and let me worry about the FAA. I will pay whatever fine they impose on you."

"I can't do that, sir. Now you are going to have to take your seat! Now!"

The captain, Tim Welsch, was black. The executive, a good old boy from the Old South was not going to let this "colored fella" tell him what to do. He was an important man, a rich man. Who did this little black punk think he was?

"I am not going to sit down! I paid good money for this flight and you are going to fly us to New Orleans, BOY!" With that, he slapped the pilot hard on the side of the head. Welsch had not anticipated a strike to the head and when he fell to the left side, his arm hooked on the steering wheel, pulling the plane sharply and violently to the left. The Lear jet started to veer to the side, and the drunk executives all fell down on the carpeting.

"He is turning violently, sir!" yelled one of the F-16 pilots. "Permission to engage!"

The Chairman of the Joint Chiefs was monitoring the situation from the Pentagon. He thought for two seconds, and then realized the risk was too great. They might not get another chance.

"Engage!" The F-16 fired a rocket into the belly of the Lear jet, which exploded into a fireball, killing everyone on board.

Detectives Jensen and Montana saw the explosion from the F-16 video being transmitted to their screens. Their expressions were grim. They did not know how many people were on board, but at least the plane could not hit the Superdome.

New Orleans. Warehouse District. 4 p.m.

The Al Hamal brothers had spent the morning applying a phony decal which read "New Orleans Police Department" over the Montgomery Police Department police car. It looked pretty decent if you didn't look too close. Then they had taken an entire pallet of C4—the C4 that they had originally planned to use for the second truck—and rigged wires to the side door of the warehouse. Anyone opening the door would blow the garage sky high.

The positioned Morse in a chair, cloth in his mouth, hands bound behind his back to the chair, legs bound to the feet of the chair. Morse knew that one way out of being bound is to keep the rope from being tied too tight. If you place your wrists apart slightly and then expand your chest as much as possible, the binds will be looser, allowing the victim more room after tying to wiggle free. Unfortunately, the Al Hamal brothers knew that trick, and tied his wrists together tightly. They punched him in the chest before tying the rope across.

"Your dumb little tricks don't work with us, Professor!" they laughed. The two brothers placed the chair in full view of the window to the side door of the garage, so that if anyone looked in, they would see Morse, open the door, and trip the explosives. Then they lifted up the bay door and drove the truck and the police car out, closing the door behind them. The warehouse was dark. Morse made note of the truck's license plate as it drove out. The only light was a light bulb with a string right over Morse's head. Morse grunted and gurgled in desperation. He was probably going to die here tonight. Morse kept thinking about the words of Henriette the prophet. He had not stopped anything. They were going to succeed.

Ils attaquent le stade quand on va jouer, pendant le jour.
L'Aigle s'approche de l'air.
Les gens fuient chercher le secours.
Les Béliers attaquent de la terre.

They attack the stadium when they are about to play, during the day,
The Eagle approaches from the air.
The people flee to seek help.
The Rams attack from the ground.

The Rams were on their way to begin the ground attack.

Somewhere over the Gulf of Mexico, 4:30 p.m.

"Good afternoon, football fans. This is Captain Caradanno speaking. The flight attendants will be handing out earphones in just a minute. Any of you wishing to see the Superbowl can turn your dials to Channel 2, and you can view the game from the screens which we are lowering from the ceiling. The pre-game should start in about a half hour, and the game begins at 6."

New Orleans Superdome. 50 yard-line. Presidential Box.

The President's three girls were thrilled. "Mom, these seats are awesome! Do you think we could get autographs after the game?"

"I don't see why not!" said the President.

She and her children scarfed down some brats and pretzels, anxious for the game to begin. Her Secret Service team was all around her, eyes darting out in all directions looking for potential threats.

New Orleans Warehouse District. 4:30 p.m.

Morse looked around him in desperation. There was nothing sharp he could use to cut the tight ropes. He could try and jump up in the chair, with the hope that the chair legs might break, thereby giving him a sharp tool, but that was a big risk. If he failed, he would be more likely to wind up on the ground tied to the chair, in a worse predicament than he was now.

There was nothing within reach, only the string of the light bulb. Maybe he could grab the rope with his teeth and then flash the light off and on, and someone might see him. Morse considered that. Even if he was successful, that would only cause someone to open the side door to the garage, blowing him to Smithereens.

In the ensuing minutes, Morse started weeping. He was really going to die here. His children would have no parents, both killed by terrorists. How could they possibly cope? Why hadn't he realized at the McDonald's that the cop was a phony? He pictured his children at his funeral, crying, his name, John Morse, etched in his tombstone. John Morse.... Then he thought of something. Morse. Maybe....

He scooted the chair over with all his strength, nudging it over about five inches, until the string from the light bulb ran across his face. Then he used his teeth to grab the light string. He turned the light off, and then back on, but he did it in a pattern. Morse Code.

He remembered his father had taught him Morse Code as a child. He wanted him to learn what his name meant. His family was actually related to Samuel Morse, the man who invented the Morse Code as a way of sending messages in wartime. He reached back into his memory banks and was surprised that he remembered all the letters' codes.

The dot was a short flash of light, and the dash was a long flash of light. He began turning the light off and on with his teeth, sketching out a message. He had no idea whether anyone would see it.

In New Orleans Harbor, Harbor Masters Billie McGhee and her husband Donny were sitting on the deck of their shrimp boat, relaxing in lawn chairs, with an old TV with bunny ears propped up on a crate. They each had a bag of Cheetos, a hamburger, and a can of Dixie Beer and were relaxing in front of the TV, waiting for the pre-game to start. Billie was a diehard Miami fan.

"You know," said Donny, "Those St. Louis Rams was idiots lettin' that Warner go. He brought their team to the Superbowl, and he gets one lousy injury and they throw him on the scrap heap."

"I can't believe he could get those Cardinals to the playoffs. Now them's some idiots," said Billie.

"Looks like we'll have good weather, though. Hope it keeps up. Our catch wasn't too good last week."

Donny popped open another beer, and then looked out toward the pier. That was odd. He had the phone in the Harbor Master's office forwarded to his cell phone, so he could watch the game on his boat. Just then, his cell phone rang.

"Is this the Harbor Master?"

"Yes, it is."

"I was walking by the warehouse over by Pier 47 and I noticed some weird flashing lights coming from the inside. I wondered if you could check it out."

"Sure. Who is this calling?"

The line went dead. Donny McGhee grabbed his flashlight and jumped down onto the pier from his boat.

"Where ya goin?"

"Somebody is reporting strange lights coming from the warehouse by 47. You wanna come check it out with me?"

"Sure." Billie jumped off the boat, and hurried to catch up to her husband. They walked down the pier and over to the small warehouse.

"Hey, Billie, look at that over there. You see that flashin'?"

Billie looked over. Sure enough, there was some weird flashing of light off and on. Wait a minute, she thought. That light is making a pattern. She and Donny had used Morse Code before with their ship's light as part of safety training.

"Hey, Donny, I think that's Morse Code!"

Donny stared at the warehouse. "Damn, I think you're right. Hey, hand me that notebook and a pen." Billie handed him the notebook. Donny watched the lights and started to write something.

"…DO NOT OPEN WARA HOUH BOOR. HELP. KNDNIP."

"Wara-houh." Billie looked at the translation. "That must be 'WAREHOUSE DOOR.' HELP. KIDNAP."

"Hey!" said Donny. "We gotta get over and help that guy." Donny and Billie sprinted over to the warehouse. They approached the side warehouse door and looked through the window, where the light was going off and on. There, tied to a chair, was a thin man with gray hair, and a rag stuffed in his mouth. He was sweating profusely and violently shaking his head back and forth.

Donny started to reach for the door, when his wife grabbed his hand. "Hey, Donny! The message said don't open the warehouse door. It is probably rigged or something. Let's get in another way." They went over to the middle of the garage and tried the bay door but it was locked. They continued further down to the other end of the building where they saw a big window. Donny took a big rock and threw it through the window. He cleared out the glass with his shirt and then tried to get through the window, but he was too fat.

"Oh, for the love of Neptune!" cried his wife, putting out her cigarette. She pushed her husband out of the way and crawled through the window opening. Donny handed her his flashlight through the window. She saw Morse at the other end of the warehouse under the light and cautiously approached him. When she got near him, she took out his gag.

"Oh, thank God!" exclaimed Morse. "Thank you so much. I thought you were going to open that door. It is rigged with all those explosives." Morse pointed to a pallet of C4 over in a corner. "Come on, we have to get out of here. Can you untie me?"

"Sure, sugarplum. Just give old Billie a minute and you will be out of there in no time." She undid Morse's ropes and he rubbed his wrists. "Let's go!" said Morse. They ran across the warehouse to the other side, where Morse crawled out through the window.

"Do you guys have a cell phone?"

"Sure do. It's on the boat, come on," said Donny and the three scrambled over to the small fishing boat.

911 Communications Center. Downtown New Orleans. 4:52 p.m.

"911."

"Yeah, my name is Carlos Bonita. I would like to report a possible terrorist plot."

"Yes, sir, go ahead."

"I was just down in the Warehouse District on Warehouse Street. There is an old warehouse there by Pier 47. Anyway, I happened to be walking by there taking a smoke, and I looked in the window of the side door, and I saw a big truck of what looked like plastic explosives in there and a couple guys loading it up. I thought you would want to know."

Two minutes later, three fire trucks, twenty police cars, the New Orleans Bomb Squad, and the local SWAT unit peeled down to the New Orleans Warehouse District, hoping to catch some real terrorists. The Al Hamal brothers laughed as they saw all the emergency responders drive by them and away from the Superdome. Americans were so gullible.

This time Morse was careful not to call the police, lest the killers track him again on the emergency channel. From the boat, he used the cell phone from the boat to call Zach, who was still at Homeland Security Headquarters in Washington.

"Zach! It's Dad! I'm safe!"

"DAD!!" yelled Zach. "I can't believe it's you!" Zach started crying. Zoey, who was sitting next to Zach in the small Homeland Security Conference Room, started jumping up and down, crying with joy.

"Is he OK?" Zach nodded to her.

"Where are you, Dad?"

"I am in the Warehouse District in New Orleans. Listen, Zach, do you still have Detective Jensen's business card? It is urgent I speak with him."

"Dad, he is standing like fifty feet away from me. They picked us up this morning for questioning and I have been here all day."

"Well, put him on the phone quickly!"

Zach dashed out with his cell phone, running towards Jensen. "It's my Dad! I have him on the phone!"

Jensen grabbed the phone and put Morse on speaker in the conference room with the other detectives and analysts.

"Morse. Where are you?

"I am in the Warehouse District in New Orleans. I am on a shrimp boat by Pier 47, I think. Listen, I saw what these guys are planning. They have a tractor trailer filled with C4 explosives, Louisiana plates, license plate CXS-990 and they are heading to the Superdome right now! They put a decal over that Montgomery Police Department police car and made it look like a New Orleans car. And they have huge machine guns, hooked on some kind of contraption on the front of the truck, so they can gun down whatever comes at them. And I also saw…" Just then there was a deafening blare of sirens as a pack of police cars came screaming around the corner towards the warehouse.

"What is that, Morse? We can't hear you."

"It's a whole bunch of police cars…. Oh, my God, I know what they're doing." He handed the cell phone to his friends on the boat, and dashed down the wooden pier toward the warehouse. The police cars parked in front, and the men jumped out of the cars, heading for the side door.

Morse ran at them head on like a crazy man. "Wait! Stop! Don't open that door!"

To Morse's great surprise, the police officers opened the side door and there was no explosion. Morse looked confused. Had the wires failed? He walked up to the warehouse with the police officers, where he had been a captive. He explained to the police who he was. One of the officers walked over to the pallet of C-4 and pulled off a clay brick. He looked at the brick curiously, and then brought it over to one of the Bomb Squad officers.

"Does this look like real C-4 to you?"

The Bomb Squad officer examined the brick closely.

"Nope. This is just modeling clay." He looked at a dozen other bricks and made the same conclusion.

The first officer called Dispatch on his shoulder radio. "Dispatch, we have a false alarm here. It looks like this was a diversion to get us away from the Superdome. Tell all the guys down by the Superdome that the terrorists are probably on their way."

Jensen was yelling into the cell phone Morse had borrowed.

"MORSE! What is happening there?"

Morse gave them the rundown, and explained how the C-4 was fake, and that this was all a diversion. "Jensen, your people need to stop that truck and that police car now!"

"OK, we will get them. Morse," said Jensen, "Hey, when you talked to your son earlier, you said something about a lead with a Miami address. What was that?"

"I found it in the glove compartment of the black van. It had Mapquest Directions to 14780 Hibernia Lane. That must be important."

"OK, thanks. Stay there, John. We will have New Orleans PD escort you back to our FBI Field Office in Baton Rouge. Then we can get you back to Washington tomorrow morning. I will make the calls."

"Detective, were you able to stop the air attack?"

"Yes, we found the guy and shot his Lear jet out of the air."

"Lear jet?"

"Yes. Why do you ask?"

"That seems a little small to be using for the big air attack of the century, don't you think?"

"Well, I guess so, but I still think he could do a lot of damage if a Lear jet crashed into the Superdome roof."

"I guess so," said Morse, unconvinced. "Detective?" asked Morse.

"Yes?"

"Will you make sure my kids are safe?"

"Sure."

"OK, I will talk to you later."

Louisiana Superdome, 50 yard line, Presidential Box. 5:05 p.m.

The President's Secret Service Agent received an urgent message in his earpiece. CHICKEN FRIED had to be moved immediately. There was an almost certain terrorist threat coming, a man in a truck loaded with C4, and machine guns mounted on the front.

"Madame President, you and your family need to come with me right now!"

The agents surrounded the surprised President and her family, shuffling her out the underground exit of the stadium reserved for rock stars and dignitaries, and threw her into the third of six black SUVs.

"Move! Move! Move!"

The SUV's pulled out of the garage, heading for the nearest safe exit.

Miami, Florida. Hibernia Lane. 5:08 p.m.

Field Agent Barry Yoman of the Miami FBI Field Office just happened to be two blocks away from Hibernia Lane on his way home when he got the call. It was urgent, a matter of national security. He pulled up to 14780 Hibernia Lane, walked up the front steps and knocked on the front door. There was no answer. He announced his presence as a police officer but still no presence. He did not have a warrant, so he went around the back of the house and peered through the basement window. There was light on the steps going into the basement. He could swear he saw red marks on the steps. That was good enough for him. Legal could straighten it out in the morning if he was wrong. He kicked in the back door and ran down the steps. There was no sound in the house. In the basement he saw a stack of cardboard boxes. When he moved the boxes, he saw two very large canvas bags. There appeared to be some blood on the outside of the canvas. He zipped open the first bag and saw a head with a bullet hole in it. Gasping, he unzipped the other bag and saw another dead body, also shot through the head.

"Dispatch! I am at 14780 Hibernia Lane, home of Bob and Nancy Eli. I have two dead bodies here, presumably the residents, each shot through the head with one bullet. Their bodies were crammed inside duffelbags in the basement." The FBI Agent, with his gun drawn ran up the stairs into the kitchen and family room, and saw nothing suspicious.

Then he ran up to the bedroom. On the dresser was a photo of Nancy Eli at work.

"Dispatch. The woman who lives here, Nancy Eli, is a Delta Flight Attendant. I repeat, a Delta Flight Attendant."

Washington, D.C. Headquarters of Homeland Security

By 5:12 p.m., the Regional FAA Liaison for Delta was on the phone with two Detectives and the Director of Homeland Security.

"Nancy was scheduled on Delta Flight 16 leaving for Los Angeles at 2:00 p.m. today. The pilot was Louis Caradonna, the co-pilot was Stephen Bishop, and the two flight attendants were Nancy Eli and Beverly Stiller. I am e-mailing you their IDs, photos, and addresses now."

By 5:22 p.m., FBI Field Agents had arrived at Louis Caradonna's house and found the two bodies zipped inside duffelbags in the basement.

By 5:31 p.m. FBI Field Agents spoke with the wife of Corporate Jet Express pilot Tim Welsch, who had called the company when her husband had not called his wife in several hours. The wife confessed that her husband had agreed to take Perez's flight to New Orleans earlier that morning. The wife confirmed that they had two children.

By 5:32, the Detectives at Homeland Security figured out that they had shot down the wrong plane.

At 5:52 p.m., the tapes from Miami Dade International Airport Security arrived via e-mail. The video footage of the gate for Flight 16 showed Perez, another Arab looking man, and two Arab looking women dressed as flight attendants board the plane. Analysts compared their photographs in the video with the photos on their ID cards provided by Delta. They did not match.

At 5:56, the FAA confirmed that Flight 16 was descending into New Orleans and was 22 minutes away from the City.

At 6:00, the Panthers won the coin toss and elected to receive.

At 6:02, a massive tractor trailer, fitted with side machine guns mounted to the hood, rolled down Highway I-10 East towards the stadium.

CHAPTER 27. CRISIS

New Orleans. 6:05 p.m.

"Dispatch, this is Unit 2 and right behind me is Unit 7. We are eastbound on I-10, just before Poydras Street, about ¼ mile west of the Superdome, and I have a truck in front of me with Louisiana plates CXS-990. That's the truck!"

The police officers put on their flashers and sirens, and drove around the truck, motioning for him to pull over. The Al Hamal brothers were not in the truck. They had paid a homeless guy $1,000 to drive the truck east on I-10 and stop the truck on Poydras street just underneath the highway overpass. Diego Sanchez, one of the two brothers, was sitting in the driver's seat of a different type of truck, monitoring the emergency police bands. When he heard the message about the truck with license CXS-990, he pressed the first button on his remote control device and the machine guns on the front of the tractor trailer truck pivoted outward from their sleeves and started firing bullets. No one was more surprised at this than the homeless man driving the truck, who had no idea the machine guns were even there.

"All units! The truck is firing from machine guns mounted on the top of the truck hood! We need to take this truck out before it gets to the Superdome. Where's our air support?"

The Army pilot of the Apache helicopter circling the stadium was ready for this contingency. He swung the helicopter over the roof of the Superdome and down towards the truck. If he had to, he would blow up the truck with a Hellfire missile.

The homeless man could see where this was going. He was going to be dead soon if he did not stop this truck. He went down the ramp of I-10 to Poydras Street, and pulled the truck to a stop just underneath the highway overpass. The Apache helicopter was hovering just on the other side. He was ready to send a Hellfire missile in the belly of the truck. The police dove out of their cars and swarmed around the truck to get the driver.

Just then, Diego Sanchez, sitting in the front seat of his own truck a short distance away, pressed the second button on his remote control panel, and the C-4 in the back of the homeless man's truck ignited. The detonation was catastrophic, and the fireball engulfed all the police officers and cars under the bridge, the hovering Apache helicopter, and a huge section of the highway as well. The concrete of the highway came down in a heap of rubble onto the top of Poydras Street. Smoke filled the air. No one would be going anywhere on those roads.

Inside the stadium, the Panthers had just scored a quick touchdown on a long bomb from Benjamin to Shane and were getting ready to kick off to the Dolphins. The Panthers' kicker placed the football on the orange tee and backed up for the kick. Just then, the explosion underneath I-10 occurred. The explosion knocked the ball off the tee, and all the fans in the stadium wondered what the huge sonic boom was. No one really worried too much, though. Not a single fan at that moment realized what had happened less than a quarter of a mile away.

6:08 p.m. Gulf of Mexico, Delta Flight 16, 10 minutes east of the Louisiana Superdome

Amy Idris had been an Air Marshall for less than a month. She flew about three to five flights a day, always sitting near the front of the plane in Seat 2B. She wore a blazer and slacks, and packed her gun in a holster that she kept under her jacket. So far, this job had not lived up to her expectations, just flying uneventful flights all day and making conversation with strangers. But she knew it was important, and she owed it to Justin, who had been murdered by the Cincinnati Bomber. She had checked in with the pilot, a Lou Caradonna, at the beginning of the flight, to let him know she would be on board, and to have him sign her flight form. She wished she could sleep, but that was not allowed. Air Marshals had to be always vigilant. Right now, she was reading a People Magazine when she got a text message on her cell phone. She glanced down at the message. It had a code number—333! — which was used by the Marshal's Service for dire emergencies, as well as the code number for the Director of the Air Marshal's Service: AM74Q@&. The message read:

THE PILOT, CO-PILOT, AND FLIGHT ATTENDANTS ON YOUR PLANE ARE ALL TERRORISTS. THEY PLAN TO FLY YOUR PLANE INTO LOUISIANA SUPERDOME IN APPROX. 10 MINUTES. IN 8-9 MINUTES, F-16 AIRCRAFT WILL RECEIVE ORDERS TO BLOW YOUR PLANE UP UNLESS YOU CAN GAIN

IMMEDIATE CONTROL OF AIRCRAFT. PRESUME FLIGHT CREW IS ARMED AND DANGEROUS. RADIO AS SOON AS YOU HAVE CONTROL OF AIRCRAFT. YOU ARE AUTHORIZED TO USE DEADLY FORCE.

Idris' heart almost stopped when she read the message. She typed back "OK." She looked around. One flight attendant was in the back of the plane, the other was in the front. If she tried to take out the flight attendant in the back first, other passengers might see her, and might not realize she was an Air Marshal. They might block her attempt to get back up to the front of the plane, and that would be disastrous. She decided to solicit help from passengers. She wrote a message on a napkin and then went back six rows, where she saw three big men in one row. She pretended to fall sideways into their row, said "Sorry," and walked back another two rows. Then she acted like she changed her mind and went back towards the front of the plane. The message on the napkin read:

"I AM AIR MARSHAL. TERRORISTS IN CONTROL OF PLANE. YOU THREE NEED TO GO TO BACK OF PLANE AND SUBDUE FLIGHT ATTENDANT IN BACK. I WILL TAKE CARE OF REST."

The three men read the message and were dumbfounded, but they had to assume that the lady was telling the truth. They all got up from their seats and started walking to the back of the plane. Idris went to the front of the plane where the bathroom was. She turned to the Arab-looking flight attendant who was seated near the sink and the drink cart.

"Excuse me," she said, leaning over to the woman and punched her in the face. The flight attendant was momentarily stunned. Idris then grabbed her cuffs and tried to cuff the flight attendant behind her back, but after she got one cuff on, the flight attendant squirmed and kicked. Idris managed to get the other side of the cuff locked onto a metal post of the seat, shackling the flight attendant by one wrist to the seat. Idris crammed three napkins into the flight attendant's mouth before she could scream and then punched her again in the face, temporarily knocking her out. Unfortunately, a business man in the front row saw the assault.

"Hey! What are you doing there?" he yelled out.

Idris took out her badge, held it in the air, and motioned with her finger to her mouth for the man to be quiet.

Ever since 9-11, the pilots' union had argued that the door to the pilot's cabin should be armored. Some of the airlines had made structural improvements to the doors, so that they could not easily be kicked in, but Air Marshal Amy Idris knew that nearly all of the doors to the pilots' cabin could not withstand a shower of bullets. Idris took out two extra clips so that she would be ready to quickly reload. At 6:10 p.m., Idris took out her service revolver, aimed it at the lock of the pilot's cabin, and screamed, "FEDERAL AIR MARSHAL!" and started blasting. The passengers on the plane went into a terrified panic.

In the rear of the plane, the flight attendant heard the gunfire and bolted up to help her friends, but the three burly men grabbed her and manhandled her into a corner by the rear bathroom.

Idris kicked in the pilot's door. She got a clean shot off on the co-pilot, killing him with a head shot. The pilot of the plane ducked down, however, and her first shot on the pilot missed, hitting the dashboard. The pilot quickly pulled up on the controls violently, and the plane lurched wildly upward. Idris fell back on the ground, but still managed to keep her gun in her hand. The yellow air masks quickly dropped from their tethers in the passenger cabin. The pilot then corrected the path of the plane, and set the plane on a crash course into the Louisiana Superdome. When he had entered the proper coordinates, which only took seconds, he dashed over to Idris and dove on her, trying to get the gun out of her hand. At 6:11 p.m., the plane began its sharp descent towards the football stadium.

The two F-16 pilots had scrambled from their air base in New Orleans and had flown at supersonic speeds towards the Delta jetliner. Their screens said they would intercept the Delta plane at 6:15 p.m., three minutes before impact with the stadium. Matt Suba was in the Situation Room at the White House with the Chairman of the Joint Chiefs, the FBI Director, the National Security Advisor, and the President's new Chief of Staff. The President, who had gotten to a secure location several blocks from the stadium, was receiving inputs and updates over a speaker phone set up in a hastily prepared office. The Director of Homeland Security, along with the Detectives from Homeland Security and the Secret Service, were live on a Cisco Telepresence video conference. The President had given the order to shoot the Delta plane over the sky if it headed for the Superdome. However, she realized that her order would necessarily result in the deaths of over 200 passengers as well as countless others on the ground killed from the plane wreckage. She gave the order that the F-16s should hold their fire until the plane was one minute away from the Dome. That could give the Air Marshall time to get control of the plane and avert a disaster. The President considered evacuating everyone from the stadium, but there could be more truck bombers waiting just outside the stadium somewhere, so that was not a great alternative.

New Orleans, 6:12 p.m. Just outside the Louisiana Superdome

After the explosion, emergency personnel were in a panic, and police cars and fire engines were driving everywhere around the stadium. In the pandemonium, a black truck with the acronym "SWAT" on the side panel quietly rolled down Howard Street, turned left on Magnolia, and right on Girod Street, along the south side of the stadium. On the south side of the Louisiana Superdome, there are two overhead walkways very close to each other connecting the Superdome to the New Orleans Hornets Basketball Arena. After a typical Saints football game, swarms of crowds take these two walkways to reach stairways which lead down to Girod Street below. The driver of the SWAT truck pulled along Girod Street, parking the truck just underneath the westernmost walkway, next to one of the concrete columns holding up the walkway. This would be one of the primary chokepoints for the crowds leaving the Superdome today. Now all the Al Hamal brothers had to do was wait for their brother in the plane. He should be due in about six minutes. They looked to the sky.

Outside New Orleans, en route to Baton Rouge.
Inside Vehicle of FBI Field Agent Brown. 6:12 p.m.

John Morse was driving to the FBI Field Office in Baton Rouge in an FBI car. He heard the report of events coming in over the FBI agent's radio.

"That's really strange," said Morse.

"What's strange?" asked his driver.

"Why would they stop short of the Superdome and just blow up a highway? It doesn't fit their M.O."

"It sounds like he wanted to get to the stadium but he got stopped."

"But he didn't try to ram the police cars to get closer to the stadium? He just stopped and then blew himself up? That doesn't sound right."

Then Morse thought a minute. Why had the terrorists not tortured him for the information he had? Why had they placed his chair directly under a light, which they knew he could use to send flashing signals? Why had they pretended to rig the door, and then used fake explosives? Why had they let him see their license plate? It was almost as if they wanted him to be rescued and to tell the FBI about the tractor trailer. Why would they do that? Perhaps the explosion by the highway was another diversion, and the real truck with explosives was somewhere else, prepared to kill fans as they left the stadium.

"Agent Brown, I need to speak with Detective Jensen about the terrorist plot. It is absolutely urgent."

Brown contacted headquarters and within a minute, Jensen was back on the phone. Morse told him about his theory.

"What about the machine guns that opened fire on the police?" asked Jensen. "Those bullets were real."

"That could have been rigged with a remote control from a distant location. I am telling you, these guys have gone to great lengths to give us all kinds of diversions. I think this is another one. How are they going to get a truck with explosives close to the stadium with all those roadblocks and police? If I were going to plan this, I would put the explosives in an emergency vehicle. I think we can rule out a police car, because it is too small to house all those explosives. If it were me, I would put the explosives in a fire truck, an ambulance, or a police truck of some kind, and then drive up to the stadium in all the confusion after the tractor trailer exploded. If I were you, I would make sure every one of your emergency vehicles is legit."

"That's a great idea, John. Thanks. We will get on that right away."

At 6:13 p.m., the New Orleans Senior 911 Dispatcher sent out an urgent message to all units to switch to Special Channel 055. Special Channel 55 could not be monitored by individuals eavesdropping on emergency bands. Seconds later, on Channel 55, the dispatcher announced:

"All units. We suspect there is another bomb. Repeat, we suspect another bomb. We are looking for any truck, especially an emergency vehicle, which looks out of place near the Superdome. Could be a fire truck, an ambulance, a SWAT truck, a truck selling T-shirts, anything. We need an inspection of any truck parked near the stadium."

At 6:13 p.m., Flight 16 was five minutes away from the stadium.

6:12 p.m., Delta Flight 16, Somewhere over Louisiana

Francisco Perez, known to his fellow terrorists as Altair, the Flying Eagle, gripped his hand on Amy Idris' wrist. Then he head butted her, slamming his forehead into her face. When Idris recoiled from the blow, Perez was able to wrestle the gun from her hand. But before he could turn to shoot, he was tackled by the business man in the front row and slammed with force into the wall. The gun went sliding across the floor over to the place where the first flight attendant was sitting. The flight attendant, having recovered from Amy Idris' initial blows, grabbed the gun with her free hand. As she turned to fire on Idris, Idris pulled Perez in front of her just in time. The three shots from the flight attendant hit Perez squarely in the chest and he went down, bleeding badly. Idris mentally counted the number of bullets fired. She was pretty sure there was only one bullet left in the clip. She kept Perez squarely in front of her so that she would not get shot.

"Hey lady!" said Idris. "You've only got one bullet left in there, so you better make it count." The flight attendant considered Idris' words.

"Throw me another clip or I will shoot one of these innocent passengers," she snarled.

"I ain't throwin' you nothin'!" said Idris.

"Well, that's fine, we will collide with the stadium in three minutes anyway. Whoever tries to get into that cockpit will get shot."

Amy Idris knew what she had to do. She owed it to Justin and all the other little kids like him. If she did not act, everyone on the plane and everyone in the stadium could die. She yelled out a carnal scream and dove on the flight attendant, who shot her in the chest. The flight attendant tried to fire again and the gun clicked. She was out of bullets. The passengers watched in stunned silence as the plane hurdled towards the Superdome with no pilot.

6:14 p.m., Headquarters of Homeland Security, Washington, D.C.

Christine Bueller, one of the computer analysts at Homeland Security, ran up to Detective Jensen.

"Detective Jensen, I have a SWAT truck outside the stadium which does not have a matching license plate."

"What do you mean?"

She pulled up satellite images on her screen. "I started pulling SAT images from every big truck parked around the Superdome, and zooming in on their license plates. Look at this SWAT truck here. Its license plate is JHF-343. But that is a license plate registered to a Dodge Pickup owned by a Chris and Carol Higgins. And look, it is parked right under the walkways to the New Orleans Arena, where all the people would come out. It is nowhere near any of the action over on the northwest side of the stadium where the road blew up. Why isn't he over there? He is just sitting there."

Jensen agreed. That had to be the right truck.

He got on the phone with New Orleans SWAT and they quickly verified that they did not have a truck with that license plate. They also said they only had two SWAT trucks, and both were on the northwest side of the stadium. That could not be their truck.

At 6:16 p.m., Jensen picked up the phone and called his Homeland Security Crisis Field Team Commander, Jim Briggs.

"Jim, this is Detective Jensen with the Secret Service. We have confirmed that there is a SWAT truck sitting on Girod Street, underneath the walkways to the Arena, on the south side of the stadium. That is not a legitimate SWAT truck. We believe it is being operated by terrorists and may have significant quantities of C4 on board. I have already checked with the sniper team on the roof of the stadium, and they say they do not have a clean shot on the drivers due to the overpasses. You need to take your team, and take out the drivers of the truck, without letting them detonate the C4 inside. You will have to surprise them, so do not go in with guns and sirens blazing. This will have to be totally covert. We believe he will detonate that C4 within two to four minutes anyway, so you have no time at all. Once you take out the terrorists, you need to get that truck out of there."

"10-4 boss, we are on it."

6:16 p.m., SWAT truck, south side of the Louisiana Superdome

The two men in the front seat were dressed as New Orleans SWAT members. Suddenly, Diego Sanchez pointed to the sky just east of the stadium.

"There is our brother! He has made it! Praise Allah for this glorious day! Our father will be so proud of us! I am so excited!"

Just then a man and a woman in Carolina Panthers jerseys and hats came running over toward the SWAT truck. The man had a bratwurst in his hand which he was eating and the woman had a Dixie Beer. They looked drunk. They swaggered up to the SWAT truck. "Hey, SWAT man!" the man yelled, laughing and wavering back and forth like a drunk.

Diego reached for his gun and silencer, but his brother put his hand over him.

"Brother, remain calm. These are just drunken Americans. I will get rid of them."

Antonio Sanchez opened the door to the SWAT truck and got out.

"Hey, buddy, we are on police business here, so…"

With that, Commander Jim Briggs, the drunk man, opened fire on Sanchez, shooting him in the head.

Diego Sanchez saw his brother die from the front seat, and quickly reached for the C4 detonator.

The woman in front of the hood dressed in the Dolphins jersey shot four shots through the windshield, killing the other Sanchez brother. They quickly ran around to the back of the truck and opened the door. There was a huge pallet of C4 with rigged timers and flashing lights. There were no other terrorists on board.

"We have taken out the terrorists on the SWAT truck. Repeat, we have taken out the two unfriendlies. There is an entire SWAT truck filled with C4. I do not know if it is set on a timer or not, but there is a detonation button on the front seat. We are in the truck now and driving it away from the stadium. Where do you want us to take it?"

"Take it North on 10 to the Mississippi River. The Bomb Squad will meet you there."

Briggs hit the gas, not knowing if the C4 would detonate at any moment.

6:16 p.m. In the sky above New Orleans

The two F-16s were flying just behind the Delta airliner. The F-16 pilots could see the Louisiana Superdome in the distance. They had just been given their orders from the President. In 60 seconds, unless they were contacted, they would take out the airliner.

At 6:15 p.m., a lawyer in the fourth row in a gray pinstriped suit stood up, asking if anyone on the plane was a pilot of any kind. Phillip Peabody, sitting in 17B, raised his hand. "I am not a pilot yet, but I have had 20 hours of training on a Cessna 172. But I have never flown anything like this." The passengers did not care. That was the best they had. "That will have to do," said the lawyer. "Quickly, come up with me to the cockpit." Peabody walked down the aisle towards the front of the plane, with other scared passengers giving him encouragement. As he walked by the first row, Perez, the terrorist pilot, despite his three bullet wounds to the chest, reached out his hand from the floor and tripped Peabody. The lawyer kicked the terrorist in the face, and helped his friend Peabody into the pilot's chair. One of the other passengers, Ed Jonas, was the owner of a Miami rifle range and knew his way around weapons. He wasn't going to take any more of this interference from terrorists. He found the extra ammo clip on the floor of the passenger cabin. Then, inserting it into the gun, he pointed the gun at Perez, and shot him four more times, making sure he would cause no further problems. He also shot the chained flight attendant. Then he pocketed the gun, returning to his seat.

"There," he said to the lawyer and Peabody. "Now go fly this plane." After a stunned moment of silence, some of the passengers clapped and yelled encouragement.

Peabody was shocked by the violence, but took the pilot's seat. Both he and the lawyer looked at each other nervously as they looked out the windshield. They were headed right for the Superdome. The new pilot put on his headset and turned the radio on the lower console to the Guard Channel, Channel 121-9.

At 6:16 p.m., Peabody spoke urgently into the plane's radio.

"MAYDAY! MAYDAY! This is Delta Flight 16. We need your assistance landing the plane. The flight crew is all dead. There was an Air Marshal who managed to kill the terrorist flying the plane, but she died as well. You only have passengers left. My name is Phillip Peabody. I am not a pilot but I have 20 hours of training in a Cessna 172. But I have never flown a commercial airline before. Please give us immediate instructions to fly the plane."

The President, who was patched in to the FAA Director, heard the announcement from the new pilot moments later. She hovered over the speaker phone.

“Advise the F-16 pilots immediately to hold their fire.”

Back in Washington, D.C. in the Situation Room, Suba could not stand this.

“Madame President,” he said from the Situation Room, “You have to shoot down that plane now. If you don’t, those people up there could accidentally fly it into the stadium!”

“I said, stand down!” the President yelled.

The F-16s got the message immediately over their radios and took their fingers away from the firing button.

The Director of the FAA had his most experienced airline pilot jump on the speaker phone.

“Mr Peabody, this is Bob Twill, I am an airline pilot. Here is what you need to do. First, look to your right, between the pilot’s chair and the co-pilot’s chair, on the lower console below the dashboard, and there is a T-shaped toggle switch. It should say ‘Auto-pilot’ next to it. Do you see it?”

“Yes.”

“OK, I need you to engage that toggle switch by locking it forward. Tell me when that’s done.”

Peabody found the switch and pressed it forward.

“Done.”

“OK, now just to the side of the toggle switch, you should see a dial on its side, kind of like a thermostat dial, that you can dial up or down. When you find it, tell me what the reading is.”

“There is no dial there.”

“What do you mean, there is no dial there? Are you sure you are looking in the right place?” asked Twill.

“I know exactly what you mean. There is no dial there! There is a bullet hole where the dial used to be!”

Twill looked at the FAA Director next to him with a grim expression. Twill thought of new instructions to give the pilot. He hoped it would work.

It was 6:17 p.m.

“Madame President!” yelled Suba over the teleconference from the Situation Room, “You have to shoot that plane down!”

6:18 p.m. Outside the New Orleans Superdome.

Several police officers standing at barricades on the east side of the stadium pointed up in the air. A huge airliner was headed right towards them.

"Oh, my God!" one said. "It's gonna hit the stadium!"

They all started running.

As the plane barreled down towards the stadium, the officers noted that it started to pitch upwards a little bit, and then it got more level. It might miss!

The plane was a few hundred feet from the stadium when it suddenly pitched upwards and barely missed hitting the stadium. It flew off into the sky over western New Orleans, heading upwards to the clouds.

On the streets outside the stadium, in the President's conference room, in the Situation Room, at the FAA Tower in New Orleans, and at Homeland Security Headquarters in Washington, D.C., there was thunderous applause, and everyone started back-slapping each other and throwing up their hands in excitement.

The FAA pilot continued to give Peabody instructions. He was ultimately able to land the airplane at New Orleans International Airport, although he destroyed the plane's landing gear during the landing. When the plane touched down and finally stopped on the runway, all the passengers erupted in applause and cheers. Peabody was given handshakes and back slaps. He was hero for a day. The FAA had fire trucks, police cars, and ambulances waiting at the airport. The Air Marshals Service took Amy Idris' body from the plane. Her heroism today would be remembered for generations.

By 6:23 p.m., Commander Briggs arrived with the SWAT truck at the Mississippi River. Bomb Squad officers quickly examined the C4. It was set to be detonated by pressing the arming mechanism. It was not on a timer. They were able to defuse the arming mechanism and the C4. The crisis at the Superdome was over.

Jensen relayed the good news to Morse on his way to Baton Rouge. He informed him that a plane would be waiting for him at 8 p.m. that night to fly him to Washington. Jensen said the President wanted to meet him and thank him. Morse was happy the whole ordeal was over.

7 p.m. Headquarters of Homeland Security. Washington, D.C.

Detective Jensen took a file and went into the interrogation room where Homeland Security was keeping Hector Santiago, known to his teammates as Ammar, the Builder. Santiago had not said anything to detectives during interrogation.

"Have you heard the news?" Jensen asked Santiago.

"What news?"

"The news about the Superbowl. One of your buddies, Francisco Perez, killed a Delta pilot and his wife, impersonated the pilot, and just drove an airliner into the Louisiana Superdome. And then when the fans tried to escape, two of your other buddies, Antonio and Diego Sanchez, blew up a truck filled with C4 and slaughtered them all. The President of the United States and about 60,000 people are dead. So your little plot is finished. Congratulations. You might as well tell me all about it now."

Santiago started laughing, small at first and then very loudly.

"Hah! You Americans are so stupid! I knew they would succeed! You cannot even see the danger signs when they are staring you in the face. It serves you right. Now we have our revenge on Mr. Bush."

"What revenge?"

"My real name is Shabaz Ma'ak Lom. I had two brothers once, Suhaim and Saif al Din. We lived in the Shaab residential district in northern Baghdad and my father sold produce in the local bazaar. We never caused anybody any trouble. On March 26, 2003, a few weeks after the Baghdad invasion began, my family was working at the produce stand. I had been sent on an errand by my father. Just then, two silver American warplanes with the red, white and blue stars flew over my head at a low altitude. I wondered what they are doing, since there were no Revolutionary Guards in the area where we lived and worked. But the Americans did not care. They bombed my family, which was only trying to sell fruit. They killed my two brothers, my mother, and my father. And that is when I answered the call to jihad. Now you Americans will know what it means to lose your families. I spit on all of your graves. I am happy about what happened tonight."

"And what are the real names of your buddies?"

"You Americans are so stupid. With all your terrorist watch lists and no-fly lists, you do not even realize it when Osama Bin Laden's own sons walk about your country. You are so stupid!"

"You're claiming that Perez and the Sanchez brothers are sons of Bin Laden?"

"It is not a claim, it is a fact. I entered into Mexico with them myself, and helped them enter the United States on student visas. What a joke that was. We did not even show up on campus for class, and no one said anything to us."

"OK, so you were the Builder?"

"Yes. They call me Ammar, which means the Builder."

"Perez was the Eagle?"

"Yes, they called him Altair, which means Flying Eagle."

"And the Sanchez brothers, they were the Rams?"

"Yes, their name Al Hamal means Ram. It is the same name that in Arabic means Aries, the ram."

"And your co-pilot, what animal was he?"

"He was not an Abisali. He was just a helper. His name was Tikah."

"What's an Abisali?"

"It means 'Warrior of the Faith'."

"And who gave you these little names?"

"The Master."

"And who is the Master?"

"Osama Bin Laden, of course."

"And the flight attendants, what were their names?"

"That was my wife and my brother's wife."

"You don't seem that broken up that your wife is dead."

"She is a martyr for the faith. She is already in paradise. I will join her soon, as soon as you Americans hang me."

"Well, that accounts for your whole group except one. Who is the Planner?"

"Mudabbir is the Planner."

"Who is Mudabbir? What is his name?"

"I do not know, Detective. But I can tell you one thing. He is very high up in your Government. He is what you would call a 'Mole'."

"You have never met him?"

"No."

"Then how did you communicate with him?"

"By text messages or e-mails and once by a DVD."

"Do you have any of these text messages, e-mails, or DVDs?"

"No, they were destroyed. We are not as stupid as you Americans."

Jensen started to leave the room, but when he got to the door, he turned back and came over to Santiago, speaking very close to his face.

"Oh, yeah, I forgot to tell you. When I said that your friends blew up the Superdome, I lied. Everyone on the plane and inside the stadium is safe. We shot the 'rams,' and they peed in their pants when they died like little lambs. And your friend the eagle, he was shot and killed by a lady police officer on the plane who probably weighed 100 pounds. He begged for his life from her when he died. He sounded a lot more like a chicken than an eagle. But you did get one thing right. We are going to hang you."

Jensen left the room with a big smile on his face. That felt good. But he was still troubled by one loose end. Who was the Planner?

CHAPTER 28. WHITE HOUSE

Monday, February 4, 2013. The White House. Washington, D.C.

John Morse was overjoyed to be back with his children. Today, they had been invited to the White House to have a long talk with the President of the United States. She was most anxious to meet them. The Morse family was waiting for their turn with the President in the Office of the Secret Service. Detective Jensen was their welcoming party, and he couldn't have been more effusive with his praise. He told Morse he was sorry he never trusted him from the beginning, but any good detective has to follow all the leads and not assume any one person is innocent. Morse was magnanimous in return, and was happy to have played such a vital part in rescuing the President.

Jensen let it slip that the President had managed to obtain an orange longboard with orange wheels, even better than the one Zach had before, and this one was going to be signed by Tony Hawke, the world's greatest skateboarder. And the President had promised that in all their photos with the President, her P.R. people would airbrush in Zach's old hair. Zach thought that was very funny. Zoey would be receiving a brand new electric and acoustic guitar, each one signed by the Jonas Brothers. Zoey was jumping up and down with excitement. And the President this morning had negotiated with the French and Italian governments to allow Morse to keep the ancient scrolls he obtained in France and Italy for one year before returning them to French and Italian museums. The French and Italian governments had assured the President that Morse would be able to claim the academic credit for discovering the scrolls. All criminal charges, of course, would be dropped.

Jensen had brought over Chinese takeout to share with Morse and his teenagers. Jensen and Morse caught up on all of the details of the last few weeks. Jensen asked Morse if he put any stock in the notion that Vice President Suba was really the "spawn of the Devil," as the scrolls had claimed.

"Well, it does seem rather preposterous, doesn't it? But the scrolls have been right about everything else!" Morse laughed.

"Well, just about everything," said Jensen.

"What do you mean?" asked Morse.

"Well, it says that this MABUS character is going to gain power by death or blackmail. The attack on the President's life was stopped, so that rules out death, doesn't it?"

"Well, for now anyway," said Morse. It was an interesting point, though. Why did it say "death OR blackmail?" It was almost as if the Prophet wasn't sure or couldn't make up her mind.

Down the hall from the Secret Service office, in the Oval Office, President Anna Scall was alone with the Vice President, Matt Suba. Despite the great success of the previous afternoon, Suba was in a horrible, angry mood.

"Anna, you know you were just lucky yesterday. You should have shot down that plane. Everyone in that stadium could have died if that pilot couldn't figure out how to work the controls."

"You have to have a little more faith in people, Matt," said the President, smiling.

"Anna, I don't have faith in many people. Especially Arabs and Muslims. They came over here, blew up an elementary school, killing hundreds of school children, killing the President of the United States and half of our Government, and now they just tried to blow up a stadium filled with 60,000 people—oh, and, by the way, the President again. Anna, you have to take decisive action now. These terrorists need a lesson. Under the Bush and Woodson doctrine, anyone who helps a terrorist is the sworn enemy of the United States. You were part of the Woodson team, Anna. You only have one choice here, and that is nuclear."

"What? I am not going to start firing off nuclear weapons!"

"Anna, with all due respect…"

"It's Madame President!"

"OK, Madame President, then with all due respect, why do we have the nuclear arsenal if we are not going to use it during war? If you don't bomb them, we are going to keep getting hit with attacks. You don't want that, do you?"

"Well, who are you proposing that I bomb?"

"Iran, Iraq, Yemen, Saudi Arabia, Pakistan, Afghanistan, Syria, Lebanon, Sudan, the West Bank, the Gaza Strip. You can spare Morocco, Jordan, and Turkey. They have never done anything to hurt us as far as I know."

"Matt, you are out of your mind!"

"Am I? That is where the terrorists come from. We know from Homeland Security that three of the terrorists involved in the Superbowl plot were born in Pakistan and are sons of Osama Bin Laden. They probably trained in camps in Afghanistan. The church bomber was from Iraq. The Cincinnati bomber was from Iran. We know that the Christmas 2009 Detroit bomber was from Yemen. Of the 19 9-11 hijackers, 15 were from Saudi Arabia, 2 were from the United Arab Emirates, and one was from Egypt. The U.S.S. Cole was attacked by terrorists who were freed by Yemeni officials and helped by the Sudanese government. In 1985, we were attacked by Palestinians. The Department of State says Syria is a state sponsor of terrorism. All of these countries are enemies of the United States."

"Matt, the shoe bomber, Richard Reid, was from England. Should we bomb England too?"

"But he trained in Pakistan and Afghanistan. We are just looking for countries which sponsor radical Islam. England is not one of those."

"Matt, this is a silly conversation. I am not going to shoot nuclear bombs over a dozen Middle East countries. You have lost your mind."

Suba grabbed her wrist roughly. "I am not being silly. I am trying to protect this country."

"Matt, you better let go of me right now."

"Madame President, I have taken the liberty of asking the Secret Service agent with the football to join us in the Oval Office." He went to the door and let the agent in.

"Thank you, Agent Griggs. Leave that on the President's desk and wait right outside the door, please."

Anna Scall was so surprised by this last move that she was utterly speechless while the guard placed the silver suitcase on the desk of the President, and then left the room.

"Anna, I will need you to enter the codes."

"Matt, I am bringing that Agent back in here. And if I hear one more word of this nonsense, I am going to have you arrested. Do you understand? She started to walk to the door.

Suba grabbed the President's wrist again, this time harder than before and shoved her back into her chair. "Madame President, you need to see this." Suba pulled out a laptop and hit a button. President Scall was troubled by what she saw on the screen.

Back in the Secret Service office, Detective Jensen was giving Professor John Morse a tour of the technology room. From this central room, the Secret Service could monitor anything going on in the White House. There were video screens everywhere. Morse and his kids were fascinated. Not many people got to come in here. Just then, one of the Secret Service agents yelled out in alarm.

"Detective Jensen, I think you need to see this."

Jensen and Morse walked over to the screen. On the screen, there was a video of Matt Suba grabbing the President's arm and roughly escorting her back to her chair.

"Boss, I don't like this. What do you want to do? He is the Vice President and she has not hit the panic button yet."

There was no audio coming from the room. An unwritten rule of the monitors in this room was that they were not supposed to listen into the President's private conversations in the Oval Office unless there was a vital national security emergency for doing so. Only Jensen could give that kind of clearance. Jensen looked on the desk of the President.

"Is that what I think it is?" he asked.

"Yes, sir, I believe that is the football."

"Turn on the audio."

"Are you sure, sir? We could get in trouble for this."

"I said, 'Turn on the damn audio!'"

The Agent pressed a button and the audio came out.

Suba was speaking to the President. "Anna, do you remember when you and I snuck off in Las Vegas back in 2011? You remember that night at the Blue Dolphin?"

"What's the Blue Dolphin?" asked Jensen.

The Agent typed in a Google search. He did not respond immediately.

"What?" asked Jensen.

"Umm, sir, it appears to be some kind of motel."

"Matt, shut up about that this instant."

"Here is a nice video of you getting it on with me. Of course, you cannot tell that it's me, but we sure can tell it's you. I think you look really good here, Anna. You should be proud of yourself. You are very fit."

"How did you get a video of that?"

"That doesn't matter. What does matter, is that there is this great website you may be familiar with called You Tube ®, which lets anybody upload any kind of video they want. I have typed in all the information here, as you can see. All I have to do is hit this SEND button, and the world sees a side to their President that they never saw before."

"You wouldn't do that."

"I will do that, unless you either enter the nuclear codes, or resign as President, so that I can do it. I have a letter of resignation prepared for you, stating that the ordeal with the terrorist attacks have left you too drained emotionally to fulfill your duties. The American people will understand that. You have been through a lot."

Scall sat there, speechless. "Matt, let's talk about this."

"Anna, I am sure you know, your Presidency will never survive a scandal like this. The American people have no problem with a female President, but they are not going to tolerate a slutty President."

Jensen went into Emergency Mode. "I want the Internet node going out of the White House disabled immediately! Nothing gets in or out! We have seconds! Get it done NOW! I need five agents to come with me!"

Jensen ran out of the Secret Service office, sprinting towards the Oval Office, with five Agents in tow. Morse thought he could help, so he and his children ran right behind the Agents. They were so pumped with adrenaline to help the President, the Agents did not even see Morse and his teenagers racing behind them.

Suba looked towards the President, and then down at his laptop. He hovered his finger directly over the button.

"You have three seconds, Anna. One, two…."

"OK, stop!" said President Scall. "I will sign your resignation letter. Give it to me. She took out a pen and wrote a signature at the bottom. She handed the letter to Suba.

At that second, Jensen and five Secret Service Agents burst into the door with their guns drawn.

"Freeze, Mr. Vice President! You are under arrest! Do NOT MOVE or we will shoot you!"

"Arrest me?" laughed Suba. "For what crime?"

"Blackmailing the President of the United States."

"Ahhh," said Suba. "So you were listening in on us. That's against an Executive Order, Tom. If anyone needs to be arrested, it is you."

"Whether it violates regulations or not is another matter, sir. The relevant point is that you are blackmailing the President. And for that you will be arrested and charged."

Suba started smiling condescendingly at Jensen. "I guess you are not a politician," said Jensen. "Because if you were, you must know that there is no way in the world that Anna here is going to allow me to be prosecuted for blackmail, because if she does, then her little sex scandal will come out, and I will be shouting about it to the highest of rooftops. You need to trust me, Agent Jensen, that is never going to happen. In addition, none of that matters, because the sitting President of the United States cannot be arrested for a crime. He can only be impeached."

"You are not the President," said Jensen.

"Oh yes, I am. Take a look at that."

Suba handed him the President's resignation letter. "What do you think of that?"

"Not very much," said Jensen.

"And why is that?" asked Suba.

"Because this resignation letter is signed, 'THIS IS PREPOSTEROUS.'"

"WHAT?" Suba grabbed the resignation letter from Jensen. He looked at the President in a rage. "You bitch!"

Suba dove over to the laptop, which was directly in front of the President, in an attempt to hit the "SEND" button. Jensen shot him in the back as he made his lunge, but he managed to hit the "SEND" button anyway.

Suba fell down to the ground of the rug, grimacing and laughing. "Well, the last laugh is on you, Anna, when the world sees that."

Jensen radioed his computer technician. "Did you shut down the node in time?"

"Yes, I shut it down. Nothing got out. And we will make sure every one of the tapes is erased showing the President."

"Good," said Jensen. "And then I have a laptop you need to clean."

Jensen deleted the photos from the laptop and deleted them again from the Recycle Bin. The analyst would remove all traces from the laptop.

"Your pictures did not get out, Suba."

"You just shot the sitting Vice President, you moron!" said Suba. "You are going to get the electric chair."

"No," said Scall. "What I saw was a crazy person, who had a mental breakdown after the exhausting terrorist attacks, who made a lunge at the President of the United States. As my protectors, the Secret Service had no other choice but to shoot. Isn't that what you all saw?"

All the agents nodded. "That's what I saw," they each said.

"That's what I saw, too," said Morse, in the doorway.

"And even if a prosecutor wanted to buck the President and arrest Detective Jensen," said President Scall, "I would give him an immediate pardon. You may recall, Matt, that is one of the powers of the President of the United States."

The life was going out of Suba. He had no other cards to play.

"One more thing I need to know," asked Jensen. "Are you Mudabbir, the Planner?"

Suba laughed on the ground, blood pouring out of his wound. "I will see all of you in hell!" With that, Matt Suba closed his eyes. The Secret Service Agent felt Suba's pulse. He was gone.

In the days that followed, Jensen met privately with the President. He explained that they would erase all the videotapes of what happened in the Oval Office, but that the media would go crazy when they heard that. The Vice President, shot by his own agents in the Oval Office? The public would want answers. When the tapes could not be produced, the media would scream cover-up. And no one could guarantee that every one of his agents as well as Morse would keep their mouths shut. But Jensen's people were loyal and they agreed to help Scall weather the coming storm.

Scall shook John Morse's hand and thanked him for his service to the country. Scall told Morse that she planned to award him with the Presidential Medal of Freedom, the highest honor which can be bestowed by the American government on a private citizen. Morse was flattered by the honor.

CHAPTER 29. MESSENGERS

Tuesday, February 5, 2013. Washington, D.C.

The day after the shooting at the White House, Morse met up with his mother, the children's grandmother, who had been shuttled by the FBI to Morse's hotel. At noon, the four of them got a quick lunch in the hotel lobby, and then got a taxi to the hotel where Zoey had left the ancient scrolls written by Scaliger, as well as the letter of Nostradamus. They handed the hotel clerk the key, and he came back moments later with his nylon bag. Morse unzipped the bag to make sure none of the documents had been damaged. He went over to a small coffee table in the lobby, and unrolled each one. None of them seemed to be damaged. He put them back in his bag and then they hailed another taxi to the airport. On the way to the airport, he got a ring on his cell phone. It was an international call. The country code looked like Italy.

"John, is that you?"

"Yes, it is."

"This is Benito Parducci calling from Verona."

"Are you OK, my friend? I heard the police were questioning you?"

"I am fine. Apparently, my Government has agreed that you will have custody of all the parchments for the next year. They are sending you the Verona scrolls tonight to your office at UCLA."

"That is great news."

"I assume you are going to make sure your old friend Benito gets some credit when the announcements are made, no?"

"Of course, absolutely."

"Oh, that is a relief. I would hate to be left out of this exciting chapter of history."

"I will call you within the next week and we will go over exactly what kind of press conference we are going to have. You can stand next to me if you want and I will give you all the credit for your assistance in Verona."

"That is great. One other thing I wanted to ask you. Did you make notes of what was written on the Verona scrolls?"

"Yes, I did," said Morse.

"Well, as I recall it, one of the last chapters made reference to the Devil gaining power and then there being a nuclear war for 200 years or something."

"Yes, that is what it said."

"John, I just received the scrolls from the Verona Police Department yesterday. Guess what? There was an additional scroll which you never saw which was stuck to the back of the last scroll."

"What do you mean?"

"There is another scroll, John. And it has one quatrain written on it. It reads:

Les anges peuvent arrêter le tir de barrage.
Les deux messagers donnent leur vie.
MABUS menace d'exercer le contrôle par le chantage
Dans La Salle de Pouvoir le Diable est fini.

The angels are able to stop the barrage,
The two messengers give their lives,
MABUS threatens to control by blackmail
In the Room of Power the Devil is finished.

Morse wrote down the words in his notebook.

"What? That is impossible!" Morse exclaimed. "How did we not see it before?"

"I don't know. I guess in all the hurry to get you to the airport…"

"Well, I would very much like to see that new scroll along with the others."

"Of course, John. We are going to loan them to you for a while."

"I shall give that last scroll a thorough examination when I receive it. If I hadn't been shot at and kidnapped so many times, I would feel like we are the butt of some centuries-old practical joke."

"Well, please let me know what you find. I am anxious to hear the result."

"Very well, my friend."

Morse looked at his notebook. Who were the two messengers?

August 1, 2013. Los Angeles, California, Home of John Morse

"Pops, I finished my Quatrain Rap for your book."

Morse had asked his son to put together a rap that he would publish at the end of his new book, "*The Prophecies of Nostradamus' Wife*." Zach flung his shaggy hair, which had now grown back as long as it was before, and was now covering half of his face. Zach pulled out a laptop on the desk, and turned up the speaker volume. He hit a few buttons, and his rap background music started blaring out. He put his green hoodie over his head, donned some sunglasses, and then bounced and waved his arms like a rap star when he sang:

Daddy is a wonk, he's a smarty and a scholar
He works all day, he don't make a lotta dollar,
His iPhone then starts a ringin' in his pants,
A priest is a callin,' he's a dude from France.

Daddy says, "Hey, Nostradamus is so whack,
But I'll bring little Zoey and my homeboy Zach,
So he flies off to France, and then I heard it tell
That he found him a secret under St. Michel.

We got all excited and our Daddy tried to calm us,
And he said, "Hey, man, it's the Vault of Nostradamus.
But kids, there's a problem that I see down the road.
The vault has a lock, and the thing's in code."

But Daddy was fly, didn't soil his Tighty-Whitey
He solved him the riddle and it said, "Aphrodite."
By the way, there's this Zeus, he's a god in this heaven,
And this dude's getting' chicks like 24-7.

Now this is the part where Zachster was a beast
See, we were double-crossed by this gangsta priest.
Pops is da man, and he's givin's us a thrilla,
He stared down the gangsta, was a stone-cold killa.

Shorty came up, said, "Hey man, you wanna war?"
She smashed up the gangsta with a piece 'a her guitar.
But Zach was da man, was the Sheriff in the Town
He stared down the gangsta and he put him DOWN.

We drove off to Agen, and Zachster was the Man-O
He found our next clue in a pipe in this piano.
But the gangstas caught up, and put us in a jam
So we shaved off our hair and we went on the lam.

But the gangstas all knew which bus we was on,
And they trailed us all the way to Carcassonne,
Doug and Ray were cool, took a bullet like a pro
Two more killas came up, which way do we go?

We ran all the way to the top of the castle
But the killa came up and was givin' us a hassle,
So Zachster the Master shot the killer off the wall
From my catapult shot took a great big fall.

So we hid in this box, and we found another clue,
But the killa came up and we don't know what to do
Killa says, "Boyz, now you all are gonna die!"
And that's when he got a candelabra to the eye.

Went off to Verona 'cause we ain't done yet,
Found the Tomb of Romeo and Juliet
Got our clue, hit the plane, and flew off in the sky
But as soon as we landed found the FBI.

I don't know what weed they was on,
But they treated my Daddy just likehe was a con,
Daddy said "Boyz, don't leave me in the lurch,
You know I told ya 'bout that bomb in the Church."

But the cops didn't listen, and we had no luck
Until they took my Daddy in a great big truck
And then all them Fibbies was runnin' here and there,
My God, we gotta stop this attack from the air.

Air Marshal lady, Little Shorty, she was brave
She whacked out the gangstas and the plane did save
Cops then listened to my Daddy with the Answers,
Oh yeah, by the way, them Dolphins beat the Panthers.

One more threat, but the cops, they done beat'em,
And they gave my Pops the Award of Freedom
Now you know my story, and you know, its' whack,
And the hero of all is my Main Man Zach!

Oonce, mama, oonce, mama oonce....

Morse laughed. "Zach, that is great stuff. Let me have it and I will give it to the publisher."

Zach gave his dad the pages, and then said he was going to go out with his friends and do some long-boarding in the driveway. Morse went into his study, where he continued to work on his manuscript.

About an hour later, Zoey started playing her new electric guitar in her room. It was very loud, but ever since the events of six months ago, he was hesitant to deny his kids anything. They had been through so much. He could work through a little noise. He tried to keep typing, but it was no use. The music was giving him a splitting headache, so he went over to the couch to lie down. A few minutes later, the doorbell rang. It was Erika Flynn, the woman with whom he had the Nostradamus debate. In an effort to patch things with her after his petty attack at the debate, Morse had let Erika read an advance copy of his book to get her thoughts and input. She was also more successful than he in marketing books, so maybe she had some tips to provide. She was delighted to look at the advance copy. These new revelations about Nostradamus were going to usher in a whole new wave of readers buying her Nostradamus books. In addition, she would probably write a new Nostradamus book herself after Morse's book was published.

Morse went outside the front door with her.

"Let's go out on the patio here. Zoey is playing her electric guitar and I cannot hear myself think." He led her over to a small patio with a table and chairs.

"What did you think of the manuscript?" asked Morse.

"Oh, it's absolutely fabulous. I have never been more excited reading a book in my whole life. I am so jealous all those things happened to you—well, maybe not the kidnapping parts." She laughed.

"Yes, I would have given you those any day."

"The part about the words on the scroll in Verona changing is absolutely mystifying and interesting, don't you think? I am not sure if you should include that part. Everyone will think you mad."

"I know what you mean. I felt kind of mad when I examined the scroll. The ink was definitely from the sixteenth century. I simply cannot explain it."

"Well, you know, John, you were always unwilling to accept any kind of supernatural explanation for anything. I hope you realize now, after seeing someone prophesize events hundreds of years later, that there is a supernatural world out there, and that often times, the supernatural explanation, although seemingly illogical, is actually the only logical explanation."

"Well, I will say this, Erika. My faith in bizarre things has certainly been strengthened through this experience. "

"Although I absolutely loved your manuscript, John, I see that you have omitted something absolutely critical."

Morse looked surprised. "What is that?"

"Why, the part about the 'two messengers,' of course. You said that in the new Verona manuscript, the prophecy was that 'two messengers' will give their lives. Don't you know what that means?"

"I am not following you," said Morse.

"In the Bible, in the Book of Revelation, Chapter 11:3, there is a discussion of the Antichrist coming to Earth. The Bible says that God's 'two messengers' will arrive on the earth and will preach as prophets for 1,260 days. Then they will die in acts of martyrdom, slain by the Beast. And then the Antichrist himself will fall, as a result of the sacrifice of the two messengers."

"OK, so?"

"In the year 354 A.D., St. Augustine was born. He was originally a pagan. He converted to Christianity after his mother, a Christian, convinced him. He went on to become one of the great Fathers of the Church, combating heresy his whole life and giving teachings on the meaning of certain Bible passages. Augustine explained in one of his early theological works that the 'two messengers' who would come to battle the Antichrist were actually Enoch and Elijah, the only two men in the Bible who did not die a natural death but who were taken by God in their lives up to heaven. Augustine explains that they really didn't go to the 'real' heaven. They kind of went to a 'Heaven Waiting Room,' of sorts, with the idea being that when the Antichrist came, they would be able to go back into the world to fight him."

"I still don't see how this connects, Erika."

"What was the name of the Air Marshal who sacrificed her life so that the passengers could get into the cockpit and steer the plane away from the Superdome?"

"Amy Idris."

"The name 'Idris' is Arabic for 'Enoch.'"

"You are kidding."

"Nope. Enoch was supposed to be the great grandson of Adam as well as the great grandfather of Noah. According to the Islamic tradition, Enoch was the inventor of astronomy, writing, and arithmetic. Guess what Amy Idris majored in during college."

"Astronomy," said Morse.

"Correct. Guess what her minor was?"

"Mathematics."

"Correct again. And the Muslims say that Enoch is supposed to defend his life with the sword against the depraved children of the Earth. I cannot think of a better title for those terrorists than the depraved children of the Earth."

"It also says that Elijah and Enoch are supposed to prophesize and preach for 1,260 days before their battle with the Antichrist. Did you know that Amy Idris was also a Methodist minister?"

"No, I did not."

"Guess how long before her death she became a Methodist minister?"

"No. Not 1,260 days?

"1,260 days, EXACTLY." said Flynn. "Almost three and a half years ago."

"But what about Elijah? Where does that fit in?"

"Do you remember your priest friend who had the vision about helping you in Agen?"

"Of course."

"What was his name?"

"He said his name was Father Gerard."

"That was the name of the saint he took as a priest. His real name was Elias St. Croix. Elias, another name for Elijah. He had been a Catholic priest for exactly 1,260 days before he was murdered. And he refused to give the killers your location, even though they briefly tortured him. Had he given in, you would have been caught and killed, and the remaining prophecies would have come true. So you see, the two messengers who gave their lives are truly Enoch and Elijah from the Bible."

"Oh, come on, that must be a coincidence.""Just like the prophecies of Henriette Nostradamus were coincidences? Come now, it is you who are being illogical, John. The word 'witness' in Greek is '*martus*.' The Greek verb *martureo*, *marturomai* means 'to witness.' We get our English word 'martyr' from the word 'witness,' because the early saints gave their lives when they acted as a witness to the truth of Jesus Christ. The two witnesses are the two martyrs from the Bible."

"That is incredible about the 1,260 days."

"The time period of 42 months, or 1,260 days, is found in many places in the Bible. In Daniel 7:25, it states that the Beast shall persecute the righteous 'for a time, two times, and a half a time.' A 'time' is a year. That means three and one half years. By the way, three and one half years ago, Matt Suba was first appointed as Governor Scall's Chief of Staff after her previous Chief of Staff was murdered."

"Seriously?"

"Yes, seriously. Here is another interesting point. The period of 42 months comes originally from the period of time about 167 B.C. in which Antiochus IV first persecuted the Syrian Jews and tried to make them give up their Jewish religion and adopt Greek ways instead. The revolt by Judah Maccabee to Antiochus' treatment led to a great rebellion. The result was that the vastly outnumbered Jews overpowered the forces of Antiochus in battle. When the victorious Jewish forces went in and re-claimed the Temple, they needed to re-consecrate the holy building with oil and to light all the lights in the Temple. Unfortunately, there was only one untainted container of holy oil left. Despite the fact that there was only one container, it miraculously lasted eight days instead of one. The Jews celebrate that holiday every year in December. The eight days of light are called Chanukah. In the days of John, the author of the Book of Revelation, this business about 42 months was understood as a prophecy concerning the destruction of the Temple by Antiochus IV. By prophesying another 42 months of torment by an oppressor, John was referencing something that the Jews feared and had already experienced. So the 42 months of rule by the Devil are directly related to the persecution of the Jews by Antiochus IV, probably another spawn of the Devil."

"Is there anything else?"

"Yes, Revelation says that for three and a half days, the two witnesses are not buried, and that after that time, they will ascend to heaven, at which point there will be a violent earthquake in which 7,000 will perish. Amy Idris was killed on February 3, 2013. She was given a hero's funeral and finally buried three and a half days later, on February 6, 2013. And on that date, you may recall, there was a massive earthquake in Cuba, in which over 7,000 people were killed. Sounds to me like a pretty good match."

"Wow, you have given me a lot to think about. I will definitely do some Bible research on this thing in Revelation before the manuscript goes to print. Well, one thing is for certain. If we are approaching the end of days, I better get the dishes in my sink cleaned up. I want to look good for the Final Coming."

"Ha, ha. Very good, John. I will let you go. But the next time you go on one of these scavenger hunts across the globe, take me with you. I would love to come along."

"Very well. I shall do that. Thanks again for your help, Erika."

"My pleasure." With that, Erika Flynn was gone.

Morse thought about her words for a minute. He saw his son Zach down the street riding his skateboard. He called to him. Zach came running up with his skateboard a moment later.

"Hey Pops, what's up?"

"Take off your skateboard helmet and go get dressed nice. And tell your sister Zoey to get dressed nice, too."

"Where are we going?"

"We are going to Church."

"Church? We haven't been to Church since Mom died."

"I know that. And I think it is high time we started going again."

"OK, I'll go get Zoey."

Morse sat on the patio steps, and said a silent prayer to his wife. If it was the end of days, he would be happy to see his wife again.

APPENDIX

HENRIETTE DE NOSTRADAME'S 58 QUATRAINS

1.

Suprême au pape lui-même, c'est le huitième,
Ceux qui protestent sont traités comme traîtres et assassiné.
Bouffi d'orgueil, il s'est marié avec la crème,
Des belles femmes: une morte, une survécu, deux divorcées, deux décapitées

Supreme to the pope himself, he is the eighth,
Those who protest are murdered and treated as traitors.
Fat with pride, he married the cream of the crop,
Beautiful women: one died, one survived, two divorced, two beheaded

King Henry VIII (1491–1597)

2.

Le Monstre de Valachie est le diable.
Il empale ses victimes avec un bâton trenchant.
Sa cruauté et son caractère impitoyables sont abominables.
Il écorche tout vif des hommes implorants.

The Monster of Wallachia is the devil.
He impales his victims with a sharp stick.
His cruelty and ruthlessness are abominable.
He skins alive pleading men.

Vlad the Impaler (1431–1476)

3.
Un loup déguisé en prêtre, il achètera la papauté.
Son avidité est insatiable, rien ne lui suffit.
Il engendra six enfants illégitimes avec ses prostiuées.
Même le meurtre de ses propres enfants ne satisfait pas son appétit.

A wolf in priest's clothing, he shall buy the papacy.
His greed is insatiable, nothing is enough for him.
He will father six illegitimate children with his whores.
Even the murder of his own children does not satisfy his appetite.

Pope Alexander VI (papacy 1492–1503)

4.
Après Pius, le prochain pape connaît la guerre, pas la paix.
Il est méchant et boit sans cesse.
Il attrapera la maladie de ses prostituées.
Et il vendra des billets au salut après la messe.

After Pius, the next pope knows war, not peace.
He is wicked and drinks all the time.
He will get disease from his whores
Then he will sell tickets to salvation after mass.

Pope Julius II (papacy 1503–1513)

5.
Le prochain pape est aussi perdu.
L'argent destiné aux pauvres va aux corridas et aux banquets.
Il coupe les mains et les pieds aux intrus.
Leurs enfants sont esclaves, leurs maisons brûlées.

The next pope is also lost.
Money for the poor goes to bull-fights and banquets.
He cuts off the hands and feet of trespassers.
Their children are slaves, their houses are burned.

Pope Leo X (papacy 1513–1521)

6.

Sur la porte il clouera sa protestation,
Quatre-vingt- quinze plaintes contre le château.
Ils exigeront son excommunication.
Il refuse de désavouer ses mots.

On the door he will nail his protest,
95 complaints on the castle.
They will demand his excommunication.
He will refuse to recant his words.

Martin Luther (1483–1546)

7.

Après encore un, le prochain pape ordonne que 8.000 soient tués.
Il croit aussi que la papauté est à vendre.
Refusant de croire en Dieu Lui-même, il est athée.
L'argent de l'Eglise, il se gêne pas de le prendre.

After another one, the next pope orders 8,000 killed
He also believes the papacy is for sale
Disbelieving in God Himself, he is an atheist
The money of the Church he feels free to take.

Pope Clement VII (papacy 1523–1534)

8.

Le prochain pape garde 45.000 prostituées.
Il est coupable de l'inceste avec sa fille et ses soeurs.
Son gendre est empoisonné.
Le meurtre et le mal noircissent son coeur.

The next pope keeps 45,000 prostitutes.
He has incest with his daughter and his sisters.
His son-in-law is poisoned.
Murder and evil blacken his heart.

Pope Paul III (papacy 1534–1549)

9.

Pendant un temps d'obscurité, une lumière.
Le savant de Cracovie cherche les cieux.
Sa théorie est tout à fait contraire,
Le soleil, pas la terre, est au milieu.

In an age of darkness, a light.
The scientist from Krakow searches the heavens.
His theory is quite contrary,
The sun, not the earth, is in the middle.

Copernicus (1473–1543)

10.

Le prochain pape n'est pas beaucoup meilleur.
Il va adopter un innocent, et après lui fera subir la sodomie.
Comme une maladie répugnante sur une belle fleur,
Son désir dégoûtant est une anomalie.

The next Pope is no better.
He will adopt an innocent, and then subject him to sodomy.
Like filthy disease on a beautiful flower,
His disgusting lust is abnormal.

Pope Julius III (papacy 1550–1555)

11.

Après encore un, le prochain pape s'amuse à torturer.
Il aime la vierge de fer et le chevalet.
La douleur incroyable que ses victimes doivent endurer.
Leurs cris de douleur vous font trembler.

After another one, the next pope takes joy in torturing.
He loves the iron-maiden and the rack.
Incredible pain his victims must endure.
Their cries of anguish make you tremble.

Pope Paul IV (papacy 1555–1559)

12.
A Novgorod 50.000 seront tués.
Il battra sa belle-fille enceinte, en causant une fausse couche.
Puis, en colère, son fils sera empalé.
Après le viol, il prend du poison par la bouche.

In Novgorod, 50,000 will be slain.
He will beat his pregnant daughter-in-law, causing her miscarriage.
Then, in anger, his son will be impaled.
After rape, he takes poison in his mouth.

Ivan the Terrible (1530–1584)

13.
Il écrit d'amants et de rois,
De fantômes et de monstres,
De faunes et de fées dans les bois,
Les pièces sont écrites par le Chantre.

He writes of lovers and of kings,
Of ghosts and monsters,
Of fauns and fairies in the woods,
The plays are written by the Bard.

Shakespeare (1564–1616)

14.
Il maîtrise l'astrologie et la physique.
Il regarde les étoiles avec sa lunette.
"La terre tourne autour du soleil," dit-il à ses critiques,
Et pour cela, on l'arrête.

He masters astrology and physics.
He looks at the stars through his telescope.
"The earth revolves around the sun," he says to his critics,
And for that, he is arrested.

Galileo (1564–1642)

15.

Le plus grand savant qui soit jamais né.
Les lois du mouvement et de la terre,
Les lois des mathématiques et de la gravité.
Déguisé, il arrêtera les faussaires.

The greatest scientist ever born.
The laws of motion and of earth,
The laws of math and gravity.
Disguised, he will arrest the counterfeiters.

Isaac Newton (1642–1727)

16.

Le four de Farriner causera un feu.
Bientôt tout Londres est englouti par les flames,
Le Maire ne fait pas ce qu'il peut,
La destruction pour tous les hommes et toutes les dames.

Farriner's oven will cause a fire.
Soon all of London is engulfed in flames,
The Mayor does not do what he can,
Destruction for all the men and ladies.

Great Fire of London (1666)

17.

Ces trois amènent le son de la musique.
Les anges sourient à leurs symphonies.
Chacun est doué et unique,
Les plus beaux sons jamais écrits.

These three bring the sound of music.
The angels smile at their symphonies.
Each is gifted and unique,
The most beautiful sounds ever written.

Bach (1685–1750), Mozart (1756–1791), Beethoven (1770–1827)

18.

Fâchés contre les impots et assoiffés de liberté,
Ils déchargeront leur thé dans la baie profonde.
Surpassés en nombre, ils battront les Anglais.
Leur drapeau aura des étoiles et des bandes.

Angry at taxes and thirsting for liberty
They will dump their tea in the deep bay.
Although outnumbered, they will defeat the English.
Their flag will have stars and stripes.

American Revolution (1776)

19.

Les dirigeants français, arrogants et détestés.
Elle dira qu'ils devraient manger de la brioche.
Les pauvres attaqueront le palais.
A la prison ils termineront leur approche.

The French rulers, arrogant and hated,
She will say they should eat cake
The poor will attack the Palace,
At the prison (Bastille) they will end their approach.

The French Revolution (1789)

20.

Un roi français, pas de royauté né,
Il perdra une campagne militaire.
Apres l'exil, il retournera mener l'armée.
Il sera écrasé par le Duc de Fer.

A French king born not of royalty,
He will lose a military campaign.
After exile, he will return to lead the army.
He will be crushed by the Iron Duke.

Napoleon Bonaparte (1769–1821)

21.

Sa théorie cause une revolution,
Du singe est venue l'humanité.
Ils ne se sont pas préparés à l'évolution.
L'espèce la plus faible ne survivra jamais.

His theory causes a revolution,
From the monkey came mankind.
They are not ready for evolution.
The weakest species will never survive.

Charles Darwin, Origin of Species (1809–1882)

22.

Grâce à lui, la maladie est arrêtée.
Il guérit ceux mordus par des animaux.
Il sait rendre potable le vin et le lait.
Pour le monde c'est un héros.

Thanks to him, sickness is stopped.
He cures those bitten by animals.
He knows how to make wine and milk safe to drink.
To the world he is a hero.

Louis Pasteur (1822–1895)

23.

Ils sont amenés en chaînes d'Afrique.
Ce sont des esclaves à cause de la couleur de leur peau.
Leurs maîtres blancs sont sadistiques.
Dans le Nouveau Monde leurs jours ne sont pas beaux.

They are brought in chains from Africa.
They are slaves by reason of the color of their skin.
Their white masters are sadistic.
In the New World, their days are not good.

American Slavery (1607–1865)

24.
Deux hommes, bien loin l'un de l'autre, veulent se parler.
Il fabrique une machine pour les rendre heureux.
Avec cette invention ils peuvent causer.
C'est tout à fait merveilleux.

Two men, far away from each other, want to talk.
He builds a machine to make them happy.
With his invention they can chat.
It's absolutely marvelous.

Alexander Graham Bell and the Telephone (1847–1922)

25.
Il exploite la force de l'électricité.
De l'obscurité il fait de la lumière.
Tout est maintenant illumine.
Nous voyons ce que nous avons besoin de faire.

He harnesses the power of electricity.
Out of darkness he brings the light.
Now all is illuminated.
We see what we need to do.

Thomas Edison and the Lightbulb (1847–1931)

26.
Le génie a l'esprit parfait.
Il dit que tout est fait d'atomes invisibles.
Malheureusement, ils utiliseront ses idées
A construire La Bombe Terrible.

The genius has a perfect mind.
He says everything is made of invisible atoms.
Unfortunately, they will use his ideas
To build the Terrible Bomb.

Albert Einstein (1879–1955)

27.

Deux frères voleront comme des oiseaux.
Ils construiront une machine qui monte aux nuages.
La vue est étonnante et le ciel beau.
Cette invention sera partagée à travers les âges.

Two brothers will fly like birds.
They will build a machine which climbs to the clouds.
The view is astonishing and the sky is beautiful.
This invention will be shared through the ages.

Wright Brothers and the Airplane (1871–1948; 1867–1912)

28.

Le monde entrera en guerre.
Les Français et les Russes prennent parti.
La bataille fait rage en Angleterre.
Des millions sont morts quand c'est fini.

The world will go to war.
The French and Russians take sides.
Battle rages in England.
Millions dead when it is finished.

World War I (1914–1918)

29.

L'équipage est abandonné.
Une voiture à quatre roues,
Elle marche toute seule, le cheval s'en est allé.
Transport facile à tous les rendez-vous.

The horse-drawn carriage is abandoned.
A carriage with four wheels,
It drives itself, the horse is gone.
Easy transportation to all appointments.

Henry Ford and the Automobile (1863–1947)

30.

Le Russe permettra à son peuple de souffrir.
Plus d'un million seront fusillés ou pendus.
D'autres seront emprisonnés pour languir.
Jusqu'à ce qu'il meure. Un tel fléau, c'est du jamais vu.

The Russian will allow his people to suffer.
Over a million will be shot or hanged.
Others will be sent to prisons to languish.
Until he dies, they have never seen such a scourge.

Joseph Stalin (1878–1953)

31.

Il y aura un Allemand qui est boucher.
Il abattra des millions de Juifs pacifiques.
Quelques-uns iront à la salle de bains se doucher.
Ils mourront plutôt de gaz toxique.

There will be a German who is a butcher.
He will slaughter millions of peace-loving Jews.
Some will go to the bathroom to take a shower.
They will die of poison gas instead.

Adolf Hitler (1889–1945)

32.

Le médecin diabloique choisit qui est épargné et qui est tué.
Il fait une injection de poison dans le coeur.
Les bras et les jambes sont amputés.
Il est barbare et ne mérite pas le nom docteur.

The evil doctor decides who is spared and who is killed.
He injects poison into the heart.
The arms and legs are cut off.
He is barbaric and does not deserve to be called doctor.

Josef Mengele (1911–1979)

33.

Le pays du soleil rouge
Subira une perte terrible.
Un arbre de nuages blancs qui bougent
Causera une mort horrible.

The land of the red sun
Will suffer a terrible loss.
A tree of white, moving clouds
Will cause a horrible death.

Hiroshima and Nagasaki (1945)

34.

L'homme bienveillant de l'Inde est un exemple pour les gens.
Il enseigne la non-violence et à se conduire pacifiquement.
Il se combat pour les pauvres, les faibles, les enfants.
Il est éclairé spirituellement.

The kind man of India is an example for people.
He teaches non-violence and how to act peaceably.
He fights for the poor, the weak, the children.
He is spiritually enlightened.

Mohatma Gandhi (1869–1948)

35.

La religeuse au foulard blanc et bleu.
A la paix elle est vraiment consacrée.
C'est une sainte qui aide les nécessiteux.
Elle aide les pauvres et donne à manger aux affamés.

The nun with the white and blue headscarf.
To peace she is truly devoted.
She is a saint who helps the needy.
She helps the poor and feeds the hungry.

Mother Theresa of Calcutta (1910–1997)

36.

Maintenant le vrai est découvert.
Ils trouvent l'échelle tordue.
Les savants ont beaucoup de savoir-faire.
A leurs théories enfin on a cru.

Now truth is discovered.
They find the twisted ladder.
The scientists have great know-how.
Finally their theories are believed.

Watson (1928–present) and Crick (1916–2004) , DNA.

37.

Le premier catholique à accéder au pouvoir.
Il détourne astucieusement une guerre.
Le pays pleure et est au désespoir.
Quand il est assassiné en un éclair.

The first Catholic to come to power.
He cleverly averts a war.
The country sorrows and despairs
When he is killed in a flash.

John F. Kennedy (1917–1963)

38.

Le prédicateur proteste aux élus.
Il enseigne l'amour de nos soeurs et nos frères.
Ses paroles aux millions ont plu.
Il est tué par un sectaire.

The preacher protests to elected officials.
He teaches to love our sisters and brothers.
Millions liked his words.
He is killed by a bigot.

Martin Luther King (1929–1968)

39.
Sur une flèche en métal ils voleront.
Ils quitteront la terre pour la noirceur au-delà.
Sur la surface de la lune ils marcheront.
Le monde entier dira, "Regardez cela!"

On an arrow of metal they will fly.
They will leave the earth to the blackness beyond.
On the surface of the moon they will walk.
All the world will say, "Look at that!"

Moon Landing (1969)

40.
En Asie il y aura un tyrant vicieux.
Ses tortures seront pires que des bombes.
Il donnera à manger à son peuple seulement un peu.
Il leur fera creuser leur propre tombe.

In Asia, there will be a vicious tyrant.
His tortures will be worse than bombs.
He will feed the people only a little.
He will make the men dig their own graves.

Pol Pot and the Khmer Rouge (1928–1998)

41.
L'Ougandais se donnera beaucoup de noms.
Il mangera de la chair humaine et mutilera sa femme - incroyable!
De ses mains, seront assassinés des milliers d'hommes.
Il ne libérera pas les Juifs bien qu'ils soient ses semblables.

The Ugandan will give himself many names.
He will eat human flesh and mutilate his wife—unbelievable!
By his hands, thousands of men will be murdered.
He will not release the Jews even though they are his fellow creatures.

Idi Amin (1925–2003)

42.

Ils fabriqueront une boîte en fer.
Dans la boîte il y a un cerveau.
N'importe quoi, cette boîte peut le faire.
Chaque jour quelquechose de nouveau.

They will make a box of iron.
In the box is a brain.
The box can do anything.
Every day is something new.

Steve Jobs (1955 to present), Personal Computers.

43.

Comme la maladie du charbon, il vient une nouvelle peste.
Elle traverse le globe, on ne peut pas la fuir.
La personne qui attrape la maladie on la déteste.
On prie le ciel de se guérir.

Like le charbon, comes a new plague.
It travels the globe, one can't escape it.
The person who contracts the disease is detested.
They pray to the sky to be cured.

AIDS Epidemic (1981 to present)

44.

La Première Dame de l'Angleterre nous a quittés.
Elle est tuée dans un tunnel mais celui qui la tuée a disparu.
Toutes les nuits des bougies ont brûlé.
Sur les portails des fleurs se sont répandues.

The First Lady of England has left us.
She is killed in a tunnel but her killer is gone.
Every night candles burned.
Flowers were spread over the gates.

Lady Diana (1961–1997)

45.
A son propre gouvernement il fait la guerre.
Au milieu du pays son complot meurtrier est accompli.
Sa bombe est faite de feu et de terre.
Son complice ne sera pas pris.

Against his own government he makes his war.
In the middle of the country, his murderous plot is accomplished.
His bomb is made of fire and earth.
His accomplice will not be caught.

Timothy McVeigh Oklahoma City Bombing (1995)

46.
De l'Empire Ottoman il est venu.
Après une guerre manquée il est fini.
On le trouvera dans un trou.
Il sera exécuté par ses ennemies.

From the Ottoman Empire he has come.
After an unsuccessful war he is finished.
He will be found in a hole.
He will be executed by his enemies.

Saddam Hussein (1937–2006)

47.
Le fils est encore plus cruel que la père.
A quiconque l'offense il donne la mort.
Il matraque un homme pendant le dîner pour sa mere.
Il enlève les femmes d'autres, les viole, et encore...

The son is even more cruel than the father.
To anyone who offends him he gives death.
He bludgeons a man at dinner for his mother.
He kidnaps the wives of others, rapes them, and again…

Uday Hussein (1964–2003)

48.

L'Arabe enverront quatre oiseaux gigantesques.
Deux tours commerciales seront rasées.
La destruction et la mort sont grotesques.
Le Pentagone sera endommagé.

The Arabian will send four gigantic birds.
Two towers of commerce will be razed.
The destruction and death are grotesque.
The pentagon will be damaged.

Osama Bin Laden and 9/11 (2001)

49.

On fait beaucoup de guerres dans le désert desséché.
Des camps les fanatiques continuent à sortir.
Mauvais traitement de prisonniers.
Les assassins se tuent et tuent d'autres en se réclamant des matryrs.

Many wars are fought in the parched desert,
From the camps, the zealots continue to go out.
Bad treatment of the prisoners.
The murderers kill themselves and others, claiming to be martyrs.

Desert Storm, Iraq War, Afghanistan War, Abu Ghraib, Terrorist Camps (1990 to present)

50.

Le père du grand orateur vient d'Afrique.
Enfant il habite une île tropicale, considérant son sort.
D'abord, on pense qu'il est magnifique,
Ensuite son soutien est au point mort.

The great orator's father is from Africa.
As a child he lives on a tropical island, contemplating his future.
At first they think he is magnificent,
Then support for him stalls.

Barack Obama (1961 to present)

51.

Les Guerriers de la Foi déclencheront la Guerre Finale.
La Torche, Le Jeune Faucon, Le Constructeur,
L'Aigle, Les Deux Béliers—
Ils sont tous sous l'autorité du Projeteur.

The Warriors of the Faith will commence the Final War
The Torch, the Young Hawk, the Builder,
The Eagle, The Two Rams—
They all report to the Planner.

Abisali (2012–2013)

52.

La Torche est en colère et derange.
Les enfants dans l'école mourront.
Leurs parents pleurent quand ils sont tués.
Dans la forteresse ils le trouveront.

The Torch is angry and deranged.
The children in the school will die.
Their parents grieve when they are killed.
In the fortress, they will find him.

Cincinnati Massacre (2012)

53.

Le Faucon s'est battu une fois pour son frère.
Il a visé le tyrant mais son coup n'était pas bien calculé.
Maltraité par l'investigateur militaire.
Il le tuera pour se venger.

The Hawk once fought for his brother.
He aimed for the tyrant but his move wasn't well-planned.
Mistreated by the military investigator.
He will kill him in vengeance.

Assassination of Secret Service Agent Gil Johnston (2013)

54.

Le Chef assistera aux obsèques du garde.
Le Constructeur cache une bombe dans la statue.
La Dame Puissante, quelque chose la retarde.
Dans l'église tous sont perdus.

The Leader will attend the funeral of the guard.
The Builder hides a bomb in the statue.
As for the Powerful Lady, something delays her.
Inside the church, all are lost.

Assassination of President Woodson at
St. Anthony of Padua Church (2013)

55.

Les remplacements sont choisis trop rapidement
Le Projeteur, MABUS , est progéniture du Diable
Il complote sa prise de pouvoir méchamment
Une fois au pouvoir, il est redoutable.

The replacements are chosen too swiftly.
The Planner, MABUS, is the spawn of the Devil.
He plots his takeover wickedly.
Once in power, he is formidable.

Suba elected VP (2013)

56.

Ils attaquent le stade quand on va jouer, pendant le jour.
L'Aigle s'approche de l'air.
Les gens fuient chercher le secours.
Les Béliers attaquent de la terre.

They attack the stadium when they are about to play, during the day,
The Eagle approaches from the air.
The people flee to seek help.
The Rams attack from the ground.

Superbowl Bombing (2013)

57.

MABUS gouverne par la mort ou le chantage.
Il se venge avec des nuages de la mort.
Le meurtre de millions cause de grand ombrage.
Une Guerre de Haine pendant deux siècles, alors...

MABUS governs by death or blackmail
He retaliates with clouds of death
His murder of millions causes great offense
A War of Hate for two centuries, then…

President Suba (MABUS) orders Nuclear Bombing of Arab countries, followed by 200 years of war between Muslims and Christians (2013-2213)

58.

Des cendres, il y a une renaissance,
Une paix finale et une durable trêve.
Il y a une nouvelle alliance
Et du bonheur comme dans un rêve.

From the ashes, there is rebirth,
A final peace and lasting truce.
There is a new alliance
And happiness as in a dream.

Peace (2213)

ABOUT THE AUTHOR

John Medler is a trial lawyer and author. He lives with his wife and six children in St. Louis, MO. This is his first published novel. If you want to connect with John online, contact him on Facebook at:

http://facebook.com/john.medler

AUTHOR NOTES

Of course, I need to first thank Nostradamus. No matter whether you believe he was a true prophet or a snake-oil selling con man, the fact remains that we still talk about his works over 500 years later, and not many men can say that.

I would also like to thank Peter Lemesurier, for his excellent scholarly reference texts on Nostradamus, including The Nostradamus Encyclopedia. Much of the information from Chapter 3, Debate, comes from information in Peter's books. It was also Peter's idea that Nostradamus might brag about successfully predicting that there would be no great flood in the year 1524. Peter pointed out in his books that the same conjunction of stars and planets occurred in Libra in 1186, yet nothing of importance occurred. Knowing that Nostradamus believed one could predict future events by looking to similar alignments of stars and planets in prior times in history, Peter suggested that it would have been natural for Nostradamus to research whether in prior history there had ever been a conjunction of the heavenly bodies similar to that which existed in 1524. Peter also pointed out that many of Nostradamus' prophecies appear to be copied or taken from other contemporary and ancient works, and Peter does an excellent job listing Nostradamus' unreferenced bibliography. I relied on much of Peter's research as reference material for Nostradamus "confession" of plagiarism. Many readers may want to learn which parts of the book concerning Nostradamus and Scaliger are true and which are the product of my overactive imagination. If you want to know any of the "real facts" about Nostradamus, Peter's books are the place to start. Peter also has excellent translations of all existing Nostradamus quatrains, some of which I used in this novel.

I would also like to thank my high school French teacher, Beryl Lemon, for assisting me with all the French translations in the book. Many times, I called upon her to be not only a translator, but also a poet, and for that I am very grateful. It is amazing how much French I have forgotten since high school!

I would also like to thank my high school classmate Jerry McCabe for all the excellent illustrations in the book. His work is inspirational.

I would also like to thank Mike Hart, the father of a friend of mine, who is a retired Delta pilot. He made sure I didn't say "press the green button" when referring to the piloting of a 747.

I would also like to thank my son Cody, who is fifteen and never stops rapping and riding his longboard (if you want to see one of his raps, go to www.youtube.com and type in "Medler Christmas Card 2009"); and my fourteen-year old daughter Natasha, who brings her guitar with her everywhere she goes, is always bored, but makes friends with everyone she meets. They were my inspiration for Zach and Zoey. While I am thanking kids, I would like to thank my other four children, Ryan, a junior at UCLA; Kevin, a freshman at Loyola of New Orleans; and Sabrina and Wendi, my two babies. They keep me forever young.

And first and last, I need to thank my perfect wife Tammy, whom I met when I was fifteen, and whom I have never stopped loving in 32 years. Without her, I would be dust.

CPSIA information can be obtained at www.ICGtesting.com
Printed in the USA
LVOW10*0706300314

379434LV00001B/3/P

9 780615 979649